A BREATH IN TIME

A BREATH IN TIME

TL DICKERSON

SAPPHIRE BOOKS

SALINAS, CALIFORNIA

Dedication

I dedicate this book to my beautiful mother, Angie Ramirez. My mother was a booklover her whole life, reading up to five books a week. Her encouragement of my writing was endless, and my confidence built with each inspiring word she spoke to me. I made some incredible mistakes in my life, but my mom never judged me. She loved me unconditionally, breathing life back into me after a stint of drug use and homelessness. She used her light to help me find my way out of the darkness, and for that, I will forever and eternally be grateful. Her passing in 2019 has left a gaping hole in my heart. I'll never know that kind of love again. But I live my life with her light still shining on me, still guiding me, and still cheering me on. I hope I've made her proud. My books will always be dedicated to her, just as my life is. Thank you, Mom, for loving me.

Acknowledgments

I'd like to thank my lobster for not only enthusiastically reading my books, but also encouraging me to keep writing. Your excitement during reading *A Breath in Time* was contagious, and I felt as though I was reading it all over again with you. Since my mother's death, I've not been able to complete a story. I have three half-written books, and that's not like me. You breathe those same reassuring words into me as my mom once did. Your empathy and understanding have meant the world to me. I know I'm not the greatest author in the world, but you certainly make me feel as though I am. You don't even know that your love and devotion has kept me going, not only in writing, but in life. Thank you, my lobster. I love you.

As always, a huge thank you to Chris Svendsen for the opportunity to write for Sapphire Books Publishing. It's truly been an honor. Much gratitude is due to you for your understanding during a difficult time in my personal life. Thank you, Chris.

Thank you, Tara Young, for taking on my self-published sophomore try at writing books. I know it had to have been a lot of work for you as it needed much polishing. It felt good to have it professionally edited and made into a real book, one I can be proud of.

To my dad, Hank Ramirez, I always save the best for last, and you are the best. You've seen me at my best and you've seen me at my worst, and through it all you stand beside me. I am indebted to you for so many things in my life, but most of all, for never abandoning me. Going through my divorce was one of the lowest points in my life. It was humbling to say the least. But just as Mom had lifted me up from the depths of darkness when I thought I would surely crumble, you helped me back to my feet, gave me a roof over my head, and encouraged me to go on. Like Mom, you never judged me for my mistakes or shortcomings. You've been my rock and my voice of reason, and I could never repay you for all that you've done for me. Thank you for loving me. I love you, Hankie.

Chapter One

It was the same thing every Sunday morning.

"Make your move, Danielle," I said.

She stared at the chessboard and warned, "You can't just willy-nilly move your pieces. Let me think."

"You've been thinking for ten minutes now."

"You can't rush these things."

I sucked my tongue piercing through the tiny gap in my front teeth, leaned back on the love seat, breathed deeply, and sighed. "Okay, okay. I'll move," she said and finally moved her knight.

"You are such a nerd."

"Why am I a nerd? Because I think things through before taking action?"

"A little bit, yes." I chuckled and moved my rook without much thought.

"And this is why I'm a nerd. Checkmate!"

"What?" I scanned the board, backtracked my steps, and examined the position of her pieces when I realized my mistake. "Damn!" I snapped my fingers. "You got me, nerd. You got me."

She giggled at me. "Play again?"

"I don't think so. I've been up all night, and it's ten a.m." She started to put the game away, and I remembered. "Hey! The concert is next Friday. You excited?"

"Always excited to see the Indigo Girls."

"How many times have you seen them now?"

"Nine times and counting." She smiled, draped her messenger bag over her shoulder, and headed for the door of my office. "Call me."

❧ ❧ ❧ ❧

I locked the doors and headed home. The bar wouldn't reopen until three p.m. Sundays were usually busy, but I let my staff handle it. I'd be in and out of the building all week, placing stock orders, and answering to Dorian Jarvie, my friend and accountant. "Are you giving booze away?" she'd ask as she examined my books for the month. But on Saturdays, I was there for the duration. I stayed on top of shit and made sure things got done.

My bar was probably the one thing in my life that I took seriously. Dorian always said, "If you really want to retire at an early age and move to Costa Rica, Parker, you better tighten up the purse strings." It was a good thing she stayed on top of me about it. She reminded me of my future intentions and kept me on track.

Dorian, Danielle, and I met when we were sophomores in college and became friends right away. We'd been close friends ever since. Danielle Bly, or Dani for short, was the wonk of our clique, always with her nose in a book and clean-cut. Didn't drink, except for an unfinished glass of wine twice a year, and didn't do drugs. She hardly ever went to my bar. It wasn't an environment she was interested in since she didn't imbibe, and watching others get drunk was a total turnoff for her.

Dorian, on the other hand, was smart as a whip but wasn't afraid to have a good time. She enjoyed liquor probably a bit too much but was one of those people who could handle it. I actually had to ask her if she was drunk because she was so good at hiding it. The only thing that gave her away was a slight slipup of words or blurting out something that was out of the ordinary for her. She was single but always in search of love. She was a tad bit overbearing at times and headstrong, and this tended to make for short-lived relationships.

❧ ❧ ❧ ❧

By the time the middle of the week rolled around, I was busy getting ready for the weekend, confirming with the band I had scheduled and making sure the bar was well stocked. I was sitting behind my desk on the phone with the band's agent when my bartender Simone walked in, took a seat in front of me, and patiently waited for me to end my call. When I hung up, I asked, "What's up?"

"I don't appreciate you scheduling me with Michelle Saturday night. Why would you do that? You know we can't stand each other."

"Okay, first of all, I'm not the manager. Jules is. I don't do scheduling. Jules does. So if you have a problem with the schedule, go see Jules." I walked over to the mini-fridge and grabbed a bottle of water. "Besides, I thought the feud was over. She doesn't talk to Gus anymore when he drops you off for your shift. Heck, Gus doesn't even stay for the one drink he used to have before going home."

"Technically, the feud is over, but I still don't want to work with her. I am not tending bar or sharing my tips with her!"

"I don't know why you get so mad about a little light flirting between them."

"He's my husband."

"Yes, he's your husband, but what you do is a far greater infraction than just some light flirting."

"There's no talking to you, Parker. Speaking of infractions, though…" Her dark brown eyes softened into a seductive stare, and she wet her lips before saying, "I need it."

"It's not Saturday night, and the bar isn't closed."

"So?" She got up from her chair and led me over to the sitting area. There were dueling black leather love seats that faced each other with a small coffee table in the middle. It was where Danielle and I played chess every Sunday morning.

She pushed me on to one of the love seats and moved the small table that was in her way. Then she crawled up between my legs and started to unbutton my jeans. Tugging them down, she said, "Come on, take these off."

I helped her pull them off, and she dragged my panties down swiftly and spread my legs as she helped herself to what she desired the most—eating pussy. She was twenty-four and my only straight employee—supposedly. She had been married to Gus for three years but told me she always had a fetish for going down on women. She never let me touch her, and she didn't touch any other part of me. She straight up just wanted to eat it.

I looked down at her as she tucked her long brunette hair behind her ears. Her eyes were closed. She clearly enjoyed what she was doing. I had always wanted to touch her big tits, a DDD, no question. But she saved those for Gus. So she said. Apparently, there was absolutely nothing wrong with their marriage. She appeared happy when I saw them together. There was only this. This deep secret of wanting to make a woman cum with her mouth.

Whatever it was, I didn't have a problem obliging her and giving her what she craved. I was thirty-eight years old with no ties to anyone. I'd dated women of all ages and races, but nothing ever got too serious. I called it the nine-month curse. I would date a girl, and after the nine-month mark, she would want to know where things were going. They never went anywhere because I was too afraid of commitment. I would feel trapped and claustrophobic and would end the relationship before it even got a true start. My only real commitment, the only one I ever took seriously, was my bar. Merge. A lesbian bar that catered to the greater Tampa Bay area.

"Oh, God, Simone!" I yelled out as I climaxed quickly and sank farther into the couch.

Our regular routine started when the bar closed at three a.m., and by four thirty a.m., the employees had cleaned up and left for the night. All but Simone, who would come through my door when the last of the staff had left. This happened every Saturday for the last six months. When we were done, we hung out and drank a couple of glasses of wine before Gus picked her up, usually just before six a.m. He was a construction worker and did side jobs on the weekend with a friend. Since they only had one car, he picked her up, and she dropped him off. Only a few minutes existed between Simone leaving through the back door and Danielle coming through the front. Danielle was the only person I trusted with a key to the bar, so she let herself in every week. She was an early riser, and by six a.m., she entered my office the same way every Sunday, with a smile on her face and coffee in her hands for both of us. How she and Simone never ran into each other in the hallway was beyond me.

Mmm...Danielle. We had been friends forever, but I always had a thing for her. I would love to fantasize about her while Simone went down on me but never let myself. Even though my mind was my own personal space and I could do what I wanted there, I didn't allow myself that pleasure. She didn't feel the same for me, so I tried not to go there in my head.

"Back to work I go. I'll talk to Jules about the schedule." Simone wiped her face and chin with her sleeve. "Thanks for the snack." She winked at me and exited my office.

My legs were weak from my orgasm, and I took my time putting my clothes back on. I buttoned my jeans and put on my sneakers. While I tied the laces, I looked at the chessboard sitting on the coffee table Simone had moved out of the way. I slid it back to the center between the two love seats and allowed myself to think about Danielle. Just for a moment before getting back to reality.

⁂

I met Dorian first. We both signed up for a communications class, a prerequisite neither of us wanted to take. The only classes I ever paid attention to were business courses or any that would teach me how to run and manage a bar. So when we found ourselves lost since writing and literature weren't our strong points, this cute little blonde sitting behind me offered to tutor both of us. After class ended, she introduced herself. Danielle. The attraction was immediate between us, but I was let down hard when her girlfriend came up behind her and gave a peck to her neck. "Who's this?" the girl asked.

"Uh, this is… I'm sorry. I didn't get your name," she said to me.

"I'm Parker. Well, Morgan Parker. My friends just call me Parker."

It was hard to look away from her. Her sandy blond hair was pulled back in a ponytail, and her loose curls fell neatly out of the hair tie. I stared into her honey brown eyes and swallowed the lump that had formed in my throat.

"Hi, Parker," her girlfriend said and introduced herself because Danielle was staring right back at me. "I'm Nicky." She raised her hand to shake mine and brought me out of my trance that was zeroed in on her girl.

After that, Nicky didn't care much for Danielle tutoring me in communications or anything else for that matter. Our tutoring sessions were only to be held in public spaces, and Danielle had to be home by a certain time. We would sit at the school library, side by side, while she looked over a paper we had to write. She pointed to the paper in front of me, reading back sentences to me as I stared at her. She felt me staring and finally looked back at me. "You use the word *just* too much throughout your text."

"I do?" She knew I couldn't care less even as I asked.

"You do," she said, still staring back at me. "Parker, if I wasn't with Nicky, I—"

"I know."

"It's bad timing."

"I know that, too."

"You have to start looking at me like a friend. Seriously. It's bad enough Nicky wants to kick your ass."

After that, I realized we weren't going to hook up and sort of moved on. I became a friend. At some point months later, she started looking at me as a friend only. We entered what I called *Friendsville*, a nice made-up town that I hated. She walked the streets freely, openly, and happily. Me, I walked the perimeter of *Friendsville*, never actually entering. Occasionally, I took a step in with one foot. Then I would look at her, and that same rush of attraction would take over. I still wanted to kiss her. That was when I would pull my foot back and continue walking the outskirts. She was the only one truly in *Friendsville*. It sucked, but if I wanted to be a part of her life, I had to know and accept my role.

So I started dating Allie, and about two months into our relationship, Danielle and Nicky broke up. It went on like this for a few years. Each of us was always with someone while the other was single. Timing was a bitch. We weren't meant to be, whether I liked it or not. As time went on, all three of us became close. Going to parties was something we often did together, but attending Tampa Bay Rays games and playing chess became a mainstay with Danielle and me. When we graduated, it wasn't long before Danielle picked up and moved across the country. California had been good to her. She enjoyed teaching at a community college and stayed for a few years before her mother's ailing health brought her back to the Tampa area. The doctors had given her mother six months to live, but she deteriorated quickly, succumbing to colon cancer in just three. Dorian and I did the best we could to console our friend, but there wasn't much we could do except be there for her.

It was during this time that Danielle and I became tighter than we had ever been. She trusted me with her feelings toward her mom, her lack of closeness and constant need for approval. She was closer with her dad, and he seemed to fill the void she felt when it came to her mom. Only now her mom was gone, and even though she got to say goodbye, she wasn't sure they really cleared the air. Guilt was left in her wake, and to blow off some of that steam, she took up running. She somehow convinced me it was a good idea to join her. I swore the woman hardly ever broke a sweat, and her breathing sounded balanced, unlike mine that sounded like a pig having a stroke. She ran along even-paced while I trudged alongside her, sweating profusely and never looking well. She always said she brought me along for the entertainment I provided.

At that time, I was seeing a woman named Tara. It was nothing serious, and we were only having some fun, but as Danielle and I got closer, she started looking at me the way she had when we first met. I'd gladly have ended it with Tara to be with her, but she insisted that the attraction she had toward me wasn't as important as the friendship we had built. Back to *Friendsville* we went.

It wasn't long after Danielle's mom died that she landed a teaching job at our old alma mater. She'd been an English professor at the University of South Florida for ten years now and in a serious relationship with a woman named April Davenport for the last three. April was a project management consultant, and the two met while April was studying for her MBA. She worked for the same consulting company for over a year and popped the question to Danielle a few months ago. Of course, Dani said yes, and they set a date for October. They were alike in many ways. They spent almost every Saturday golfing. Tennis was a big activity they shared, and going to the theater was high on their list of common interests. Although April was away a lot on business, they seemed happy when they were together. They made it work, and I envied that. Yes, April was the final nail in a coffin filled with *what-ifs.*

☙ ☙ ☙ ☙

Thursday morning, I drove to Danielle's house for our weekly run. She ran every morning except Sundays, and I tried my best to run at least three times a week, just enough to keep up with her. She liked to run before her first class of the morning and said it gave her a boost of energy that lasted all day. When I pulled up to her white-columned, two-story slate gray house with navy blue shutters, I knew I was in the epicenter of North Hyde Park. To say the neighborhood was affluent was an understatement.

She was already outside, bent over, stretching, and looking adorable in her blue and yellow running shorts. Her Asics were a flashy mix of pink, purple, and orange, and were the last thing I noticed as she spread her legs and leaned to one side. Her back was to me, and I sneaked a peek at her cute little ass. The shorts clung to her just right, but as I walked toward her and got a better view, she stood and turned to me.

"You're late," she pointed out, grabbed her ankle, and brought it up to the back of her thigh as she stretched her quad muscle.

"Good morning to you, too."

"You're never late. What happened?"

"Thought I set my alarm, but turns out, not so much. I'm only ten minutes late, jeez!"

"You're finally here?" April asked as she walked out the front door, briefcase in hand. "I thought she was going to lose her mind."

"Seriously?" I asked Danielle.

"I'm getting my period," she divulged.

"Way too much information."

April kissed her goodbye, hopped in her red Lexus, and drove off in the direction of work. Danielle zoned in on me. "Well?"

"Well, what?"

"Are you going to stretch? You have to stretch, or you're going to cramp."

"I think you're cramping enough for the both of us," I chided, barely doing a couple of stretches. "Come on. Let's go."

"Suit yourself. Don't look for sympathy from me if you ball up in pain on the ground."

"Okay! Let's go, grumpy!"

We began at a light jog, getting the juices flowing, and building up to a nice pace. She knew she had a limited window of opportunity to talk with me before I became a gasping mess, unable to do anything but try to make it through the run to the finish. "How's the bar? Were you able to book the Damzels?" she asked.

"Bar is great, and yes, got the Damzels. Any chance of you coming out Saturday night to see them?

I know you like them."

"I do, but you know I don't fit in at the bar. I've never done the bar thing."

"Yeah, I know. Just wish you would learn how to relax every now and then."

She turned her head to look at me and insisted, "I do relax. I don't like bars is all."

"Yeah, yeah."

"Man, I really dodged a bullet when it came to you."

Now it was my turn to look over at her. Confused, I asked, "What's that supposed to mean?"

"It means we're very different. You own a bar, you smoke weed, you ride a motorcycle. Should I go on?"

"Wow! Really? And I only occasionally smoke weed. Once or twice a month does not a stoner make. That would be Cookie." I chuckled and tried to maintain my breathing at the same time.

"Cookie's a bad influence on you."

"Cookie is my oldest and dearest friend. I wouldn't get rid of her for the world. I don't care how much pot she smokes." Cookie Micheletti was short with long, light brown hair and crystal blue eyes, and had one of the foulest mouths I had ever heard. The F bomb was used frequently. She cussed like a truck driver but was the most loyal person I knew. She was a habitual pot smoker and often was a bad influence on me. Danielle was right when she said that. I just never admitted to it. Whatever trouble or drama I had ever been in had been with Cookie.

I started to breathe jaggedly now, no longer able to keep a steady pace, and I was about to be done with this idle chitchat. "Dani, you need to shut up now. I have to concentrate on my breathing."

We ran side by side for the first two and a half miles, but as we turned the bend and headed back in the direction of her house, mile three kicked my ass. She was right, I should have stretched. I hated when she was right. By mile four, I went down, balled up on the ground in pain with a charley horse to the back of my calf.

"Damn it, Parker!" She knelt next to me, took my leg as she massaged the knot, and lifted my foot to stretch the muscle.

"Ow! Ow!" I yelped.

"I told you to stretch!"

"I know! Ow! Ow! Why are you helping me? You said you wouldn't."

"I said I wouldn't have sympathy for you. Of course I would help you. You're my friend."

To this day, I still hated hearing that word. Friend. Yuck! The word didn't even flow naturally from my mouth. I gazed into her eyes just long enough to ask myself for the katrillionth time if I still wanted to kiss her, hoping against all hope that I wouldn't. *Son of a bitch!* Yes, I did. It was awful this torch I'd carried for her for so many years.

"Is that better?" she asked, still massaging the area.

"Yeah, it's good. Thanks."

She helped me up, and we cut our run short. Not by much. I almost made it. We headed back to her house, walking this time. She and April had lived in North Hyde Park for just over a year, and the ritzy neighborhood was second nature for Danielle. She was used to this life, having been raised in a wealthy family. She was always daddy's little girl, evident in his gift last year on her thirty-seventh birthday, a silver BMW Roadster.

As we walked down the sidewalk, the birds were singing, and a gentle breeze rustled through the leaves of the trees that lined the street. It was another beautiful Florida day, and outside of the birds chirping, the only other sound was that of lawn mowers. Landscaping and pool care were big businesses here, and in North Hyde Park, they took it seriously. The streets were adorned with one huge home after the other, all with flawlessly manicured yards.

When we got back to her house, we stood by my car and planned for the concert tomorrow. She gave me a quick hug, and as I opened my car door, she asked, "Why no bike today?"

"Because I didn't feel like hearing the speech today." I put the word speech in air quotes.

She smiled and assured me, "I only give the speech," she said as she too added air quotes, "because I don't want anything to happen to you. You're one of my best friends."

"Yeah, whatever. Me and Dorian will pick you girls up at six thirty."

"Okay. We'll be ready."

❧❧❧❧

The next night, we arrived in Dorian's Tahoe and walked the pathway filled with jacaranda and Japanese fern trees to the front steps of the porch. The sun was on its descent, an extraordinary bright orange, indicating it would be hot tomorrow. It hung softly in the mix of a pink and purple sky. The sound of cicadas filled the warm evening air as we climbed the steps and rang the doorbell. We were greeted by the barking of JoJo, their Jack Russell terrier, and April opened the door. He instantly jumped up and down, wagging his tail, excited to see friends. Off he went, across the room in search of a toy to bring back.

"Where's Danielle?" Dorian asked.

"She'll be down in a minute."

"Well, tell her to get a move on. Emily and Amy wait for no one."

JoJo raced back into the room with a toy in his mouth and ran up to me. He knew I'd throw the toy every time. He loved me for that. A lot of times when April was away on business, I brought my Shih Tzu, Addie, and had a play date for the dogs. Danielle got lonely when April was away, so we spent a lot of time together.

I threw the toy, and JoJo bolted through the living room, grabbed it in his teeth, and shook it vigorously. I heard footsteps coming down the staircase and glanced up to see Danielle appear in the room. "Hey!" she said, giving us both a hug. "I'm ready. You ready? Let's do this."

I patted the top of JoJo's head and headed for the door. It was a short ride to the small venue that the Indigo Girls were performing at, and April insisted on driving.

Once we were on the highway, she blared the stereo through the car speakers. She wasn't playing Indigo Girls music, though she should have been. It was tradition when we saw them that the car ride was filled with their songs. Dani popped the greatest hits in, and April shot her a look. "I don't care! You're listening to them," Danielle warned. April gave in, though she wasn't happy about it. She wasn't a big fan but went for Danielle. She was usually able to get out of it. I guess Dani wasn't having it this time.

Dorian and I were sitting in the back, and we all sang to our favorites. When one song ended, I watched Danielle reach across the center console and hold April's hand, almost consoling her for having to come with us tonight. It'd been so many years that I'd been friends with Danielle, and April had been with her for a few of them. One would think I'd be over this shit by now. It annoyed me to watch them hold hands, their fingers interlaced. It wasn't that I had a problem with PDA. It was that I had a problem watching Dani and April's PDA.

⁂

When we were all settled into our seats at the concert hall, Dorian and I excused ourselves and went directly to the bar for a drink. We stood in line, waiting our turn, when Dorian asked, "It still bothers you to watch her hold hands with someone else, doesn't it?"

"What are you talking about?"

"Don't front! Who do you think you're talking to, anyway? You know exactly what I'm talking about."

I raked my fingers through my hair. "Yes. Okay? Are you happy now?"

"Why would it make me happy to watch my best friend pine over a woman that has consistently shot her down all these years?"

We finally reached the bartender and ordered three beers, one for us and one for April. "I really wish you would get over her already," she said as she set the cash on the bar. "There are plenty of women out there. For Christ's sake, you own a lesbian bar."

"Yeah, but…"

"No buts, Parker. She's getting married." She left a tip, and we walked away sipping our drinks and strolled back to the showroom.

Once we were back in our seats and we sat through yet another horrible opening act, the Indigo Girls took the stage. The crowd was ignited, and the room burst into song, singing jubilantly and swaying in their seats. Dorian and Danielle were seated in the middle of me and April, and I took full advantage, using Dorian as a shield to sneak peeks at Dani. She couldn't see me staring, and I watched her, admiring her as I did. She sat with her legs parted slightly but comfortably in front of her; her hands rested on her thighs. Her jeans hugged her thighs in such a way that I wished my hands were there instead of her own. I quickly turned away as Dorian leaned back in her seat, not realizing she was blowing my cover. I barely averted my stare as I caught Danielle glance at me out of the corner of my eye.

Halfway through the show, people had made their way out to the aisles to dance. I wasn't surprised when Dani got up from her seat and slid past us to join the others. She didn't need anyone to dance with her as she rocked her hips and snapped her fingers to the beat. April wasn't fazed by Dani's sudden exit and remained seated herself, trying her best not to look annoyed. Dorian was happy to sit and sip on her beer, and I took my opportunity to get up and scoot past several people to dance with Danielle. Rhythm wasn't one of my strong suits, but I did my best not to look like a complete idiot. Most times, I was pretty good at hiding my feelings for her, but sometimes when I had a drink or two, my facial expressions could get away from me, and I didn't realize how I was looking at her. With only a beer in me, she smiled at me and shook her head. I immediately realized my face was looking at her the way it wanted, and I smiled back as I shrugged apologetically.

Just as the girls started singing *Galileo*, Dorian joined us. The three of us put our arms around one another while we swayed and sang to our favorite Indigo Girls song. When the song came out years ago, there was a line in it about letting the next life off the hook and about things that had to be overcome in the last life. It reminded us of the actress Shirley MacLaine, who had written a book about reincarnation. Each time the line was sung, the three of us would shout out, "Shirley!" It was the same thing every time and wouldn't be an Indigo Girls concert if they didn't sing that song. Like clockwork, the words were sung, and we all chimed in, "Shirley!" It was stupid, but we laughed. April thought we were silly and never took part, but we couldn't care less. The three of us had been friends for so long, it was second nature to be silly together.

When the concert was over, Dorian dropped me off at my house on Branch Avenue. Seminole Heights had been my home for the last four years. It was just north of Tampa and was an easy fifteen-minute drive to Merge. I traversed the walkway to the front door of my Japanese-style bungalow and climbed the steps to the porch. The porch swing rocked lightly in the warm breeze of this late spring night, and as I put the key in the door, I heard Addie barking impatiently.

I swung the door open, and she jumped up at me repeatedly, happy to see me and panting wildly. She followed me through my newly renovated living room, past the baby grand piano, and to the backdoor to let her out. The baby grand? I remembered when I purchased it. I had absolutely no clue how to play it, but Danielle did. She thought Iit was foolish to spend so much money, not knowing how to play a lick, but I enjoyed listening to her play so much that I had to have it. It was such a great conversation piece, too, and gave my living room a touch of class, truly the focal point of the room.

❧❧❧❧

Saturday night was in full effect at Merge with a packed house for the Damzels. Dorian had been here for a few hours already, knocking back several drinks before the show even started. She was on her usual stool at the corner of the bar and was flirting heavily with Simone. No one had any idea about the semi-fling she and I had going for the past six months. Dorian loved flirting with Michelle, too. As much as Simone insisted she was straight, I insisted that she not tell the patrons that. I believed her tips would decline if they knew. Lesbians loved a good fantasy, anyway, so let them fantasize and give up the cash.

Cookie was at the other end of the bar, talking, always talking. She loved mixing it up with the ladies and always left her relationships in ruins, except for the one time a woman named Shady broke her heart. She was never quite the same. Even over the music coming from the jukebox, she was the loudest person in the room. Her hearty laugh was heard all the way across the bar, and she was animated as she told a story to a few young lesbians. Her hands were in constant motion, and she had the full attention of the group.

The show was about to begin, and food and drinks were flowing. The crowd loved the Damzels, who played cover songs and had a few originals. They were a local favorite and played all over Tampa. As always, a few rowdy types were here. The type who can't handle their liquor and shouldn't be drinking. A few young butch girls from the university were also here tonight, and they were fired up. Too much testosterone and too much liquor was not a good mix, and I knew it was only a matter of time before a fight broke out. I could feel it, and I didn't tolerate fighting in my bar. I employed two thick, well-built women to bounce for me. Renee and Trudy. I didn't worry about a thing when these two were here.

Three songs in, and right on cue, the pickled young butch girls got into it with some other frighteningly butch girls, and some pushing began. When one was pushed into the guitarist from the Damzels, the guitarist pushed her right back into play. My bouncers had enough and rushed the small fight before it turned into something bigger. By the time they got to the door, I met them there and personally informed them not to come back. "You've been ejected permanently." There were no second chances when it came to fighting. I found it distasteful and unbecoming to watch women fist fight. Especially at a bar...my bar.

⁂

When closing time approached, Simone gave me that look. That look that asked if we were still on for our weekly rendezvous. I gave her a small nod and walked away, trying my best to continue this secret. I was pretty sure Jules surmised something was going on between us, but if neither of us admitted it, then it wasn't true.

Dorian was still in the same spot I left her in at the beginning of the night. I had a seat next to her and motioned for Simone to bring me a beer. "Well, how was your night? Did you enjoy the band?" I asked.

"I did. They're awesome! Not as awesome as the Indigo Girls but still awesome."

"They brought in a good crowd. I think I'll have them come back soon."

"I'll tell you who should come back. Come back to my house. Those twins over there."

I peered across the bar and made a line from Dorian's eyes to a tall brunette standing at the other end of the bar. "What twins?"

"Right there. Standing there by themselves."

Ahh, the telltale sign that my friend had exceeded her alcohol limitations. I laughed out loud and realized my mistake as she asked, "What are you laughing at?"

"Nothing. I'm not laughing at anything! Hey, why don't I introduce you?"

"Yeah? Okay. Bring 'em over!" Amazing how she never slurred, never had that glazed-over look that so many drunk people got. I'd never know if she didn't say something peculiar.

I walked up to the woman and introduced myself. As I pointed across the room at Dorian, I explained that I'd like to have some fun with my intoxicated friend. I told her Dorian thought there were two of her and that she would like to bring her and her twin home tonight. She giggled and accepted my invitation to screw with her.

Dorian waited patiently for us to make our way

over to her. "Dorian, this is Dahlia," I said.

"Hi, Dahlia. What a pretty name! What's your sister's name?"

Dahlia smiled and attempted to control her laughter. She looked to me, wondering what to say. "Her sister's name is Darrah. Don't be rude. Say hi," I ordered.

"Hi, Darrah. It's a pleasure." She extended her hand, and Dahlia shook it. She was a good sport and was just as entertained as I was. "Can I buy you a drink?" Dorian asked.

"Well, the bar is about to close, and I still have to drive home, but thank you. Maybe another time."

"What about your sister?"

"She doesn't drink." Dahlia giggled again.

"Oh! Okay. Well, can I get your phone number then?"

I didn't know if Dahlia gave her the correct number or not, but I was surprised when she asked Simone for a pen and grabbed a napkin from the bar. She took her time, wrote her name and number on it, and handed it to Dorian, who in turn asked Darrah for her number, as well. Dahlia glanced at me once again with a questioning look, and I shrugged and gestured for her to write it again. She chuckled, nodded, and wrote her number on another napkin. I knew Dorian was drunk because she held both napkins up, side by side, and didn't recognize it was the same exact number with different names. I couldn't control it anymore and burst out laughing.

"Why are you laughing?" she asked.

"It's just been a really good night!" I patted my friend on the back, and Dahlia excused herself.

"Can I call you tomorrow?" Dorian asked her.

"Yes, you can."

"How 'bout you, Darrah?"

She played along one final time. "Yes, I would like that."

As Dahlia walked toward the front door, I walked with her and thanked her for playing along. Before she opened the door, I asked, "Did you give her the wrong number? I would understand if you did."

The corners of her lips turned upward. "Actually, I gave her the right number. She's cute. When she sobers up, tell her to call me."

She exited the bar, and I turned around to find Dorian flirting with Simone again. *Boy, she's on fire tonight.* When I took a closer look at her, I noticed that Dahlia was right. She was cute. She wasn't that tall, about 5'5". She had an average build and body. Her hair was dark brown, short with the classic sapphic side-swept bangs. Every once in a while, she came into the bar on a Saturday night with the bangs slicked up, bringing out a bit of a punk style, but she usually wore it plain because of her job. She had been working with the same accounting firm for eight years now and was aiming at making partner.

The eyelids above her sandalwood-colored eyes appeared heavy as I approached her and Simone at the bar, and I knew it was time for her to go home. I took my cellphone out of my pocket and called a cab for her. She never argued with me about driving drunk and consented to the taxi ride home. When the car arrived, I walked her out and noticed how straight she walked. I knew she was wasted, but she hid it so well. If it were me, I'd be walking like the room was slanted to the right. Just as she was about to get in the cab, she turned to me and asked, "Those twins were hot, right?"

"My friend, they were smokin' hot and totally into you."

"Yeah?"

"Of course! Dorian Jarvie always gets the hot girl!"

"You're a good friend, Parker."

"Yeah, I know. Now get in the car."

❦ ❦ ❦ ❦

Dorian got in, I closed the door, and went back inside. The bar was almost empty now except for a few regular stragglers finishing up their drinks and my staff, who were busy cleaning up and counting their tips. Simone and I never acknowledged each other, rather we saved those looks for our alone time. The bar wasn't completely empty of everyone until four thirty a.m. when I heard a soft knock at my door. Simone. She didn't wait for me to let her in. Instead, she opened the door slowly and closed and locked it behind her.

"Is everyone gone?" I asked.

"Yep. I locked the front and back doors."

"Good girl. Now what is it you crave like a crackhead craves the pipe?"

She snickered at this and moved toward me. "You know exactly what I crave."

I was sitting behind my desk, and she spun the chair around so that I was facing her. She dropped to her knees and settled between my legs. I watched her as she intently zoned in on my pants, unbuttoning them, and pulling at them.

When she received no help from me in taking

them off, she looked up at me, and I asked, "Are you ever going to let me kiss you?"

"You already know the answer to that, Parker."

"I keep hoping you'll change your mind."

"You know the deal. I'm married," she said for the hundredth time.

"You know you're not straight, right?"

"Are we going to start this again?" She rolled her eyes.

"Why don't you just admit it? Straight girls don't eat pussy, especially the way you devour it."

"I love my husband. Now give this to me and stop wasting time." She cupped my crotch and squeezed it before pulling me out of my jeans and underwear. I spread my legs and lifted them up and over the arms of my chair, exposing my pussy, and watching her salivate as I did. "You have the prettiest pussy I've ever seen."

"Yeah? Why don't you get a closer look then?" I set my hand on the back of her head and guided her to my waiting, wet center.

She didn't use her hands at all, preferring to push her whole face in, sticking her tongue out right away, hungry for what her husband could not give her. Her wet tongue only made me wetter, and the sound of her eating me turned me on even more. She moaned into me while she enjoyed slurping up my stickiness.

I leaned my head back in the chair. "Jesus Christ, you eat my pussy so good!" I reached for her breasts, and as always, she pushed my hand away. Her strokes were paced evenly, knowing how to bring me to climax as she had six months' worth of practice. "Oh! Oh, yeah! Aww, shit, I'm gonna cum!" I lost myself in my orgasm, allowing her to lash at my hardened clit to the very end.

"Nothin' like lickin' the boss," she joked and wiped her mouth on the sleeve of her work shirt. She ate me once a week whether I needed it or not. I knew it was a superficial relationship without any real affection from either of us, but I had needs like anyone else.

After the deed was done, we sat on one of the love seats and enjoyed a glass of wine together. After our third glass, I glanced down at my watch and realized that Gus was late this morning. I hoped he wasn't much later. Danielle would be here shortly, and I didn't want her to get the wrong idea. I didn't want her to think I was a pig or something, and she would have too many questions that I wouldn't want to answer. So I preferred to keep them separated. Simone and I would remain on the down low, as it should be. Right before my nerves started to shake about the time, I heard Gus's truck pull up. "He's here!" I exclaimed and jumped to my feet.

"Wow! Do you wanna get rid of me or what?" she asked with a bewildered expression.

"Oh, no, no! It's nothing like that. Just extra tired this morning. Can't wait to get home. Sorry if I seemed abrupt."

I walked over to the door, and she took her time getting up, almost as if she knew I was lying. It wasn't that she never met Danielle. She had. Only that was in a bar setting with plenty of people around and Dani acting weird because she didn't like bars. For some reason, I didn't want them to know each other on any substantive level. I was funny that way with Dani. Simone left with some suspicion about my behavior, but this was never supposed to be romantic. We didn't lay in each other's arms after she went down on me. She was casual sex, and that was the way I wanted it to remain.

❧ ❧ ❧ ❧

Once Simone was gone, it wasn't long before I heard a light rapping at my office door. The door swung open, and Danielle appeared in my office, coffee in hand for both of us. "Good morning."

She handed me a cup, and I returned her *good morning* with a "Hey, you're early." I was hoping she couldn't see me sweating as I faintly heard the backdoor close. Simone was gone. *Thank God!*

"Only a little. Would you like me to come back in ten minutes?" she kidded, smiled at me, and set her coffee cup on the small table that held the chessboard. She plopped down on the sofa, crossed her legs, and sipped her coffee. She was dressed in dark green shorts and a USF T-shirt that fit her perfectly as it clung to her bosom and accentuated her hardened nipples. She took the hair tie from her ponytail and shook it loose. Her hair was down only for a second as she was about to pull it back once more and retie it. But that second that her hair spilled around her face and down her shoulders was like a punch to the heart. She was so beautiful when her hair was down that I had a difficult time trying to look away from her. She didn't wear any makeup. She didn't have to. She was a natural beauty, at least to me. My heart stopped in that second, along with my breathing. I regained my breath only after she had tied her thick mane back into a ponytail.

"Why are there two wine glasses sitting here? Did you have company?" She smiled and toyed with me.

"Uh, no. I, uh..."

"Why are you stuttering?" She grinned at me. "You're a single woman. You can have a glass of wine with someone. What's wrong with you?"

"Nothing. Really. Forget about the wine. Let's play chess."

Danielle accepted my blow-off and instead said, "You go first."

I moved a pawn forward. She did the same, and the game began. We played for a couple of hours before my body had enough, and I needed to sleep. We wrapped things up, and I let her out the door before me. I closed the door to my office and followed her down the hall. "Stop looking at my ass!" she warned without stopping or turning around.

"How do you know I'm looking at your ass?"

"Because I can feel the heat from the lasers coming out of your eyes. Now stop!"

"It's terrible how well you know me." I chuckled as we walked through the bar area and to the front door.

Before we exited, we hugged each other goodbye. She was an inch or two shorter than me, and she wrapped her arms around my waist. I, in turn, enclosed my arms around her shoulders. She chose to make our hugs of short duration, never wanting to lead me on in any way. But it was in these brief moments that I consistently took the opportunity to smell the top of her hair. The fragrance of wildflowers wafted through my senses, and I wanted to lean down and kiss her. I knew better, though.

She broke our embrace and gently pushed me back a step, placing the appropriate amount of space between us. "Thursday morning run?"

"Can't this week. I have a meeting with a contractor to talk about a possible addition to the bar."

"Yeah?"

"Yeah. I'll tell you about it Friday night at Natalie's birthday party."

We parted ways, and I departed the bar in the direction of home.

Chapter Two

*K*nock, *knock, knock*! Addie ran straight to the front door, barking and growling as if she was a big, bad German shepherd. "You wanna let me open the door?" I asked her as I tried to get her out of the way. When I finally opened the door, Cookie and some girl I'd never met before were standing there.

"Hey," she said and sidestepped past me into the house while introducing her friend. "This is Kylie. Kylie, Parker."

"Hi," I said and shook her hand.

"Nice to meet you."

All conversation stopped as Addie stole the show. She was the center of attention when people came over. They both talked to her in a baby talk voice, petting and playing with her. Every time I heard Cookie talk in that voice, it cracked me up. It wasn't all the time that she let her soft side show. Usually, she showed that tough New York City attitude side of her. This was apparent in her natural pissed off-looking face. She wasn't really mad all the time, but her face suggested otherwise. It was a defense mechanism, I guess. Most people found her unapproachable and intimidating, and only a special few got to see this sweet side.

As I watched Cookie play with my dog, I reminisced for a moment in my head, remembering our very first encounter. She was fourteen when her parents moved her from New York City to the Tampa area. Her father was laid off from a company he had worked at for seventeen years. He moved his wife, Cookie, and her brother, Roger, in with his sister, Dolores, and her family. His brother-in-law got him a job at the plant where he worked. They lived with Dolores for the summer, and by the start of autumn, they rented their own small house. Roger was a couple of years older than Cookie and started the school year as a junior. Cookie started her freshman year with me. She sat a couple of seats in front of me in homeroom. Our last names put us close to each other in each class we shared. Her first name was Delfina, and she was eternally grateful that her dad nicknamed her Cookie when she was a toddler.

Our friendship started after we had an argument in gym class over the rules of basketball. She didn't know or understand them. She couldn't or wouldn't get the concept of the game, and to this day, she still didn't. However, she was impressed with my *cogliones*. Of course, I looked at her like she had three heads until she translated, "You got balls." We quickly became friends. When she found out firsthand what I was going through at home, living with an abusive, alcoholic father, we became best friends.

She listened to my stories of how I hated my father for being such a loser. My dad drove an eighteen-wheeler cross-country and wasn't home most of the time, which we kids were happy about. It meant peace for a couple of weeks. I told Cookie about the time he came home from being on the road, and the three of us kids were lying in front of the TV watching a show. He took one look at us and asked my mother,

"Why ain't these kids crying?" *Whack*! He slapped all three of us and made us wail. "That's better." He was a sick bastard that way. There were times he would enter our room in the middle of the night while we were sleeping and just start swinging. Ever since, I've had trouble sleeping throughout the night. As a child, it got so bad that I would fall asleep with one eye slightly open. I still did. It creeped my friends out, and they never believed I was really sleeping. I was a night owl most nights, up until after eight or nine in the morning sometimes. Because I was trained not to sleep comfortably throughout the night, I tossed and turned when I did. The dark reminded me of him, a living nightmare.

My mother, my siblings, and I took more than our fair share of beatings. Ten years after my college graduation, my father killed my mother, just as he always said he would. I'd never gotten over the guilt of being unable to save her. But he would never know an ounce of peace and would rot in prison like the piece of shit that he was until his final breath.

From his jail cell, my father had written to me several times, begging for forgiveness. Prison turned him into a Bible thumper. It was his way of staying clean and sober. Asking for my forgiveness couldn't have been easy for him, but reading the letter I sent back to him had to have been even harder. There was no forgiveness to be had. He made my childhood a living hell and kept my mother captive in her own home. If not for Cookie's family, I didn't know what would have become of me. My older brother, Domenic, followed in his footsteps as he continued the cycle of alcoholism and domestic violence. His wife and children were just as afraid of him as we once were of our own father. Needless to say, I didn't have a relationship with him. My little sister, Lynn, moved out of state and as far away from all of us as soon as she graduated from high school. We talked occasionally throughout the years and rarely saw each other. Strange how I still had family, yet I felt like a fucking orphan. Cookie was more of a sister to me than my own.

And that was all because I showed up at school one morning with a black eye. That was the last straw for Cookie. She asked her parents if I could move in with them, and I spent my sophomore through senior years living with them on a full-time basis. They treated me like one of their own, and it was because of her family that I made the decision to go to college. I couldn't save my mother, much as I wanted to, but I needed to save myself. Cookie didn't have the grades to go to college, nor did she want to, and started working in a local pharmaceutical factory right out of high school. It was a good job for someone with no higher education. She worked on a production line, watching things like ibuprofen pills come down a conveyor belt and picking out the defective ones. She said it was easy work for great pay, and she still worked there. I remember times in our early days when I would visit her on her break to smoke a joint. She would come out in her lab coat, scrub cap, and mask, and I would laugh at her every time. She looked ridiculous in the getup, but it was mandatory. I hadn't gone to her job to smoke a joint in years. I outgrew doing it every day in my early twenties, and now I only did it occasionally. Usually when Cookie wouldn't take no for an answer. And honestly, I probably needed it at those times. It did help relieve some stress.

Tonight was no different. She was on the floor with Addie when she peered up at me with her piercing blue eyes. "Are you ready? Fuckin' get ready! Let's smoke a fuckin' joint and go!"

"Natalie's party starts at seven. It's good to be fashionably late. And it'll take me five minutes to change."

"Well, go change already. Go, go, go!" she said as she shushed me along.

"All right already. Jeez!"

Kylie was looking at me and smiling. She was cute. Her hair was black, and she wore a short fauxhawk with the sides cut short. The top was longer and purposely messy. Her haircut suited her oblong face, and her chiseled facial features included high cheekbones and a petite nose. She was tall and thin, not the gym type but naturally thin. I couldn't help but stare at her long legs, as she was in shorts and sitting on my couch with one leg crossed over the other. Her most captivating feature, though, were her sterling gray eyes that held an air of mystery. She was young, probably no more than twenty-eight.

I looked at them and wondered if they were together, but before I could ask, Cookie was on top of it, knowing me so well. "We're just friends. She works with me at the factory. Now fuckin' go get ready!" Kylie and I smiled at each other, and I turned to go to my bedroom to change. I traded my sweatpants for jeans, my T-shirt for, well, a better T-shirt, and my old sneakers for new ones. I looked in the mirror and cursed myself for having a bad hair day. My hair was dark brown, medium length with straight layers and parted on the side. The humidity of the day had absorbed the shine, and it looked like straw. I attempted to put more gel in it but could tell it wasn't getting better. My brown eyes looked tired, but I was wide awake and ready to have some fun tonight. I examined myself further in the mirror, always self-conscious of my crooked nose ever since my father broke it when I was fifteen. Good times.

When I returned to the living room, Cookie and Kylie were sitting in a cloud of smoke with goofy grins on their faces. Kylie handed me what was left of the joint, and I graciously declined. Cookie took it and handed it to me again, only for me to refuse once more. "Just fuckin' take it!" she bullied.

"I don't want it! I'm not in the mood for that right now. I'd rather drink."

"Drink later. Smoke now."

"No!"

"Take it!"

"No!"

"I'm just gonna keep at you till you take it."

"Fine." I caved and took what was left of the joint. I inhaled slowly, and as I held it in, added, "She was right. You are a bad influence."

"Who was right?"

"Danielle."

"Fuck Danielle! Little snot!"

"Stop!"

"I don't know why she doesn't like me. I'm an absolute fucking delight. She needs to stop being such a little fuckin' tight ass."

"Easy," I warned as I put my hand up to stop her. I looked over at Kylie and attempted to change the conversation. "So, Kylie, are you from around here?"

"Trinity, born and raised."

Her inquisitive gaze checked me out more than

once, and the corners of her mouth turned upward into a cute smile, indicating to me that she was interested. There was a genuine attraction between the two of us. It was obvious. Her T-shirt with the Harley-Davidson logo gave her a cute boyish look, and the fact that she cut the shirt to show off her flat stomach was sexy as hell.

"Do you ride or do you just like biker T-shirts?" I asked.

"I ride."

"Really? What do you ride?"

"A burgundy Harley Street 500. It's used. An '08. But she's my baby. You're asking about bikes. Do you ride?"

"Yeah," I said excitedly. "I have a purple Fat Boy Lo. I fucking love it."

"We should ride some time." She flirted with me with her eyes as she invited me out.

"I'd like that."

❧❧❧❧

By the time we got to the hall, the party was in full swing. The parking lot was filled with cars, and as we neared the front door, the sound of laughter and loud conversation could be heard along with earsplitting music. The room was crowded with all sorts of people, most of them lesbians from the small circle we all rolled in. The entire team of Muff Mashers, my sponsored softball team, was here. The birthday girl, Natalie, was our star pitcher. We eventually reached the gift table, which was loaded up with presents, and the sheet cake was decked out with Tampa Bay Rays decorations. Natalie was a diehard fan, and it was apparent as we walked up to a large round table with a big crowd around it watching the Rays play the Red Sox on someone's cellphone. One of Danielle's and my biggest loves was going to see the Rays play. We hadn't been to a game yet this season, but I was sure we would get a few good games in before it was all said and done. The only reason she wasn't involved in this game right now was because April wasn't a typical sports-loving dyke. She had a thing for golf and tennis, nothing else. She said it was a waste of brain power to sit and watch a sport that was less interesting than watching paint dry. But Dani and I still thought of it as a great American pastime, and it bound us together despite April's disinterest.

Cookie tapped Natalie on the shoulder, and when she turned around, she excitedly said, "Cookie! Parker!" She gave us both a bear hug, and Cookie introduced Kylie. We wished her a happy birthday and asked where her other half was. She pointed in the direction of a table off to the corner where her girlfriend, Elise, was sitting with Danielle, April, and a few others.

I excused myself from Cookie and Kylie and went to say hello. I meandered over to their table, and Danielle spotted me immediately. She got up and gave me a welcoming hug. April, being the dude that she was, gave me a half hug and a handshake. "Where's Dorian?" I asked Dani.

"Strange thing. Said to tell you she has a phone date with the twins. And then she laughed. What is it, some kind of inside joke?"

"No, no. It's a long story. I'll tell ya later." I snickered.

During this discussion with Dani, Elise removed

herself from a conversation she was having with two other guests to come say hi to me. She hugged me and directed me to the buffet table. "Eat and eat plenty! There's way too much food."

I ended up in line with Kylie, waiting to pick from an array of food spread from one end of the table to the other. Above the loud music, we heard the roar of the group watching the baseball game, cheering and yelling. "They really get into it, huh?" she asked.

"Yeah, we get a little crazy for the Rays around here. Do you like baseball?"

"No, not really. Not into sports, really."

"What? What kind of lesbian are you?" I joked.

"The kind that likes girls." She shot me a sexy look with a playful grin.

The line moved, and we moved with it. "So are you seeing anyone?" I investigated as I reached for a dinner roll.

Her chortle was intriguing as she responded, "Not yet." With a teasing grin and a quick gaze, we finished filling our plates and sat with Danielle and April. A couple of other people were also seated with us. I sat next to Danielle. Kylie sat next to me, and I was monkey in the middle. Dani squinted and nodded in Kylie's direction, pretty much asking me who she was. I introduced them, and they shook hands over my plate. While Kylie looked down at her dish and ate, Dani mouthed the words, *Are you with her?*

"Not yet," I said out loud.

Kylie lifted her head. "What? Not yet what?"

"Uh, she just asked me if the baseball game was over, and I said not yet."

"Nice save." Danielle smirked.

Cookie pulled out an empty chair by Kylie and

sat with a loaded plate. She looked around the table and greeted everyone until she got to Danielle. The glare said it all. It upset me that the two people who cared most about me couldn't stand each other. They both knew I wasn't willing to give up either of them, so they did their best to tolerate each other. They came from opposite sides of the tracks. Danielle came from a wealthy family, career-oriented, and driven. Cookie was raised by a lower middle-class family. It was rebel versus athlete, pothead versus success. For Cookie, life was one big party. For Danielle, it was about goals. Their only common denominator was me.

As the festivities progressed and the keg had been hit harder than a hooker at a bachelor party, the DJ slowed things down a bit. Couples, straight and gay, made their way to the floor, including Danielle and April. I watched as April took Dani in her arms. She reached down to place her hands on Dani's hips, and they swayed to the music.

Dorian found it funny that April looked a lot like me, saying she didn't get why Danielle didn't just go for the real thing. She had about the same build as me, a medium frame, not petite but solid. Her hair was almost the same color as mine, just a little shorter. Honestly, she could be my sister. Only difference was, she had way more in common with Danielle than I did. She liked golf. I thought golf sucked. She enjoyed reading classic literature. I barely picked up a magazine. She played the trumpet. I couldn't hold a note. I was happy for them...mostly. I didn't know what kept us friends for all these years. Besides a love for the game of chess and a shared love for sports, we were complete opposites. But they say opposites attract, right?

I guess I liked April for the most part. And for all that they had in common, the things they didn't have in common, well, Danielle didn't talk about them. But I will. I had a problem with the way she controlled Danielle. The only time Dani was allowed to watch sports or any shows that she liked was when April was away on business. And God forbid she did anything to the house without permission. April wouldn't even let Danielle paint a room on her own, insisting that she didn't know how. For Christ's sake, a five-year-old could paint a wall, but Danielle didn't rock the boat, maintaining that she had to pick her battles, and painting wasn't one of them. I guess in some ways she had changed Dani, but overall, she told me she was happy, and looking in from the outside, they appeared that way.

A little later, the gifts were opened, the cake was cut, and I had knocked back a few beers. Kylie had been flirting with me all evening, and I had welcomed it, invited it even. I wasn't sure how fast I wanted to move with this young woman, though. She wasn't like Simone. She knew she was gay, and she wasn't ashamed of it. She certainly didn't hide it. With Simone, there was no fear that she would ask me for anything in return. It was strictly sexual. But Kylie. I didn't know what she was looking for, and if it was a relationship, I already knew I was out.

They rented a VFW hall for this party, and it was one of those deals where the renter set up and broke everything down. When Elise asked me to help, I didn't think she realized how tuned up I was. I wasn't drunk, but I had a nice buzz going. Nonetheless, I washed chafing pans, baking trays, etc. A large Tupperware bowl sat in the sink, filled with soap and water, and

I reached into it to grab for silverware at the bottom. I didn't notice the knife and had no idea I sliced my finger open until I brought it out of the water. Blood oozed from the bottom of my index finger, dripping into the sink. Danielle, who was next to me packing up leftover food, rushed to my aid.

"Dani, there's a first-aid kit in the bathroom," Elise said and pointed in that direction. She handed me a paper towel to wrap around my finger.

"Come on, Parker." Danielle maneuvered me out of the kitchen. "Hold your finger tight, okay?"

We entered the single bathroom, and she found the first-aid kit right away while I locked the door and stepped in front of the sink. She turned on the faucet. "Hold your finger under the water."

I did what she said as she rummaged through the kit. She found Neosporin and a variety of bandages and gauze.

"Let me see it." She took my finger and dabbed it with a clean paper towel. "I hope you don't need stitches. It looks pretty deep, and the hunk of meat hanging off your finger is disgusting." She looked up from my cut, and we both laughed. She knew I couldn't stomach the sight of my own blood, but she demanded I look at it.

"You know I won't."

"Why not? C'mon. Look!"

"No. Stop!"

She laughed again, that cute little giggle that got my heart going. I struggled to look away from her face. Her sweet face. "I'm so glad you wear your hair up all the time," I blurted out.

"What?" she asked, grinning but a bit confused by my statement that came out of left field.

"Your hair. I'm glad you wear it up most of the time."

Her eyebrows scrunched together. "Why?"

I didn't answer her. She glanced up at me from dressing my wound. "Why?" she repeated.

With a profound and everlasting affection for her, I said, "Because when you wear your hair down..." I paused for a split second, peering over her pretty face, and professed, "You are so beautiful that I have to remind myself to breathe."

She looked down as if she didn't want to hear that, took a deep breath, and continued bandaging my finger, ignoring what I said and attempting to move on. However, I continued to stare at her face. My desire for her never ceased, even after almost two decades. She felt me staring and didn't bother to look up. "Parker, why are you looking at me like that?"

"Like what?"

"Like you want to kiss me."

"Because for eighteen years, I've wondered what it would be like to kiss you, to taste your lips. I've always imagined that they taste like strawberries."

She looked from my bandaged finger, examined my face, and searched my eyes. "Just do it."

"Excuse me?"

"Just do it. You've been wondering all these years, so just do it, and let's get this out of the way."

I was stunned. Never would I have expected her to give me the green light on physical contact. She was giving me permission. Like an idiot, I stuttered, "Um, I, uh, I..."

"If I have to say it again, I'm probably going to change my mind."

I wasn't going to let that happen. I planted my

lips on hers. She was somewhat hesitant at first as if she didn't think I would have the moxie to go through with it. But I had wanted this for so long, I wasn't letting this opportunity pass. Once she felt how gentle I was, she relaxed enough to let me kiss her. I brushed my lips over hers, lightly kissing them and then sweeping my lips over hers again. Her lips were velvety and soft against mine. Our kiss was gentle and tender. This powerful energy built up between us. I stepped closer to her and parted my mouth, offering her my tongue and not expecting to be invited into hers. Yet she did. She did invite me in. Our tongues met for the first time, touching and circling around each other before I brushed my lips against hers again, kissing her and opening my mouth to feel her once more. She didn't even complain about my tongue piercing that she always cringed at. Instead, she let the kiss linger for a while.

When she ended it, she took a step back and away from me. I took this as a sign that she didn't feel anything in the kiss, and I said, "I know. You just think of me as a friend."

Just then, someone pounded on the door and yelled, "Hurry up! You've been in there forever!"

Danielle never said a word as she gathered the first-aid kit and put it where she found it. She looked at me one last time before she unlocked and opened the door. The woman banging on the door rushed in and closed it behind her. We walked to the main room where everyone was gathered, and Danielle wasted no time taking April by the hand and hightailing it out of there. Of course she ran out of there. Her close friend of nearly twenty years had just shoved her tongue down her throat. She was probably grossed out.

When Cookie pulled up to my house, Kylie and I exchanged phone numbers, and though I had every intention of kissing her at the end of this night, what took place in the bathroom with Danielle was foremost in my mind right now. I climbed the steps to my porch, turned, and waved goodbye, watching them drive off in the darkness. I let myself in and let Addie out. Once she finished her business and ran back in, I locked up the house and retired for the night.

※ ※ ※ ※

Saturday was difficult for me. I walked around in a fog. I replayed that kiss over and over in my head and couldn't get Danielle off my mind. Her lips were sweet and warm, and even though I knew it would never take place again, I felt a comfort in having remedied my curiosity.

Merge opened at three p.m. like usual. I opened the bar at that time every day for my old-timers, who started to leave around eight when the college girls came. Simone was already behind the bar when, much to her dismay, Michelle walked through the door. "What's she doing here?" Simone asked me. Tricia was my other bartender tonight, not Michelle for this reason.

"I don't know."

"Well, you need to get rid of her, Parker! I already have a partner for tonight." Simone used her thumb to point behind her where Tricia was slicing limes and lemons.

Michelle put her pocketbook under the bar and readied herself to work.

"Uh-uh, bitch!" Simone yelled.

"Who you callin' a bitch? Bitch!"

"Whoa! Whoa! Whoa! Hey! Not here! No way!" I looked from one to the other. "My office, now!"

They followed me down the hall to my office. Simone was the last one in and closed the door behind her. I sat behind my desk, and they sat in front of me. I reached into my pocket and pulled out my cell to call Jules. "Where are you?" I asked, waiting for a response before saying, "Well, stop smoking your cigarette and come to my office, please."

"Parker, she can't help herself, she—" Simone attempted to say.

I waved her off. "Wait!"

Moments later, Jules walked through the door. "What's up?" she asked but didn't wait for a reply, seeing Michelle and Simone sitting there, both with angry faces. "Shit," she said and started in. "Listen, it was a mistake on the schedule."

"Again?" I asked.

"Ya know what's wrong, Parker? That I don't get to work Saturdays anymore because of Queen Douchery," Michelle said.

"What did you call me, bitch?"

"Simone, enough!" I slapped my hands on the desk. "If the two of you can't find a way to get along, then one of you will have to go!"

"And I guess that would be me, right, Parker? Because you don't fuck me anymore! You're fucking her now, aren't you? It's 'cause she has bigger tits than me."

"What?" Simone barked out. "You fucked her?"

"That was a long time ago," I said to Simone and looked at Michelle. "That was a long time ago. And how did this become about me, anyway? Ya know what, Michelle, go home, and I'll talk to you Monday. The rest of you, get the fuck out of my office and do some Goddamn work!" My voice had escalated into an angry and enraged tone, and as Jules was about to slither out the door, I yelled, "Stop scheduling them together!"

I didn't know how I owned a lesbian bar and employed two bisexual women bartenders fighting over a man. Gus certainly wasn't that handsome for these two to hate each other like this. I knew I couldn't have these internal problems in my place of business. I needed the employees to get along. After all, a happy employee was a productive employee, and that was my aim. Whether I had to force that happiness on them was a different story.

The night was busy, and having Common Bond play was a smart move. They were a local lesbian duo and extremely popular with the younger crowd. While they played their last set of the night, we announced last call. Simone inconspicuously grabbed my attention and gave me the eye, indicating we were on after we closed. I wasn't really in the mood and was awfully punchy. I hadn't heard from Danielle all day or night, and I didn't even know if she was coming to play chess this morning. The last thing I wanted was for things to get weird between us.

I sat behind my desk when Simone strutted in, chipper and happy, a far cry from the beginning of her shift. "Did you have a good night?"

"I killed it! Have Common Bond back soon. They really brought them in!"

"Yeah, I was pretty thrilled with business tonight. And no fights! I'm always happy when there are no fights. These young butch girls don't know when to quit, always puffin' out their chests when they have too much to drink."

"Some of them are cute, though." Simone smiled.

"You just wanna eat their pussies."

"Mmm, speaking of eating pussy."

"I don't know, Simone. I don't know if I'm in the mood."

"What? You not in the mood? What's up with you tonight?"

I leaned back in the chair, lifted my head toward the ceiling, and let out a deep sigh. "Haven't been able to focus all day or night. Guess I'm feeling stressed out for no reason." *Oh, there's a reason.*

She got up from the chair and came around to my side, offering her hand to me. "C'mon." She grabbed my hand, lifted me out of my seat, and led me to the love seat. She pushed me back and knelt between my legs. "Let me relax you," she whispered and unbuckled my belt, loosened my pants, and yanked them off. Once she got my bottom half bare, she looked up and encouraged me, "Come on, Parker. This is usually a fun time. Why the long face?"

"I can't talk about it."

"I want to cheer you up." She dragged her fingertips over my naked thighs and caressed them. She tried to get my motor running. My feet were on the coffee table where the chessboard was. But the board had been moved from the center and was off to the side. My foot rested against the side of it. I wanted to move it back to the center and out of the way, but she began her clit-lashing session, and I forgot all about it. The feel of her wet tongue sliding over my nub made it throb with yearning for release. It took a while for me to climax, though, and she stopped. "You never take this long. Something is not right with you tonight, and you're not telling me."

"It's nothing. Really. Everything is fine." I pushed her head back down, and she returned to beating my clit. Just because I couldn't cum didn't mean it didn't feel fantastic. It did. I allowed myself to fantasize about Danielle. Now that something physical actually happened between us, my mind permitted the images of the kiss to play and replay, again and again. With each image, I sank deeper and deeper into the cushion of the leather couch.

My clit was so hard, and if it was possible, I was wetter. I was so close. "Mm-hmm," she muttered into my pussy, talking as she licked, "You're so wet."

Then the image of Dani's face between my legs entered my mind, and the orgasm that followed was explosive. "Uh, uh, uh, uh..." I rubbed my clit all over Simone's tongue and came in her mouth. "Oh, God! Yeah!" My body jolted from pleasure, and I involuntarily kicked the chessboard. The pieces scattered to the floor.

The couch had taken possession of me, and I was one with it. I couldn't have moved if my life depended on it. "You okay?" Simone asked as she wiped her chin over her shoulder.

"Yeah, why?"

"Because you've never cum like that for me. Holy cow! I want to do it again."

She dropped her head back down, ready to go at it once more, but I pushed her head up and giggled. "No, no. That's all I can take for tonight." I put my pants back on, and we shared a glass of wine. The talks we had after these weekly romps were good for me, even though I'd never been completely honest with her about my thoughts and feelings. I was good at protecting my heart. I had plenty of practice, caging it up all these years with Dani.

Simone talked about Gus more than anything else, but tonight, I hadn't heard a word about him. He seemed nonexistent lately as she sipped her wine and caressed my arm, her fingertips sending goosies up and down my body. She never did this. We didn't touch. Those were her rules. I wasn't sure what was going on, but before I could ask, she leaned in to kiss me. I was about to break the lip lock she had on me but decided that if she was breaking boundaries tonight, so would I. Apparently, breaking rules and boundaries was my new thing, so I went with it and brought my hands to her shapely bosom. At first, she started to take my hand away, but then she took her hand from mine and let me touch her. Her nipples stiffened between my thumb and index finger, and I was so happy the stupid cut was on my left hand. She moaned, and her breathing became shallow and shaky. I was going to make my move. I was just about to fuck her when she stopped me. I couldn't argue. It was the most she let me near her, let alone touch her. "I can't," she said.

"It's okay."

"I want to, but—"

"It's okay. Really."

Not long after, Gus was outside honking the horn. She kissed me goodbye, and I had yet to figure out what had just happened. This was the same woman who shouted her love for this man from mountaintops. Not so much tonight.

Simone left, and I waited for Danielle. By six twenty, I was pretty sure I was being stood up. When she didn't show by six forty-five, I gathered my shit and threw it in my backpack. As I swung the backpack over my shoulder and grabbed my keys off the desk to leave, there she was standing in the doorway. Her hair was naturally tied back in a ponytail, and her gaze begged to understand what she found most perplexing. I knew she wasn't in her right state of mind, but she attempted to act normal. "Leaving so soon?" she said.

"I got caught in traffic. An accident. I guess I should have sent you a text."

"Why didn't you? Were you hoping I'd already be gone?"

"No, Parker. I'd really like to move on from the other night. Can we do that?"

"I've been doin' that for eighteen years, so yeah, we can do that." I knew that kiss couldn't happen again. She was spoken for, and our friendship would be in jeopardy, but I'd always have that kiss.

She handed me a coffee, and we sat on opposite sofas. She straightened out the pieces on the board. "Hey! You're missing a couple of pawns, and where's the queen?"

I wanted to tell her I knocked them off the table coming to her face, but instead said, "Oh, I, uh, I accidentally tripped against the table, and I guess some of the pieces fell off."

She hunted around the table and searched the floor before finally exclaiming, "Got it!" And then she spotted the other pieces. "There they are!" She set up the board, and we played. We tried to make small talk, but it was strained and a little awkward.

"What did you and April do yesterday?" I asked.

"Played golf."

"Did you win?"

"We played partners, and no, we lost to a creepy straight couple that we got snookered into playing with. Pretty sure they wanted to swing with us."

"Eww." I chuckled.

We drank our coffees, and even though we sort of talked, Danielle hadn't looked at me. I knew she wasn't her normal self today because she was off her game in a bad way. I took advantage of that and beat her in the first match.

"Have you been practicing?" she asked.

"No, you just suck this morning."

I got a small giggle out of her, and we began our second game. I was so focused on the board that my head was down and my gaze zoned in on my pieces. I hadn't realized how much time I spent to move my bishop. I exclaimed, "There! Your move!" And when I lifted my head, she was looking at me. Like she had the very first time we met. My stomach dropped, and I had to catch my breath before asking, "Dani, why are you looking at me like that?"

She sucked in her bottom lip. "I...I haven't stopped thinking of that kiss since it happened."

"What? Yeah, right," I said in disbelief.

"I liked it," she confessed.

The room was quiet except for the ticking of the grandfather clock in the corner and my heart beating out of control over her words.

"This is a joke, right? You're fuckin' with me."

Her face remained serious, and her gaze was fixed on me. She wasn't kidding. Once I realized this, I simply moved the table out of the way so there weren't any barriers between us. I sat with my legs slightly apart, and I leaned forward, resting my elbows on my knees and crossing my arms.

"Do they?" she asked me, and my confusion mounted.

"Do they what? What are you talking about?" I returned her question with a question.

"Do my lips taste like strawberries?"

I watched her face as she rubbed the tops of her thighs slowly, restlessly, and obviously battling temptation. I knew I shouldn't have, but I slid off the couch and onto the floor, crawled the few feet to get to her, and knelt between her legs. She pulled back some and put her hands to her sides, afraid to touch me. She knew she shouldn't touch me. I placed my hands on her thighs, caressed them with my palms, and grasped her muscles.

"Yes," I said as I broke our stare and leaned forward to kiss her. I took her hands that were almost hidden, looped them around my neck, and placed my own hands around her waist. My lips parted, and she did the same. Our tongues reunited, and the sweetness that I tasted the other night resumed. Her kiss was tender and soft, slow and deliberate. A barely audible, quick hum escaped her lips, "Mmm..." That quick little *hum* compelled me to press against her and shift her from a sitting position to a horizontal one. Her eyes were closed, and I couldn't help but gaze at her while we kissed. She was so beautiful, and I was certain this was a dream. That was until a love song started playing right next to my ear.

"My phone!" she yelled and pushed me away. "Hi, honey." April. My stomach sank with a small pang of guilt. "Uh, actually, we just finished our last game, and I'm about to leave." She looked at me while she talked. "Yeah, babe, I can pick up creamer. I'll see you soon. Yeah, I love you, too. Okay, yes, hi to Parker, too. I will."

She ended the call and abruptly got up from the couch. "Parker, we can't do that again. It was a mistake. You know that, right?"

"But you said you couldn't stop thinking about it."

"I know, but it's something I'm going to have to forget."

"Forget?"

"I'm with April. She's my fiancée. We're getting married."

I guess I had lost track of reality, but she made sure to slap me across the face with it. She gave me a quick, half hug and raced out the door. I was left standing with my heart up my ass. It wasn't a big deal. I had repeatedly pushed my feelings for Danielle aside for almost two decades. I would do it again. Though in the past, I never knew what her lips tasted like. I couldn't believe she told me she liked it. She liked kissing me. I liked kissing her, too. She was right in stopping it. She was going to marry April. It wasn't in Danielle's biological makeup to cheat. She was very matter-of-fact, and everything was black and white. Everything was planned. Nothing ever left to surprise, and maybe that wasn't always a good thing because life didn't come wrapped neatly in perfect packaging. Sometimes, life kicked you right in the teeth when you were least expecting it, and here I was spitting them out on the floor like a ripped-open box of Chiclets.

By Tuesday, I had shoved the thought of Danielle to the back of my mind. I busied myself and searched the internet for new talent to perform at the bar. A promoter I did a lot of business with, Ted, kept pushing for Used Lug Nutz, a heavy metal band, to play. I wasn't sure of the particular clientele they would bring in and kept putting them off.

Then I talked to the general contractor again about the possible addition to the bar, and no day would be complete without having to referee a Simone versus Michelle battle. Simone wasn't even working or physically there, but Michelle couldn't leave it alone. "Are you fucking her?" she asked.

Without moving my head from my laptop, I looked at her and calmly answered, "That's none of your business."

"So you are. So gross!"

"You're standing in my office, and I'm not sure why. I know it's not to interrogate me about my sex life." I focused on the computer screen again. "Do you like working here?"

"Well, yeah."

"Then get out of my office and take that attitude with you."

With one final evil squint to me, she turned and left. There was so much negativity between them that I may just have to smudge the building. No sooner did Michelle leave than Dorian rambled through the door. "What's wrong with her?" she asked. "She looks pretty pissed off."

"The same bullshit! Simone."

"Why don't you just get it over with and fuck 'em both? Threesome!"

"What?" I looked at her incredulously. "Are you insane? They hate each other." And in that split second of waiting for her reply, I pictured what that might look like, me sandwiched between two hot women. The image was tainted quickly as the inevitable fighting took place, even in my fantasy.

"If they could get past their hatred of each other...Man! That would be hot," she said.

"Dorian, I'm not fucking my bartenders."

"You mean now?"

I laughed out loud at this because Dorian only knew about what happened with Michelle when she started working for me. Michelle and I had a fling for the first six months she was here. Like Simone, it was kept a secret. Unlike Simone, Michelle let me touch her. However, Michelle had failed to lock my office door one night after closing hours, and Dorian, drunk and wandering around the bar, walked in on us. I tried to swear her to secrecy, but it only took her telling one person for the entire bar to find out. I had to cut the affair off or get rid of Michelle. And since she needed the job in a bad way, I cut it off. It didn't go over so well with Michelle, but I couldn't have a soap opera-like atmosphere in my bar. She seemed to get used to it, and life went on—until Simone. I didn't think Michelle ever really wanted Gus. That was just to piss off Simone because she surmised something was going on between us. I had been able to keep Simone a secret for months, and even though Dorian had questioned me in the past about her, I believed I had finally convinced her that nothing was going on.

Ignoring her entirely, I asked, "To what do I owe the pleasure of your visit?"

"You need to have a pool party."

"Excuse me?"

"You gotta have a pool party. I've been talking to Dahlia on the phone every day since we met, but she says she wants our first date to be in public."

"Public? Why? Does she think you're a serial killer?" I chuckled.

"It's not funny. She says she would feel more comfortable around people. So you have to have a pool party."

"Why not just meet at a restaurant?"

"Because then I wouldn't get to see her in a bikini. And I really wanna see her in a bikini."

"It's a little short notice, don't ya think?"

"Okay, well, don't have it this weekend. Have it the following Sunday." She waited for my answer and nonchalantly included, "You owe me."

It was true. I did owe her. I did my best not to fall into any addictions. My father was the worst addict I knew, but the gambling bug got the best of me about six years ago. Gambling in backrooms of lesbian, biker gang, clubhouses almost got my legs broken until Dorian lent me the money to get out of debt. I almost lost the bar that time. "A pool party it is. Two weeks from now."

She bear-hugged me. "Thanks. I'll send out an email to invite everyone."

I had plenty to do between now and then. I had to prepare my house for guests, buy all the food and booze, and decide on a band or DJ. Either way, my neighbors were going to hate me.

Chapter Three

Thursday morning, I woke up to a big sun and an even bigger blue sky. The temps were in the mid-eighties, and I decided I didn't care if I had to suffer through another one of Danielle's speeches about the dangers of riding a motorcycle. Even though I drove a Jeep and could take the top off, it was just too nice a day, and I needed to ride. I put my helmet on, despite the fact it wasn't required, thanks to the state of Florida. Funny how I would wear the helmet but never attempted to cover up any exposed skin. I was in shorts, a tank top, and running sneakers. Not the first choice for riding a bike, but I didn't care. I hopped on my hog and revved it up. Man, I loved the loud sound of a Harley.

With a little traffic, it took me fifteen minutes to get to North Hyde Park for my run with Dani. When I pulled up, she was already shaking her head. I knew what was coming, and I tried to persuade her instead. "Come on! Hop on the back! Let me take you for a ride."

"Are you kidding me? Yeah, right!"

"Come on! I won't hurt you. I promise."

"No."

"Just around the corner."

I was stunned that she was actually thinking it over. She looked around, bit her lip, and clearly debated with herself over the decision. I took my helmet off and offered it to her. "Here. Put this on."

"Only around the block and no shenanigans."

"No shenanigans. I promise." I crossed my heart.

She took the helmet from me and put it on, but it was a little crooked on her head because of her ponytail. I tried to straighten it out some, but it was of no use.

"It would fit better if you took the pony out," I said.

"I'm not taking my pony out."

"Why?" I snickered, a little puzzled.

"Because of what you said."

It took me a second, but I realized it was from what I said in the bathroom at Natalie's party. "Oh! What do you think, you're leading me on if you let your hair down?"

"Well, I don't know."

"Stop! I'm sorry I said what I said. You're my friend, Dani. I would never want you to feel uncomfortable around me. So go ahead and let your hair down so the helmet fits properly...please."

She hesitated but eventually took the hair tie out, and with her hands, shook her long golden hair loose. Once the helmet was on, I adjusted the strap under her chin and purposely didn't make eye contact with her.

"That's better," I said and patted the back of my seat. "Come on. Hop up."

With a little apprehension and a bit of fear, she threw her right leg over the seat and slid on. I sat back on my seat and put the bike in gear. As it shimmied forward some, she reached for my shoulders.

"That's not gonna work. Put your hands around my waist and hold on."

I could tell she was nervous, but she listened. When I took off, I felt her grip around me tighten, and she said, "Not so fast!"

"Dani, I'm doin' twenty miles per hour and barely able to hold the bike up. We have to go faster." I turned the throttle to pick up speed. "Trust me."

While I rode, I adjusted my right-side mirror. Only I adjusted it so that her face was smack in the center. I didn't think she realized, but I periodically glanced from the road to her face. The face shield was up on her forehead, and she pointed her face in the direction of the sun. Her eyes were closed, and she enjoyed the warmth as it shone over her face. Her eyelashes laid like feathers, spread below her eyes, and I quickly averted mine when she opened them to observe her surroundings.

On our second trip around the neighborhood, I felt her relax and loosen her grip a little. While we rode down the street, I felt her hand on my left shoulder blade, softly rubbing over my tattoo. She had no idea that the tattoo she was touching was put there for her. She just knew it had been there a long time. The night I had it done, I was with Cookie, of course, and even though I wasn't completely sober and maybe a bit stoned, I had the artist create a rather large heart with a lit torch stabbing the center and a banner that read *HOPE*. Before he colored it in, I asked him to write Danielle's name in the middle of the heart so I would always know it was there. Her name written on my heart. Then I made him color it in. I was the only one who knew it was there, yet here she was circling over and tracing her finger around it. The sensation of her caressing my skin was enough to melt me right there under her touch. But as I pulled it together, I glanced at my rearview and caught her looking at me. I smiled, and she smiled back at me, her dimples deepening as her smile widened. She was so pretty, and I loved having her on the back of my bike.

I still wasn't sure what possessed her to climb on the bike with me today, but I loved it so much that I made a mental note of what her hands felt like around me, and then I pulled in her driveway. I wasn't at all surprised when the helmet came off and the ponytail was put back in place right away. It was okay, though. She made my day just by taking a short ride with me.

∿ ∿ ⦆ ⦆

We stretched for our run, and April came out the front door with a suitcase in tow. She tossed it in the trunk of her car, walked over to Danielle, and hugged her. "I have to go. I'll call you when I land. Okay?"

"Okay. I'll miss you."

"I won't be gone long. Dallas is always a short trip. You know that."

I watched as she kissed her. When she turned away from Danielle, she looked over at me and said, "Take care of my girl, Parker."

"Naturally." *Oh, if you only knew.*

She got in her car, blew Dani a kiss, and drove away. No more was said as we finished stretching and began our run. Conversation didn't exist as it usually did, and I didn't press Dani to find out why. Maybe she was just trying to find a way to cope with recent events. I believed I was coping with it a little better than she was, but only because I had so much more practice turning it off. This time, it was harder. I knew what her mouth felt like on mine. Nonetheless, I still knew my role in her life. *Friend.*

By the time we finished and got back to her house, I was a hot sweaty mess. As I tried to regain a balanced breath, she asked, "Are you busy tomorrow?"

"No. Why?" I paced back and forth with my hands above my head, trying to stretch out a cramp in my side.

"April will be away for a few days. I was wondering if you want to bring Addie by for a play date with JoJo and maybe have some dinner, watch a movie. I don't feel like being alone the whole time she's gone."

"Yeah, sure. That sounds good. I'll see you to-morrow night then." I stepped toward her, gave her a quick hug, and made sure not to linger too long. As I hopped back on my bike and put my helmet on, she followed behind just to be sure to get part of *the speech* in. "Please be careful on that thing. I really do worry about you."

"Dani, I've been riding my whole life. I think I got this!"

She didn't seem convinced. "It's not you, it's the drivers that don't see you!"

I gave her a warm smile and assured her I would see her tomorrow. With a turn of the key, the beast came alive, and I rode off down the street.

※ ※ ※ ※

After I spent the next day at the bar preparing for this weekend's business, I headed home to shower, change, and pick up Addie. On my way to Hyde Park, the weather drastically changed. Gray clouds were rolling in, and the wind was picking up.

When Addie and I approached the front door, Danielle and JoJo were waiting for us. The barking started, and the inevitable butt sniffing began. I didn't know why we always found this funny, but we did. I followed Dani through the house to the backyard with the dogs in tow. We walked out to the pool area and continued to the large yard next to the pool. JoJo raced up to me with an old, beat-up toy in his mouth, and after I wrestled him for it, I threw it across the lawn. Both dogs chased after it, and even though JoJo got to it first, they both ran back, side by side, the toy half in his mouth, half in hers.

While we played with the dogs, we chatted about our day. I still debated if I wanted to shell out money for an addition to the bar, and Danielle talked about her new students and taking on summer classes. Dusk soon turned to night, and a light drizzle came down from the sky. We gathered the dogs and went inside. "Are you hungry?" I asked.

"I'm starving. What are you in the mood for?"

"Pizza."

"Pizza?"

"Well, what do you want?"

"Chinese. No, wait. The new Greek place in town. They deliver."

"Deal. I can go for some Greek food."

The food soon arrived, and we fixed our plates as we got comfortable in front of the TV. We scrolled through a bunch of movie titles before we settled on a horror movie. She wasn't all that keen on the selection, but I refused to watch the goofy love story she wanted. The movie was about an exorcism of a demon possessing a teenage boy. Every time the music became eerie and creepy and you knew something scary was going to happen, Danielle squinted and looked away. "What do you have me watching? Eww… what is that evil-looking thing?"

"Stop talking and just watch."

Just then, they showed the boy asleep in his bed. The demon came out of the closet and towered above him. He was about to attack when Dani looked away. "Tell me when it's over." She had her eyes closed and covered her face with her hands as she waited for me to tell her it was over.

But just as she couldn't resist playing with me at times, neither could I. "Okay. You can look." She peeked through her fingers, and the demon pounced on the boy and wrapped his claws around the kid's throat.

"Damn it, Parker!" She punched my arm. "Why would you do that to me?" I couldn't stop laughing from the innocence she displayed at times. For such a strong, intelligent, professional woman, she had certain child-like attributes. And this was one of the things that made her so attractive to me. For instance, when she wore those corny bunny pajamas, I giggled every time I saw her in them.

As the movie approached the end and Danielle had disfigured the pillow she clutched for the past half-hour, the rain came down in torrents. Thunder could be heard in the distance, and she turned to me. "Maybe you and Addie should stay. It's pretty late, and the rain is really coming down."

"Are you sure?" I knew she was a little uneasy about what had taken place between us recently.

"Yeah. I'd rather not worry about you driving home in this weather, and besides, look at them." She pointed to the dogs curled up next to each other asleep on JoJo's small bed. "They look too comfortable to disturb."

I agreed, and she shut off the TV. We climbed the staircase to the bigger guest room. I followed her in, and she asked, "Do you need another blanket? Pillow?"

"No. I think I'm good."

"Okay then." She looked at me as if she wanted to hug me but thought better of it. "Well, good night."

"Good night."

❧ ❧ ❧ ❧

Danielle left the door cracked just in case the dogs wanted to come in and headed for the master bedroom. Once alone in the room, I took a look around. The whole house screamed seaside, and this guest room was no different. The walls were painted a soft green and were covered with scenic beach paintings placed evenly to balance out the room. On each side of the white, four-poster canopy bed were seahorse end tables with shell lamps in the center of each. At the end of the bed sat an upholstered, tufted bench. Everything matched, right down to the area rug under the bed.

The hardwood floors creaked as I walked over and closed the drapes. I turned one of the end table lamps on and turned off the main light. Addie came racing through the door, sprang up on the bench, and onto the bed. Seconds after, JoJo did the same. "JoJo, why aren't you with your mother? You wanna sleep with Addie, huh?" He rolled onto his back and offered me his tummy. I smiled and pet him. "Okay, you can stay."

While the dogs settled in at the end of the bed, I stripped down to my bikini underwear, took my bra off from underneath my T-shirt, and took all the decorative pillows off the bed. There were so many. After I placed them on the chair in the corner, I turned down the covers and climbed in. The sound of the rain beat against the windowpane. It relaxed me enough that I closed my eyes. This wasn't the first time I had stayed the night when April was away. Danielle got lonely quickly and didn't care too much for staying in this big house by herself. It wasn't all the time, but occasionally, she asked me to stay.

The wind picked up now, and the thunder moved closer. A flash of lightning appeared, and *Boom!* The thunder echoed outside. I opened my eyes, looked around the room once more, and closed them again. *Bang!* The thunder sounded like it was right over the house. The dogs panted at the foot of the bed, but my attention was diverted from them to the door slowly creaking open. I opened my eyes to see Danielle enter the room.

"Hey, are you awake?" she asked softly.

"What's wrong?"

"Well, besides the fact that my dog is a traitor and we watched that scary movie, the thunder is sort of unnerving. Can I stay in here with you?"

I propped myself up on my elbows and stared at her a bit baffled. Was this some kind of test? If it was, I would surely fail. Temptation was a real bitch, even as she stood there in those ridiculous pink and yellow bunny pajamas. I didn't feel as though there was much choice in the matter, and I found it difficult to resist her.

"Sure," I appeased her, while the inside of my stomach uncontrollably shook.

She scampered across the room and stood by the bed, unsure and somewhat apprehensive about getting into bed with me.

Crash! The thunder exploded, rumbled, and shook the house. Danielle quickly dived under the covers. We both lay on our backs and watched the lightning flash like a strobe across the room, waiting for the next big boom. When it came, I realized that, though I thought she was my prey, it turned out, I was hers.

Kabang! We flinched from the shaking of the ground, and she turned on her side to face me. As more thunder erupted, she inched closer and closer to me. When the next roar of thunder came, it may as well have cracked right in the room. I never heard or felt thunder so close. My body jerked slightly from the sound, and Danielle asked, "Are you okay?"

She placed her hand on my stomach, and I refused to look at her. If I looked at her, we were going to have sex. So, instead, I closed my eyes and answered, "Yes."

She didn't remove her hand. Rather, she rubbed over my stomach, gently brushed her fingertips over my T-shirt, and sent goose bumps up and down my body. My hands were at my sides as I tried desperately not to touch her. It was just yesterday morning that she didn't want me to get the wrong idea. I didn't know what idea I was supposed to take from this as she grazed over my belly with the palm of her hand. She slowly lifted my T-shirt just enough to place her hand on my warm skin.

It was still pouring outside, the rain pelting the

window with force and the wind howling past. Lightning filled the room again, and out of the corner of my eye, I saw her studying me. I would not look at her. I didn't think she understood that once we did this, we couldn't undo this. I didn't want her to regret it or feel guilty about it, but she would.

While these thoughts raced through my mind, her fingertips caressed my bare skin. It was like I slapped invisible restraints on my own wrists. I clamped down on the bed and tried to resist her. But her touch felt so good. Her gaze had yet to leave my face, and I closed my eyes as she traced over my ribs, outlining each one with her fingers.

I didn't know how I kept it together when her leg slid over my thigh, and she gradually but steadily began grinding. Heat permeated through her pajama bottoms, and it took everything I had to keep my hips still. I felt her hot breath in my ear, and she whispered, "Why won't you look at me?"

"Because I'm trying to control myself."

"Maybe I don't want you to control yourself."

She lifted herself upright as she straddled my thigh. One hand rested on my stomach, and the other steadied her weight on the bed. She started from right above my knee and dragged her pussy all the way up my thigh. She repeated this several times as she attempted to entice me or at the very least to make me open my eyes. Finally, she reached for my face and demanded, "Look at me!"

"I can't."

"Why?"

"Because things are gonna happen."

"Open your eyes, Parker."

When I did, she placed her hands behind her

head and pulled the hair tie out. I was completely entranced by her as she shook her hair back and forth, letting it fall around her shoulders. I didn't realize my jaw had dropped, and I whispered, "Wow," out loud.

I couldn't close my eyes now if I wanted to, and I didn't want to. She knew exactly what she was doing. She was so incredibly beautiful sitting on top of me that she really did take my breath away. Her memory apparently had clung to my words from the night of our first kiss, and she reminded me, "Breathe."

I gazed upon her angelic face as she continued her seduction of me. Each thrust on my leg brought her pussy closer and closer to mine. She was about to slide right on top of it, and I warned, "Danielle, I'm not going to be able to control myself if you go there. I won't be held responsible for what takes place."

There was no response. Instead, our gazes locked as she grinded her pussy directly on top of mine. This provoked some heavy breathing from me, and I reached my breaking point. My hips rose to meet hers, and I grinded back into her. My underwear and her pajama bottoms were all that stood between us. The invisible restraints dissolved, and I set my hands on her waist momentarily before I brought them down to her ass. I cupped her cheeks and aided her in rubbing her pussy on mine. Our gazes were still on each other as she rocked on me. What started out at a slow pace had now picked up speed, and I wanted the barrier gone…now. I pulled at her bottoms, dragged them down over her ass, and squeezed. "Take these off," I ordered.

"What's going to happen if I take them off?"

I licked my lips. "I'm going to make you cum like you've never cum before." And I meant it.

"You're awfully sure of yourself."

"I have been so hot for you for so long, there's nothing I wouldn't do to please you. Yeah, I'm sure of myself."

She leaned down to kiss me, all the while sliding her pussy back and forth over top of mine. "Mmm…" She quietly moaned. Her breath was heavy as I rolled her from the top to the bottom and placed myself between her legs. I moved a strand of hair from her face and looked into her eyes. She wrapped her hands around the back of my neck and pulled me closer. She teased me with her tongue and enclosed her mouth around mine. We fit so perfectly together. I slid down her torso and lifted her pajama top up, just enough to expose her tightly toned stomach. Her ab muscles and her navel were surrounded by a few beauty marks. I kissed all around her belly button and tugged on her pajama bottoms slightly, teasing myself by uncovering her pussy inch by inch, never completely revealing it. Unveiling her mound, I kissed it. Her hips never stopped moving. I knew I turned her on when she lifted her pussy up to my mouth and practically begged me to lick it.

Her gaze was on me, her lips slightly parted, and the intensity in the room built. Her breathing was short and quick as she anticipated the feel of my tongue on her small gem. "Yeah…" she murmured, her hips rising once again to provoke me.

At last, I pulled them down to the tops of her thighs, divulging her entire pussy. A well-manicured little patch of hair in the shape of a square was right above her bald pussy lips, and I kissed around the area where her slit began. She jerked her hips upward again, persuading me to connect with her clit. My eyes rolled to the back of my head as I closed them and dipped my tongue into her. I took one long stroke up her and made sure to use the ball of my tongue piercing to slide over it. Her body jolted from the current sent from my touch. "Oh. Oh, yeah," she muttered. Her face twisted in pleasure.

My tongue connected with her hardened jewel repeatedly, and I drank her in as I craved her body and soul. In between strokes, I said, "Oh, you're so wet. And you taste so fucking good." I intentionally licked just below her clitoris so that the very top of my piercing rubbed directly on top of it. Interchanging my tongue and lips, I urgently made out with her pussy and stroked her into a tizzy. Her back arched, and she bucked frantically, thrusting up and down on my tongue. "Oh, Parker, your tongue pierc—" she whispered, but then, "Oh, Parker! I think I'm gonna…I'm gonna…Oh, God!" And she did. Her legs tensed as she released her orgasm onto my already soaked face, and I consumed all of her. Her chest rose and fell with each heavy breath she took. No words were spoken as she pulled me up to her. I put my head on her chest and listened to her pounding heart. Her arms encircled me, and she held me until we drifted off to sleep.

Chapter Four

The sun rose on this quiet and still morning as droplets of rain still clung to the windowpane. Rays of sunlight beamed onto Danielle's peaceful, sleeping face, and her long eyelashes fluttered lightly as she was still in dreamland. My mind was in disbelief over what took place last night. I wasn't sure if it was real until I ran my fingers over her silky skin and discovered her pajamas were still around her legs. I watched her sleep and cased over her body. My desire was just as strong as it had been the night before. I wanted more this time, and I slowly unbuttoned her pajama top. The little bunny faces on her pajamas gawked at me almost mockingly until I let loose the last button and opened her top, revealing her small, perky breasts. Gently, I brushed my fingertips over the area between them, and her nipples hardened immediately, standing erect for me. All resistance was chucked out the window as I took one into my mouth and sucked on it lightly. My tongue circled around it, and I felt it get harder between my lips. I fondled her other breast with my hand, cupping it and caressing her nipple. Her rib cage showed with each breath, and her long lashes opened, contemplating me as I reveled in her. "Good morning," I whispered on my descent. I wanted to taste her again. Her pajama bottoms were an unwanted obstacle this morning, and I removed them swiftly.

I spread her legs wide and kissed over the small, dark blond patch of hair before I opened her with my tongue. Her pussy was made even wetter by my tongue doing a tap dance on her hooded gem. I found the stickiness of her opening, dipped my tongue in, and thrusted it as deeply as I could before I slid it all the way back up to her clit again. "Oh, Parker." She moaned and set her hand on the back of my head. While I spoke French to her pussy, I reached up and took both her breasts in my hands. I squeezed them gently and rolled her nipples between my fingers. "Oh, God. Uh…Your mouth feels so good on me. Yeah…" Her body was in constant motion as it squirmed and writhed. But I had a good hold on her hips, and my mouth was clamped in position. She was going to feel me. I would not be denied. "Oh…uhh…yeah…yeah…" Her orgasm was an explosion, and her pussy became a sopping puddle of cum. Her body shuddered before she pushed my head away, unable to take anymore.

I slid back up the length of her body and straddled her. Bending over, I laid soft kisses on her face, on her lips, and around her mouth. She reached down between my legs and rubbed her palm and fingers over my pussy. I was still in my panties until she grabbed the sides and tugged them down over my backside and over my thighs. Too impatient to feel me, she didn't bother taking them all the way off. Instead, she slid her fingers over my clit and sank them into me. Moaning could be heard from both of us until—*Brnnng, brnng!* She pulled her fingers from me, my juices clinging to them, and she wiped them on her bunny jammies. Poor bunnies had cum all over them now, their faces held a stunned look. "Hello?" she said as she picked up the house phone and quickly jumped from the bed. "Oh, hey, baby! My phone? I, uh, I must have left it downstairs last night. Sorry."

I knew I was being bold when I came up behind her, lifted her blond hair, and kissed her neck. I was still horny, and my pussy wanted to feel her again. She squirmed out of my hold. "You're coming home early? Like when?" There was a nervousness in her voice that she could hardly control. "No, of course I want you to come home. Don't be silly." She put her pajama bottoms on as she spoke and went to her bedroom to continue her conversation with April. I could still hear her talking but could no longer decipher what was being said. My clit was still rock hard, but I knew we were done here.

❧❧❧❧

As I put on my clothes from the previous night, I noticed the dogs sitting up on the bed staring at me, and I realized they hadn't been out yet. "Come on, babies! Let's go outside!" They followed me down the steps, and I let them out the back slider. I stepped out with them and watched them sniff around for a good spot to pee. The sun was shining, doing its best to dry the dew that was left on each blade of grass.

About ten minutes passed before Danielle appeared outside with two cups of coffee in her hands. She offered me one. "April's coming home by noon. She's packing up and headed to the airport now."

"Oh." I glanced at my watch. "It's only seven thirty. Maybe we could continue what we were doing." I stepped closer to her and put my hands on her waist.

"Parker, we can't." She was saying it but let me kiss her nonetheless. The sun warmed our faces as we stood there making out. She started to put her arms around my neck, but it was as if there was an invisible force that pulled her away from me. Guilt. She broke our kiss and looked me dead in the face. "We can't. This is wrong, and you know it's wrong. It's a mistake."

"It's not a mistake. You knew exactly what you were doing last night when you got in bed with me."

"Then I need to get a grip! I love April! We're getting married. This isn't like me, and you know that. I don't cheat."

"Well, you did last night."

"Are you going to let this go?"

I looked into her eyes. "But it was good, wasn't it?" I leaned forward once more and tasted her lips.

"Mmm…yes, it was good. Better than good," she whispered and backed up. "But it stops here. I mean it, Parker. No more!"

"Let's not forget who seduced who here." I was annoyed now and walked back into the house. She came in after me, and I placed my coffee cup in the sink. When I turned around, she was right there. I stepped to the side and grabbed my keys off the kitchen table.

"Wait! Where are you going?" she asked.

"I'm leaving! Isn't that what you want?"

"Please don't leave like this. I don't want you to be mad at me."

"Maybe you should have thought about that before you called me a mistake for the second time. I mean, what the fuck, Danielle? You know how I've felt about you for years. This is the way it's gonna go down? I'm a fucking mistake?"

"I don't mean it like that. I'm just a bit confused,

and I'm not sure I know what the hell I'm doing anymore."

"Let me know when you figure it out." I headed for the front door, and as I opened it, I turned to look at her one last time before I left. Her bottom lip quivered, and tears streamed down her face. This was an instant tension breaker. She knew how to get to me, and her tears turned me into mush. "No. Don't do that. Don't cry, please."

"But you hate me."

I wrapped my arms around her, trying to comfort her and understand how she felt because this was the first time in her life she had been unfaithful, and she truly didn't know how to handle what happened. I knew this was a bad idea. *Damn my libido!* "I don't hate you. I could never hate you. I lo…" I stopped dead in my tracks, and she peered up at me through her tears.

She knew what I was about to say but didn't force me to finish. "I'm sorry," she said and touched my cheek.

I took her hand from my face and held it in mine. "Listen, I'm a little confused myself. I'm gonna go." I tried to put on my best face when I said, "I'll see you tomorrow morning for chess, right?"

She wiped away her tears and hugged me once more. "Right."

It killed my insides to leave her standing there as she looked so unsure of her own feelings. I knew where I stood with mine. My heart had loved her from the very first time I saw her. That much was true. But she seemed shell-shocked. I knew it wasn't something she planned. Neither did I, but it happened. I didn't know where we were supposed to go from here, but I knew our friendship was changed forever.

I wasn't supposed to know what her body looked like, but I did. I wasn't supposed to know what she tasted like, but I did. I wasn't supposed to know how she sounded when she came, but I did. Those things were supposed to be reserved for April, yet I knew them. Even though I had no right, I couldn't help but get jealous when I thought of them together in bed. It wasn't something I was accustomed to, imagining the two of them having sex. Quite frankly, this was the first time I ever thought of her with anyone else. Why now? Just because I had a taste of her now? Literally? I liked April and all, but I was in love with Danielle. I always had been. Letting go of this wasn't going to be easy. The line had been blurred, yet I knew if she offered herself to me again, I would take it. I couldn't help it. I was like a sponge soaking up her love.

❧❧❧❧

It was hard for me to concentrate or focus on any one thing throughout the day, other than the image of Danielle's face in ecstasy and calling out my name. I had wished for it for so long, and it was always bad timing. Why this was happening now, I wasn't quite sure because, yet again, it was more bad timing. On my short drive to Merge later that afternoon, though, my thoughts switched from us to her and April, and the very thought of it sucked the life out of me. Because I overthought things, it was the only thing I could think about now, even if it wasn't happening. Jealousy ran deep, and presently, it was at the core of my soul. I didn't want April to touch her. I didn't want them touching each other. I needed to pull it together. *Come on, Parker! You're better than this.*

I entered the back door of the bar and immediately ran into Jules as she went into the stockroom. "Hey! What's up? What are you doing?" I asked.

"Rotating our stock of beer and cleaning out the tap lines."

"Great! Make sure the CO2 pressure is correct. I want a nice flow coming out of those taps."

"You got it, boss!" Just as I walked away, she added, "Oh! I almost forgot to tell you. The softball league starts this week. I have a roster list for you, and they'll need a check for the entry fee and uniforms."

"Already? Damn! That came up quickly. Okay. Gimme the roster later, and I'll give you a check."

The Merge Muff Mashers were league champs last season. It was good business, and I enjoyed giving back to the community. My friend Lisa Spalducci was the coach and a childhood friend from kindergarten up. She had such a bubbly personality, her face always held the biggest smile, and her eyes had a permanent gleam in them. One of my few straight friends, she had been married to Scott for ten years now. Funny how a straight woman coached my mostly gay softball team. However, in her tipsy moments from too much wine, she admitted she had a strong curiosity to have sex with a woman. Though she never followed through with it, it was still there. And coaching a predominantly lesbian softball team was like swimming in a small pond of fish just waiting to be scooped up. It was bound to happen.

As the evening progressed, the Used Lug Nutz took the stage. I surveyed the room and the crowd. This was the first time I ever had a heavy metal band play at the bar, and I was a little anxious about the kind of element it brought into my establishment. I wasn't happy right off the motherfucking bat. I didn't care that the band was dressed in black leather and bandannas. That didn't bother me. It was the fandom they brought with them. These girls were rough. Not the usual preppie college girls who frequented the place. They smoked cigarettes at jet speed, one after the other, and I was pretty sure I smelled pot. It was so crowded that I couldn't tell where exactly it came from, and quite honestly, I wouldn't have been surprised if Cookie was the culprit.

When I found Cookie in the crowd, her eyes were wide as she looked over at me and mouthed the words, "What the fuck?" She wasn't smoking weed. But there was a rotund woman standing next to her who overshadowed her and basically muscled her out of the way to make a bigger circle for her and her friends to smoke. They were huddled together in little packs, and one was more butch than the other. I was appalled when one of them had the audacity to spit on my floor right in front of me.

"Hey!" I yelled, puffing up, but quickly shied away and stepped back as a woman with a crew cut and tattoos covering her face and neck stepped toward me. She stood about six inches above me and peered down into my eyes. She squinted, and her eyebrows inverted as she said, "You got a problem with it?"

I looked her up and down and decided I liked my teeth. "Nope. No problem."

There were too many of them. The bar was packed in like sardines. No way were Trudy and Renee going to be able to handle this. When I glanced over at them, I caught Renee's gaze instantly. She shook her head and appeared at a loss. The animals that came into my bar were now drunk and stoked for a fight. You know that feeling you get in the pit of your stomach that tells you shit's about to go down? Yeah, shit was about to go down.

During the band's third break, their last one of this God-awful night, I stood with Trudy and Renee when we noticed a huddle being guarded by a watchdog. "What's goin' on over there?" I asked them.

"I don't know, but it doesn't look good." Trudy said.

The two bouncers separated and made their way around this powwow, only to look back at me and shake their heads yet again. Trudy pushed her way back through the throng of people and informed me, "Yeah, they're doin' coke. Or meth. Or who knows what."

"Well, how the fuck are we gonna get rid of them?" I asked.

Just then, we noticed and heard yelling and screaming coming from across the other end of the bar, and when the pushing and shoving commenced, I noticed Cookie squirming her way out of the bustle. By the time she got to me, she was in full panic mode. This was not the usual Cookie behavior. When Cookie was scared, it was time to be scared.

"Fuck!" I shouted before all hell broke loose in my bar. A beer bottle whizzed past my head and cracked on the wall behind me, splashing and oozing down.

"Whoa!" I yelled, barely moving my head out of the way.

Chaos had broken out, and my head was spinning. I felt caught in the middle of a war zone in my own place of business. This was not good. Among the commotion, a chair was picked up by a heathen who brought it over her head and swung it at the woman next to her, knocking her to the ground. When I raced over to help the woman up, I was pushed to the floor with her. At this point, people tripped over us, and I wiggled my way out before being trampled. The woman I was trying to help had disappeared, and I felt a hand grab me by the scruff of my shirt. I whipped around, kung fu style, and expected a fist to the face, but it was Cookie trying to get me out of the fray.

"Parker, what the fuck kind of fuckin' band did you bring in for these fuckin' motherfuckin'…I don't know what the fuck they are!"

"Dude, I don't know, but if I get through this tonight, never ag—"

A group tussle moved all of us across the bar involuntarily. I lost sight of Cookie once again and dived out of the massive movement to behind the bar. I found Simone crouched back there, hiding and shaken up.

"What the hell, Parker?" she yelled and peeked up just above the bar to see what else was taking place. She quickly bobbed her head back down. "I didn't sign up for this shit! Not kidding!"

The sound of glasses and bottles being broken was nothing in comparison to hearing all my windows being shattered.

"Did you call the cops?" I asked.

"No, I didn't call the cops!" she said indignantly.

"Hey! Do you smell that?"

We both sniffed the air around us, turning from one side of the room to the other and looked back at each other.

"That's a fire. Holy shit! That's a fire!" I

screamed, clamored to my feet, and ran to the phone on the wall. By the time I babbled my way through the 911 call, I saw not only the blinds on the windows ablaze, but also my beloved pool table. Some people were still fighting, but the smart ones ran for the door. Renee and Jules sprayed the flames with a fire extinguisher, but it did nothing. The flames just got bigger and spread to the wood bar. I dragged my fingers through my hair, looked around, and shook my head in disbelief. *What just happened here? Did I just watch my bar literally go up in flames?*

I was still behind the bar as I watched this debacle unfold. I hung the phone up just to hear more glasses being broken. When I looked over, I saw Jules being slid across the top of the bar by a burly-looking dyke and thrown in my direction. When she came to a halt in front of me, her face slowly turned upward. "You gotta get rid of these fuckin' people."

"Ya think?" I helped her off the bar and turned back to the fiasco at hand. "I thought you were trying to help put out the fire."

"I was. Until two of those crazy bitches took the fire extinguisher and threw it out the window, then they, well, you saw what they did after that!"

Sirens could be heard, and seconds later, firefighters rushed through the door. While they attempted to contain the fire, police officers also arrived and helped the remaining people. Smoke enveloped the entire property by now. When all of us, including me and my staff, were safely outside, I watched in horror as my life's dream went up in a poof. I was stunned. As if I wasn't in enough emotional turmoil today, this was not what I needed.

❧❧❧❧

After the last of the fire was extinguished and questions from the police answered as best as possible, they told me I should just go home. It was five a.m. by this time, and going home wasn't an option. I couldn't part with what was left of the wreckage. Simone gave me a hug, not waiting for Gus this morning. Knowing eating pussy was out of the question, she took a cab home. Cookie attempted to talk me into going home, too, but she finally gave in and took off, as well. By five thirty, I was alone. I walked back into my charred bar and stood in the middle of the ashes. I looked around. Shards of broken glass glimmered and sparkled in the early morning rays of sun. Every step I took was met with crunching under my shoes from all the debris and remnants of the apparent cyclone that spun through my place of business. I was numb and probably in shock.

I didn't realize how long I had been standing there until I heard, "Oh, my God! What the hell happened?"

Turning around to meet Danielle's gaze was just too hard to do. I had yet to even cry over what took place here tonight. But when I didn't turn around right away, she moved closer to me and slowly spun me around. We came eye to eye, and in that moment, I finally broke down. Tears escaped my eyes in torrents, and I sobbed uncontrollably as she took me in her arms and held me close. She didn't press me for more information just yet. She simply let me cry. We had our own issues to work out together, but for now, my friend just held me and let me get it out.

When I was calm enough and ready, I explained

the whole story to Danielle. She didn't interrupt me. She listened intently, her focus zoning in on me as she took it all in. After I caught her up to speed, she refrained from the usual speech about why she didn't frequent bars. She didn't break my balls or tell me I was foolish for letting a heavy metal band play here since it wasn't that kind of bar. No, instead, when I finished the story, she beelined for the utility closet and pulled out a couple of brooms. She handed me one and got to work with no further questions. I followed suit, pulled my big girl panties up, and grabbed it from her.

Inch by square inch, I knelt with the pan as she swept the rubble into it. We filled the dumpster quickly and cleaned up what we could. It took us a few hours, but we finally finished and stood there once again scanning the room. The walls were burnt to a crisp, and most of the bar was demolished. I couldn't even recognize my pool table, as it was part of the death of a dream. I realized my insurance would pay for most of the renovation, but this wasn't going to be easy. And it was certainly going to be a time-consuming bastard! My bar wouldn't be reopened for at least a month or more. In the meantime, my financial situation would suffer because of it.

After I hung my head for the umpteenth time this morning, Danielle stepped up to me and lifted my chin with her fingertips, so loving I almost forgot about the bar for a split second. "You're going to be okay. Do you understand?" I looked away from her, but she pulled me back. "Parker, do you understand me? You will not cave to this." Again, I turned my face from her because I knew what she was alluding to. "Hey! No gambling! Do *you* understand? Look at me."

I brought my attention back to her and answered

as I knew I should. "Yes."

"Don't lie, like the last time I found out from Dorian. And only because she couldn't take handling you alone. You were depressed and out of control. Please don't get depressed. It saddens me when you feel so horrible."

Her fingertips were still on my chin, and her gaze turned from friend to more than friend in a heartbeat. And just like that, she leaned up to kiss me. She laid her lips upon mine and didn't move. As fast as it started, it ended, and our heads lay against each other momentarily. "Why am I finding it so hard to go back to being just your friend?" She wrapped her arms around me again and whispered, "It's not fair."

"Nothing about this has been fair for the last eighteen years, Dani."

"But why now?"

"I don't have an answer for you."

I pulled myself away and placed my hands on her hips to step her back a bit. "I really think I need some normalcy right now. I can't deal with the back and forth. It's like a roller-coaster ride. Only it never ends."

"Do you want to play a game of chess before I leave?"

"I love how you totally avoided what I just said. Ya know what, yeah, let's play."

The back of the house was still intact, and we walked down the hallway toward my office. Once there, we took our respective seats on the couch with the chessboard between us, only we didn't play. I waited for her to make her first move, but I felt her look at me every time I looked down at the board. "Stop," I warned. The intense attraction we felt the very first time we met repeated itself. All because of a simple kiss in the bathroom at a friend's party. I had to know.

"Danielle, what was it about that kiss that night that made you feel this way for me? I want to know."

She settled back into the love seat, shifted her weight, and crossed her legs. I could see her thinking, and she finally said, "I don't know. It was something about the way your face looked when you leaned into me." She contemplated a second more, before adding, "Your lips were so soft. You were so gentle." And she still wasn't finished as she uncrossed her legs and leaned forward above the chessboard. "I could feel your heart."

Wow! At this point, she got up and headed for the door. "Wait! Where are you going?" I asked, baffled after the sweet things she just said to me.

"I should go before something else happens. I'm only going to feel like crap again. I have to think of April."

I got up to follow her and shut the door that she had just opened. Standing behind her, I nuzzled my face into the side of her neck, taking in all of her. I craved the scent of her and kissed her lightly. When I shimmied her around to face me, she looked up at me. She seemed to know what she *should* do but knew what she felt for me. In the time between her lips meeting mine was this colossal moment, where the connection was made, where the connection was real, and the magnetism that existed between us was too strong a force to keep us apart. And finally, we kissed. The sweet feeling of passion released inside me, and I wanted her. Now. The kiss heightened and intensified as we unbuttoned each other's jeans quickly. Both of us wanted to feel the other in a hurry, as if it was the last time this would ever happen again. Almost like, *fuck it, let's make it worth it.*

Danielle wasn't as quick as me, though. While she just got her hand down my pants, mine was already down hers, past her underwear, and right to her pussy. My fingers slid through her slit and into the wetness of her opening. I plunged them into her, eliciting a groan of approval into my ear. She never did get her hand where she wanted it. I took over, and she let me. I fucked her against my office door, and she held on to me around my neck and took each thrust I gave while pounding the door behind her. I had her pinned, and I whispered in her ear, "Oh, Danielle. We could have been doing this for years."

"Uh-huh. What was I…oh, yeah…what was I…oh, God, Parker…what was I thinking?" She was about to cum for me when there was a banging on the door, and it wasn't us. "Dani! Parker! You guys playin' chess?"

"April!" Danielle whisper-screamed to me while she leaned her weight against the door long enough for us to button our pants back up.

"Guys!" April pushed from the other side and eventually pushed through. "Hey! Everything all right?" She looked confused as she looked at us, and I was almost afraid we weren't going to be able to pull this off. "Hey, Parker," she said while extending a hand out to shake mine. I barely wiped my fingers on my pants when she walked in, but I didn't want her to think I was rude, so I shook her hand. I could feel the stickiness of Danielle's pussy juice as I pulled my hand away from hers. She didn't notice, but my heart was beating out of my chest.

Danielle gave her a small peck to the lips. "What are you doing here, hon?"

"Before I say why I'm here…Um, what the hell happened to your bar? Why does it look char-broiled?"

"An unfortunate incident, if you will. Honestly, I'm not ready to talk about it. It's taken me this long to calm down and accept it. Dani can tell you all about it later. Why are you here again?"

"Well, I've been away a lot and really haven't seen you," she said as she looked to Danielle. "Thought maybe when you're done with your game, I could take you out for breakfast." She glanced at the board, saw the pieces hadn't even been moved, and asked, "Did you even play?" She looked from the board to Danielle. "You're white as a ghost, babe! You okay?" A look of concern replaced the one of confusion, and Danielle looked like she was about to hurl.

"No, no. I'm okay. Just feeling a little faint. I think I need to sit down." She grabbed hold of the armrest and gently sat in a chair off to the right of the door where we stood. I went to the mini fridge, pulled out a cold bottle of water, and handed it to her. Her gaze caught mine, but she immediately looked away to remain calm.

While she sipped from the bottle, April continued, "I was going to take you out for breakfast, but if you're not feeling well…"

"No, really, I'm fine. Feeling better already. Let's go. Shall we?"

"All right. Parker, would you like to join us? Looks like you could use some breakfast after whatever took place here last night."

"Nah, I'm good. Besides, you don't need a third wheel around while you're trying to spend time with your girl."

"Third wheel? You're practically sisters."

Eww…Danielle and I made eye contact for a brief moment, and an expression of absolute horror came over her face at April's words. She shook the taste out of her mouth and straightened her face. It was so quick that April never even noticed. And in that moment, I knew what we were doing was deceitful and despicable. This was definitely not who Dani was. I was afraid I opened Pandora's Box with that kiss. Part of me found this daring side of her wildly attractive, but the other part was afraid of the turmoil and drama this affair could bring if found out. I put Danielle in a bad situation, but even though my heart was reasonable enough to understand that this, too, was not our time, my heart yearned for what it had craved for so long. I knew I needed to stop this now to save her from herself.

"Well, that is true, but I'm gonna pass. It's been a long night, and my head needs a pillow. Tomorrow's a new day, and I need to come up with a game plan for how to get my bar up and running again." I gathered my book bag and grabbed my keys.

"Yeah, babe. Parker's had a rough night," Danielle said to April, then turned to me, and added, "Get some sleep. I'll call you tomorrow." She gave me a hug so as to act normal but promptly ended the embrace. April went out the door first with Danielle in tow. But before Dani was out of sight, she turned to give me a small wave.

Chapter Five

The next day, I met the contractor at my obliterated bar. The damage ended up being more than I had anticipated, and while we were ending our conversation, Dorian came through the front door. She took one good look around and said, "Jesus H. Christ! What did they do?" She ran her hand over what was left of the oak bar and shook her head. "Didn't I tell you not to book that band?" She whipped her head around at me. "This is bad, Parker!"

Jeff, the contractor, took his cue at hearing this. "We'll start tomorrow" was all he said and walked out the door.

I turned back to Dorian. "Really, Dorian? Are you really going to break my stones? Do I look like I'm in any mood to have my stones broken? I can assure you, my friend, that I've been sick to my stomach since this happened. There is nothing you can say to make me feel worse." Images of the chaotic scene replayed in my head. "The worst of all animals set up shop in my bar and destroyed it. I'm sick over this! Yet another mistake!"

"No! Absolutely not! You are not playing the victim in this! Cut that shit out right now!" After she looked at the boarded-up windows, she saw what was left of the pool table and noticed the burned-up insulation hanging from the rafters. She peered back at me with a look of concern. "No gambling! You got me?"

I clearly didn't want to hear this and headed for my office.

"Stop!"

"What?" I asked, not bothering to turn around.

"I'm not kidding. I won't pick up the pieces this time if you do. Know that!"

"I got it." I disappeared through the door that connected the hallway to my office.

I heard her come through the door behind me, and she followed me down the corridor. Once inside, she asked, "How long will it take to renovate?"

"He said it could take a month or more. There's a lot of smoke damage. It's all going to have to be replaced."

"Is your insurance picking up the tab here?"

"Don't know. Just put my claim in today. Gotta wait." I took a deep breath. "Dorian, this pool party, I—"

"No need to finish that sentence. I get it! Funds are going to be tight for a while."

"Sorry. I guess I'll tell everyone the party's off."

"Who said the party was off?"

"Well, I just assumed that—"

Again, she interrupted me, waving her hand. "Stop! Listen, I know I'm a cheap bitch sometimes, but I really like this girl. We talk every day, and I'm counting the days to that party. Please don't cancel. I'll take care of it all!"

I couldn't believe what I just heard. I smiled and said, "This girl's got to have a golden pussy for you to shell out dough." The smile that came across her face was enough for me. "Okay. You got it! It's on!"

The next few days were long and hard. Outside of checking on the reconstruction of Merge, my days seemed pretty mundane. I didn't know what to do with myself, and that was never good. I suffered from depression, and though I hadn't been depressed for years now, this was a critical time to get through without falling into that dark abyss. I still took anti-depressants, but situational circumstances could throw me off regardless. I tried to fill my time walking Addie and talking to friends, but I hadn't heard from Danielle since the incident in my office. She'd only texted me a couple of times to make sure I was okay, which basically meant making sure I wasn't overwhelmingly depressed. I was feeling sad, not only for my bar, but for what was happening with Danielle and our friendship. As much as I wanted her and wanted to be with her, this wasn't how I wanted it to happen—by cheating. She sucked at it anyway. So we stayed away from each other all week as if distance would solve the feelings and somehow put an end to it.

Saturday was spent preparing the pool and yard for the next day's party. Dorian bought all the food and booze, just as she said she would. She spared no expense. She decorated my yard like it was a luau and included strings of pink and purple lights strewn over and around my fence, all the way around the property. Multicolored balloons were placed selectively where she thought best, big blow-up palm trees were set on the corners of the pool, and I let her do it all. She even went as far as to buy neon glow sticks and necklaces. She gave the backyard the works, and I had to admit, it looked spectacular. This was the summer kickoff, and everyone was going to be here.

⁂

When Sunday morning arrived, I was surprisingly chipper. The sun was shining, the birds were singing, and I felt calm. I jumped in the shower and jerked off right away. It always put me in a good mood, and I loved to start my day rubbing one out. I didn't put my swimsuit on first thing. Instead, I chose to wear a pair of cut-off jeans and an orange tank top with the Merge logo on it to show off my preseason tan. My hair was a little longer than usual as I needed a haircut, so it hung over my right eye.

On my way to the kitchen, I passed a picture of me, Danielle, and Dorian, framed and sitting by itself on a round accent table. I stopped to pick it up and examined the image. It was taken last summer on our seasonal camping trip. The three of us in front of our community of tents, as there were usually about twenty lesbians who attended this annual function. I set the picture down and continued on my way to the kitchen for some much-needed coffee.

While I scrambled a couple of eggs, I thought about Danielle. It was a week since we last saw each other. I knew she was trying to put some distance between us, but I didn't care much for it. I was used to talking to her all the time, so her absence had been quite noticeable. Going back to being friends seemed almost impossible, but I had to try, or I was going to lose her altogether. I couldn't handle the thought of that. We needed to talk. She and April were supposed to be coming today, so if I got an opportunity to be alone with her, I had to straighten this out. I loved this physical side of us that we discovered, but if the guilt was going to divide us as friends, then we had to stop. I convinced myself of this all morning.

I was lucky enough that a friend of mine was available today to DJ. Bobbi was an attractive woman with beautiful, thin dreadlocks parted on the side. The one side curled around her face and ear. She preferred to call them locks because some dreadlocks were dreadful, and hers were not. Her arms were covered in a tattoo sleeve. A free spirit, she was one of the best DJs in the area. She called herself DJ Nubian Queen, and though her beats and cuts were wicked, her smile lit up a room. She took her time setting up her equipment, tested the sound system, and adjusted the EQ for the right bass and treble. She started the music up right away, scratching and warming up.

Dorian was the first to arrive. She came an hour earlier than the party was expected to start. She wanted to help me with last-minute preparations. I had a dozen coolers that we stuffed with ice, beer, soda, and water. The fridge was stocked with burgers, hot dogs, and chicken breasts and legs. I didn't think we could have more potato salad, macaroni salad, or deviled eggs. She filled party bowls with chips and pretzels and went about taking pool toys and rafts out of the shed, along with the horseshoes and volleyball net. Everything was ready to go. Dorian looked a little antsy, nipping at her nails and shaking her leg, as she sat in a lounge chair by the grill.

"You okay?" I asked.

"Yeah. Just a little nervous."

"I don't know why. You've been talking to this woman for three weeks now."

"I know, but this is our first real date."

"You'll be fine. It's obvious she likes you, or she wouldn't talk on the phone with you every day and night."

"Yeah, but I really like her. I don't want to blow it. You know I'm good at that."

"You won't. Maybe go easy on the liquor today. You don't need her thinking you see two of her again."

We both giggled at that, and it was enough to calm her down. "Yeah, you're right. It's probably a good idea to lay off the booze."

As we finished our conversation, the first of many expected guests arrived. One by one, the entire Merge Muff Mashers softball team showed up. Having won their very first game of the season this morning, they wasted no time jumping in the pool. Before you knew it, uniform T-shirts and bras were stripped off, and beautiful boobs were everywhere. Dorian and I turned and looked at each other, smiles stretched across our faces. There was nothing more beautiful than bare boobs. Cece was the first to swap her shirt for naked breasts and flaunted them to anyone who would look. She was the star shortstop, just turned thirty with rock-hard abs that you could bounce a quarter off of. Her long blond, highlighted hair gleamed in the sun's rays as her wet curls clung against her neck. Her golden-brown tan only added to her attractiveness.

While the half-naked girls in the pool played chicken, I wandered back into my house to get the burgers and hot dogs out of the fridge. Only I didn't get that far as I heard loud motorcycles pulling up my driveway. I went outside to find Cookie, Tristan, and Kylie getting off their bikes as they rested them on their kickstands.

Tristan was the first to say hi. She worked with Cookie. Her ebony skin glistened in the sunlight, and our gazes caught for just a second. She had short hair, almost a crew cut, with one side dyed in rainbow colors. We hooked up a couple of times, stoned and drunk, and fell into bed easily. She was one of my few butch affairs, but damn, did she fuck me good.

"I can't believe you're here this early," I said, stunned at my always-late friend's early arrival.

"You said there's food and beer, right?" Cookie chuckled.

"And naked women, too. My softball team decided to celebrate with no tan lines."

"Ooh…oh, my! Well, get the hell outta the way already!" She pushed me aside and headed for the party with Tristan close behind her. But Kylie stopped our progress by stopping short of the door and stepped in front of me.

"I was hoping I would have seen you by now for that ride. You said you like to ride, right?" She purposely tried to throw me off guard, and she may have had Danielle and April not walked up the drive at that very moment.

"Hi," Danielle said, extending her hand. "Kylie, is it?" She intentionally interrupted the flirting she had walked in on, and I felt a slight jealousy radiating from her. I hoped April wasn't feeling that, too.

After exchanging welcomes and greetings, we headed toward the party. I acted like I didn't feel tension from Dani and chose to ignore her attitude toward Kylie. Once by the pool, I noticed Dorian taking enjoyment in handing out the glow sticks and glow necklaces to the naked softball team, and as more guests arrived, plenty of other women stripped off their T-shirts and bathing suit tops, too.

Laughter was contagious as Dorian clasped a necklace around one of their necks. She clearly took pleasure flirting with all these girls right up until Dahlia came through the fence gate. She pushed the girl with the necklace to the side and beelined for Dahlia, who waited with a wide smile and open arms. They embraced as if they missed each other forever.

I left my love-stricken friend with the object of her affection and went back to the kitchen to retrieve the burgers and hot dogs I originally went in for. Addie followed me back out the slider and disappeared into a sea of lesbians. The party quickly grew, and as I handed the tray of meats to my griller friend Fran, the ground pounded and vibrated from the music Bobbi spun. Sizzling was heard when she threw the first burger onto the grill, and smoke emanated while she continued to place more in rows from front to back.

The coolers stared at me, and I took my time picking through them to find just the right beer for myself. I popped the cap and took a swig. "Ahh, ice cold, baby," I said out loud to no one. I scanned the pool and surrounding areas and noticed everyone was having a good time. Laughing, music, dancing, and games were the theme of the day, but for me... I was always scanning the crowd for Danielle. And there she was, standing by the patio table with April. Just as I was about to avert my gaze, she caught my eye. She grinned a crooked smile at me and promptly removed her tunic cover-up while I watched. She never took her face from mine, as she let the cover-up slip from her shoulders and to the ground. She knew exactly what she was doing, and the sight of her beautifully tanned body in that ultra-white bikini made my clit stand at attention and salute her. I smiled back at her and swallowed the lump in my throat while I tried to control the urge to bum rush her and rip that bikini right off her.

I was jarred from my daydream by a set of hands wrapped around my waist from behind. I turned, startled, to a very excited Shady.

"Parker!" She hugged me tightly and couldn't control the look of joy at seeing me.

"Shady! Oh, my God! It's been like two years! How did you know I was having a party?" I asked, completely baffled by her appearance. Shady, pronounced *cha-dee* in Spanish, was the gorgeous Latina who Cookie was desperately in love with. They were together for seven years. Her dark thick hair hung in long graceful curls over her shoulders. Her face was well-modeled and feminine. Her eyes were like midnight. She was animated in her actions as she threw her hands in the air, and in that raspy, sexy accent of hers, proclaimed, "I know everything, *chica*!"

While I pointed her to the food and beer, I couldn't help but spot Cookie, whose face was one of sheer shock and panic. This was the first time she had seen her ex in two years. When Shady left Cookie for another woman, Cookie was never the same and never got serious with anyone after.

By the time I reached the table where she and Kylie sat, she was already out of her seat, asking, "What the fuck is she doin' here?"

"You're asking me? I haven't seen her in two years just like you." I took a swig of my beer and glanced in her direction. "But damn! She looks good!"

"I'm goin' in." And with that, she moved in Shady's

direction.

A few hours into the party, my pool was packed with lesbians. Horseshoes were being played by some of my older friends, while the younger ones started a game of beer pong on the picnic table. Things were in full force, and everyone seemed to be having fun. April was standing there talking to a few of the Muff Mashers teammates and clearly got her peeks in on Cece's nipples, which were rock hard under a tank top she threw on after having frolicked in the pool bare-breasted. Danielle sat at the table next to them and looked distant and distracted. She didn't join the conversation at all.

In the meantime, Kylie appeared beside me with her beer in hand.

"Great party," she said as she offered her bottle to tap mine.

"Not bad for short notice."

"Not bad for long notice," she agreed and quickly changed the subject. "So are we ever goin' out or what?"

"Are you asking me on a date?"

Her slate gray gaze burned into mine. "Actually, yes."

She was asking me out, and all I could do was keep looking over at Danielle, who was now sitting by herself. April entered the beer pong game and partnered with Cece. Dani looked so bored all of the sudden. I felt bad that April left her there alone.

"Um...does your silence mean no?" Kylie snapped me back to our conversation.

"Mean no to what?" I asked as my attention slowly diverted from Dani back to Kylie.

"Parker, do you wanna go out with me or not?"

"Huh? What? I mean, yes, we can go out some time."

She noticed my distraction, gently turned my face, and directed me to focus on her. Her steel-colored eyes peered into mine. She sent goose bumps down my arms.

"That wasn't very convincing. I'm serious. There's a beef and beer Wednesday night at Randolph's Bar and Grill. It's for a good cause. Would you go with me?"

"I would be delighted. Yes."

She was still looking in my eyes when, to my surprise, she brought her hand to my face and leaned in to kiss me. I pulled back slightly as I wasn't expecting it, but she reeled me in and pressed her lips to mine. It was only for a second, and even though it was nice, it took me off guard.

"I've been wanting to do that since the night I met you. Sorry if I freaked you out," she said, smiling but still being serious.

"No, uh, no. I mean, uh," I babbled and stuttered, not knowing what to say. When I looked back to the pool area, I caught Danielle's gaze. Guess she saw that kiss because she didn't look pleased, but there was nothing I could do about that. I was a single woman. She was the one who wasn't. And as long as she was with April, nothing more could happen. I was trying to save her from herself. I was used to the pain, but she wasn't. This wasn't how I wanted *us* to start. I wanted her to be happy, even if it wasn't with me.

My attention was quickly diverted from Danielle to Kylie again as she shifted my face to meet hers once more.

"Why are you always so distracted and distant?

Is there something I should know?" she nervously asked, a little bewildered.

"No. Really. I'm not distracted. Just trying to be a good hostess is all."

By the time I turned around to see Dani again, she was gone. April was still playing beer pong and still gawking at Cece, oblivious to the fact that her wife-to-be had disappeared. As always, Danielle would be the designated driver tonight. I searched the yard, the pool, the horseshoe pit, but she was nowhere to be found. Just as I was about to look inside the house, Sherri, the centerfielder, approached and stopped me just shy of my sliding door. She was smiling peculiarly, almost as if she just got away with something huge.

"What's up, Sher? What's the devious smile all about?"

She looked to the left, to the right, and all surrounding areas before looking back at me. "Here, take these." She placed three little pills in my palm and closed my hand into a fist.

"What's this?" I asked, my eyebrows pointing inward in confusion.

"Molly," she asserted. "Have you ever tried it?"

"No, I haven't. Listen, the most I do is smoke a little weed now and then. I don't do anything else. Like, seriously, my experimental days are long over."

"Take them anyway. You never know. You may want to try them with someone you want to have sex with. Like, everything feels so good, but sex is a hundred times better. Every touch sends you straight to the moon."

"I don't know, Sher."

"Just hold on to 'em."

I shoved them into my pocket, and I was about

to step inside when I peered behind me once more to be sure I didn't miss seeing Dani anywhere outside. Nope. No Dani. However, I did see Shady and Cookie off to the side by themselves. Their conversation appeared intense, and their gazes never left each other as Cookie's hands flailed about. Her Italian hand movements were no match for the Latina in Shady, who not only moved her hands around, but moved her head and neck, as well. Both were animated, but it was better than the silent treatment I had seen them give each other in the past.

I stepped through the door, and the noise from the party outside faded. All was quiet except for the lovely sound of music being played on the piano. I entered my living room to see Danielle playing the baby grand. She didn't realize I was standing there right away as I watched her intently. The melody she played struck emotions in me, and I gazed at her from behind, which allowed me the freedom to feel what I felt for her without her seeing me. She was a natural. As soon as her fingertips hit the first key, the piano came to life.

Slowly, I took a seat next to her on the piano bench. She didn't flinch or appear surprised by my presence. It was almost as if she was expecting me. We sat there silently for some time. She played her heart out, all her feelings emanating through her fingertips and making the piano sing. Finally, without ever missing a beat or turning her head, she asked, "Do you like her?"

She stunned me with her question. What difference did it make, anyway? I didn't know how to answer, so I just said, "I don't know. Yes. Maybe. She's all right, I guess. Don't really know her."

"Looks like you know her mouth."

"Seriously?" I could feel my face scowl before I proceeded. "You're the one that's with someone. I'm single. Remember?" I turned on the bench toward her. "You're the one getting married. You've made that perfectly clear to me."

At this, she stopped playing and turned to face me. "Parker, I am such a focused person. You know this. But I have been so distracted. I can't stop thinking about you, and I don't want to think about you, not like this."

"You have to stop thinking about me. You have to."

"What? Where did that come from? Ya know, you kissed me first!" She wheeled back around to the piano, obviously ticked off at my words, but she wasn't done.

"Are we playing a blame game here because I'm pretty sure you told me to kiss you."

She went from being annoyed to emotional in a heartbeat, turning once more on the bench and facing me. She peered in my eyes and caressed my face, with a look of want on hers.

"No." I took her hand from my cheek.

"But why? Why all of a sudden?"

"Exactly. Why all of a sudden? You're so back and forth, my head is spinning. First, you don't want me. Then you want me. Then you tell me what we did was a mistake when you clearly seduced me that night at your house."

"I'm confused."

"Then I need to make it clear because this hurts too much."

Just then, Simone clamored in through the back

slider. "Hey…" she said excitedly, happy to see me after not seeing me for a week. However, as she looked from me to Danielle and back, she seemed to realize the tension between us. "Uh, maybe I'll wait for you outside, Parker."

She stepped back outside. Danielle began playing again, but once she did, I got up from the piano bench. She abruptly got up, too, and asked, "Where are you going?"

"Back to my party. Don't want to be a terrible host. Maybe you should go outside, too. Your wife-to-be is out there."

But as I turned to walk out the back slider, she stopped me and placed her hand on my shoulder. "Wait."

"What?"

She took me by the hand and led me into my bedroom. "Whoa! What are we doing in here?" I asked.

"Shh…" She covered my lips with the palm of her hand but promptly replaced it with her mouth.

For a split second, I lost myself to her and enjoyed the succulent taste of strawberries on her lips. As much as I didn't want to, I stopped it. I had to. When the kiss was broken, her beautiful eyes looked into mine, and I swore I saw the sun rise and set in them. I looked away and said, "Go outside to your fiancée, Dani."

"Hey! What's going on in here? Thought the party was outside." Dorian barreled through the door with nothing but questions and a drink in her hand.

"Dorian, what are you doin'?" I pointed at the drink she was sipping on. "I thought you were going to stay sober today."

"Oh, relax! It's only one. Just enough to take the edge off."

"Where's Dahlia?"

"Changing into her swimsuit." She glanced back and forth between us. "What's going on in here? Everything all right?" She looked back to Dani. "You're white as a ghost. What's wrong with you?"

I wished I could tell her she looked like that because we were just making out and nearly got caught. This was the shit I was talking about. This incessant guilt she felt whenever we were intimate.

"Just not feeling so well, I guess," she finally answered after a long pause.

"Feel better quickly before Cece scoops your woman up."

"Yeah, right! April would never."

"Sure about that?" Dorian pointed out my bedroom window at April, who was now giving Cece a lesson in throwing horseshoes, standing behind her with one hand on her waist, the other taking Cece's hand and tossing the horseshoe together. "She's getting awfully friendly with her. Just sayin'."

Danielle's face scrunched up in disgust as she peered out the window at April cozying up to a hot, younger version of her. She turned abruptly and left the room. Dorian looked a bit confused, shrugged, and left behind her.

I stood there at my bedroom window and slipped the pills Sherri had given me into my nightstand drawer. When I glanced back up, I got a good look at Dahlia, now in a purple and pink bikini. She dipped a foot in the shallow end of the pool and proceeded down the pool steps, beckoning Dorian to join her. Dorian couldn't get out of her T-shirt fast enough, having already been in her one-piece bathing suit and swim trunks. They were both in the pool now, and I got to witness their first kiss. So sweet, the way Dahlia placed her arms around Dorian's neck. She was much taller than Dorian, but somehow, they seemed to fit perfectly. I was happy for her. She hadn't dated anyone since she and Sydney broke up over a year ago. They split because Dorian was a workaholic. Getting to the top had always been a huge motivator, but it left little time to spend with anyone, even her girlfriend. Yes, work was a relationship killer for Dorian. Ever since the break-up, though, she slowed down at work. Still worked like hell to make partner but took most weekends off now to enjoy life. It was a shame she couldn't figure that out while she and Sydney were together, but such was life.

Chapter Six

By the time I returned outside, a good portion of the Muff Mashers were dancing in front of Bobbi as she played the most current dance jams. The girls were still half naked, and dancing turned into dirty dancing. They were all smiling, laughing, and grinding on one another. When I approached Sherri, who appeared to be in her own world, nuzzling her face into Leah's neck. I tapped her on the shoulder. "I take it you took those pills?"

"The Molly? Oh, hell yeah, I took the Molly, and now I'm about to take Leah and maybe a few more ladies," she said as she pinched Leah's ass. Leah stood with her backside to her, and she suggested, "You should take one, too."

"I'm good, thanks." I took a look at the girls dancing, rubbing on one another, and looked back at Sherri. "Did you give that shit to all of them?"

"Yes, I did! If I'm lucky, we'll all be fucking in your backyard in the next hour."

I couldn't lie. The image of tanned, hot, sweaty bodies rubbing and sliding all over one another was a welcome one. I certainly wouldn't be upset if that happened. But I was just trying to keep track of everyone, especially my closest friends. Cookie and Shady were standing and animated just a half hour ago, and now they sat at the picnic table as they exchanged flailing hands for holding hands and calmly talked with an intent gaze. I hadn't seen them so intimate in years, and though I was stunned a little, the sparkle in Cookie's eyes said it all. She wasn't over her. Never was. Though she didn't say, it was pretty clear Shady was single now, or she wouldn't have shown up here. And the longer their conversation went on, the more convinced I became that she came here specifically looking for Cookie.

I spotted Dahlia sitting on the side of the pool, hanging her feet in the water. Dorian wasn't sitting next to her. Tristan was. Another swig of beer, and I scanned the party and wondered where the hell Dorian disappeared to. People multiplied with each hour that passed, but even through the crowd of partiers, I saw Dorian standing alone as she talked excitedly to a big magnolia tree in the side yard. Granted, it was a nice tree but a tree nonetheless. It was definitely not Dahlia. Tristan was a smooth operator if I must say so myself. It didn't take her long to get into my pants. Before I knew it, I was out of my underwear and in her bed. She was a great lay, and I needed to get Dorian away from the tree and back to Dahlia before it was too late. As I strolled up to her, I heard her talking and laughing.

"Dorian, what are you doin'? Who are you talking to?"

"Don't be silly, Parker! And don't be rude, say hi."

"To who?"

"To my friend here, of course!"

"Dorian, you're talking to a fucking tree." I tried to keep my voice down but threw my hands in the air in frustration. "I thought you were going to lay off the booze today. You do realize Dahlia is being hit on by

Tristan, right?"

"I know. That's why I'm over here. She's good-looking, with a great body and great abs. I mean, look at her," she said while she nodded in Tristan's direction. "I don't look like that."

"It's not about looks all the time, and what's wrong with you anyway?" I questioned. "That woman has been talking on the phone with you every day and anticipating spending some time with you today. Now are you going to stand here like an idiot talking to a tree, or are you going to grow a pair and go claim the woman you want to be with?"

She gathered her thoughts, and then herself, took a big breath, and exhaled. No more words were spoken. She gave me a sincere hug and walked toward Dahlia. I could tell Dahlia really liked her because she instantly blew off Tristan once Dorian sat by her side.

April was still throwing horseshoes with Cece, and I was surprised to see Kylie throwing horseshoes from the other end teamed up with Danielle, of all people. I wasn't sure how to take this new friendship, especially since it wasn't but an hour ago that Danielle seemed jealous toward her. Kylie sipped her beer while Dani drank a soft drink. They seemed to be getting along, and I didn't know what to make of it. As confusion turned into wild bewilderment, watching the two of them act so jovial together, Simone moseyed up to me, her hair and body dripping with beads of water after having just gotten out of the pool. She towel-dried herself and asked, "Is there something going on between you and Danielle?"

"What? No. Why would you ask such a thing?"

"Well, the way you were looking at each other was a telltale sign. You're both pretty intense."

"Nothing's going on. You know Dani is one of my best friends."

"That doesn't matter. Sometimes, even the best of friends have been known to fall for each other."

"Yeah, well, we're just friends, okay?" I snapped. "She's getting married, for crying out loud."

"If you say so."

"I say so," I argued, peeved at this conversation.

"Okay, okay! Don't get so upset," she said and quickly changed topics. "I haven't tasted you in a couple of weeks now. Mama needs her fix." She winked at me and licked her lips in anticipation of a good pussy licking.

"Maybe later." I sighed and watched Danielle and Kylie interact so pleasantly.

While Simone waited for a better answer, Cookie appeared in front of me, holding Shady's hand.

"We're out!" was all she said. I looked from her to Shady with curious wonderment, and her thin lips curled into a mischievous grin, not saying a word. Cookie point blank offered, "No fuckin' promises!"

That was enough for me. They were leaving together, with a strong possibility of reconciliation. This was good. I would like nothing more than to see these two hook back up. Cookie had been a shell of a person since they split, and even though I could tell she didn't trust Shady, I could also detect the love in her eyes that she still harbored for her. I always liked Shady, even if I didn't care for how she did my friend at the end of their relationship. Her reason for cheating, and ultimately leaving for someone else, was lack of attention from Cookie. It seemed Cookie would rather hang out with her friends and leave Shady at home alone than spend alone time together. Cookie wasn't the most affectionate person in the world, but when she loved, she loved hard and deeply. She knew she had a part in Shady's departure. She just didn't know how to change it.

I walked them out to the driveway, and Cookie climbed on her bike. Shady jumped on the back. Her arms circled Cookie's waist, and in a moment, they were gone, squealing wheels and speeding down my residential street. She did nothing quietly.

A smile spread across my face when Dorian and Dahlia came bursting through the front door. Dahlia was headed home, and Dorian was walking her out. After thanking me for my hospitality and a great time, they walked to her car, Dahlia leading her by the hand. I didn't think I had ever seen Dorian so giddy over a female. Don't get me wrong, she had fallen for women before. But she had never given up control, never allowed herself to completely commit, always with a wall up. Even if the wall was penetrated by a few, it still stood.

⚜ ⚜ ⚜ ⚜

When I was finished gawking at them, I returned to my party. My party that had now turned into an apparent orgy. The softball team was high on Molly and groping one another freely now. Even the straight ones couldn't help but caress the arms and legs of their gay counterparts. They traded out their husbands and boyfriends for butch women with short hair and tattoos today. Who was to know? I wasn't completely surprised to see Lisa in the middle of this foray. I didn't think she was high, but she had been drinking, and when she drank, she got a little gay. She may have been the coach of the team, but I was pretty sure her players were about to teach her a thing or two. And it wasn't going to be about softball.

It was sort of like who's on first? Except it was more like, who's on the first baseman? Sherri was the ringleader in this festival of touching, directing who she thought would go best with whom. It wasn't long before faces were in crotches and fingers were in holes. The moans emanating from my yard were almost enough to drown out Bobbi's beats. Bobbi, being the comical person she was, started scratching records to the rhythm of their moans, causing laughter to erupt from the pit of my stomach and vibrate through the air.

The lineup went as follows: Natalie, the pitcher, was in a long-term, committed relationship, so she was scratched; the catcher was on her knees giving oral to the short fielder; the right fielder and third baseman were tag teaming the shortstop; the first and second baseman were pussy locked in a sixty-nine position. But by far, the most interesting and entertaining sex fiend among them was the left fielder, who apparently didn't need anyone but herself to get off, rubbing her own clit like a monkey yanking his own chain.

Sherri, who drugged all of them, went around the whole group with a glow stick, rubbing it on every open pussy she could find as if they were cats in heat. Each one backed their ass up to meet the neon poker made of foam and plastic that flashed multiple colors of light.

"What the fuck?" I heard Dorian come up from behind me. She put her hand around my shoulder and joked, "Wow! Your very first orgy, Parker! Well done, my friend." After a few more minutes of watching this live porno in front of us, she offered, "You should jump in. It's your house after all."

A devious smirk covered my face as I pondered the very thought, and my attention to this group fuck was only distracted when I felt someone bump into me. It was Simone, and she was drooling at all the wet pussy in front of her just sitting there out in the open, waiting to be eaten and slurped up. I could tell she was trying to contain and restrain herself because no one knew about her deepest, darkest secret but me. It was entertaining to watch her study the group so intently.

"Um…" is what I heard next. I looked over my shoulder to see Danielle looking aghast with her hand covering her mouth. "You've never had a party like this. What are they doing?"

"What do you think they're doing?" I noticed April concentrating on Cece, who joined in the fun and was being fucked by some girl I didn't even know. Her gaze zoned in on April's as the chick fucked her relentlessly with three fingers, and I didn't know how Danielle was oblivious to this. This flirtation and seduction concerned me, but I had to have faith that April would never do anything to hurt Dani. Something in my gut was telling me otherwise, and I couldn't shake the feeling as I observed the attraction between them.

"I don't understand why they can't control themselves. They're like animals," Danielle said, baffled by the sight of about ten women intensely pleasuring one another.

"Dani, they're all doing Molly," I explained.

"Who?"

"Molly! They're on Molly!"

"Jesus, Parker! Who the hell is Molly? Do I know

her? Which one is she?" She scoped the pile of women intertwined together, cocked her head to the side, and tried to figure out which one was Molly.

I turned to April, who was trying not to laugh, and shook my head at Danielle's naïvety. She was almost child-like in her innocence of certain things. Drugs were one of them. She could read the shit out of any book and summarize it for you in four bullet points, but street smarts? Not so much.

"What? What's so funny?" she asked April.

"Nothing, hon, really."

"Well, which one is Molly already?" She pointed to the wicked soirée.

"They are all Molly." I waved my hand over the group like a wand.

"I don't get it."

"April, please take your fiancée home and maybe explain some things to her on your drive there."

"Come on, hon. Let's go. We need to have a talk." April guided Dani by the shoulder to go and thanked me for a good time.

However, before they got to the fence gate, Danielle stopped and squirmed free of April's hold on her shoulder to give me a hug goodbye. When she did, she pulled me close, and whispered in my ear, "Behave."

My arms gave her a good squeeze before reluctantly letting her go. They walked away, and I could faintly hear her say to April, "Which one is Molly, and why is she such a slut?"

I giggled. I knew how that conversation was going to go when they got in the car. Funny, behaving wasn't on my list of things to do, and stuffing my feelings down deep for Danielle always led to sex with other women. It was like a defense mechanism.

I stared at the gaggle of women fucking and sucking one another and couldn't help but get aroused. And the sounds coming from them were even more enticing. My trance was unwillingly broken by Kylie and Tristan, who were about to leave.

"We're gonna head out." Kylie opened her arms to give me a farewell hug.

"What? Not interested?" I nodded at all the girls mixed together in a ball of sweaty, heated sex. "That's a lot of pussy."

She leaned in for that hug, and in my ear, softly said, "I'm just interested in yours. Any chance of that happening tonight?"

Her hold on me tightened, and she nuzzled her face into my neck. She was awfully brazen, but I liked it. A jealous look came over Simone, who cased us from across the lawn. She was steaming mad as if we were a sure thing. We were not. I liked to keep my options open. But before I could give Kylie an answer, I noticed Tristan standing by the circle of pussy. Only she wasn't just standing there. She decided to poke around the group—literally. Her favorite seemed to be a girl who was licking another. Her ass was straight up in the air, begging to be fucked, and Tristan obliged. She had two fingers inside of this girl, and she backed her ass up into Tristan's fingers, her pussy swallowed them whole. She pulled them out, stickiness glistening to her fingers, and rubbed them together. She played with it before plunging them back into her, which elicited a string of pleasurable moans.

Kylie seemed to be getting turned on by the entire show, but her focus was on me. I was still in the clutch of her embrace, and she tightened her grip on me. The nuzzling of my neck turned into light kissing and sucking on the delicate skin there. Without a doubt, I was horny. How could I not be? But I wanted Kylie when I wanted Kylie, and tonight was not the night. I needed to be in control of when and where it happened, if it ever happened. Amazing how I controlled every relationship I had, no matter how short or how long, but the minute Danielle walked in the room, I became a puddle of mush. I tried to control things with Dani, but that wasn't how it usually ended up. I'd do anything to be with that woman. Anything.

I finally chose this time to answer Kylie's original question of spending the night. "Not tonight, okay? Another time."

"Suit yourself." She was peeved as she peeled herself off me. She lifted Tristan by the scruff of her shirt and made her retrieve her fingers from the warm spot in some stranger's hole.

"I'll call you," Kylie said with a wink and a wave as she lost her attitude fairly quickly.

They departed and left the entertainment for me and the crowd that had gathered around them. That Molly must've been some strong-ass shit because these girls were not stopping; one came after the next. I didn't see Dorian anymore as I scanned the party. I would've been surprised she left this debauchery, but she was into Dahlia in a deep and meaningful way. Too bad for her. I couldn't stop watching, and just as I unbuttoned my jean shorts, I felt a hand grab hold of mine. I looked up to see Simone. She smirked seductively as she led me into my house.

Once we were in my bedroom, things picked up speed. No words were spoken. Simone pushed me onto my bed. She hadn't gone down on me for a couple of weeks, and it was apparent when she ripped my jean shorts off me. She needed what she needed, and so did I. I welcomed the feel of her mouth on me. Her wet tongue slid over my clit repeatedly, and although I thought I was game for just getting off, it turned out I wanted some affection, too. But I was seeking that affection from a woman who deemed herself incapable of that kind of emotion toward another woman.

I attempted it anyway by sliding her up the length of my body and placing my lips on hers. I didn't expect her to respond positively to this, but it was almost as though she could feel that I needed her. I needed her close. I needed that intimacy. She kissed me, full on, just as she had during our last encounter. After a while, she worked her way down my neck, down my throat, and to my hardened nipple that she released from the constraints of my bra. My breathing became measured, and my pussy became wetter as her mouth wrapped around it. "Oh, fuck!" I yelped, delighted in the pleasure she yielded.

Some things didn't change. As I went to cup her dangling breasts, Simone promptly pushed my hand aside. My persistence in repeating the action did not get rewarded, and she pushed my hand aside again. "No," she said firmly. She pressed my wrists into the mattress and took control. I didn't allow anyone to control me and immediately put her on her back. She looked at me with concern and started to push me off, until I climbed up her and straddled her face. "Oh," she said, seemingly pleased at this turn of events.

No time was wasted as she munched away on

me like a fat kid who hadn't eaten cake in months. She knew my body better than any lover I ever had, and it didn't take long for me to cum. I came hard for her, and she refused to stop. She was eager for more, but I was spent and collapsed on top of her. It was nice, the closeness we shared tonight. And as we lay there, content in each other's arms, resting peacefully, I could hear the moaning from outside subside, along with the music. My party had ended without me present, and I didn't even care. Falling asleep was easy after an orgasm like that, and I slept restfully until about four thirty a.m. when I awoke to an empty bed. Simone had slipped out like a thief in the night and left me alone.

My thoughts promptly turned to Danielle. At first, I giggled out loud, thinking about the fact that she didn't know what Molly was. However, giggling soon turned to weeping as I let myself feel. I loved her. I was always trying to stifle it, trying to shove it down deep within me, but tonight, I let it surface, and it hurt like hell. I lay there missing what we never had. The tears were somehow different this time because I now knew what it was like to kiss her, to make love to her, to hold her in my arms. The tears were hot as they blazed a trail down my cheek and dripped off my ear onto my pillow.

"Oh, Dani," I whispered out loud. I took hold of the extra pillow on my bed and held it tightly to me. The pain oozed from my heart while the moon mocked me through the window. The intense emotion finally exhausted me. Sleep forced itself upon me once more.

Chapter Seven

Sunlight bustled through the blinds and cascaded upon my face, slowly rousing me with its warmth. Morning had arrived. I knew this whole day would be spent cleaning up from the party, but I woke up just as horny as when I went to bed. I lay there, softly stroking over the skin of my stomach, giving myself goose bumps. My nipples hardened, and I lightly grazed over them while my mind dug through a multitude of fantasies in my memory bank. Even though I didn't allow myself the simple pleasure, as a result of emotionally killing myself over the years, I chose Danielle fantasy number forty-two, one of my favorites.

My eyes were closed as I watched her enter the room. She wore only a T-shirt and panties as she climbed onto the bed. She crawled over me while I lay on my back in anticipation. Her beauty mesmerized me, and I was entranced. She straddled me and placed her hands on my chest to balance herself. I caressed her thighs and stroked her silky-smooth skin. I grabbed her ass as I squeezed and pulled her down to me. Grinding my pussy into hers only became more intense as she lifted her shirt over her head and released her pert little boobs. I reached up to her face and lightly dragged my fingertips down her cheek while I grazed over her bottom lip with my thumb, longing to feel her mouth on mine. Finally, I pulled her face to mine and kissed her gently. My heart pounded a mile a minute as the kiss deepened, and I felt her body meld into mine. Her breasts slid over mine again and again with each motion of her hips, and my hips bucked back in response.

My pussy ached for her, and I slid her out of her panties. My own hand was down my underwear already, rubbing my clit incessantly. However, my emotions for her got tangled into the fantasy, and it was not welcomed this morning. I just wanted to get off and get on with my day, so my brain switched images from love to raunch. The scenes of Danielle faded and were replaced with Simone and Kylie and Tristan and the whole lineup of women I was attracted to, and they kept coming, one after the other until… "Oh, my God!" I yelled out my climax and relieved my torment.

Masturbation completed for the day, I rolled over, popped the lid of my medication bottle, and swallowed the little jagged pill that kept me depression-free. I was about to get out of bed when I saw I had a new text message. It was from Danielle. My heart sank to my stomach. I read, "Lunch?" I thought about my choices: clean up or have lunch with a hot-ass professor. I chose the latter. I was on the road in less than an hour.

※ ※ ※ ※

Driving up to the college always made my heart flutter with fond memories of my time spent there. Not much had changed since I attended the school. The buildings and halls were the same. I entered the building where Danielle's office was located and walked down a long corridor lined with classrooms

                    TL Dickerson

and offices. Hers was all the way at the end, the last one on the right. The door was cracked, and I could see and hear her ending a conversation with a male student. They discussed a paper with a bad grade.

"All you have to do is put the work in, David. It shouldn't be this hard," she reprimanded him.

"But, Professor Bly, I did put the work in."

"Your paper suggests otherwise." She peered over at the door because it made a creaking noise when I opened it and immediately ended their discussion when she saw me. "We'll talk about this more in class," she said and bid him farewell. He turned and headed for the door and squeezed past me.

Her office was the epitome of higher education. Her degrees and accolades lined the wall behind her massive walnut desk. The dark wood implied class and authority with its claw feet and intricate hand-carved woodwork. Victorian in appearance, it was an antique her father had gifted her when she moved back from California and landed the job at the university. The cherry wood bookcase by the window was illuminated by rays of sunlight. It showcased the great classics stretching the span of the shelf.

The lush gray carpet cushioned my sneakers as I walked into the office and gave her an obligatory hug. "Hi," I said as I made my way to her desk and spotted a new framed picture of her and April at their latest golf tournament. "You about ready?"

"Yes, I am. Pizza?"

"Pizza? What, no salad?"

"Don't feel like it today. I'm in the mood for grease."

I looked at her in disbelief because I knew she stayed away from junk food as a general rule, but she insisted, "I'll run a couple of extra miles. Don't look at me like that."

Just as she grabbed her pocketbook, my cell rang. It was Dorian. "Hey, what are you doing?" she asked.

"I'm about to go to lunch with Danielle. Why? What's up?"

I tried listening to Dorian, but Danielle was fixing her hair. She took her ponytail out, shook her hair loose, and made sure to make eye contact with me as she did. Then she pulled her thick mane back once again and tied it tight. I told Dorian to meet us at Mancusso's Pizzeria and did my best to avert my gaze. Every time I looked in Danielle's eyes, I fell in love all over again. She stepped toward me.

"Stop!" I said out loud.

"Stop what?" Dorian asked.

"Not you. I'll see you in fifteen minutes."

My vow not to become involved was shattered like the broken glass that covered my bar as she continued her approach. She stood inches in front of me now.

"Dani, what are you doing?"

"What I wanted to do yesterday, but you were too busy sucking face with that young girl."

"That young girl that you were playing horseshoes with so nicely?"

"I guess I was checking her out. Do you like her more than me?"

"You're engaged. You remind me of it quite often. Don't you remember?"

Resisting her was futile. Being in her office, seeing her in that skirt suit with one too many buttons undone on her blouse, I lost myself to her. Her kiss was slow and thoughtful, so sure that I would pull away, but her lips were more persuasive than I cared to admit. The longer I allowed the kiss to continue, the more confident I could feel her getting, and the intensity grew. Her tongue infiltrated my mouth as it demanded more. She was intrigued by my tongue piercing. I could tell because she tugged on it each time she sucked on my tongue. What choice did I have but to succumb to her? My mind knew to resist, but my body was like, *Bring it!* The blood coursed through my veins like an awakened river. My arms circled her, and my hands explored the small of her back, pulling her closer. The sound of our lips smacking together enticed me to continue my exploration to her cheek, her ear, and down her neck. I suckled the heat of her flesh.

"This isn't fair," I whispered into the nape of her neck.

"No, it's not," she agreed but didn't stop me from dragging her skirt upward. After I hiked it up over her buttocks, I grabbed her naked flesh. I caressed her ass cheeks and moved her thong down to the tops of her thighs. Her meaty, round little ass undulated forward some. It was hungry for more touch. I inched her closer and closer to her desk, all the while our mouths feasted on each other. Once I had her against her own desk, I lifted her up by her ass and sat her on it. Papers and folders shifted and crumpled under her. I separated her legs with my body and tugged her closer, close enough that my pussy, although covered by my jeans, smashed against hers. Her thong was twisted, half on, half off, until my frustration with it got the best of me. Blinded by the intense heat between us and unable to control myself, I ripped it off her. Our kiss was broken, and her eyes showed shock at my assertiveness. What appeared to be annoyance at first quickly dissipated and morphed into an expression of want. She liked it, and she silently let me know as she took my hand and directed it to her throbbing, wet center. The hot tide of passion raged through both of us, and I sank my fingers into her.

"Uhh…" she muttered a short moan of consent.

The feelings I had for her for years consumed me, and whatever restraint I had been able to sustain thus far was diminished in seconds. Her hands had a tight grasp on my shoulders as I penetrated and sliced through her wetness with ease. Her hips bucked and invited me to fill her completely as her body involuntarily tremored with each thrust. Each movement brought her face closer and closer to my neck. She kissed me and brought her hands behind my head, cupped it, and closed whatever space there was left between us.

"Oh, Parker," she whispered, our faces cheek to cheek.

She was panting now, short, brisk breaths, and I knew she was about to climax. Her grip on the nape of my neck became tighter, and it took everything she had to remain quiet. The sound of students buzzing to class could be heard in the hallway. They giggled and chatted, oblivious to what was taking place only a few feet away, separated merely by a thin wood door that wasn't even locked.

Her orgasm finished, she started to unbutton my jean shorts in hopes of reciprocating. I wanted nothing more than to feel her, but I refrained. For starters, the fact that the door was unlocked made me more nervous every second we were in each other's embrace. I felt like I was just able to bring her to climax without being detected. I didn't think we could get away with it much longer. Moreover, I felt like I may reach the point of no return if I let her. She had yet to take her time in exploring my body. The reality was that she was still getting married to someone else. Silently, she was not taking *no* for an answer. She reached for my zipper again, and once again, I pushed her hand aside.

"Why? Why won't you let me?" she asked, miffed by my refusal.

"We should go. Dorian's meeting us at the restaurant."

"Dorian can wait," she said and aimed for my crotch.

"No. Danielle, no." I grabbed her hands and put them by her sides. "I said no."

"But why?"

"Because it's not right, and I'm trying to save you from a shitload of guilt. And in the meantime, trying to save myself altogether. After we do stuff, you feel guilty, and I can't take that." I dragged my fingers through my much too long hair, totally disheartened. "Seriously, am I going to be your mistress? Your fling on the side? You're going to begin your marriage having an affair with your best friend?" I didn't wait for a reply. Instead, I continued, "Because that's not going to work...for either of us, and especially not April."

"It could."

"Are you insane? Who am I even talking to? What's going on with you?"

She let out a deep sigh. Her head shook back and forth and hung low when she answered as sincerely as possible. "I don't know. I'm not okay with this, but then you come around me and everything changes, even if only for a moment."

"Moments of indiscretion that have to stop." I pelted her with a bunch of unanswerable questions. "Why now? Why after all these years? You could have had me at any point in your life. Why now?"

"I don't know, Parker. It's like…It's like all these feelings, the attraction, the chemistry, I had turned them off for so long, tucked them away, hidden from everyone, especially me. I really thought we were in *Friendsville*." Her gaze dropped from my eyes to my lips. Her stare lingered there like a child desperate for a piece of candy, before she recognized, "Until that kiss. I blame that kiss for unleashing something that was better left alone, better left undisturbed. I never wanted to lose your friendship, but your lips have me second-guessing everything I've ever known to be true." Her thumb brushed over my bottom lip, and before I could stop her, she leaned in toward me and tasted her guilty pleasure once more. Oh, like the sweet taste of strawberries on a summer day. But my heart needed some kind of protection. It was bad enough I tortured it on some level and never allowed it to love anyone else but her. And now that she was here, right here in front of me, giving me the physical part of what I always yearned for, something in me saw more than just a little emotional pain to come if I let this continue. She was getting married to someone who wasn't me. No, my heart couldn't possibly take the beating if we stayed this course.

Going against everything I ever felt for her, I ignored the fire in my groin. I lifted my hands, put them on her shoulders, and peeled myself away from her. It was like an old wound that ached on a rainy day. I was used to the pain, but her eyes told me that she was not. "Let's go meet Dorian," I said as my heart broke for the millionth time.

Once outside in the sunshine, we walked across the vast parking lot to her silver Roadster. "What? You don't want to go in my Jeep? Top's already down."

"Do I look like I'm dressed to climb up into your Jeep?" she sarcastically asked as she pointed to her attire.

"No, but I'd pay good money to see that." I giggled and imagined her trying to climb into my Jeep that had a six-inch lift on it, in high heels no less.

We got into her sports car, and she put the top down before driving off campus. The sky was a beautiful baby blue, and the white clouds that dotted the sky scattered in poofs like big fluffy pillows. She had her sunglasses on, so I couldn't see her eyes as she lifted her face to meet the sun. We cruised down the street just fast enough to gather a whipping wind through my hair, and I raked my fingers through it. I watched her shift gears in her high heels. It was amusing because she pushed that clutch in like she was wearing running shoes.

❧❧❧❧

Dorian was waiting in her car when we pulled into the spot next to her. She opened the door and stepped out wearing a navy blue pantsuit. She had never worn a skirt or a dress to her job. She was a true butch but always the epitome of professionalism.

"What took you so long? You should have been here fifteen minutes ago," she said.

"It's all good. We're here now." I opened the front door to Mancusso's for them to enter.

The tan walls of the pizzeria were adorned with Italian paintings, and artificial green ivy was spread around the perimeter of the ceiling. It gave the room a much-needed splash of color. The tall plants that were placed purposely in the corners emanated a cozy atmosphere, and the huge bay window in the front of the dining room permitted sunlight to stream through as it casted its rays on the classic wood tables with white linens and chairs. It was a nice place, and the three of us frequently met for lunch here. We all pulled out a chair and took a seat.

While Dorian perused the menu, I felt Danielle's gaze on me. Without looking back at her, I gently shook my head. It was my way of telling her to cut it out. And a slight head bob in Dorian's direction was my way of indicating Dorian would notice if she didn't.

"What are you guys getting?" Dorian asked without looking up from the menu.

We didn't answer right away, and Danielle got more brazen with each passing minute. The white linen tablecloth hung low enough to the floor that it hid from view the fact that her foot, out of her high heel shoe, had now made its way to my bare legs. Lightly, she petted my freshly shaven legs with her toes, up and down. She made me jump in my seat, and I shook the table, consequently rattling the silverware on the surface above.

"Jesus, Parker! What's up with you? You okay?" Dorian wondered.

"Sorry. Bug." I swatted at the air.

Danielle smirked and giggled under her breath.

She removed her foot momentarily and scanned the menu. If she was trying to lighten my mood after the serious talk we just had, making me uneasy in front of our close friend wasn't the way to do it. "I think I just want a slice of pizza." Danielle peered at me. "How about you, Parker? What are you having?" But as she got her last words out, I once again felt her foot brush against my leg. I didn't jump this time but pulled my phone from my pocket and texted her while answering her question out loud.

"I think I'll just have a slice, too."

Meanwhile, I texted her, *What the fuck are you doing? STOP!* Her notification sounded on her phone, and she retrieved it from her purse, read it, then looked up at me. But while she was in the process of texting me back, her foot returned. Only this time, she grazed my thigh and landed smack dab on my crotch. This sent me reeling in my seat once more. I banged my elbow on the edge of the table, sending my fork falling to the floor and making a ruckus.

"What the—" Dorian snapped but was interrupted by the server, who was ready to take our order.

"Hi. My name is Mindy, and I'll be your server today. Are you ready to order, or do you need a few more minutes?" We each gave the woman our order, and she turned to walk away.

"Okay. So where are we going camping this year, ladies? It's almost that time," Dorian said as she rubbed her hands briskly together.

Our annual camping trip had started with just a few of our friends but had since transformed into quite the event. Five years later, at least thirty lesbians now attended. The last one was a blast! We always tried to pick a state park because they tended to be the nicest and cleanest as opposed to some privately owned campgrounds. So, after discussing it at length and getting nowhere, we let Dorian pick. Faver Dykes State Park. It was beautiful and serene with some of the best hiking trails around. Of course, we didn't know that at the time. She picked our destination based solely on its name.

These camping trips were mostly drunken fests. We tried doing as little camping activities as possible. Last year, Coakley, a friend of ours, popped open a beer at the crack of dawn. She called it breakfast. I was pretty sure we all stayed intoxicated the entire weekend. That was, everyone but Danielle. Instead of drinking, she usually helped out the drunks who couldn't hold their liquor and got sick. She was great at holding heads or holding hair out of the way while people puked. She hated when they got so drunk, they lost control of themselves, and she found this to be a total turnoff. However, it wasn't in her nature to turn her back on a fellow human being who ended up sick as a dog. She would always say, "This is why I don't drink. You want to know why I don't drink? This is why I don't drink." She added, "I need to have control of myself and my actions." This was true of her non drinking, but her sober actions had taken on a whole other meaning as of late.

Just as I pondered this, once again, I felt the pantyhosed toes of hers graze my calf, which caused me to bang my knee against the top of the table, rattling dishes and silverware alike. She found my nervousness entertaining and chuckled and grinned, until we both went wide-eyed and pale as a ghost when Dorian asked, "Okay. What's going on? Really? Are you two fucking?"

"Why would you even say that, Dorian? Of course not," I anxiously responded.

"I don't know. Something's going on. You've been acting all weird since we got here, and you," she pointed at Danielle, "you've had a shit-eating grin on your face since we sat down. I've known you both for far too long to not know when something is going on." She looked from me to Dani and back to me. "And something is going on. So who wants to be the first to fess up?"

Dani and I sat there silently, hoping she wouldn't notice we weren't saying anything, but Dorian wouldn't let it be. "Someone say something! Okay, now it's getting weird." She sipped from her glass of water and waited as patiently as she could, her eyes, like watching tennis, back and forth from me to Danielle.

"There's nothing to fess up to. So, hey, how did things go with you and Dahlia last night after you left?" I desperately tried one last time to deflect the focus off our apparent affair. I shifted my legs in a way that Danielle couldn't touch me again, not realizing she would mistake Dorian's leg for mine. Just then, Dorian visibly jumped in her seat and hit her knee on the table.

"Whoa!" Her eyes grew as round as half dollars, and her mouth gaped open. "Um…let's try this one more time, and I'm not about that lying shit. We've been friends for too long. Now tell me!"

Again, neither of us responded, not willing to include Dorian in this secret. She didn't know how to act when told a secret. It wasn't that she couldn't keep one, it was just that her excitement was hard to contain. Once she found a secret out, she asked one question after the other, badgering and interrogating the poor soul who made the mistake of telling her in the first place. This particular news might throw her over the edge, and I didn't know how prepared either of us were for that. One of us had to say something. The silence was loud, and seconds felt like hours.

"Spill it!" Dorian ordered.

"Uh…uh…" Danielle stuttered, her face filled with fear and guilt. Ah, yes, the guilt. The reason I was trying to keep my hands off her. I didn't want her to regret me or wish things hadn't happened. But damn! The more I tried to say no, the more she came at me.

"Parker, would you like to give it a go? Because the big-time, award-studded literary expert and English professor has become a babbling idiot."

"Dorian, listen, it's complicated."

"Parker, no!" Dani pleaded.

"Danielle, if you didn't want this to come out, you shouldn't have played footsie with Dorian. Ya made it pretty impossible to lie." I returned my attention to Dorian. "Okay. So…" I wasn't able to get it out but tried again. "Okay. So…"

Dorian rolled her eyes, inhaled deeply, and exhaled a lungful of air as she got more annoyed.

"Okay, okay. So, some things have happened between us as of late," I began, not really knowing what to do with my hands. I fidgeted and sucked the ball of my tongue piercing through my two front teeth. It was a bad habit I had when I was nervous.

"Some things?" She turned to Danielle, who was still clearly in denial. "Aren't you getting married to April?"

"Yes, I am marrying April."

"Then why? I mean, have your plans changed?

Are you breaking it off with her?" And so the game of one hundred questions started.

Danielle glanced at me before ramming a dagger into my chest cavity. "No. Nothing has changed. I'm still going to marry her."

"I don't understand then," Dorian said.

"I don't know. I don't have an answer for you."

"So let me get this straight. You're getting married to April, but you're having an affair with Parker."

My eyebrows scrunched together, and my eyes narrowed at the words. My head was about to pop.

"All these years, and you wait until you're about to get married to someone else?" Dorian didn't realize she was adding more fuel to my fire.

"I think Parker was right when she said it's complicated."

"Pssh…" uncontrollably escaped my mouth.

"Can we go back to talking about where we're going camping this year? This is getting a little uncomfortable." Danielle squirmed in her seat.

"Really? You weren't uncomfortable rubbing your foot on my crotch just minutes ago," I retorted.

"Parker!!"

"No, Dani! This is bullshit!" I yelled but quickly brought my tone down to a more subdued level as I looked around at other diners who had abruptly lifted their heads to see what the disturbance was. In a more hushed tone but just as strained, I continued my tirade. "You want to know what's uncomfortable? I'll tell you what's uncomfortable." I picked up my fork and tapped it on the table. "Trying to save my heart from being crushed. That's uncomfortable." I may have chewed the piercing right out of my tongue while my temper rose with each uncomfortable statement. "Watching you go home with April instead of me. That's uncomfortable." I pointed the fork at her. "Trying to do the right thing by you in ending this before it really gets started and having you be wishy-washy about it. That's uncomfortable." My frustration could not be more evident as I dropped the fork onto the table, ending in a clank to the surface.

Dorian sat there patiently but finally could take no more. "I don't know where either of your brains have gone, but it seems all common sense has been lost. All these years you've had opportunity after opportunity to be together, and you wait until you're getting married?" Dorian focused on Danielle. "I gotta tell you, Dani. This is not like you. And you," she turned to face me, "you've been hiding this from me? My two best friends keeping shit from me. That's great, guys!"

"We are changing this conversation right now!" Danielle interrupted and pointed her index finger down to the table. "Where are we camping this year?" She was unwavering in her quest to kill this topic of discussion, and her last words to Dorian before leaving the restaurant were, "You say nothing to no one. Do you understand?" Manipulating situations was one of Dani's strong points, and this situation was no different. I swore she got it as a child. She played one parent against the other to achieve the desired outcome.

The drive back to the college was quiet. She slumped forward with a death grip on the steering wheel, and the skin around her eyes was bunched together in a pained stare. When she pulled into her reserved parking space, she put the car in park and shifted in her seat to face me. She took a second, her gaze lingering on me, not sure what to say, but one thing was for sure…she knew I was still infuriated. Finally, she spurted, "So what? You're not going to talk to me?"

I had been staring straight ahead the whole time, my eyes were piercing mad, but I turned my face to her and stabbed her with my words. "This ends right here, right now. You're getting married, and you have no intentions of ending that. I will not be your mistress. I won't!" My body turned in her direction to align with my face. I demanded her full attention. "You know how I feel about you, but you can't have your cake and eat it, too. We're not meant to be together, and I need to accept that."

I had one foot out of the car door, but she stopped me, reached for my shoulder, and brought my attention to her once more. "You know I care about you, right? I can't picture my life without you in it. I promise I'll stop behaving the way I have around you, okay? Because ultimately, I know you're right… that this is wrong. I want to be faithful to her, and it shouldn't be this hard. It's just that…It's just that I've discovered these feelings for you, and now I have to stuff them down."

"You could reconsider getting married. You don't have to do this."

She stared blankly at the teachers and staff walking to and from their cars. "I love her, Parker. The plans have been made, and I'm going to spend my life with her."

"I gotta go." I was so annoyed. I stepped out of the car completely. The pain of her words impaled my pathetic heart and soul. All that I'd felt for her all these years culminated and came to a head like a zit about to burst. I leaned forward, ducked my head into her car, and proclaimed, "Do not ever touch me again. I mean it. Don't kiss me. Don't look at me with those dreamy eyes. Don't you dare! It's back to *Friendsville* for us. You got it?"

She pursed her lips and pouted slightly, seemingly stunned by my words. She was used to getting her way and almost didn't know how to take me. She knew she had me for so long and probably didn't believe the things I just said, but I meant them. Having her this way wasn't an option.

"Well, wait," she stammered and ran her hands back and forth over the steering wheel. "Will I see you Thursday? For our run?"

"I don't think so. I need some time. Don't call me. I'll call you when I'm ready." I knew full well I wouldn't. I walked to my Jeep, climbed in, and was fuming mad at what just occurred. I wasn't mad that Dorian knew now. I was relieved that she found out. Not having anyone to talk to about this had been draining. When I started the engine, I took a peek in the rearview mirror and noticed Danielle was still sitting in her car. I realized she was crying, wiping away her tears with the back of her hand. It was gut wrenching to watch, but my pride had gotten the best of me. I put the Jeep in gear and drove away.

Chapter Eight

Leaving Danielle so upset in her car wasn't easy, but I needed to get away from her, pronto. I was heated, and not in a good way, but once I pulled up in front of Merge, my anger about Danielle dissipated, and anxiety took its place. Construction was bustling, and the sounds of hammers and drills greeted me as I walked through the front doors. The work had only started a few days ago. All the Sheetrock had been ripped down, stained with soot from the fire. The remnants of my beautiful oak bar were being demolished. I couldn't resist the urge to shake my head, reliving that horrid night of destruction and chaos. My stomach flip-flopped at the thought.

I made my way around the workers rebuilding my dream bar and slid through the double doors that led to the back of the house. The hallway was so empty and lifeless without the usual hubbub of staff going about their regular routines. I entered my office and took a seat behind the desk. A sinking feeling sat in the pit of my stomach as I browsed the internet, not reading a thing, but just staring at the screen. That wooden stare was the one that scared me. It was one of the telltale signs of an impending bout of depression. My psychiatrist told me I would have days like this and that it was okay as long as it passed within a few days.

It had been six years since my last episode,

when my mother was murdered. A part of me blamed myself for her demise, even though I knew I wasn't the reason. It was one of the most difficult times of my life to get through. I tried to get her away from my father so many times over the years, but she wouldn't go. The fear of what he might do to her if she left was too much for her to bear. Sadly, in the end, it didn't matter if she stayed or not. He was bound to kill her. I hoped he suffered for every tear she ever shed during his time of abuse. Maybe he would choke on the crocodile tears he shed for his own actions, tears that meant nothing because my father didn't have a soul. He threatened to kill her since I was a child, and even though he had come close a couple of times, she survived the broken arms and ribs. She survived him punching her so hard he broke her eye socket in four places and survived him wrapping his hands around her neck while choking her until she was blue in the face. For as much as he used her as a human punching bag, beating her to a bloody pulp at times, it was odd the way she died. He simply pushed her, and she tripped backward, hit her head on the corner of the coffee table in the living room, and died. To this day, I felt the loss of my mother deeply. Though my father still lived, be it in prison or not, I felt like an orphan, and had for a long time.

At that time, I found myself doing self-destructive things. I began drinking heavily and experimented with hard-core drugs. I started to see my father in me, which made me take a step back and stop the onslaught of the same addiction he had. Instead, I put the drugs and alcohol in check, only to realize my true addiction lay in playing poker. It started out simple, exchanging one addiction for another. The further I sank into the darkness, the more deep rooted my addiction became. It consumed me and changed the person I was.

When I started borrowing money from loan sharks, I knew I was on a horrible and ugly downslope in my life. I played in all sorts of grimy, rundown backrooms. Backrooms of restaurants, motels, and people's houses became a second home to me, but when I got mixed up with a rough group of lesbians who considered themselves a biker gang, things really took a turn for the worse. These girls were rough, similar to the type who destroyed my bar. Bitterness was on the menu every day. To say they were misfits would be a compliment. They were butch lesbians, hard lesbians, tattooed and pierced lesbians. They took their poker games seriously, and if you didn't pay up, they weren't opposed to getting physical. They were thugs. A couple of them had the teardrop eye tattoo, which meant they served time in jail. One girl had even made it a rainbow teardrop.

Then it got to the point where I couldn't pay the loan sharks back, I completely lost my mind, and bet the bar in a heated cutthroat match of Texas Hold 'Em. I knew it was wrong, but I was too far gone to realize my mistake...until it was too late. I held a straight, ace through five, and insisted in my head that there was no way I could lose. Playing cards with gang members was one thing, but when the head honcho was involved in the game, the atmosphere was tense.

Tiny was her name, though there was nothing tiny about her. The leader of the pack was big and not just overweight. She was tall, thick, and as rough as they came. Nails, nuts, and bolts were what she ate for breakfast, and she couldn't wait to feast on me. Half her grill was missing, and I didn't know if it was from all the meth she snorted or if she just had bad teeth. But the thing that scared me the most about her were her huge hands. They were like mitts, like the paws of a great Dane.

"Call," I said.

"You have no more money to bet with, Parker," Tiny said with a cigarette hanging out of her mouth.

"No, but I have the bar."

The room went silent. A pin drop would have spoiled the moment. The smoke was thick in the air and hung in the specter of light from the bulb above us. The smell of stale beer permeated the room, and Tiny blew small smoke rings from her mouth while she waited patiently for me to reveal my hand. Confidence and a bit of arrogance were obvious in my demeanor, as I laid my straight down on the green felt table, so sure I was about to win a boatload of money. However, all color drained from my face, and I was whiter than a ghost when Tiny spread her cards out— ten, jack, queen, king, ace.

She laughed a hard, diabolical laugh, even with the cigarette still hanging from her lips. I thought I would pass out from sheer shock or at the very least have a fucking heart attack, but she wouldn't let that happen. She repeatedly slapped me on the back and congratulated herself on being the new owner of a bar. She gave me a week to get my paperwork in order, then I was to pay the piper.

Just as I reached the front door, Tiny stopped me and sternly said, "Leave town and I will hunt you down like a rabid dog." I glanced at her hand on my shoulder, shrugged it off, and reached for the door, but once more, she stopped me. "Parker?" I returned her gaze, and she added, "I'll kill you." Needless to say, I left there sick to my stomach.

By the middle of the week, I still hadn't told anyone about losing the bar or the fact that this time next week my staff would have a new boss or find themselves unemployed. Dorian happened to come in for happy hour one evening, and we talked about everything but what I had done. I was behind the bar, directly in front of her. I poured her another bourbon when Tiny entered through the front door abruptly and with an entourage of her burliest gang members. She walked around the place, studying it, and pointing to areas of the room she wanted to change.

"I want the pool table over here." She pointed to the opposite corner of the room. One of her goons wrote down her every word on a notepad as she followed her from one end to the other.

Dorian clearly looked confused and wondered out loud, "What's going on, Parker? Who are these people?"

"Uh…uh…"

She squinted at me, knowing when I stuttered that something awful had happened, and I didn't want to admit to it.

"Parker, why is that woman verbally redecorating your bar?"

Before I could respond with the truth, Tiny came behind the bar and started taking inventory of the liquor on the shelves.

"You gettin' those papers together? I want a nice, smooth transition, and the first thing I'm doin' is changin' the name from Merge to Tiny's Ale House. Got a nice ring to it, doesn't it?" She laid her big paw on my shoulder and gave it a little squeeze.

That last statement made Dorian's eyes widen,

and the concern on her face was undeniable. "Parker?" she agonized again.

I waited for Tiny to be on her way. She approached the front door and turned back to me. "You have three days." She and her cronies exited, and the door slowly shut behind them.

"Parker, what did you do?"

"I lost the bar in a poker game last Wednesday," I confessed, humiliated and desperate.

Dorian's jaw dropped. She was aghast. "No way. That's not true," she said as calmly as she could. She lifted her whiskey glass to her lips and took a healthy swig. "You would never. This bar is your world. It's everything you've worked for your entire life. You would never." She was in denial, but the longer I held my silence, the more inclined she was to believe that I did lose the bar in a card game. For the first time, the reality of my actions brought tears to my eyes. Before I knew it, I bawled like a baby and was being cradled in Dorian's arms. She didn't know what to do with me because she had never seen me cry like that, so she just held me.

After a while, with tears dripping off my chin and snot running from my nose, she finally spoke. "It hasn't sunk in entirely yet for me, but I'll be damned if you're going to lose this place. You worked too hard to build this business. I can't watch you throw it away."

"There's nothing I can do. She won fair and square. They'll kill me if I renege."

"You're not reneging, but you're going to give her the money you owe her."

"Do you know how much the bar is worth?" I thought she didn't realize the kind of money I would need.

"You know what, I really don't. But neither does she. Everyone has their price."

"I don't have that kind of money."

"No, but I do."

I backed up out of her embrace, and that little bitch Pride took over. "What? No! No way! I can't ask you to do that." I was distraught but hellbent on not accepting anyone's help.

"You didn't ask me! I offered. Stop with the pride shit! You need me right now, and I'm here, and I'm able."

"But it's too much."

"Not for family. That's what we are, right? I mean, you're like a sister to me." She picked up her snifter and took a warm sip. "Nobody's changing the name of this bar to Tiny's!" She slammed the glass on the bar. "No more gambling! I know you haven't been right since your mom passed away, and I realize you're depressed, but the gambling has to stop." She sliced her hand over her throat as she implied for me to cut it out.

"Parker? You there?" I was roused from reminiscing and looked up to see Jeff, the contractor. He peeked his head in my office door.

"Yeah, Jeff." I gestured for him to come in.

He approached my desk a little suspiciously, almost as if he didn't want to tell me what he was about to.

"Well, I don't know how to tell you this, so I'm just gonna come out with it." He paused briefly and went on, "As we work, we're finding more and more damage. The metal rafters melted and twisted from the fire, and the concrete under the floor has also cracked in several areas. It's going to take us longer to complete the job, and the cost has substantially gone up." He was at the door when he turned to me one last time. "I'm sorry, Parker, but I promise when it's all done, you'll be more than pleased. It's going to be beautiful, and your business will be booming again in no time."

I nodded, thanked him for informing me, and went back to staring at the computer screen. This day had not been good to me. First with Danielle denying us again, and now this. The fact that I left my backyard a disaster area from the party yesterday also weighed on my mind and made me not want to go home.

When I finally got the gumption to leave, I passed through the wreckage of my bar once more. The strong smell of smoke still clung to the air and remaining debris. I made a beeline to the front door with tunnel vision. I didn't want to see the destruction anymore. I didn't have much faith that the insurance company would cover one hundred percent of the renovation, but I couldn't even think about that right now. It was all so overwhelming, and all I wanted to do was hide under a rock somewhere and never have to deal with it.

❧ ❧ ❧ ❧

I climbed in my Jeep, buckled up, and sped home. When I pulled into my driveway, I noticed Cookie and Kylie's motorcycles there. Granted, Cookie had a key to my house, but she hardly ever used it.

I entered my house yelling, "Cookie!" Nothing. I walked farther and yelled once more, "Cookie!" Again, nothing. By the time I made it to the back slider, I saw them outside, sitting at the patio table, smoking a joint. The entire yard was cleaned up, all the pool toys and rafts had been put away, and coolers were emptied and washed out. I couldn't believe my eyes as I walked outside and approached them.

"Holy shit!" I exclaimed and took a seat with them. "I can't believe you guys did all this. Seriously! It was a mess! I was dreading coming home to it."

"We can't deny that the place was trashed. There's a pile of women's underwear over by the back door," Kylie said and winked at me. "Even though the place was in shambles, we cleaned up. We decided you would never come for an evening ride if we didn't." She had successfully disarmed me with her smile, and I felt I had put her off long enough.

"Ya know what? Let's go! I could stand a nice cruise at dusk."

"Let's finish this joint first. Here!" Cookie handed me the doobie.

"I'm good," I said, but she wouldn't take no for an answer. It was the same thing every time. "Cookie, no!"

She shook it at me and gestured for me to take it. "Goddamn it! No!" I yelled.

"Parker?"

"Yes," I responded.

"Take the fuckin' thing!"

Kylie couldn't control her laughter and practically spit out her water as she covered her mouth with her hand. I finally took the joint and indulged, knowing I could probably use it to calm my anxiety. I held in the first hit, and when I exhaled, I asked, "Not for nothin', but you and Shady seemed to be reconciling yesterday. Would I be correct in saying that? Would you like to expand on the subject?"

"I don't fucking know. I'm still a little stunned how she just showed up here." She grabbed the joint from me. "Part of me was happy to see her, and the other part of me wanted to knock her fuckin' teeth out." She exhaled a large cloud of smoke. "It's not exactly like I'm over her leaving me for someone else. I mean, no one's ever hurt me so badly."

"But you left with her. You didn't look like you wanted to punch her. You looked like you wanted to fuck her." I laughed, and Kylie joined in the fun.

"I didn't just look like I wanted to fuck her," she said. Her face turned serious. "I did fuck her!" Now the three of us were laughing, and damn, it felt good. I had such a shitty couple of weeks, and I didn't like how I had been feeling in my head. The pot not only made my head giddy, but the fogginess lifted and dissolved, even if only for a short time.

"Seriously, Cook, what was the end result?"

"Don't know! She doesn't know! I mean, she's no longer with that fuckin' skeevy whore, and even though she came to your party in search of me yesterday, she says she doesn't want to jump right back into the relationship we had. All I know is that I'm seeing her again tomorrow night. Guess we'll see what the fuck happens from there." She grabbed the keys to her bike. "Fuck her! Let's roll!"

Kylie held the door open for me, but as I passed through, she lightly took hold of my arm and stopped me in my tracks. Cookie was already on her bike, and as I turned back to Kylie and asked, "What?" she planted her lips on mine without permission and parted my mouth with her tongue. Her kiss was firm, the kind of kiss you give someone when they've made you wait for a long time.

It was only broken when Cookie started yelling, "Cut me a fuckin' break, will ya? C'mon already!"

As Kylie backed away from me, her gaze never left mine. She didn't speak. She didn't have to. Her eyes spoke to me in ways her words could not. It was obvious that she liked me. Maybe a little more than I cared to admit. There was a connection, yes, but she was so young. Sure, we would have a great time rolling around in the sack together, but her age made her incapable of a long-term relationship…said me. I think I was always drawn to young girls because they were less prone to wanting anything more than sex. It was so much easier to end it when there were no real feelings involved. Was I going to sleep with Kylie? More than likely, yes. Just because I didn't want anything serious didn't mean my libido was dead. I was moist down there from a simple, short kiss from her, so it was bound to happen if she kept chasing me. No doubt it would be good. It was just that my heart wasn't in it. I could only hope that she didn't feel another way.

❧ ❧ ❧ ❧

Madeira Beach, or Mad Beach as we locals liked to call it, was one of my favorite places to cruise. As we hopped on the Tom Stuart Causeway, I felt my adrenaline pump through my veins. Kylie and I rode Harleys, and although Cookie had a Harley, she had one of those God-awful crotch rockets, too, and today she had chosen the latter to ride. I must admit, I hated when she rode it. Not because there was anything wrong with it. They were nice and fun to ride if you were mature enough. Cookie was not. She was one of those riders who people complained about. She weaved in and out of traffic and sped like the devil, completely oblivious to anyone else on the road. As far as Cookie was concerned, it was her road.

Once we were on the highway, that was just what she did. Kylie and I rode side by side, while Cookie switched lanes, passed us with an impish grin on her face, and eased back into the lane in front of us. Then, she took off, her bike buzzed like lightning, and passed car after car, while she cut numerous people off. That was the thing about Cookie, she just didn't care, and her carefree attitude was what I loved about her. But not this. This was dangerous, and she knew how I felt about it. Kylie and I looked at each other and shrugged. We both knew there was no controlling her, so we continued our ride until she slowed enough for us to catch up.

We eventually ended up on Gulf Boulevard, and we settled into the right lane as we took the opportunity to enjoy the summer breeze and scenery. Cookie even slowed her roll enough to bask in the sunshine and breathe in that ocean air. Condominiums and apartment buildings lined either side of the strip, and the smell of the sea pervaded my senses. The roar of my Fat Boy had a calming effect on me, and we cruised to the end of Mad Beach before we turned around.

No ride would be complete without a round at the Old Oar House, or as Cookie and I liked to call it, the Old Whore House. A biker's haven, it was a dive bar, but we loved the roughness of it and enjoyed ice cold beer fresh from the tap. While we waited for our wings, we played a game of darts. Kylie doted over me, and her attention was welcomed. I knew this thing with her wasn't going anywhere except bed. After the day I had, I allowed her to take my mind off things.

Right before our food came, she went to the bathroom. "You gonna follow her?" Cookie asked with one corner of her mouth pulled into a slight smile and suggestive sparkle in her eye.

"What? Why would I?"

"Weren't you just making out on your fuckin' porch?"

"Yeah, so?"

"So what the fuck are you waitin' for?"

"Do you really want me to answer that?"

"No!" she yelled and zinged a dart at the board. She looked at me and reiterated, "No! Damn it, Parker! When are you gonna let that pipe dream fuckin' go?"

"I don't know how."

"She's getting married, and she hasn't shown an ounce of interest in you since her mother died. Isn't that right?"

"Well..."

She squinted, and her eyebrows wrinkled together in suspicion. "What the fuck does that mean?"

"Uh..."

"Parker, what the fuck are you doin'? What are you not tellin' me?"

I threw my dart and chose to ignore her, but I missed the board completely.

"Nice shot!" she mocked.

"You were staring at me. I hate when you do that!"

"Parker?"

"Okay, okay!" I took a deep breath and slowly exhaled before I continued, "So some things have happened between Danielle and me."

"What kinda things?"

"We've sorta been fooling around a little."

"Holy shit!" she exclaimed. I grabbed her by the shoulders to calm her down, but she wasn't having it. She was flabbergasted and excitable, and I understood, but Kylie walked up behind her as she began to say, "You're fucking Dan..." I slapped her hard across the face. I didn't mean to, but I didn't want her to finish that sentence within earshot of Kylie. The stunned look on Cookie's face was almost comical, but the red welt on her cheek was not. It was fire engine red, and I was afraid she was about to haul off and clock me one close-fisted. I took a couple of steps backward and noticed Kylie, still standing behind Cookie, with her hand covering her mouth in disbelief at what she just witnessed.

"You get one of those! The next time, your hand comes back minus a few fuckin' fingers. You got that?"

"Sorry. I didn't mean it," I apologized, and as I did, she turned around to see Kylie there.

She hadn't noticed her before and nodded in acknowledgment, understanding why I just wailed on her face. "Oh...now I get it."

"Get what? I left for a few minutes and came back to a slap contest. Who's winning, by the way?" Kylie laughed, a little bewildered by the dynamic of our friendship.

I acted as though I didn't pop my best friend across the face just moments ago, and we went back to throwing darts and drinking our beer. It was our golden rule that when we rode, we had a one-drink limit set. We stuck to that firmly. Yes, smoking pot also impaired a person, but she had always felt that we were still in control of ourselves after smoking. The only time Cookie ever had an accident was after drinking, so even though most people would think one is no better than the other, that wasn't the case with Cookie. That time, she crashed into a guardrail while she came around a bend one night after drinking several beers. That was enough to enact the rule.

I was with her that night and rode behind her, watching as she hit the rail. She flew off her cycle though the air and landed in a swamp. She wasn't crazy about the idea of smelling like swamp when she waded through it to get out. It was a horrible stench, but it was better than her flying into a tree. The swamp water broke her impact, and being drunk left her body loose, so she was able to take the hit.

By the time we finished up, the sun was on its descent. The causeway was serene and peaceful during the ride back. The sky was a nice mix of red and orange, and the sun hung low over the horizon. It was a clear evening, and the humidity was unusually low for this time of year. I was glad I went out with them.

❧❧❧❧

When we got back to my house, Cookie and Kylie hung out for a bit. Long enough for Cookie to roll a joint and smoke it. Each time she handed it to me, I declined, and each time I declined, she pressed. Satisfied with the one hit I took, she didn't pass it back. "I told you, you have to take at least one hit just to be fuckin' social."

"Yeah, yeah! So are you going to be social this year and come on the camping trip? You missed it last year," I chided as I flipped through the channels on the TV aimlessly.

"Camping trip?" Kylie asked. "I like camping."

"These fucking girls and their fucking camping!" Cookie yelled. "I didn't go last year because I didn't feel like dealing with Danielle again. Every year, it's the same thing! She sits in a beach chair and reads the Goddamned *Wall Street Journal* while everyone else sets up the tents and the site." She tugged hard on the joint, fuming at her memory. She blew it out just as hard as she had inhaled. "She really pisses me off!!"

"God! Why do you two seem to hate each other so much?" Kylie interjected.

"Because she's a little snob who doesn't drink, doesn't party, doesn't know how to have a good time," Cookie said.

"And she thinks you influence me in evil ways!" I shot back. "Which isn't completely unwarranted."

Kylie burst out laughing, seemingly entertained by two old friends who bickered in front of her like a married couple. "So where's the camping trip this year?" she asked.

"Faver Dykes State Park. It's in two weeks. You want to come? We leave on a Friday and come back on Monday morning," I said.

"I'd love to. Only I'd have to meet you on Saturday. I work Fridays, swing shift."

Kylie worked at the factory with Cookie. They had weekends off but worked second-shift hours, four o'clock to midnight. She had only been working there a few months, and Cookie took her under her wing. She was the wild, big sister we all aspired to be, until we turned about twenty-five and realized there was more to life than partying.

When the evening came to a close, Cookie rose from the couch and nodded in the direction of my front door. "Come on, Ky! Let's get the fuck outta here."

"Gimme a second with Parker alone, okay? I'll meet you out front."

Cookie took a deep breath while she rolled her eyes and sauntered out the door. She didn't bother to say goodbye to me. Maybe she and Danielle weren't so different. She just didn't know it. When the door closed behind her and she was out of view, Kylie stood and slowly headed for the door. She expected I would follow, and I did.

"I had a great time with you tonight," she said as her eyes seemed to undress me. She took a chance by adding, "I could stay if you want."

I knew she meant for the night, and I wasn't ready for that. I giggled, a little shy all of a sudden. So out of character for me, but I leaned into her and whispered in her ear, "No." I straightened and reached to open the door, but there was no hesitation when she placed her hand on mine, somewhat forcefully, and just went for it. She pressed her lips to mine, and her tongue coerced its way into my mouth as she turned my whole body against the door. I wasn't accustomed to being manhandled and quickly turned the tables by shifting her into the door instead. I couldn't deny I liked her. My body wouldn't allow me to deny it while my clit throbbed behind my shorts.

"Are you sure?" she whispered back in my ear.

My pussy was screaming to let her stay, but my head knew it was a bad idea. This young woman had allure with a bit of charm to her, and though she was quite compelling, I opened the door and bid her *adieu*.

Chapter Nine

Two weeks passed swiftly, and before I knew it, the big camping trip weekend had arrived. Faver Dykes State Park was our destination, a two-hour-and-forty-minute trek from the west coast to the east. Maybe giving Dorian free reign to choose the campground hadn't been the best decision. Her sense of humor was at best silly. For the past two weeks, I had to suffer through *dyke* jokes, then *faver* jokes, and which *dyke* was going to do what *faver* to whom. She had a way of amusing herself and often laughed out loud to her own jokes. It was annoying, yet endearing and part of the reason I loved her so.

There were about thirty women going this year. Last year, we only needed three sites, but this year, we needed four. *The more the merrier,* I always said. While I waited for Dorian and Dahlia to pick me up, I skimmed through my Facebook page and looked at pictures from the pool party. They looked so cute together that day. This was Dahlia's first camping trip with us, and she was a welcome addition to our clique. The last two weeks had been kind to my buddy, who had gone into somewhat of a hibernation. I hadn't seen or heard from her since the day after the party, except for a text I received from her stating that the sex was phenomenal and that she could get used to this, followed by a *ttyl*. It sucked not having her around during this time. The last day I talked to her was the last day I talked to Danielle.

By the time they pulled up in Dorian's Tahoe, I was packed and ready to go. After we exchanged hellos, hugs, and a few pleasantries, the three of us threw my camping gear in the back of the SUV.

"You sure you have everything? Who has Addie?" Dorian asked with an insane eye for detail.

"I have everything, and Addie is staying with my neighbor. Have you spoken with Dani and April? Have they left yet, or are we piggybacking?"

Her look was one of faint amusement as her eyebrows raised in surprise. "You haven't talked to her?"

"Not since lunch that day."

"That was two weeks ago," she pointed out the obvious, picked up a cooler, and chucked it in the back. "Is this how it's going to go down between you? You talk to each other every day, and all of a sudden, you fool around a little, and bibbidi-bobbidi-boo, friendship's over?"

"It's a little more complicated than that."

"Oh, for crying out loud! I'm so tired of hearing about how complicated it is. How complicated could it be? The two of you are bangin'! It's pretty simple to me. Just cut the extracurricular shit, and your problem is solved."

"Would it be? You're kidding, right?" I helped her lift a long tote full of camping necessities and heaved it into the back. "I'm in love with her." I knew she already knew that, but I kept going. "It's different now." I gained her total attention, placed a hand on her shoulder, and looked her in the eyes. "I think she's in love with me, too."

"Did she say that to you?" Dorian immediately

shot back.

"Well, no, not exactly." I took my hand away from her shoulder and broke the momentary intensity of our conversation. The entire time, Dahlia stood there. She didn't seem to know what to do or say. She only met Danielle once at the pool party, but she was introduced to a bunch of people that day, and I didn't think she remembered which one was Danielle. She was sure to ask Dorian later, no doubt.

"Then I wouldn't jump the gun on that one. She's still wearing an engagement ring. And as much as you would like the ring to be from you," she said, about to disappoint me but needing me to see it for what it was, "it's not. It's from April. You do understand that, right?"

I turned my attention to the ground. "Yes, I understand that, but when she looks at me," I said and looked into her eyes, "I feel it. It's different now."

"Look, I'm not going to deny that there's always been something there between you, but she hasn't left April, and it doesn't look like she's going to. Be careful. You may end up losing her altogether. It's not your time."

Not our time! Not our time! I'm so sick of it not being our time. It's never going to be our time. Why can't I get that through my thick skull? Frustrated and annoyed, I threw the last of our supplies in the vehicle and hopped in the backseat. I didn't bother responding to her reality check.

As Dorian drove down the highway, she blared the stereo. It became impossible to be involved in their conversation. So instead, I leaned back in my seat and settled in for a long ride across the state of Florida. When I wasn't thinking about Dani, I thought about the bar. When I wasn't thinking about the bar, I was hellbent on thinking about Dani. I was disappointed in the snail-like progress of the renovations. Construction had been slow. All the same could be said of Danielle and me. Somehow, I had to put my feelings on the backburner again and have a good time this weekend. Kylie and Cookie would be there tomorrow, and I looked forward to my next encounter with Kylie. My next brush with Danielle was yet to be determined. We were used to hearing each other's voice every day, so either she was pretty pissed off, or she thought I was. Either way, I was about to find out.

Dorian and Dahlia held hands most of the ride there and periodically sneaked cute glances at each other. Dorian usually had a way with overpowering a relationship. She took the dominant role, but this time seemed different. She couldn't do enough to please this woman, who found everything Dorian said funny. She had a sweet, adorable giggle to her.

The mundaneness of the highway and the drone of the vehicle made me sleepy. My eyes grew heavy, and I eventually fell asleep. It wasn't long after that I slowly regained consciousness and heard voices as the SUV came to a stop. "We're here!"

⁂

When I opened my eyes, Dorian and Dahlia were already opening their doors and stepping out. I sat straight up and scanned my surroundings. Pellicer Creek was right in front of me. The water was so calm and tranquil. A small fishing dock and boat ramp sat off to the left, perfect for launching canoes. I stayed in the car while they went to check us in and to find out where our sites were located.

The screen door shut behind them as they exited the welcome center and got back in the truck. We drove away from the water and down a dusty, bumpy dirt road. Trees on either side of us became thicker as we reached the epicenter of campsites. RVs, campers, and tents lined each tiny cubbyhole, set back in a thicket of trees and bushes. We couldn't see the creek from here, but it was probably a short trail walk through the woods.

We pulled off the road into one of the empty campsites and got out. Two were side by side with a bush buffer separating them. The other two were across the way. The trees provided much-needed shade from the sun, which was smoldering at ninety-five degrees. The humidity hung thick, and sweat formed on my brow almost instantly. I perused our site while I grabbed stuff from the back of the Tahoe.

As I peered across the dirt road, I saw that part of the softball team took up the site diagonally to the right of us. I pulled out a few coolers and lined them up next to the picnic table. One cooler had hot dogs, burgers, eggs, and bacon already covered in ice. But we still needed more ice for the cooler filled with beer. Dorian noticed me and said, "Don't worry! We'll get ice. We passed a small mom-and-pop store about five miles down the road from here. We'll get it later."

She headed back to the truck and pulled our tents out. While she set up the needed pieces on the ground, I noticed more trucks, SUVs, and cars arriving. The other half of the softball team was on the other side of a thicket next to us. They laughed loudly while they popped beer cans open as they wasted no time getting their party on. Their voices carried through the bushes, and soon, women were walking back and forth, helping one another set up for the weekend.

During all the disorder, Danielle and April pulled up in April's red Lexus. Her car stuck out like a sore thumb amid trucks and hooptie cars that were a good twenty years old. April got out first. She sported a navy polo shirt with her golf club's insignia embroidered on the left side of her chest. Her matching visor hung low over her eyes as she shut the car door and walked toward us. She doled out hugs to Dorian and Dahlia, and I watched Danielle get out of the car.

She was dressed in university mesh shorts and a gray Tampa Rays tank top. The fact that she was mismatched indicated to me that she was still fucked up about us. She was not in her neat, comfortable world like she was used to, and it showed in ways like this. She always matched. Whatever the outfit, she was color coordinated. But here she wore an MLB tank with college shorts, dark blue and light blue against green and yellow. She had on multicolored running shoes, and sunglasses covered her eyes. The only thing that appeared normal to me was that her hair was pulled back.

As she casually strode toward us, I could tell, even through her shades, that she contemplated whether to hug me or not. So as not to draw attention, she gave me a half hug, only embracing me with one hand, the other in the pocket of her shorts.

"Hey," she said somberly.

"Hey," I returned the same half hug she gave me.

We weren't off to a good start as far as I could tell. Neither of us knew how to behave with the other. Seeking to get away from each other, we separated in a hurry and started in different directions. However, our opposite paths were immediately brought back together with a simple, "Why don't you and Dani go to that store down the road for some ice? We need this beer to get cold right away," April offered as she retrieved more beer from her car. For Danielle to say *no* would have sent up red flags for our whole group, so she agreed.

"Here! Take the truck," Dorian ordered and threw the keys at me.

I looked over at Danielle, who still had her sunglasses on, and I hopped into the driver's seat. We rode back in the direction of the store. No words were spoken. The tension was so thick, it could've been cut with a knife. By the time I came out of the store and threw the several bags of ice in the backseat, I'd had enough. I got back in the driver's seat and turned my body toward her entirely.

"Enough! Take the glasses off," I said firmly. I was waiting for a snide remark, but none came. Instead, she removed the sunglasses and looked intently into my eyes. Just like that, my heart melted. But I couldn't let her see that this was killing me. "Are you going to talk to me?"

"You haven't called or texted me for two weeks. I get that you're mad at me, but two weeks? Really?" She put the sunglasses back on. "I thought we were still friends."

"We are. I just needed some time."

"And this time you needed, did you accomplish what you wanted?"

"What did I want?" I needed to hear it from her.

"You said you wanted to get over me," she said and didn't wait for me to speak. "Are you?" She averted her face and lowered her head. "Are you over me?"

The sixty seconds of silence that followed felt like an eternity, and when I finally spoke, I lied. "Yes. Yes, I am. It only took me eighteen years, but yes, I'm finally over you."

"Oh" was all she said. And when she attempted to touch my cheek, I brushed her hand away. "No, Danielle. If you want to touch someone's face like that, it should be April's, not mine."

"But…"

"But nothing. I'm trying to save us both from some serious emotional pain."

"Are you still my friend?"

"I'm always going to be your friend. Nothing's changed there. It's just that you made up your mind to stay with her," I said. "You can't have it both ways, and now that you've made your choice, I'm going to make sure you stick to it. Because quite frankly, it hurts to watch you two together."

"I don't want to hurt you. You know that, right? Parker, please tell me you know I would never intentionally hurt you."

I took a quick, deep breath. "I know that."

I started the engine, but before I could throw the truck in reverse, she swung her arms around me and gave me a tight hug. I couldn't push her off because she would not let go. "I've missed you so much," she confessed. "Please don't stay away from me for so long ever again."

I knew I shouldn't have, but I sank into her embrace and enjoyed the feel of her arms around me as I inhaled her scent. She wasn't wearing perfume. She just smelled like Danielle, and it was intoxicating. Our heads were so close together, our lips mere inches apart. Temptation got the better of me, and I let her kiss me. Before she could slip her tongue into my mouth, I halted her. "Stop, Dani."

She didn't back up, rather she leaned close to my ear and whispered, "You're a liar." She started nibbling at my earlobe, and honestly, she wore me down.

"Why are you doing this?"

"I know it's wrong, and I'm good, until I get around you, and then…and then…"

"And then what?"

"And then I'm not so good anymore."

"Do you feel guilty when you go back to April after we've kissed and fooled around some?"

"Well, yes, of course I do."

"Then you need to stop! You're not leaving her. You say you love her. You feel guilty. So what do you think that does to me? Do you know how much it hurts every time you say you're still going to marry her? Do you?"

"My God, Parker, I am so sorry. The fact that you make my panties wet just looking at you is absolutely no excuse for hurting you." She shifted back into her seat. "I promise I'll stop. Okay? I promise. You're my best friend. I don't want to lose you."

Unfortunately, it was like neither one of us heard ourselves, as if neither one of us was even around for the conversation we just had. We held hands on the ride back. The last time we held hands was when we first met. After she and Nicky broke up and I was dating someone at the time, we would watch TV together on the couch, blanket on top of us, and hold hands underneath. I knew why we held hands back then, but why now? Same reasons? Was it some kind of goodbye to that part of us for good? Was it because we actually did want to be together? Or was it because we changed the entire dynamic of our friendship in a matter of weeks? Whatever the case, we held hands until we came to a stop at our campsite. We gave each other one last affectionate look and separated our hands. I didn't want her to get out and run right for April, but that was what happened. I watched while April gave her a peck on the lips as Danielle handed her a bag of ice.

Everything had been assembled while we were gone, and it felt like I entered a big tent city. A couple of our friends had small campers amid the tents, and everyone was busy icing up their beer. I poured ice on top of ours when April suddenly appeared next to me as she dug through the cooler adjacent to the one I filled. She fished out a can of beer, popped the can, and took a few gulps, but she stared at me the whole time. I could see her out of the corner of my eye.

"You know I can't stand being here, right?" She looked dead at me, as if I was the root of her displeasure. "If it wasn't for you and this Goddamned camping trip, I'd be golfing tomorrow morning." She took another swig of beer. "I mean, really, some of the girls are even talking about not showering the whole weekend. Something about roughing it." She swallowed another mouthful and arrogantly stewed, "That's gross." She looked absolutely disgusted at me, turned, and walked away. I stood there with my mouth hanging open, trying to figure out if she really just said that shit to me. I let her retreat without saying a word. If she only knew what went on behind her back, her definition of gross might have changed.

April and I resembled each other in physical appearance, but that was where the similarities ended.

Our personalities were completely opposite. Her smug attitude was getting on my gay nerves lately. It couldn't have anything to do with the fact that I was hopelessly in love with her soon-to-be wife. I didn't know what I was going to do or how I was going to get past this, but it was necessary for my friendship with Danielle to survive. It figured that as I was thinking about how to be just friends again, I spied Danielle sneaking glances at me even as she hugged April. Only her eyes were struck with uncertainty. I knew she felt torn, and I didn't know how to help her. How could I? I didn't know how to help myself. She was on her own with this one, as was I.

A couple of hours into our trip and a few beers later, the ladies were already acting up. There were about twenty of us altogether tonight, and we expected ten more tomorrow. The ages of our campers ranged from their early twenties to early sixties. It usually happened that way. But during this trip, there were a couple of underaged girls, both twenty years old. They were close enough to legal but not. We told them to buy their beer at home, but like most young people, they didn't listen. The rules of the park didn't allow us to drink alcohol, but we figured as long as we were inconspicuous, it would be okay. It was sort of an unspoken rule that if you kept your booze undercover and used a coozie on your beer can, they wouldn't break your balls about it.

I stepped away from our site and Danielle as I roamed from one tent city to the next. I said hello to all my friends and moved through the tents until I stumbled across Sherri, who was putting air in a blow-up canoe.

"Hey, Parker!" she said.

"Hey, Sherri."

"Wanna come canoeing with us?"

"Who's all going?"

"Me and Cece."

My gaze wandered and finally landed on Cece, who was leaning against a tree with a woman standing in front of her. The woman's back was turned to me. Cece blushed and giggled while the woman flirted with her. When the woman turned around, I was shocked to see it was April. She glared at me, almost mad at me for catching her flirting with someone other than Danielle. When she dashed away like a little bitch, Cece came over to us. "Hi, Parker!"

"Hi, Cece."

"Are you coming canoeing with us?"

"Eh, I don't think so." I shrugged.

"Are you sure? We're gonna drink a couple beers out there and enjoy the scenery." She took her hand and lightly stroked my arm.

It was at this point that I realized they popped a Molly, and not only were they high, but they had been drinking, too. This wasn't Cookie, who could handle her high. These two were goofy without being impaired. I wasn't comfortable with them going out in the water like this. The boat inflated, they both jumped in, and grabbed an oar. It took some time, but I finally convinced them not to go. Rather, they left their canoe where it was and came with me to my campsite. The smell of weed wafted through the warm breeze that rattled the leaves on the trees. Laughter could be heard as we passed by one of the tents that belonged to the youngest members of our group. Cece and Sherri stopped dead in their tracks.

"Where's that coming from?" they asked each

other, hellbent on following the scent. Visible smoke emanated from the youngsters' tent, and Cece and Sherri didn't wait for an invitation. They had already started pulling on the zipper to the entrance of the tent as they stammered, "Hey! Let us in! We have treats, too."

Inside the tent, the girls could be heard yammering but eventually said, "Yo! Who's there?"

When the tent finally opened, Sherri and Cece proceeded to enter with Sherri going in last and looking back at me. "You comin'?"

"Nah. I'm gonna head back to my tent." I started walking away but turned back and said, "Sherri!" She stopped just shy of being entirely inside the tent and whirled her head around to meet me. "Be discreet, will ya? There's park rangers all over the place."

"Will do!" She quickly zipped the tent back up and concealed their activity but were still rowdy and loud once inside. Those young girls had no idea what they were in for with these two Mollied-up troublemakers. They were sure to find out, and I wouldn't be surprised if there was some moaning coming out of that tent soon. All four sites were filled with activity, and once we finished everything we needed to do, we decided to play volleyball. They had a great volleyball pit that was nicely framed out and filled with beach sand. This park was likeable, properly kept, and well-maintained. It was top of the line in the way of state parks, and we were happy with our choice this year.

Chapter Ten

The girls grabbed a ball, and we made our way past other campsites, along the water, and to the play area. Picking teams should have been easy, but this particular group of lesbians was difficult, each swearing she was the alpha dog. They each named themselves team leaders so they could pick who would be on their team.

After about ten minutes of bickering, we finally decided on leaders, and the teams were chosen. Somehow, I ended up on the same team as Danielle. April chose to sit out, but I noticed her getting chummy again with Cece, who had left Sherri with those young girls. They talked and laughed as they seemed to know each other a little bit more than they should. As the game went on, I periodically glanced over at them. I couldn't get the sinking feeling out of my gut. It was that tiny voice inside that said *something is wrong* and screamed that they were more than just friends. I held court in my head and judged April based on the laughter they shared in. Part of me thought *something was rotten in the state of Denmark*, to quote Shakespeare. Part of me thought I was reading too much into it because I was sleeping with her fiancée. But that was all stopped now. Or so I thought, until the volleyball was hit high into the air, and Danielle and I both went for it. We collided and landed on the ground, her on top of me. What was only a split second seemed like an eternity as she lay on me, gazing into my eyes and melting me like ice on hot tar. She left me defenseless. We were about to kiss until I felt her hand on my ribs. She pushed herself up and offered her hand to me. I latched on to it and let her help me up. One last lovesick look was exchanged between us before play resumed.

We played several rounds until we were all pooped and gave it up for the rest of the day. It was dusk and time for dinner. On our way back to our site, we passed the underaged girls. Their picnic table was bogged down with bottles of hard liquor, and a huge bag of weed was next to it, completely exposed for anyone to see. The three of them were higher than kites, and as I walked by, I told them to put the shit away, to be more subtle and inconspicuous since there were families with kids staying here, too. They laughed me off as if I were kidding, called me Mother Teresa, and bowed to me as I moved past them.

I shook my head and continued to our campsite. Their carelessness was unnerving, but I brushed it aside and helped Dorian make hot dogs and burgers on the portable grill. I couldn't help but notice Danielle quietly take a seat on April's lap in one of the camping chairs, throwing her arms around her neck and giving her a quick kiss. She faced me then, grabbed April's hands, and pulled them around her waist. When she realized I was watching, she looked at the ground. It was awkward and uncomfortable, and the part of me that wanted her so desperately wanted nothing more than to punch April square in the face. The rational side of me knew I needed to accept things the way they were and not force this, but it wasn't easy.

While we all ate, Sherri, Cece, and those two

young women came stumbling through our site, hanging on to each other and snickering as they headed in the direction of the neighboring site. Loud conversation and even louder laughter could be heard. Danielle was oblivious to them as she ate. She didn't detect April scoping out Cece. There was no covering up the lingering eye contact between them. Cece maneuvered her way between April and Dani's chairs. Just as they were almost out of view, Cece turned her head back and peered over her shoulder to take one last peek at April. A knowing smile came across Cece's face, and the corner of April's mouth turned upward slightly, a crooked half smirk covering her countenance. Something was going on. I made a pact with myself and swore that if I found out that April was cheating that I was going for it with Danielle. I would stop trying to be so considerate of their relationship and go full throttle in my quest to steal her from April. Because if April was being unfaithful, she didn't deserve to be with my sweet Danielle. My sweet Danielle, who seemed more involved with eating her hamburger than with her fiancée, who she thought would never betray her.

❧❧❧❧

Just before I was about to call it a night, Dorian and I had a nightcap. April and Dani had gone to the restroom. The fire was ablaze, and Dahlia bid us both good night. Halfway into the tent, she turned back to Dorian. "Don't make me wait too long." She winked seductively at her and disappeared into the tent. Once we heard the zip on the tent, Dorian and I talked for a while. The stars were bright and in multitude, spread across the night sky, and helped the moon illuminate the Earth below.

"Are you okay?" Dorian took a drink from her beer and poked at the fire with her walking stick. The walking stick was a branch she had found years ago on one of our many camping trips. Everyone had carved their names into it over time, and it became a mainstay on our annual trip.

"I'm all right." I knew what she wanted to talk about.

"I still can't believe you didn't talk to her for two whole weeks. When's the last time that's happened?"

"I don't think ever."

"Wow! Then I guess you don't know what happened last week."

She had my full attention now, and I leaned forward. "No. What happened?"

She stopped poking the fire, and like a high school girl excitedly talking gossip, said, "Well, you know that prestigious teaching award she won?"

"Yeah."

"Well, the award dinner was last Wednesday, and April was supposed to accompany her."

"Yeah? So what's the big news in that?"

"April didn't go. They got into a fight, and Dani went by herself."

My face snapped toward her. "What? April always goes to those functions with her. What did they fight about?"

"Get this. A pile of dishes in the sink that Dani promised to clean up but didn't get around to."

"Really?"

"I know. It seems so miniscule. Hardly something to fight about, which leads me to believe there's more to it than dirty dishes. I would say I think there might be trouble in paradise, but we both know there's trouble in paradise because you're banging her."

"I'm not bangin' her," I said adamantly.

She cocked her head sideways, and with a knowing look, mockingly said, "*Really*?"

"Dorian, it happened once, and we didn't even get to finish," I lied.

"You didn't?"

"No."

"I hope you've come to your senses. No good can come from this, and trust me, karma is a bitch. This isn't the way to get with her."

"I realize this. I'm trying to stay away from her, which isn't easy every time she plants those dreamy eyes on me. Not for nothing, but my entire body tingles when she looks at me that way." I took a moment to feel that familiar rush I got right to my crotch with the thought of how Dani gleamed at me.

"I must admit, her eyes did sparkle at you the day we had lunch. I hadn't seen her look at you that way since college." She poked at the fire again, and a log fell from the top of the pile to the side. The impact set loose some flyaway sparks and ash. "But unless she intends to leave April, you really need to make a conscious effort to leave her be in that way."

"Well, she definitely intends to stay with April. As much as she comes at me with a desire I've never seen in her is as much as she has made it perfectly clear to me that she's still marrying April. And the more I try to push her away, the more she won't let me. I don't know what she wants, and I'm not about getting hurt by the love of my life."

"I would say I didn't know that, but you never

had to say it out loud for me to see it all over your face for, well, a lot of years." She tried her best to change the subject. "Is that girl Kylie coming out this weekend? I know you said Cookie isn't coming until tomorrow."

"Actually, she's coming with Cookie."

"That should get your mind off Danielle for a while. She's cute…and single." She chuckled and stabbed at the fire once again. "I worry about you, Parker."

I got up out of my chair, took my last mouthful of water, and bid Dorian good night. It was a good thing I did, too, because just as I unzipped my tent, Dahlia came out of theirs. She wondered what was taking Dorian so long to come to bed.

Silence had settled in and around our campsite, and I changed into a pair of cut-off sweatpants and a beat-up T-shirt. I crawled onto the air mattress and attempted to get comfortable. It was so humid that the very idea of pulling the thin blanket on the bed over me made me sweat. I decided to take the T-shirt off and hoped to cool off enough to fall asleep. Although it was quiet, I could faintly hear those young girls and smell the distinct aroma of pot as it drifted through the night air. Sherri and Cece were still partying with them. I could hear Cece's raspy voice through the woods. I shifted slightly on the bed, still trying to find a good spot, when much to my chagrin, I heard voices coming from the tent next to me. The more the noises continued, the more it became clear that someone was having sex. But before I could realize who it was, I heard, "Yeah…Oh, Dani, yeah, lick it."

A sickness swelled up from the pit of my stomach to the very core of my soul. Was I really going to have to lie here and listen to them have sex? Their tent was just inches from mine. They were so close they sounded like they were in my tent with me. This was no threesome, though, and as their moans became clearer and somewhat louder, I covered my face with my pillow, desperately trying to dim their sounds.

I couldn't believe Danielle's audacity, fucking April right next to me and not so discreetly. Was this my payback for pushing her away? For trying to do the right thing by her? The familiar sound of panting permeated my tent. The familiar sound of Danielle panting. However, once I could hear the sound of Dani's wetness and my tent visibly started to move, I had enough. Just as I sat up in the bed, I heard Dani moaning, "Fuck me…fuck me." Her words were drawn out, and I could no longer lay idle. I was listening to the woman of my dreams being finger-fucked by someone else. I put my shirt back on and popped my head out of my tent. I thought I would go for a walk until they were done.

Instead, I poked my head out only to find two park rangers entering our site. They appeared intimidating. That was, until they opened their mouths. The one ranger was a young man no older than twenty-three. He was obviously attempting to grow facial hair, without much luck. A few whiskers surrounded his chin area, and he was tall and lanky. He was the lazy, passive type, but her…nope. The female ranger, who was no doubt gay, apparently had a hard-on for throwing her weight around. The two of them were like *Dumb and Dumber,* and I couldn't wait to hear why they were sneaking around our campsite.

The big bull dyke introduced herself as Ranger DeLaurentis, but let's just call her Sergeant Douchebag.

"Everyone out of their tents," she demanded in a shaky, quiet tone. But her tone became more dominant and forceful when no one responded. "I said everyone out of their tents! This isn't a joke! I'm about to start reading everyone their Miranda rights if you don't get out!" She shined a flashlight in my eyes when she noticed me exiting my tent.

"Who are you?" she asked.

"Uh, my name is Parker."

"Is this site in your name? What about the neighboring site?"

"This one's in my name. The other one is in Danielle's name," I stood completely now. "What's going on?"

"I'm going to need your driver's license, and I'm going to need the same from…Danielle, is it?"

"I can give you mine, but I'm pretty sure Danielle is predisposed presently." I could still hear April and Danielle having sex, apparently clueless to what was taking place.

"What's she doing in there?" She flashed her light on their tent, her face scrunched up.

"If you don't know what those sounds are, then I can't help you." I knew I was being sarcastic but wasn't interested in a filter, either.

Her eyes widened at me. "Well, she needs to get out here right away."

"You have yet to tell us why you're here."

"We found an awfully big bag of marijuana sitting in plain view on the picnic table over there, and someone's getting arrested tonight. Maybe several people if I don't get some compliance. Now get her out here!"

Reluctantly, I got close to the entrance of their

tent and called out, "Dani." No response, but more groaning was heard. Once more and with a little more bravado, I loudly said, "Dani!"

"What?" she screamed.

By this time, Dorian and Dahlia stood outside in their pajamas, and others from surrounding sites came over in hopes of finding out what all the ruckus was about. I tried one more time. "Danielle, come outside! A park ranger wants to speak with you."

"Yeah, right!" She swore I was messing with her.

"It's not a joke, Danielle," I tried again. However, Sergeant Douchebag had lost her patience and stepped up to the tent. She took it upon herself to unzip the tent and shined her flashlight inside.

"Hey!" April snapped. "Get that light out of here!"

"I said get out of that tent and bring your driver's license with you…now!" she ordered.

Finally, Danielle appeared as she finished pulling up her shorts and buttoning them. She glanced at me before addressing the ranger.

"Is that campsite under your name?" the ranger asked.

"Yes, it is. Can I ask what's going on? I was busy sleeping."

"Yeah, you were busy sleeping, all right." Sergeant Douchebag snickered. "Someone at that site left a rather large bag of marijuana on the picnic table. We've been watching all day. If that someone doesn't claim ownership to it, I'm going to have to arrest you." The ranger went on, "Are there any drugs at this site or the other sites you've rented?"

"Not to my knowledge, no." Fear crept into Danielle's voice as she handed over her license. "Whoever it is, please speak up! I can't lose my teaching cert. Please!" She perused the small crowd of our own campers who were now crowding our site, all curious to see what was happening. When no one came forth to claim the weed, Sergeant Douchebag started reading Danielle her rights. As she did, I watched Sherri run back and forth behind them in the woods, stashing their beer, and God only knows what else, all over the place.

These two rangers are idiots! The young male ranger tried to reason with his partner and said they could just confiscate the drugs and order them to leave the park by morning. She shrugged him off and continued reading Dani her rights. It seemed like this was her first bust, and even though her voice cracked and was unsure, she eventually finished the process.

"You're going to have to come with me," Sergeant Douchebag ordered.

She put her hands on Danielle's shoulders, and Dani shook her off. "Don't touch me!"

"Well, you're going to have to come with me!" she repeated as her tone became louder.

"I'll go with you, but you don't need to touch me!" Dani was stern. She was visibly shaking and on the verge of tears.

"It's mine!" one of the young women confessed, much to everyone's surprise. She stepped forward, and Sergeant Douchebag led her to her patrol car. Come to find out, when those young girls stopped at that mom-and-pop liquor store next to the park, the clerk recognized that they were underage. But instead of refusing them the purchase of alcohol, the clerk asked if they were going camping. When the girls said yes, the clerk called the park. The rangers had been watching them all day, waiting for the opportunity to nab them. They should have listened to us when we said to buy their alcohol at home. Before they put her in the car, they checked her license.

"You're on a roll, kid," Sergeant Douchebag chided. "Underage drinking and illegal substances? Any other charges you would like brought against you?" She opened the back door and ordered, "Get in!"

Before Sergeant Douchebag and her sidekick departed, they warned us, "All of you need to clear out of here in the morning before ten o'clock." The girl climbed in the back, and the ranger shut the door. She turned to us one last time. "By ten o'clock, all four sites out!"

All we could hear was the sound of their vehicle slowly driving away. Tires rolled over the gravel of the dirt road. When their headlights were no longer visible, we all took a moment to breathe.

"That sucks we have to leave in the morning." Sherri groaned.

"What does that mean exactly?" Dahlia asked.

"It means we'll discuss it in the morning," Dorian chimed in.

In the meantime, Danielle was over this debacle and started for their tent. Before she went in, she looked at me, and I shot her a look that would have buried her deep within the Earth. She pursed her lips and looked down. She knew she had infuriated me by having sex with April just inches from me. There was nothing she could do but go in the tent and call it a night. I didn't know if April asked for sex or if Danielle offered it. All I knew was that it was like taking a lightning rod to my heart, jolting me back to reality, whether I liked it or not. She disappeared into her tent and called, "Come on, April!"

However, April was too busy making time with Cece again to even hear or care what Dani said. I took a second to watch these two, who were undoubtedly flirting. I didn't think I had ever seen April smile as much as I did when she was around Cece. Eye contact was how they talked. These two had it bad for each other, even if they weren't supposed to. No one knew better than I what it was like to have the hots for someone I shouldn't. They never saw me looking at them. After all, everyone had returned to their own tents. From Danielle's tent, once again, I heard, "April!"

It was only then that April finally wrapped it up and said good night. They gave each other a hug, but their embrace lasted a little longer than it should have. Their eye contact lasted a little longer than it should have, too. They shared a telling smile before separating for the night. April unzipped her tent, but as she did, I made the mistake of shifting my weight from one leg to the other. The sticks and stones I had been standing on broke and grinded together under my feet, and April's face whipped toward me. Her gaze met mine, and I could tell she was trying to figure out how much I saw. Her hesitation only lasted a brief second, but I could tell I was in her head now.

Chapter Eleven

I awoke to the sound of voices outside my tent. I blinked and tried to wake up before I rolled off the air mattress. After I threw on a T-shirt and a pair of shorts, I stumbled to the front of the tent and peeked my head out. It was an overcast, gray, and dreary day, but I perked up slightly when Dorian handed me a cup of coffee and greeted me, "Good morning."

"Good morning," I responded as I found it hard to wake up. I squirmed the rest of the way out of my tent and sat in a camping chair, sipped my java, and watched a mix of women surrounding Dorian, who held her phone in her hand. They were all staring at it, and I asked, "Are there naked ladies on that phone or something? I've never seen anyone stare at a phone so intensely."

"We're looking for the nearest campground that'll let us drink," Dorian answered.

"Are we going home?" one girl asked.

Dorian, who was in control of the phone and the map on it, vehemently said, "Hell no, we're not going home! We didn't travel all this way to go right back home." She put her nose back down and studied whatever it was they were looking at on the screen.

While they all debated where we should move this party, I heard the tent in front of my chair unzip. Danielle crawled out, hair in a ponytail as always, and went right for the coffeepot. She was still sleepy, and this baffled me because she was such an early riser. It was eight o'clock and way past her usual rise-and-shine hour. Must have been all the sex.

After she fixed herself a cup of coffee, she plopped down in the chair next to me. She never made eye contact and took a sip from her cup. "Good morning."

"Mornin'," I left out the *good* part because I was still mad at her. She didn't have to fuck her fiancée right next to me. For crying out loud, they may as well have been in bed with me. I would say that maybe she didn't have a choice, but that was ridiculous to suggest. Of course, she could have said no, but she didn't, and she knew I was only inches from them. I really didn't need to hear that shit. I was the one who didn't have a choice.

We sat there in silence for a few minutes before she asked, "Are you mad at me or something?"

I glared at her just as I had the night before. "Was it good?" I asked. She sucked in the side of her cheek, looked at me with pure disgust, and got up to walk away. I let her. I wasn't going to chase her. I had done plenty of that through the years. I was done. If she wanted me, she could come get me. I watched as she walked down the trail in the direction of the restrooms.

In the meantime, Cece and Sherri meandered over to our site. They joined the circle around Dorian. Sherri already had a beer wrapped in a coozie. Yes, it was eight o'clock in the morning, but drinking and getting stoned were a cornerstone of these camping excursions. As they all discussed where we were going next, April climbed out of her tent. Once she saw Cece, her face lit up, and before she zoomed in for some flirting, she scoped the area for Danielle. Danielle not in sight, she went right for her. They got nice and cozy and stood way too close. And they knew they were standing too close because they quickly separated as Danielle re-entered our campsite, her hair wet from a shower. Something was definitely going on, and I wasn't going to be satisfied until I found out.

"Yeah, but can we drink?" I heard Dorian ask the person on the other end of the phone.

When she hung up, she announced, "We're going to Prairie Pines Campground, ladies! She ended the call and ordered, "Pack it up and move it out!"

While we were all busy breaking down tents and packing our gear, I called Cookie to tell her the change in plans. I told her the story of Sergeant Douchebag, and all she concluded was, "What a bunch of assholes!" Our conversation ended with, "I gotta pick up Kylie and Tristan, and we'll be on our fuckin' way."

"Wait...Tristan?" I was confused.

"Yeah. I don't know. She said something about hoping the girl she finger-fucked at your party will be there."

I burst into laughter as she brought back the image of the Mollied orgy at my barbecue. Cookie had already left with Shady, so she missed the debauchery. The thing of it was, the girl who took in Tristan's fingers was actually on this trip. Her name was Rita, the first baseman, and she was hell on wheels, or at least hell in a pair of cleats. I couldn't wait to see how this panned out.

"Okay. I'll see you all there," I said, and before I concluded our conversation, I bolstered, "And, Cookie, please don't be the reason we get thrown out of the next place." She didn't bother to answer me, she just hung up. With everything packed up, we all jumped in our vehicles and piggybacked out of the park. We paraded by the ranger station, and I was glad Cookie wasn't with us yet because she would have given the one-finger salute to them as we passed.

⁂

Our convoy traveled down the interstate about an hour and a half inland to Prairie Pines. We were stunned at the park as we weaved through woods and thicket. Passing a small lake that looked more like a swamp, I wondered why we had just come from a beautiful, oceanic area with a scenic view of Pellicer Creek to what could only be described as a creepy, rundown campground. But then I remembered that above all else, we were allowed to drink here.

We had to close the windows as the bugs and insects buzzed in and out of the Tahoe. It irritated all of us, evident as the three of us swatted the air. The deeper we traversed into the woods, the more we questioned our decision to come here. We came to a stop at the welcoming center, which was nothing more than a shabby shack. It needed a new roof, and the eaves dangled off the top. Parts of the siding were missing, and the screen door was broken, crooked, and didn't shut all the way.

While Dorian went inside to register, Dahlia and I took a short stroll around the tiny shack. The first thing we encountered was the playground. It was all metal, rusted, and toxic, from the monkey bars and the slide to the swings. There were actual rust holes through the slide, and the seesaw was cocked off its metal balance beam, and half of it lay on the ground. The fence surrounding the playground was dilapidated and rusted, as well, and the gate at the entrance hung off its moorings. Dahlia and I looked at each other, horrified. I was glad we didn't have children with us.

We continued our exploration of our new surroundings and came across the inground pool, if that was what you could call it. I expected to see the creature from the Black Lagoon crawl out of it. To say it was disgusting would have been an understatement. The pool hadn't been used in years. It couldn't have been. The water was obviously never drained. A thick layer of green goo stretched across the expanse and was so cloudy, I couldn't see the bottom. Some of the tiles from within the sides were cracked or missing.

"Eww…" Dahlia said, grossed out at the sight of slime that floated and caked to the top of the water.

"What? It's perfect for skinny dipping," I teased as she crinkled her nose at the thought.

We wandered to the bathrooms where we were even more appalled. When we peeked at the showers, we whipped back the ragged plastic shower curtain and found a hole in the wall. For real. Just a hole. I grabbed for the controls, turned the water on, and watched as water dribbled out of the wall. If April had a problem with girls not showering, they really weren't going to clean themselves after they saw this. Dahlia looked at me. "Are they serious with this?"

"I believe so."

"It's disgusting in here!"

"Yeah, I'd rather take a shit in the woods," I said because the rest of the bathroom was just as dirty and unsanitary. "What did we get ourselves into?"

We finally exited the restrooms and returned to

Dorian, who waited by the truck for us.

"Well, is it as fancy in there as it is in there?" She pointed to the shack.

"Oh, I think you'll like the restrooms way better," Dahlia jested.

I never did go up to Danielle when they all went in the shack to check in. She didn't bother to come near me, either. I guess this was what we were going to do the rest of this trip…avoid each other.

Our convoy slithered its way down a narrow trail, leading us to several secluded sites. A couple of them were directly in the sun with barely any shade. One site stuck out the most to me, entirely covered with trees and foliage, definitely the most private. Dorian and I chose it at the same time. Even though Dani stayed in the same site with us, she made sure to stay as far away from me as possible. We passed by each other without saying a word or exchanging a look. It was awkward, but I was still infuriated with her.

As we unloaded the Tahoe, we heard a bunch of hooting and hollering that got louder and louder until we realized it was Cookie, Kylie, and Tristan. They barreled down the bumpy dirt trail and came to a halt right in front of me as they laughed. When they opened the doors to Kylie's Dodge Ram, the pungent smell of pot drifted from the cabin.

"A little stoned, are we?" I grinned and poked fun at them.

"A little? We've been getting' fuckin' high since we left Tampa," Cookie poked back and took a look around. She was good until she spotted Danielle, who was seated in a beach chair reading the *Wall Street Journal*. Everyone else was busy constructing their tents, and the usual complaint came from Cookie. "And this is what I can't fuckin' stand about her, Parker."

"I know, I know," I agreed. "We're not speaking right now anyway."

"What? Yeah?"

Before I could get my next sentence out, Kylie came around the truck and promptly wrapped her arms around me, hugged me, and brazenly gave me a kiss. Danielle lifted her head from the paper and happened to catch that kiss. She rolled her eyes, clearly disgusted by what she saw, and put her nose back in the paper. As I caught the eyeroll, I took Kylie by the hand and walked around to the other side of the truck, out of Danielle's view. I didn't need Kylie seeing her attitude toward us, especially since the last thing Kylie recalled about her was them buddying up to play horseshoes. She had no idea that Dani felt the same way about me as she did.

Helping Cookie put her tent together was always a bitch because it was old and big as hell. It was a brown monstrosity that she called the Taj Mahal. I didn't know how many people fit in that thing. It came complete with a porch area and awning.

"I hate this fucking thing, Cook!" I declared as I staked a corner into the ground. "Wouldn't kill you to buy a new one. Maybe even one from the twenty-first century."

"Hey! This tent is a classic!"

"A classic what?"

"You didn't bitch about it two years ago when Amy threw your ass out of your own tent. You don't remember rolling into the Taj, freezing and begging to get warm?"

I remembered it well. It was unseasonably chilly at night that weekend. Amy was another passing fancy of mine, and she told me she had feelings for me that night. It didn't go over well when I told her I didn't feel the same. She kicked me out of the tent without hesitation, and I paced around our site. I didn't want to wake anyone, but I didn't have a blanket or even a sweatshirt, and freezing wasn't on my agenda. After Cookie F-bombed me left and right because I woke her up, she let me in and let me share her sleeping bag. Amy left the next day, and that was that.

It was barely noon, and the drinking had commenced. The fact that we didn't have to hide our alcohol was evident as girls walked from site to site, beer in hand and without concern for concealment. The woods that surrounded us were thick, and if we attempted to trek through it, we would be infested with ticks, chiggers, and poison ivy. We swatted at annoying insects, and it got old really quick. We ended up dousing ourselves in bug spray.

There weren't as many things to do around here, so some of us started a basketball game. The court had cracked concrete and was spider-webbed in certain areas, and the rusted hoop was without netting. Cookie, Kylie, Tristan, Dorian, and I made up one team, and the other team had April, Danielle, Sherri, Cece, and a girl named Taryn, who was a regular at the bar and typically attended these trips. After we cleared off debris, which included sticks, rocks, and empty beer cans, that were left on the playing area, we started the game. It didn't take long for Cookie to be up to her old ways of not knowing a damn thing about basketball. Taryn passed the ball to Dani, who was ultimately manhandled to the ground.

"Cookie! You can't do that!" I yelled as I offered Dani my hand. She wasn't sure how to react to my voluntary gesture, and all I said was, "I don't have to talk to you to know we're still friends." I made sure no one else heard me, and she finally took my hand, allowing me to help her up. When play resumed, Kylie dribbled the ball up the lane and passed it to me. My shot went in, and she gave a little pat to my bottom as I passed by her. There was no getting away from Dani, who spotted that, and as she passed by me, she shoulder-bumped me. She was not pleased with these small physical interactions that Kylie and I enjoyed. Too bad. I liked Kylie's company, and I was comfortable in her presence. Again, play resumed. Everyone defended against their respective counterparts, except for Cookie. She basically molested Taryn to the point of pushing her to the ground, too.

"Cookie!" I yelled once more and walked toward her. "This is not football! You can't do that!"

"Who the fuck says I can't?"

"The rules of basketball, that's who!" I clamored. She knew she tested my patience, and I was pretty sure she took some pleasure in that. But when she gave Cece a good shove to the ground, I'd had enough.

"That's it! Go sit over there!" I pointed to the bench on the side of the court where Dahlia was spectating, and she laughed at this scene between friends.

"You're throwing me outta the game?"

"Fuck, yeah! Sit!"

She flipped me the middle finger as she walked to the sidelines. The teams were uneven now, and Taryn offered to sit out. After we shifted the teams around, Cece was now on my team, and Kylie teamed up with April's squad. We started playing again while Cookie shouted obscenities at me from the bench, obviously rooting for the opposite team. While we passed the ball around, Cece was plainly being groped by April and didn't seem to mind one bit. The fact that Danielle was the only one not seeing this did not go unnoticed.

"Isn't she getting married to your friend Dani?" Kylie whispered in my ear. I nodded in agreement, and the game continued like this until my team ultimately won. We all sweated profusely as perspiration beaded on our foreheads and dripped down our T-shirts, drenching them.

"Oh, I feel disgusting and icky," Sherri offered.

"Then go take a shower," April said matter-of-factly. Danielle was ahead of us and out of earshot during this exchange of words.

"Are you kidding? This weekend's about roughing it. Nope, no shower for me until I get home Monday."

"Wow! That is absolutely disgusting, Sher!" April said.

"It is what it is, and I wouldn't dare use the showers here," Sherri said, and while we walked back to our campsite, she added, "What do you care, anyway? I'm not sleeping with you."

I didn't know what that comment was about, but April threw her nose up in true snob fashion. While we walked down the trail, I felt Kylie grab my hand. At first, I was taken aback by the PDA, but then I eased into it and allowed it to happen. We held hands all the way back. In the meantime, Danielle, who had slowed enough to rejoin the rest of the pack, saw this small display of affection and reached for April's hand.

However, April pushed her hand away. Something was going on for sure.

As the day passed, Kylie got more and more brazen. When women hit on me in front of my friends, it didn't bother me. But damn, did it bother Danielle. For someone who was a *mistake*, she sure hadn't let me out of her sight. Each time Kylie kissed me, I saw Danielle stare us down. Daggers were shot at me. Her gaze filled with fire, and I believed if she had the option, I would've been maimed and dead right now. I didn't know what she wanted from me. One minute, she was kissing me and cumming for me. The next, she was all over April, trying to cleanse herself of her guilty, dirty, pleasurable sin. I refused to allow her to have it both ways. She didn't get to cum for me, then cum for April. It didn't work like that, so I cut her off and didn't give her a choice in going back to *Friendsville*. It hurt too much. Listening to them fuck last night was traumatizing, and it didn't help her in her quest to continue things with me. It only made me angrier. So, if Kylie showed me some attention, and it got to her, good!

⁂

Around dinnertime, Dorian broke out the grill. "Tonight, it's London broil, people." While she was busy preparing a steak dinner, I realized some of the women who had been drinking since noon were quite inebriated at this point. Laughing was contagious, and they were like children who chased one another around from site to site as they played a makeshift game of tag. The campground sucked, but the girls were happy. They didn't have to hide their beer, and they didn't have to behave nearly as much at this place.

Smoke from the grill filled the air, and I hoped it would chase the flying insects away. As I watched Cookie swat the back of her neck for the hundredth time, I finally shoved some citronella candles into the ground and made sure to surround our area with them. Then I collected some tinder from the woods and made a fire in the ring. I piled it up in the center when Kylie came over to help me. She looked really cute and was very attentive. I knew she was trying to get in my pants tonight. But while we talked, giggled, and flirted with each other, I glanced over toward the coolers. Several women dug through them and picked out the beer they wanted. One of those women happened to be Danielle. *What the...*I was confused by this as Dani rarely drank. And when she did, it was always wine. She never even finished the glass. When she popped open a can and took a swig, I couldn't help but excuse myself from Kylie and go over to her.

"What are you doing?" I probed.

"Having a drink. I'm not allowed?" she shot back.

"Of course you're allowed. You're a grown-ass woman. It's just that you don't drink."

"Maybe I'm taking up a new hobby, a new pastime."

"I know you're doing this because you don't like what's going on with Kylie, but you need to get over yourself. This is not going to help." I pointed to the beer she held.

She glared at me and guzzled a good mouthful down the hatch.

"You don't even like beer," I said.

This was evident as she crinkled up her face after

each swallow. "I do now. You don't have to worry about me, Parker. I'm a big girl."

"Really? Then maybe you ought to pull your big girl panties up and act like one." Disgusted, I left her standing there with her beer. I hoped April took care of her later when she puked because I wouldn't. Danielle was definitely not in her right state of mind.

When I returned to the fire, Kylie asked, "Everything okay? That interaction seemed pretty intense."

I rolled my eyes and shook my head. "Yeah, everything is fine. She's just lost her mind is all."

"What do you mean she's lost her mind?"

"She doesn't drink."

Kylie looked over at Danielle, who eyeballed her over the brim of her beer can. "Looks like she's taken it up today," she pointed out. "Why is she looking at me like she wants to kill me? We got along so well at your pool party."

"It's not you she wants to kill," I corrected. "It's me."

Just then, Cookie flew up to us and broke up our conversation. "Yo! You gotta see this! Hurry!" she excitedly said.

We followed her through a trail to the neighboring site to find a crowd circling something or someone. All that could be heard was loud talking and hysterical laughter. Everyone had their cellphone out to record. We had no idea what they were recording as we fought our way through the surrounding people. When we finally got to the center, we found Buckley, drunk and stuck in her camping chair. When she sat down, she fell right through. She couldn't get out of it to save her life.

"You're some great friends!" Buckley struggled

to get up, only to completely fall to the side.

After everyone had their fun, they helped her out of the gaping hole in her chair. "It's all fun and games until y'all need your air conditioning unit repaired!" Buckley chastised.

We met one summer when the air conditioning broke in the bar. She and her wife, Tonya, became regulars after that, and we all became good friends. The couple came every year on this camping trip, and she stayed loaded the entire weekend. I wasn't surprised to see her crack open a beer at dawn. She drank it like coffee. She was crazy fun and always a hoot to hang out with.

By the time we got back to our site, Dorian had dinner ready for our small group of friends. The steak was perfect, and I complimented her on her grilling skills. "It's fucking delicious, Dorian!" And everyone chimed in to thank her for our meal.

While I ate, I periodically glanced over at Dani, who was now on her second beer. We made eye contact for a moment, and God, I still fucking wanted her. As hurt and mad as I was, I couldn't stop loving her. I didn't know how to make things right, and I wasn't sure that they would ever be again.

April wasn't being very nice to her. She left her alone and hung out with everyone but her. Every time Cece was around, April was right there sidling up to her. That was a far cry from last night when she wanted to fuck her wife-to-be. But Dani was already too drunk after two beers to see what was going on between them. Danielle tried to keep it together but only because other friends had come over to chat with her. She talked and occasionally laughed, but it wasn't her real laugh. Her laugh was light and giddy. This one was forced as if she was disguising her inner battle.

I felt obligated somehow to talk to April about Danielle's drinking. I wouldn't normally, but normally, Dani didn't drink, and I was concerned. She already looked disgusted with me when I approached them.

"Can I talk to you for a second, please?" I interrupted.

She reluctantly stepped away from Cece with that cocky attitude of hers. "What is it, Parker?"

"Your fiancée is drinking. You don't find anything strange about that? She doesn't drink, April. And why aren't you keeping an eye on her?"

"She's a grown, responsible woman. If she wants to drink, she can drink. It's that easy."

"But she's going to get sick later," I informed her. But she didn't look fazed, and I didn't get it. "You don't seem concerned at all."

"She's fine. She'll just pass out in the tent later. Let it go, will ya?" When I didn't leave right away, she told me we were finished. "You can go." She didn't bother to wait for a response. Instead, she rudely turned her back to me and began talking to Cece again.

Chapter Twelve

I did my best to forget about Dani by choosing to be involved in Cookie's clique instead. Rita hung out with us because of Tristan, and it looked like they would hook up tonight. Guess Rita still remembered what Tristan's fingers felt like. Cookie awaited Shady's arrival while she roasted a marshmallow over the fire as a joint hung out of her mouth. Kylie and I talked, and I relaxed enough to enjoy her. Every now and then, she would lean over and kiss me. She wasn't making out with me, but she was still turning me on.

"Here." Cookie handed me the joint she just lit.

"No, I don't want it."

"Just take it," she said.

"I don't want it," I snapped.

"I said fuckin' take it! You're gonna fuckin' need it tonight."

"What are you talking about?"

"That woman over there," she pointed at Danielle, who swayed a little, still with a beer in her hand, "she's gonna ruin your fuckin' night is what's gonna fuckin' happen."

"No, she's not. Her wife can take care of her."

Kylie got up and went to the cooler for another beer. Cookie schooled me. "Parker, Dani's been lookin' over here all fuckin' night, watching you and Kylie kiss and touch. You mark my words, you're going to take care of her later, not April. You're the one she wants to take care of her." She looked over at Danielle and back at me. "She does not want you to hook up with Kylie." Again, she glanced over at Danielle, then back to me. She clicked her lighter and relit the joint. "Now think about what I just fuckin' said and hit this joint."

I couldn't argue with her. As the day grew later and evening turned into night, it appeared Cookie was right. April was flat-out cold toward Danielle, and I couldn't help but watch Dani getting drunker by the hour. The fact that she hung out with Buckley now, the biggest drunkard on the trip, indicated she had sunk to a new low for herself. For someone who disliked alcohol as much as she did, she was slamming them down.

I took that joint from Cookie and hit it hard. I hadn't touched any alcohol today, but I thought Cookie might be right about Danielle needing me tonight. It wasn't too often that she was wrong. Cookie was loaded with street smarts but never had a desire to pick up a book. This had been one of the big differences between her and Dani. Dani didn't have a lick of street smarts but could read the shit out of a book.

Wanting to spend some time as a group, the girls decided to play a game. Everyone grabbed their camping chairs and formed a circle around the fire. There were about fifteen of us playing, and Sherri announced, "We're going to play a game called Thumper. This is how it works." She pulled up her chair and intently scanned the group. "Everyone is going to clap their thighs repeatedly." She beat her thighs as if they were tom-toms, and continued, "I'll start by grabbing my ear." She pinched her lobe. "Then the next person will repeat my action, and then add their own. The next in line will repeat my action, then the second person's, and then make up their own. And it goes around the circle so on and so forth. If someone gets them wrong or forgets one, they're out of the game. What do you think? Wanna try it?"

The girls agreed to play, and the game began. Everyone thumped their thighs, and Sherri started it out just as she had explained. She pinched her ear and thumped again. Kylie went next. She pinched her ear and made an X over her heart with her finger. She started thumping again, and it was my turn. I pinched my ear, crossed my heart, tapped the top of my head, and thumped again. The circle was large, and it took a while to go all the way around.

Even as we thumped, Kylie smiled and leaned over to steal a kiss. She became more and more confident and comfortable each time I let her. Danielle never missed it. She was all the way on the other side of the circle and scowled at me. But the scowl turned into a puppy dog look. She looked saddened by the affection Kylie showed me. This last time, not only did she watch as Kylie kissed me, but she downright stared at me, taking swigs of beer with each blink of her beautiful honey brown eyes. And every time she attempted to gain some attention from April, she was brushed aside. April had abandoned her by this time for Cece. It was so obvious to me. I didn't understand how Dani ignored it.

We made it past one round of Thumper with only one person getting tossed from the game, and to my astonishment, it wasn't Dani. How she got through all those signs without messing up was beyond me.

 TL Dickerson

However, by the second round, the booze had clearly affected her motor skills. Touching her nose was damn near impossible, and each time she spoke, her words slurred together incoherently. Although the girls found her funny and amusing, I knew better. She wasn't trying to be funny or amusing. At this point, she was just attempting to speak and move properly. When she was thrown out of the game, she wobbled in the direction of the coolers again. As she rifled through the ice in search of another beer, I excused myself from the game temporarily to check on her. I was still pissed at her, but being pissed didn't take away from the fact that I still loved her. Someone needed to check on her because April apparently refused.

"Hey! You okay?" I asked.

"Why wouldn't I blee?" She looked as if she would punch me square in the face.

"Please stop drinking. This isn't you!"

"Who am I?" She turned her body so that she faced me completely. "Who am I, Parker? Really? I don't even recog…recog…*hiccup*! I don't even recognize myshelf thanymore."

"Dani, I know you're confused about a lot of things, but this isn't the answer." I pointed to the can of beer she just popped open.

"You're going to shleep with her tonight. Aren't chu?"

"That shouldn't matter. I mean, after all, didn't you fuck April last night in a tent that was no more than ten inches from mine?"

She pouted at me as she looked to the ground. She continued to sway. "All of a sudden, you have nothing to say?" I stared hard at her as I recalled the sounds that came from that tent.

"Jussgo, Parker!" she slurred a bit too loudly, even with all the thumping from the game.

Nonetheless, I said, "You wanna take your tone down?"

"Not really! I shaid go!" She placed her hands on my stomach, pushing me backward. The more I tried to stand my ground, the more she pushed.

"Stop! Dani, stop!" I grabbed her by the arms, halting her progress and aggression toward me. I noticed Cookie and Kylie looking wide-eyed at us, and I attempted to calm her down once more.

But when Dorian got up from the group and came over to investigate, I realized maybe I should have just walked away when Dani wanted me to. "Um, ladies, I realize you've been friends for a long time, but people are starting to stare at you, wondering what's going on." She peered back over her shoulder at the circle of campers, who had now stopped playing the game. When her attention returned to us, she continued, "If you don't want anyone to figure out what's going on between the two of you, I suggest you leave each other alone." Before she went back to the group, she looked hard at Danielle. "You are wasted! What the hell?" Her attention switched from Danielle to me, and she instructed, "Parker, go back to Kylie."

"Yeah, go kack to Bylie," Dani mimicked her as best she could.

I walked away and didn't know what I felt. When I took my seat next to Kylie again, I couldn't help but look over at Dorian, who tried her hardest to take Danielle's beer away. Once she finally gave up and came back, Dani's gaze locked on mine one last time before she turned and stumbled through the woods to a neighboring site.

Dorian, Cookie, and I exchanged a concerned look, and when I glanced over at April, she didn't seem to care one bit. I was baffled by her indifference. Pulling her aside again would only add to the commotion, but I admit, I was sickened by her lack of attention toward the woman she supposedly loved and even more disgusted by her attention toward Cece. I struggled with myself and tried to stay away from Danielle in this way, but each smile, each giggle shared between them had weakened my will to do the right thing. The woman I had been in love with for years was drunk, wandering around the woods, and here I sat playing Thumper? I took a deep breath and desperately tried to go on with my night.

When the game ended, the party started to break up. I approached April one last time. "Hey, have you seen Dani?"

"Well, since I've been sitting right here for the last hour, I'm gonna say no," she said with that awful, arrogant attitude.

"What the fuck is wrong with you, anyway? Your girl is trashed! Doesn't that bother you? Why are you not giving a shit? Are you guys fighting or something?" I was eager for an answer that made any sense.

Before she responded, Danielle staggered out of the darkness of the woods with her beer in hand. I didn't even recognize my intelligent, professional, had-it-all-together friend. She was a walking, slurring wrecking ball, ready to slam into any obstacle in her way.

"See? There she is." April threw in one last dig, "Go back to your new girlfriend and mind your own business."

As I hesitantly backed away, my gaze was still glued to hers like a ferocious predator. I was about to enter my own tent where Kylie waited for me. I looked back at the fire where Danielle clumsily fell into a chair. April urged her to come to sleep, but I heard Dani ramble, "I wanna sit by the fire forabit." Her eyes were heavy, and her head bobbed slightly as her equilibrium was clearly off.

April left her there and disappeared into their tent. Danielle sipped from her can and stared at me. She was silent, and the only sounds left tonight were the crackling of the fire and the creaking of insects and frogs involved in their nocturnal ritual. I wanted to go to her, but it would only cause another argument, and I didn't want her to make a scene. The embarrassment she would feel in the morning would have overwhelmed her, so I broke our eye contact and slipped into my tent.

Once inside, I realized that Kylie expected to score with me tonight, and part of me wanted that. She had worked on me all day, so I tried to loosen up and go with it. She rested on her side and propped herself up on her elbow. Her gray eyes seared into mine. From there, her gaze traveled my face until her focus landed on my lips. She beckoned me to lay with her and patted the empty spot next to her. My grin widened at the sight of her soft side, and I crawled over to her. However, rather than lie next to her, I gently pushed her onto her back and continued my crawl on top of her. I took the lead and placed my lips on hers. Her mouth parted for me as she took in my tongue and lightly sucked on it. Her hands explored my body, caressed my back, and traced my spine down to my ass.

We sank into each other when I heard a noise outside. Danielle tripped and fell with a thump and a yelp, and I needed to excuse myself to check on her. The kissing stopped as I peeled myself from Kylie. "Wait! Where are you going?" She was confused by the sudden break in heat.

"I have to check on her."

"Who?"

"Danielle," I answered as if she should've already known.

Kylie pushed herself on her side again, her left leg up and bent. She paused for a second and finally asked, "Do you have a thing for her?"

I practically spit the water out of the bottle I sipped. She got up to pat me on the back, and I sputtered, "Why would you ask such a thing?"

"I don't know. You looked like a quarreling couple just a few hours ago. Sorry if I misunderstood." She then added, "Did I?"

"Um, well, no. I mean, yes. I mean..." I took a moment to collect myself and started over. "What I mean to say is, Danielle is one of my closest and dearest friends. Maybe we're a little unusually close, but it's because of our history. I'm sorry if it came off as more than that." I lied, but the question was, did Kylie think I was lying? She didn't say anymore, and as I unzipped the tent, I turned back. "I'll be right back."

I ducked my head out of the tent and scanned the area. Looking around the fire, I didn't see Danielle anywhere. When I made my way over to Dani and April's tent, I quietly called out, "Dani? April?" No one answered. I unzipped their tent and peeked inside. There was an empty air mattress. I knew April came in here a while ago. Where the hell did she go? And where the hell was Danielle?

"Holy shit!" I jumped as I felt someone touch my shoulder.

"It's just me," Dorian whispered and looked around the tent as she saw the same thing I did. "Where are they? Do you think they're together?"

"I don't know, but I'm not going to be able to rest until I find out."

"Come on. I'll go with you."

With only Dorian's flashlight, we crept through the wooded trail to the next campsite. It was dark and quiet, and everyone was asleep. Buckley's snoring helped disguise our footsteps as we walked over loose brush, and we got back on the trail to the next site. Danielle was nowhere to be found, and I worried she may have passed out in the woods.

"Where is she?" Dorian asked softly.

"Wait. Do you hear that?" I stopped dead in my tracks. We both stood still, listening for what, I wasn't sure.

"You go that way. I'll go this way," she said.

"But you have the flashlight."

"Then use your phone for light."

It wasn't as bright as her flashlight but bright enough to see where I was stepping. We separated. I heard a noise and walked toward it. As I got closer to the rusted playground, I heard a faint voice. I passed the seesaw when the voice gained some clarity. There was a little fort-type structure next to the swings, and it sounded like it was coming from in there.

When I was close enough, I heard, "Listen, it's

just for a little while." The voice sounded familiar, but a second voice could be heard, this one not as clearly. The first voice spoke again. "It's only until her father dies. Once he croaks, she'll collect a healthy inheritance, and that's when I'll divorce her. I'll take half, and we can be together then."

I finally realized that it was April who spoke, and I was horrified by her words. Who she was talking to had yet to be determined, but it was true, Danielle's father's health was failing. He had recently been diagnosed with liver cancer. His doctors started him on chemo a few months ago, and even though the fatality rate was high, Danielle carried immense hope for his recovery. The thought of losing both parents to cancer was unbearable to her. I was the only one she opened up to about it. She didn't talk about it often, though, because she said it made it too real.

With one fluid motion, I swung the door open to that tiny fort with one intention—to see who April was saying these awful things to. When the door flew open, I caught April and Cece tongue locked and cradled in each other's embrace. They both jumped, surprised at being caught in the act, and instead of being upset, April became enraged. "Really, Parker? Get out!" She started toward me. I took a step back and straddled the threshold, but she continued to push me out. She followed me outside of the rusted fort, and her piercing look shot straight through my soul. "Don't you dare tell Danielle! You got that?"

"Why shouldn't I tell her? You do realize she's wandering around the woods drunk out of her mind, right?"

"I'll tell you why you shouldn't tell her. Because if you do, she's only going to think you're saying it to get with her."

Confusion took over, and I asked, "What do you mean by that?"

"It means I'm not an idiot. I've known for a long time that you like her. Do you think I don't see the way you look at her? You think I don't see you checking her out?"

"I, uh…I…"

"Yeah, you keep *I, uh,* and keep your mouth shut, too! I don't know how much you heard, but I'll make sure you never see Danielle again. Do you understand?"

"You can't keep her from me. And we've been friends for too long for her not to believe me." I took a step back toward the woods. "I'm telling her exactly what I saw."

As I turned in the direction of the trail, I heard her take a run at me. I turned to face her, and she tackled me to the ground with great force. While I lay on my back, I struggled to break free from her, but she was straddling me and had leverage. I must admit, she was stronger than I ever gave her credit for. Trying to scratch her eyeballs out didn't work as she grabbed my hands and pinned me to the ground entirely.

"Don't fight it, Parker," she said while I continued to kick my legs in an effort to remove her from me.

"Fuck you, April!" Spit spewed as I yelled, and she removed one of her hands and grabbed me by the throat.

With my one free hand, I clutched at the collar of her shirt. She tightened her grip. I was finding it difficult to breathe but still managed to say, "What are you gonna do, kill me?"

"I fucking should." Suddenly, both her hands were around my neck, squeezing the life from me slowly. She purposefully dug her fingernails into my skin. "Are you going to tell her?"

"Yes," I said, barely able to squeak out the word and feeling my face turn blue from lack of oxygen. "Go ahead, kill me."

Out of the corner of my eye, I could see Cece standing there, frightened at what she was witnessing. Her eyes were big as her mind appeared to digest what was happening.

"Clearly, you don't care about your own life, so how about I go one further?"

I continued to struggle with her, and with her next words, my body went limp. "If you so much as mention that you even saw me here tonight, so help me God, I will kill Danielle. You may not care about your existence but I know you care about hers."

She was right. I did care about Danielle more than I did myself. I always had.

Her actions toward me and the plan I overheard convinced me April was downright evil. Choking me to within an inch of my life was enough proof that she meant what she said.

"Be a real shame if something happened to the brakes on her Roadster. Imagine what that would be like. No more precious Danielle in your life. Don't think for one minute that I wouldn't do it." She looked into my eyes with a ruthlessness that burned into my very soul. Her voice lowered into a guttural tone. "You will not fuck this up for me. Do you understand?" The venom that spilled from her was enough for me to lay still, complying with her threat. She wanted to hear it, though. She wanted to hear it from me. "Do you understand?"

"Yes."

She released her talons from my neck and proceeded to get off of me. I swiftly got to my feet, rubbing my throat as I did. "I thought you loved her," I said.

She ignored me, took Cece by the hand, and walked back to the little fort. Cece entered first, but as April set foot inside, she glared at me one last time. "Remember what I said, Parker."

"I don't believe that you would do what you said." I absolutely believed what she said but wanted to hear something different.

"Test me." She grinned wickedly at me.

My insides were shaken, and my hands trembled involuntarily. I was stunned as I turned and walked in the direction of the restrooms to search for Dorian. What just happened? I couldn't believe that April was cheating. Even though I knew what Danielle and I were doing was the same thing, I was still shocked. Even more shocked that she had a plan to rob Dani. But the capper for me was her threatening to take Danielle's life. The thought of it made me queasy, and I stopped briefly to gather myself.

When I reached the restroom, I found Danielle sobbing in Dorian's arms. She muttered something incoherently into Dorian's shoulder but immediately tried to pull it together when she saw me. She swayed as she stood in one spot, and the more she tried to balance herself, the more unstable she became. Dorian looked at me, and without saying a word, she understood that she should leave us alone. I wanted to tell Dorian what I had transpired only minutes ago, but that was going to have to wait. She hugged Dani one more time and bounced out the door.

We stood there and stared at each other. We didn't say anything for what seemed like hours. Dani's eyes were bloodshot, and she couldn't keep still. When her eyes filled with tears, my immediate reaction was to grab her and hold her close to me. At first, she hesitated, but then her body went limp, and she wrapped her arms around my waist as she laid her head on my shoulder. I let her cry for a while, and before I knew it, I started crying, too. I held her so tightly. I didn't want to let go. Her pain became my pain, and all I wanted was to take it away from her, to make it all better. Before I let go of her, she whispered, "I love you, Parker."

As I backed away from her, my hands were still on her shoulders, and I held her at arm's length. "What did you say?"

"I'm so confused," she said.

"No. What did you just say? You said you love me."

She touched her lips with her fingers as if she didn't realize she spoke it out loud. "I can't say it again."

"You love me?"

"I didn't say that."

"Why are you playing with me?"

"Playing withshu? You think I'm playing with-shu?"

"If I'm understanding your version of drunken English, then yes, I do think you're playing with me."

"Yeah, because that's what you've always shknown me to do, right? Play with people," she said sarcastically. "I'm a big user."

"That's not what I said."

She turned away and leaned her head on the wall. She lightly banged her head against it.

"Dani, stop!"

She stopped and asked, "Did you sleep with her?"

"Does it matter?"

"I don't know."

"Yes, you do."

She turned clumsily back to me. "I don't want you to." She pleaded with me with her bloodshot, tear-soaked eyes as she gently brushed her fingertips over my lips. "I don't want you to."

Her face suddenly turned a nice shade of white, and she raced to a toilet. She threw open the bathroom stall door, dropped to her knees, and hurled everything she had eaten and drunk today. It wasn't one of her finer moments. I diligently knelt beside her and held her forehead while the rest of it came up.

While this went on, I heard the door to the restroom open, and a loud voice said, "I have to pee so bad!"

I looked out of the stall door to see Shady and Cookie approach us. Danielle vomited again, this time with a vengeance. The sight of Dani throwing up and the stench of the alcohol from the puke, mixed with the already weird smell of this bathroom, was enough for Shady to say, "You know what, I'll just pee outside."

But Cookie wasn't as quick to go. Rather, she stood beside me, towered over Danielle, and made fun of her. "A little too much fuckin' fun, huh, Professor Bly?" She laughed and patted Dani on the back. "Don't worry! It'll all come out eventually. You keep fuckin' hurlin'."

"Cookie, leave that girl alone! C'mon!" Shady scoffed and left the restroom.

Cookie followed, but not without one more dig at Danielle. "Stick to literature! Ya know, something you can handle 'cause it ain't this, darlin'. You suck at it!"

"Hold on to me," I advised Danielle, put my arm around her waist, and did my best to stand her up. She was finished doing her business and needed to get fresh air.

We staggered through the woods and shuffled into trees as we walked. The only light we had was from my cellphone, and my battery was almost dead. "Come on, Dani. Ya gotta help out a little," I said. Holding her up got tougher the farther along we went, and eventually, I had to stop. I had to practically drag her the rest of the way back to the campsite.

I was mad at her, no question. She ruined my night, just as Cookie said she would. But my love for her came first and ran deep. It always had. The last part of our trek was spent with Danielle repeatedly apologizing to me.

"I'm shorry, Parker," she mumbled, and three seconds later repeated, "Parker?"

"Yes?"

"I'm shorry."

"I know. It's okay."

"No, it's not."

"You're right, it's not, but this is what it is, and I can't leave you alone."

I was pretty sure she passed out the last few feet to my tent, as she became deadweight against my side. I unzipped the tent and threw her inside. Inside, where Kylie was still waiting for me.

"Uh…" she said as she moved over involuntarily, and Danielle fell into her. Her face contorted in confusion and a touch of anger. I nodded in the direction of outside, and when we walked out, she asked, "Why is she in your tent? I thought we were gonna spend the night together."

"Kylie, she's trashed and incapable of…well, quite frankly, she's incapable of anything."

"Clearly. However, doesn't she have a fiancée? Why isn't she taking care of her?"

"That's a whole other story." I thought about April's behavior earlier and didn't know how to explain it. "Kylie, I'm sorry."

She directed her attention away from me. "It's okay."

"Well, even I didn't believe that just now," I said. "I'll make it up to you. I swear!" She didn't look convinced, and I added, "What kind of friend would I be if I left her alone like this? God forbid we find her in the morning dead." Her eyes widened, and I explained, "She doesn't drink. She's not used to it. She could roll on her back and choke on her own vomit in her sleep. I couldn't live with myself if that happened."

Finally, she realized my plight, and even though she still seemed disappointed, she conceded, "Okay. You're right!" She stepped toward me. "I don't want to force this. I can be patient." It sounded like she tried to convince herself more than me. As she leaned in to kiss me, a painful moan came from the tent, and then, "Blaah!"

The sound of throw-up was an instant kiss killer, and Kylie shook her head, crossed the center of our site, and disappeared inside the Taj Mahal with Cookie and Shady. Kylie listened to Cookie bitch about being an unwanted third wheel, but their tent soon went quiet. It wouldn't have been such a big deal had Tristan not hooked up with Rita, but she was spending the night in her small camper parked in the same site as Cece and Sherri.

Once I was back in my own dwelling, I scoped the area around Danielle. I searched for where she vomited since I never gave her something to throw up in. Unfortunately, she vomited into one of my hiking boots. I threw the boot outside and retrieved the small waste basket from Dorian's Tahoe. When I went back in the tent, I put the basket next to her head. I was going to sleep on the opposite side of the tent but chose to curl up to her. My arms folded around her, and she briefly came to semi-consciousness. Enough to whisper for the second time tonight, "I love you, Parker."

There was no question as to whom she spoke when she blurted out my name. She was aware enough to know she wasn't in April's arms. She knew exactly who she was talking to and where she was. I didn't know what to do with this statement, words I would've died a thousand times to hear. The fact of the matter was, our circumstance hadn't changed, and she may not even remember saying it to me when she sobered up. I set myself up to be crushed, yet I couldn't stop what was already in motion, even when I tried. Gently, I pulled the hair tie from her ponytail, combed my fingertips through her hair, and kissed her cheek. She reeked of alcohol and puke, and still she was the most beautiful woman in the world to me. She was passed out for good now. I whispered back what she had known for years. "I love you, too, my sweet, sweet Danielle."

Chapter Thirteen

Come and get it!" I just about jumped out of my skin as I heard that breakfast call. I was pretty sure Danielle was even less amused than I was as she stirred. "Who is that? Kill them!" she mumbled under her putrid breath and buried her head under the pillow. When she rolled onto her back and turned her face toward me, I could see her mind racing to remember the events of yesterday and last night. "Oh, my God! I'm so sorry." She covered her face with her hand as she recalled at least some of it.

The smell of brewed coffee was a welcome one but apparently not so much for Danielle. She snatched the basket next to her and dry heaved into it. Nothing but some bile came up at this point as she repeatedly spit into the can. Her hair was a mess. Half of it was smooshed to the side of her head, the other half sprang out in every direction. She was in disarray, looked like hell, and was pale white from the night before.

"How do you feel?" I already knew the answer.

"I feel like a big, heaping pile of cow dung."

"You smell like it, too." I tried to get a smile out of her.

She cracked a cock-eyed grin before her face vanished into the bucket again. "I feel terrible." She pulled her head back up. "April didn't help me at all, did she?" While the minutes passed, her brain put some things together, and she came to the conclusion,

"April didn't help me at all."

I wanted to tell her what happened at the playground, but April's vengeful words replayed in my head. "No. She didn't."

Her head hung low as she heard this, and disappointment seeped from her voice. "Will you help me walk to the showers? I think I'm still a little drunk." She tried to change the subject. When I helped her out of the tent, she was still a little shaky on her feet. But it was nothing compared to last night.

Dorian scrambled eggs and fried bacon as we walked through our site. The smell forced Danielle into the woods to heave again. When we were on the annual trip a few years ago, she couldn't wait for breakfast. Her impatience drove her into the next campsite searching for food. Our friends in that site felt bad for her and thought we weren't feeding this poor soul. I snatched the plate from her hands as she had opened her mouth to take a bite because I had gone looking for her to tell her breakfast was ready. "They're feeding you and you're over here acting like they're not?" Buckley rhetorically asked as she set Danielle's plate on another table. Ahh, memories.

"Is she okay?" Dorian asked. "Does she want some eggs?"

"Does she look like she can hold down eggs? She can't even hold her own bodily fluids down, let alone eat."

Danielle stopped at her tent and gathered some clean clothes. I guess April was still asleep because no words were spoken while she was in there. She came right back out, and we walked past Cookie, who ate steak and eggs at a picnic table along with Shady, Kylie, Tristan, and Rita. She couldn't help but get a few jabs in on Danielle. "Lookin' good, Professor!" she teased and couldn't resist, "And the puke all down the front of your fuckin' shirt is just as attractive as you this morning."

Dani peered down to see the dried vomit that clung to her T-shirt. She flipped Cookie the bird. Usually, she just ignored Cookie, but today, she surprised all of us.

When we were out of earshot, she admitted, "I'm so humiliated."

"Don't be! We've all been there."

"This isn't me, Parker. I don't do things like this."

"Well, you did this time, and you're going to pay for it most of today. Be prepared."

"Wait…did I hit you last night?"

"Not exactly. More like pushing."

She stopped dead in her tracks and gained my full attention. "Oh, my God! I'm so, so sorry."

"It's okay."

"It is not okay." She touched my arm. "I've never laid my hands on anyone in my life. But you? I can't believe I put my hands on you. And knowing what you've been through in your childhood with the abuse and the—"

"Hey, hey, it's okay! Stop!" I interrupted. I knew this wasn't who she was and that she was just stressed and didn't cope with it very well.

"And you still took care of me?"

"Well, yeah. Of course."

"But I've been treating you terribly. I didn't deserve your care."

"Okay, just stop already. You know I'd do any-thing for you."

Our conversation took another turn as she stumbled over what she wanted to ask me so desperately. "Did you…Did you? Ya know, did you…"

"Did I what?"

"Did you and Kylie…you know?"

"If you're asking me if I had sex with her, the answer's no. You pretty much asked me not to."

"I did?"

"Yes."

"I'm sorry."

"No, you're not," I corrected her. "Listen, things are awkward enough between the two of us lately. I don't think I wanna talk about her with you."

"Awkward? Wait, things are awkward?" she challenged.

"They're not?"

We both chose to end this discussion, and we finally arrived at the shabby restrooms. We stepped inside, and she began undressing. I averted my eyes as I didn't want to gawk, and she said, "You act like you've never seen me naked."

"Just trying to be respectful."

She put her flip-flops on and got into the shower stall, turned on the water, and watched it dribble out of the hole in the wall.

"I'm gonna give you some privacy, okay?" I dragged the beat-up, crusty shower curtain over and covered her.

"Wait. Would you wash my back?" She handed me the bar of soap.

I looked around to see if anyone else was in the vicinity, and against my better judgment, I took the soap. She turned her back to me. I ran the soap over her skin and tried not to let myself get aroused by her soft, silkiness under my touch.

"Mmm…that feels nice." She delighted in the back rub. "Thank you." She turned back around to face me. "And thank you for taking care of me last night. I know you don't believe me, but I am sorry I ruined your evening."

"I know I've already said this, but I would do anything for you, Dani. You know that, right?" I would give my life for her.

We stood there staring at each other for a moment; her hair was wet and matted to her face and neck. We were about to lose ourselves in a kiss when all of a sudden, a familiar voice said, "Okay, Parker, you've done your friendly deed, and although I appreciate you taking care of my girl, I'm here now." She squeezed between us and covered Danielle's bare body. "You can go now," she said as she relieved me of my voluntary duty.

When I turned to leave, I heard Danielle ask, "Where were you last night? I needed you and you weren't there."

"I was angry with you for being so irresponsible. Since when do you drink? It wasn't becoming, and I was turned off by it completely."

"So you left me? Nice, April."

I could hear the sarcasm in Danielle's voice, but April seemed unmoved. *Maybe if you pulled your tongue out of Cece's mouth long enough, you could have been there for Dani the way you should have.* I left them alone and went back to our site a little weirded out and more confused than ever. Not confused over what I felt for Danielle but confused by the situation. I couldn't get past the image of April making out with Cece or hearing the evil, greedy things she said about

Danielle's dying father. Worse, I couldn't stop feeling her hands around my neck still or seeing the evilness in her eyes and hearing the malice in her voice when she said she would kill Dani. I always knew April had an arrogant streak in her, but this mean streak was something new. The more I stewed over it, the more I wondered why I held back. But then I pictured Danielle lying in a coffin, dead. Making it real in my head was a misery and anguish I never wanted to know. Just imagining the pain of her permanent absence from my life, from this earth, no, I couldn't bear it. I had to remain silent to Dani.

❧❧❧❧

When I arrived back at our site, the girls were just finishing up breakfast. My stomach growled, and I was disappointed I missed out. "Don't worry. I saved a plate for you," Dorian said as if she read my mind. "How is she?"

"Still feeling sick and probably will be all day."

"I would say I don't know what possessed her to drink like that last night, but knowing what I know…" she said without finishing.

"I gotta tell you something."

"What is it?"

But before I could get the words out, Dahlia popped out of nowhere, and it only took a simple graze of Dorian's arm to lose her attention. As if I didn't exist, they started making out in front of me, and I realized this dire conversation was going to have to wait. I took a seat and ate my breakfast that consisted of cold eggs and cold bacon, but beggars couldn't be choosers, and I was grateful Dorian thought of me.

It was about ten in the morning, and Buckley had a beer in her hand. She wasn't alone since most of the women either drank, got stoned, or did both, so early. Of course, Cookie was the center of attention as she sat under the shade of a beach umbrella and rolled one joint after another. She lined them up on the picnic table. "What are you doing?" I asked.

"Preparing."

"Preparing for what?"

"Preparing for the motherfucking day naturally," she asserted as she licked the gum of the paper to finish rolling what appeared to be joint number eleven. She couldn't help herself when she changed topics. "How's Goody fucking Two-Shoes this morning? She looks like death, by the way."

"No time for that! I need to tell you what happened last night."

"*Hola, chica!*" Shady came up behind me and put her arms around my waist. "*Qué pedo?*"

"I'm never going to get to tell this story, am I?" I asked no one in particular.

"What story, *chica*?" Shady asked with a puzzled expression. "Why do you look so serious?"

Although I wanted to tell Cookie what took place, I didn't want to include Shady in this loop. Too many people knowing wouldn't be good, and I needed to handle this gently. The last thing I needed was for this to get back to Danielle, but I trusted Cookie and Dorian.

✦ ✦ ✦ ✦

The midmorning sun was strong, and its rays were merciless combined with high humidity. A few of the women were topless and sunbathing while Tristan was in her glory. She not only lathered sunscreen on Rita, but also rubbed lotion onto the backs of the other lovely ladies sprawled out on their bellies as they lay on lounge chairs, Cece among them. It was funny to observe Tristan in action. She was such a smooth operator. Even after the lotion was thoroughly rubbed into Cece's back, Tristan continued massaging her. Cece showed no signs of putting a stop to it and appeared to be enjoying the doting and attention.

I didn't know if these girls had taken Molly or not, but I figured I might get to witness my second orgy in weeks. I looked around to see if anyone else witnessed what I saw, but my gaze stopped on April as she and Danielle materialized from the woods. Her jaw dropped, and her eyes widened at the sight of Tristan groping her mistress. However, she went from wide-eyed to squinty glare quickly, and had she been a cartoon, there would've been a burst of steam shooting from her ears.

While April continued her jealousy, Danielle was oblivious. As they entered our site, Danielle towel-dried her hair and dabbed behind her ears. She looked a lot better. She was still hungover, but at least she was clean now. Her expression suggested she was still pissed at April for leaving her last night, and she broke away from her when they reached their tent. She went in and left April outside. She didn't get an invite, either, as Danielle zipped the doorway up and sealed April out.

Once Danielle was out of sight, April sauntered over to the topless sun worshippers and leaned down to whisper in Cece's ear. I didn't know what she said, but Cece was up and off her lounge chair in a flash.

April made eye contact with me before she led Cece into the woods and away from our camp. She had a huge set of balls the way she cuddled up to Cece with Danielle just yards away. And although Dani didn't see any of this, surely everyone else did. April was reckless, and maybe I wouldn't have to be the one to drop the ax on her after all.

I stood there in the middle of a sea of tents and looked around at everyone. Tristan still tried to get into the bikini bottoms of the sunbathers. Shady sat on Cookie's lap and shared a joint. Dorian and Dahlia cleaned up after breakfast, and Kylie sat at the picnic table playing cards with an already drunk Buckley. All these options, plenty of people to hang out with, and all I kept doing was glancing over at Danielle's tent. I knew I should've just stayed away from her, but I was drawn to her. I started to turn to walk away, but a greater force than me swung me back around, and before I knew it, I knelt in front of her tent. "Dani?"

"What?"

"Are you okay?"

"Not really."

"Can I get you something? Bread, some ginger ale?"

"No, thanks. I don't know if I can keep anything down today."

"Can I come in?" I was tired of speaking to the outside of the tent.

⁂

I heard the zipper come down, and the flap opened. I got on my knees and crawled inside. Danielle lay on her back on the air mattress with her eyes closed, and I started to sit next to her. But visions of April making out with Cece filled my head, and instinctively, I climbed on the bed with her. I took it one step further and slid on top of her. My body covered hers. Her eyes fluttered open as she felt the weight of me on her. She didn't tell me to get off her.

She didn't say anything at all. Her gaze locked with mine. She brought her hand up to my face and brushed the hair from my eyes as she caressed my cheek. She licked her lips in anticipation of our impending kiss, and then it happened. Our lips met, slow and soft at first. This was the first time we felt unrushed, and unconcerned, about being caught. It wasn't as if our situation had changed. In all fairness, April could've walked in on us at any point, but I didn't give a shit. This had been in the making for years. We tried to fend it off or wish it away. But it was meant to be. We were meant to be.

All nerves dissolved for both of us. Her lips were the missing piece to the puzzle that was my life, and fighting it was a struggle I was no longer willing to suffer. I put April on the back burner, instead of Danielle, and seduced her with smoothness and ease. It wasn't difficult. She'd been attracted to me for as long as I had been to her, no matter how comfortable *Friendsville* was. We meshed in a desire neither of us could deny anymore.

"Mmm," she hummed lightly in approval, and our kissing became more impassioned and heated. We breathed in unison, each breath heavier than the one before, until our bodies were compelled to move on each other. My hips thrust down on her while hers grinded up to meet mine. I heard people walking and talking as they passed the tent, but it wasn't enough to get us to stop.

The sounds of our kissing created a fire in my shorts, and each breath and each moan warranted my hips to move faster. I fucked her without a dick, but she didn't care as she grabbed my ass with both hands, directing my grind. From her lips, my mouth slid down and over her throat. I kissed the hollow of her neck and sucked on her tender flesh. We were being careless, but we seemed to throw caution to the wind as we got hotter and hotter. Our bodies smoldered, and before I could make my move, she rested her fingers on the edge of my shorts and pushed them down. "I want you," she whispered and licked my lobe as she dipped her tongue into my ear. She pulled my shorts down and took advantage while she squeezed my ass in the palm of her hand.

"Anybody seen Parker?" I heard Dorian. She was right by the tent, and we were startled free from each other as she scraped the outside of the tent with her fingernails. "Danielle?"

"Yes," Danielle answered while I scrambled to my feet and quickly pulled up my shorts.

"Where's Parker? We need more ice."

"Ice?" Danielle repeated. We looked at each other, read each other's minds, and she added, "We can go get ice."

"Parker's in there?" she probed and unzipped the flap. She poked her head inside the tent and studied us. "What are you two doing in here? Up to no good, are we?" A devilish grin overtook her face.

"Why? Do you want to join us?" I grabbed hold of her by the scruff of her T-shirt and pulled her all the way inside the tent. She practically fell in, and I could tell she had been drinking, too. She giggled and pushed me back onto the bed with Danielle. She was buzzed, for sure, because she dived headfirst on the bed and squirmed her way in between us, when normally her face would've turned beet red about being invited into a threesome. It was only when she got a little tuned up that she became so bold and willing to test the boundaries of her comfort zone.

"Dorian, why are you drinking? I thought you were trying to be good around Dahlia."

"Meh, Tristan's hittin' on her again." She shrugged.

"So that's it? Every time Tristan comes around, you just give up?" I didn't seek an answer and continued, "That's one hell of a copout! Tristan won't be the reason you lose her. Your insecurity will be." She buried her head in my shoulder and I kissed the top of her head. "Now cut it out! There's nothing wrong with you. You're way better than Tristan!"

"Am I?"

"Dorian," I lifted her head up, "Tristan has nothing to offer Dahlia except a romp in the hay." She shook her head, clearly not wanting to hear what I was saying. I grabbed hold of her and looked her in her eyes. "You have way more to offer than just sex. She obviously wants more than that. Talking on the phone with you for hours on end, making sure you had a first date, these aren't things a woman does if she only wants sex. The Tristans of the world come a dime a dozen. You're better than that!"

"You're a good friend, Parker."

"You always say that." I laughed.

"Because it's true. Thanks for saying all that. You always make me feel better." She spun onto her back, still in the middle of us, and turned to face Danielle.

"You know you belong with Parker, right?"

"Jesus, Dorian! You reek of alcohol! Exactly how much did you have to drink?" Dani waved her hand in front of her face and attempted to rid the air space of the stench of liquor.

"Regardless, do you hear me?"

Danielle looked across to me, and I just smiled. That smile that said *You know she's right!* Still no answer from Dani, Dorian offered, "You're already fucking, and I mean, dear Lord, there's been these pent-up feelings for each other for years. Why don't you just give in to it?"

Danielle rolled off the bed, brushed her hair, and pulled it back into a ponytail. Without ever responding to Dorian, she said, "Let's go get ice."

Dorian's laughter rippled through the tent at Danielle's snub of her observation. "You can ignore me all you want. You know I'm right!" Dorian got up from the bed and straightened herself up. "How do I look?"

I chuckled and raked my fingers through her hair. "There! Pretty as a picture! Now go out there and stake claim to your woman." She was halfway out of the tent when I added, "And, Dorian…"

"Yeah?" She swung her head around to meet me.

"Don't talk to any trees when you do."

"Right," she agreed and left us alone once more.

Chapter Fourteen

The silence was filled with an unmeasurable degree of longing. Fire smoldered in Danielle's gold-flecked, honey brown eyes, and I could feel her desire for me. The harder she tried to ignore the truth, the more it persisted. She knew Dorian was right, even if she didn't say it out loud. Her fingertips grazed over my bottom lip, and instinctively, I kissed them and dragged my own cheek against the palm of her hand. "I don't want to talk. I just want to be with you," she confessed.

"We can't…at least not here." I looked around the tent, and all signs of April's presence stared me in the face. The thought of her walking in on us wasn't pleasant, either.

"Let's go get ice," she said, but the tone of her voice suggested more than buying ice, and I wasn't strong enough to stop it. And after what I witnessed with April last night, I didn't care.

"Let's go," I concurred.

꧁꧂

The road was long and winding and lined with thick woods on either side. There wasn't a house or a store for miles. Definitely not the state park we started out at this weekend. There was more life there for sure.

As I drove, Danielle shimmied next to me and rested her head on my shoulder. Her hand caressed my thigh, and I felt her warm breath on my neck before she planted a few small pecks there. My concentration was shaken, and staying on the road became a difficult task. She teased the shit out of me, and I was about to put an end to that. While we careened down the street, small trails appeared in between the trees. I veered off onto one of them. She didn't question my decision because she knew exactly what my intentions were. I couldn't come to a halt fast enough, and the minute I threw the gear in park, we both raced to the rear, lowered the backseats, and crafted a makeshift bed.

The prolonged anticipation was almost unbearable, and the sense of urgency drove us to cling to each other immediately. She kissed me just as urgently, no longer slow and soft, but forceful and ravenous. She was as eager and erratic as a summer storm, as she ached for me to touch her. I returned her kiss with reckless abandon and a savage intensity. My heart pounded wildly as her mouth descended over my neck and kissed the pulsing hollow at the base of my throat. The heady sensation she evoked was like being drugged, and I lost all self-control.

My breath came in long, surrendering moans as she drew the skin of my neck into her mouth, clamped down, and sucked harshly. "Oh, yeah," I drew out. She lifted my T-shirt up enough to place her hands on my skin. Her touch set my body aflame with divine ecstasy. There was no disguising my body's reaction, and my hips involuntarily moved toward her. The full weight of her body rested on mine, and I was surprised at her brazenness as she kicked my legs open with her knee.

I never let anyone take control, but I surrendered completely to her masterful seduction.

Her lips, her mouth, and her hands possessed me in a way no one ever had. It was almost as if I had been waiting, saving myself for her, yet having no idea how aggressive she would be. My fantasies had basically been about me touching her. I knew precisely how I would, but I never imagined for one second that she could be a top. I preferred being the top, but with Danielle, I felt comfortable being the bottom if that was what she wanted. The only real preference was satisfying her in whatever way she wanted, and right now, she had my legs spread eagle as she thrusted her groin on mine. "We don't have much time," I said.

"You're right! We don't!" She ripped off my shorts in a hurry and tossed my panties to the front seat. I was busy pushing her shorts down, too. Our T-shirts were left on, but we hiked each other's bras up, over our breasts, and exposed them enough to fondle and suck on them. She dangled her tits over my face as she teased me a little before she sank one into my awaiting mouth. Short but heavy breaths escaped her lips as her arousal intensified. Her deep breathing accompanied soft moans when she leaned down to devour my nipples one at a time while my hands gently twisted and pinched hers. Deciding that foreplay was over, she rushed to shift positions. She climbed on top of me and positioned her pussy over top of mine.

She took my leg and forced it over as she spread me open like a pair of scissors. We were both soaking wet, and she opened her pussy lips with her fingers. I did the same. She slowly slid her clit directly over mine, back and forth, and the sensation drove me wild. Not because I never tribbed or scissored, but because I've never done that with Danielle.

"I never get to do this," she whispered in my ear.

Feeling her clit rubbing on mine compelled me to grab her ass and aid her in her motion. I controlled the rhythm by rocking with her, and our moans were only overshadowed by the wet, smacking sound of our pussies snapping together. She steadied herself by holding me down, one hand in front pressing one leg down, and the other behind her, keeping my other leg pinned to the floor. She had me straddled and immobilized, while she had her way with me. I gasped in sweet agony as the real world spun and turned on its axis outside of the car. There was no controlling the waves of pure bliss that throbbed through both of us. She rode me fast and furious now, as she found a tempo that bound our bodies together. Her raw act of possession ended in the flooding of undeniable joy when she cried out, "Oh, God! Oh, yeah!" She collapsed on top of me, and her head leaned on mine. "You didn't cum." She was disappointed.

"It's okay."

"No, it's not."

"It's not?"

"No. It's not complete. I want you to cum."

"We don't have time to keep going. We still have to get the damn ice."

"I don't give a shit about the damn ice!"

"Okay, truck driver Joe with that foul mouth!"

She wasn't taking no for an answer, and her fingers penetrated me, eliciting a groan of approval. "Do you like that?" she asked softly in my ear.

"Yes." I lifted my hips to meet the thrust of her two slender fingers inside of me. She slid in and out of my wetness, which had now become a puddle for her. Having a dream that was over a decade long come to fruition was almost unbelievable.

To feel her inside of me and to know it wasn't just another one of my fantasies was surreal. She fucked me harder now, each thrust a reminder that it was really her. "I want you to cum for me," she demanded sweetly. But even though her voice was soft, her fingers were hard.

She pushed into me deliberately and begged me to climax. "Oh, Dani." I was almost there. "Faster, baby." She was willing to do whatever it took for me to get there. Hearing her pound my center threw me over the edge, and then, "Oh, yes! Oh, yes!"

"Yes! Yes!" she sang along with me as I wailed out my pleasure.

What felt like the longest orgasm I'd ever had ended with me gasping for breath, completely spent. I pulled her close to me. There was no pulling away. There was no guilt. There was no mistake. Not this time. She didn't give a rat's ass as to where April was or how long we had been gone. No, she relaxed her body on me and peacefully laid her head on my chest.

"You know we have to go, right?" I didn't want her to lose track of time.

"Just a few more minutes," she mumbled into my chest.

Time was a bitch! Always with her, time was a bitch. But I gave her the few minutes she requested and caressed the soft skin of her back. I gently grazed over her flesh and lingered on her buttocks. "You feel so good," she confessed. "I don't want it to end."

I knew she already knew how I felt about her, had for years, but I had never said the words out loud.

Each time I opened my mouth to say it, I forced it shut. I felt like if I said it, I'd only hear about how she was marrying April. Honestly, I was tired of making her choose between me and April, and I realized this was the route I took since this started. Maybe it was time for a new approach. Obviously, I would've liked nothing more than for Danielle to be with me. Letting her know April's evil plan may have shifted that decision into my favor, but damn April for intimidating me with threats to Dani's life. Even if I did tell Danielle about all of this, she wouldn't believe her dear April was so sinister. April's threat was warranted, and she knew she shoved an invisible gag down my throat.

However, what April didn't know wouldn't hurt her. In that moment, I decided I would let Danielle have her cake and eat it, too. Being morally shaken had ceased. Never would I have suspected April of not only being a cheat, but also a downright thief and a possible murderer. This was a woman who had a six-figure salary. She didn't need money. Why she felt she needed to wish death on Danielle's father and steal half of her inheritance was beyond me. My loyalty was with Dani, and even though she didn't know it, I had to stop their wedding from happening one way or another. Somehow, I had to shed light on the real April as despicable as she was.

Before we got dressed, I asked, "Uh, when we started, ya know, fooling around, you said you never get to do that. Can I ask why?"

Danielle knew exactly what I was talking about. "She doesn't let me," she simply said.

"What?" I thought this was absolutely ridiculous. "Why not?"

"I don't know. She says she doesn't get it."

"Get what?"

"Doesn't get the appeal. Says it's too much work, and it doesn't feel as good as my tongue."

"All right. I didn't need to hear all that."

"You asked." I dummied up because that was true and continued listening to her. "I can't even tell you the last time she let me do that. She seems to be turned off by it."

"Turned off by you rubbing your pretty pussy on her? There's something wrong with her. I'd let you do that all day, every day," I confessed. "You are so beautiful, Danielle. She should let you do whatever turns you on. What a foolish woman!"

✦ ✦ ✦ ✦

When we returned with ice, the girls were having a softball catch. Cookie ran up to the SUV and helped me carry the bags of ice. She greeted Danielle with a "Hi." Cookie must have been drunk. It was almost as if the Earth went off its tilt and the planets shifted out of alignment. Cookie and Danielle courteous to each other?

"How are things going with Shady? You've been inseparable since she arrived," I probed.

"I'm trying not to get my hopes up. I mean, she and her girlfriend haven't been broken up for more than two or three weeks, and I'm pretty sure she's been trying to get back with Shady. Just a..." She looked over to Shady, who smiled and laughed with Buckley. "Just trying to keep my fuckin' heart in check. I don't think I could take being hurt by her again. It's bad enough the first fucking time was like having her reach into my chest, tear out my heart, and stomp on it repeatedly. And after she fuckin' stomped on it, she picked it up, and threw it at the fuckin' wall!"

"Well, you do paint quite a picture, don't you?" I snickered.

"Forget me! What's going on with little Miss Muffet? I notice April getting awfully chummy with Cece. What's up with that?"

I looked around, not wanting anyone in earshot, and noticed Danielle talking with Dorian and Dahlia. "Cookie, I gotta tell you what happened last night."

"What happened?"

"Hey!" Sherri interrupted and squashed my second attempt to tell Cookie about April. "I've got this fat-ass blunt, Cookie! C'mon, let's go smoke it!"

Cookie glanced at me with her piercing blue eyes to let me know she was sorry, and Sherri pulled her away. *Damn it!* Foiled again. I stood at the Tahoe alone now and was about to close the driver's door, when out of nowhere, April appeared as I closed it. A look of hatred loomed from her eyes, and my glare displayed the same. I kept rehashing what she said as she waited for Danielle's father's demise, all for the sake of money. I would have sworn April would have died for Dani. She was a chameleon who disguised herself as a decent person and was damn good at it because none of us would have thought any other way.

"Keeping your mouth shut, I hope?" she snapped.

"Maybe," I rumbled back.

"You better!"

"You wouldn't dare do what you said you would."

"Do you really want to wager Danielle's life? I'll make sure you never see her again," she threatened. "I'll make sure no one sees her again. She'll never believe you, anyway."

"You seem pretty sure of that, yet you seem quite shaken even thinking of me telling her." I closed the car door. "When did you become so slimy?"

"Fuck you, Parker!"

"No! Fuck you, April! If you think I'm gonna let you fuck Danielle over like that, you've got another thing coming!" My face turned beet red, and my insides were shaking. It took everything I had not to punch her in the face.

"Don't push me." She gritted her teeth as she turned and walked away.

She walked up to Danielle, who was still talking with Dorian and Dahlia. April slid her arm around Danielle's shoulder. Danielle's face instantly changed to disgust. She shook her arm off her, and it became clearer that there was division between them. Danielle apparently wasn't over the fact that April left her alone last night in the condition she was in. Forgiveness was not on the menu today, and April knew it.

Although Dani and I didn't have sex again on the camping trip, she didn't let me out of her sight. It became her mission to make sure Kylie and I didn't hook up that final night, and when Kylie attempted to visit my tent later, I blew her off. She didn't understand why, and I didn't blame her for not buying my excuse. Headaches were worn out and old, but she took the hint and slept in the Taj Mahal for the second night. I felt bad, and I meant what I said when I cut Danielle off, but with the revelation of April's affair, I wanted Danielle more than ever.

The camping trip ended with several new tidbits of information gained. Dorian and Dahlia had made it official. They were a bona fide couple. Cookie and Shady were trying to work it out. Kylie stopped talking to me altogether, and that was fine. I only chased one woman in my life. But the capper of the entire weekend happened Tuesday night. I received a text from Danielle. She told me that April didn't want her to be friends with me anymore. When I asked why, she said April didn't trust me, that she thought I still had the hots for her. She wanted Dani to stay away from me, but some bonds couldn't be broken.

April made sure we didn't see each other for a few weeks, and it caused more than one fight between them. Danielle would text me from her office and delete it by the time she got home. Being between a rock and a hard place wasn't a pleasant place for me, but not seeing or hearing from each other was something we weren't going to let happen. If nothing else, April had set in motion resentment that she never could have imagined. Danielle resented the control and the jealousy. And she surely resented the interference.

Even though we exchanged texts and got to talk a few times, I missed her. April threw a damper on our usual routine. There were no more Thursday morning runs, no more Sunday morning chess games, no more parties, and Rays games were out of the question. I guess I would feel ten times more depressed if Danielle didn't really want to see or hear from me, but she did. So I held on to that. "When can I see you?" I asked during one of our stolen conversations.

"I don't know. She hasn't even been away on business recently, and I think she's doing it on purpose, making sure I don't see you." She took a deep breath and sighed. "I miss you."

It was true April hadn't been away like she usually was. It was slowly killing me, April getting her way. And her awful secret was still on the tip of my tongue with no one to tell. Dorian had been holed up with Dahlia since we got back from camping. Cookie was busy trying to rekindle a relationship she felt was stolen from her so long ago. There was no one to tell, and quite frankly, it made me nuts.

Chapter Fifteen

I took a late morning ride to Merge to examine and inspect the progress. It had been nearly two months since reconstruction had started, and Jeff had told me it would be another four weeks before the place was up and running. Because it was Sunday, workers weren't there, and I crept through the front door. I didn't know why. It wasn't like I hadn't been in and out of the building since the project began. Not everything was in shambles. At least it was beginning to look more like a bar again.

The cracked foundation had been repaired, and hardwood flooring had been laid. The rafters were repaired, and everything was sealed in with drywall and a fresh ceiling. The windows were reframed and replaced, but the Sheetrock hadn't been completed yet. I had a fresh canvas to work with, and I was glad I chose to go with two bars. I had them placed catty-corner to each other. I could now shut Michelle up about having lost Saturday nights to Simone. They would have their own bar and wouldn't have to share tips. Simone would probably still find something to bitch about when it came to her, but at least it wouldn't be about this stuff anymore. I was still excitedly waiting for my custom-made billiards table to arrive.

I filed through the double doors and strolled down the corridor until I was in my office and seated behind my desk. I spun around in the chair a few times because it amused me, and when I came to a stop, I faced the love seats and coffee table, the chessboard, and all the pieces that were still in their usual positions. I felt pretty bummed that I hadn't seen Danielle, and I was pissed off at April for it. As I grappled with the idea of what happened to us, my cellphone vibrated in my pocket. I was thrilled to see it was a text from Danielle. Maybe I thought her up.

Hi. I'm texting from the bathroom and have to be quick. She's going to Houston tomorrow on business. I have a couple morning classes and I'll be by. Can't wait to see you! Gotta go!

I didn't text her back. No need to, and I didn't want to chance that April might see it. But my lips did curl into a genuine smile, and my heart fluttered to the sky. She had just made my day. I was satisfied and got up to leave. When I opened the door, I almost jumped out of my own skin. "Holy crap!" I yelled and clutched my chest.

"It's only me! You're awfully jumpy." Simone popped out of nowhere.

"You scared the piss out of me!"

"Oh, God, I hope not!" She pushed me back into the office. "I happened to be driving by. Gus has a job right down the street. I drive by all the time because I miss the place…and the things that used to happen in here." She winked at me. "What are you doing here, anyway? I didn't expect to see your bike outside when I drove past. Figured I'd stop and say hi."

She had backed me into one of the love seats, and I fell backward onto it. "I didn't have much to do today, so I figured I'd stop in and check on the place," I answered, though she wasn't listening. Her mind was elsewhere, which meant on my pussy. She knelt between my legs, and her hands were on my zipper at the speed of light. She yanked it down, and I knew where she was headed. For the first time ever, I said, "No, Simone."

"What?" She snapped her head up at me. "You never say no, and when you try to, I'm always able to change your mind." She ignored my refusal and pulled at my pants as she tried to take them down. I took her hands in mine and brought her attention from my crotch to my face. "No, Simone. Not tonight, okay?" I pulled my jeans back up and zipped them.

"I don't understand, Parker. I haven't seen or heard from you in weeks. I need it." She cupped my pussy through my pants.

"I just have a lot on my mind right now. I can't concentrate on that. I'm sorry."

"You suck!" She bumped into the coffee table, which forced the pieces to knock together and slightly shift. She picked one of the pieces up, studied it, and looked at me. "Is she the reason why?"

"What are you talking about?"

"I was at a Muff Masher game the other night. Overheard Cece telling Sherri that you're having an affair with her."

How did she find out? The only people who knew were Cookie and Dorian, and they would never betray my trust.

"Where did she get an idea like that? That's absurd!"

"She said April told her. Sounded pretty pissed, too, from what I understand."

April was making shit up now and projected her own affair as mine. Was this her cover? "Don't believe everything you hear, Simone," I warned and turned her toward the door.

"I can't believe you won't let me," she bitched, and I continued to propel her down the hall, through the double doors, and out the entrance to the bar.

I locked the doors and turned to her. "I'll call you." I didn't wait for her response as I threw my leg over my bike, started the engine, and rode off down the street.

There was nothing for me to feel bad about. Our fling was less than superficial, and all I really wanted to do was see Danielle. It was with Danielle that I felt most alive. It was with Danielle that I felt complete. This was it for me. I was either going to be with Danielle, or I would never fall in love again. It was that simple. There was no one else on this Earth more suited for me. I knew our backgrounds were completely opposite and we were raised very differently, but we were so naturally comfortable together that we finished each other's sentences. I didn't think we'd ever spent this much time away from each other. It was hard to contain my excitement as I knew we would be together tomorrow. I spent the rest of my day giddy with thoughts of her.

❧ ❧ ❧ ❧

The next day, I patiently waited for Danielle's arrival. I tried to pass time as I sucked my tongue piercing through the tiny gap between my two front teeth. Addie was just as excited. She felt my energy while she stood at attention at the front door and wagged her tail. Her sense was keen, no doubt.

Danielle pulled up in her Beemer. The convertible top was down, and she stepped out in a hurry, unconcerned with locking the doors. She wore a skirt suit and heels, and I knew she came straight from class. I opened the door and watched her through the storm door. As she sauntered up the walkway, much to my surprise, she was already unbuttoning her suit jacket and taking her hair down. She was smoking hot, and she knew it! By the time she reached the door, her blouse was unbuttoned. I opened the storm door, and she forced me back into the house before I could even say hello. There wasn't any greeting or even a smile that suggested she was happy to see me. I only knew how happy she was by the taste of her tongue in my mouth. She was making up for lost time, and three weeks' worth of sexual build-up was about to erupt and explode between us.

We made out the entire way to my bedroom. Pushing me onto the bed, she proceeded to finish undressing in front of me. Her craving was evident as she climbed on the bed and laid her naked body on me. She grazed her mouth all over mine before she separated my lips and poked her tongue inside. "Mmm," she murmured. "I've missed you so much."

Frantically, she pulled my T-shirt over my head, but she pulled it off inside out, and the collar caught the top of my open mouth. She tugged at it, and I couldn't get unstuck from my shirt. My mouth was being stretched, and she didn't understand until I yelped, "Ow! Ow! Ow!"

"Oh, no! I'm so sorry!" she apologized as she realized she was about to rip my head off.

It was just enough to break the tension. Not that the sexual tension wasn't fabulous, but I think in that moment we recognized there was no rush. No rush and no guilt. Certainly not on my part, and from the look of it, not on hers, either. April's threats of keeping us apart had backfired. We giggled at the small T-shirt mishap, and things slowed down. The entire day belonged to us, and we were about to enjoy each other's bodies several times that afternoon.

Once Danielle had me out of my clothes, she pressed herself to me, her flesh burned hot against mine. Any more heat between us, and my house would be engulfed in flames. Her lips kissed their way down to my neck, and without inhibitions, she inhaled the scent of me and clamped her mouth on my throat. She sucked so hard it became painful, but it was a good kind of pain. I didn't want her to stop and would be completely content if she left bruises. I was hers, and she knew it. My cries reverberated through the room, and the more I moaned and hummed with pleasure, the more excited she became. She had so naturally slid her body between my legs, and her pelvis uncontrollably grinded into mine. If she had a dick, I believed she would've fucked me right through the wall and into the next room. My pussy throbbed with each thrust from her. "Uh...ooh, I want to do it to you." She grunted and waited for my approval.

"Do it. Take it." I allowed her to do whatever she wanted.

She positioned her legs like a pair of scissors over top and in between my thighs. With her hands wrapped around my leg, she held on to it above her shoulder. She rubbed her pussy over mine and slid back and forth. "Oh, yeah," she purred. She stopped momentarily to open her pussy lips farther and pressed her clit directly onto mine. Our erect, pulsating pearls rubbed together, which prompted a series of moans and groans. Her thrusts were deliberate, and she slid back as if she were winding up to jerk forward. She knew what she was doing, and she was good at it.

We were both so wet as our pussies clapped together. I couldn't get close enough to her, and she sensed this. She changed positions and placed herself between my legs. She grabbed me by my bent knees, opened my legs as wide as they could go, and pushed them back almost to my ears. She squatted over my very exposed slit and began grinding her clit on mine again. We were face to face now, and the connection our eyes made was deep and electrifying. I didn't think I was capable of orgasming like this but, "Oh! Oh, God! Oh, Danielle!" I impulsively grabbed her chunky ass and assisted her in rocking back and forth on me. My body went limp, my eyes closed, and all I felt were baby kisses all over my face, my ears, and my shoulders.

"I've never cum like that." I huffed and puffed as I tried to catch my breath. "You're really good at that. Um, why doesn't she let you do it again?"

"Because she's a foolish woman," she replied while she slithered up my body.

"Where do you think you're going?"

"I'm going to get mine." She chuckled and straddled my face. She positioned herself just right and spread her pink folds around my mouth. I inserted my tongue and lapped up her dripping arousal, which was filled with excessive desire. She rode my tongue piercing like a champ. The taste of her was so enticing, but I could not quench my thirst, not on her first orgasm, second, or third. Our energy level was second to none as we desperately attempted to make up for nearly twenty years. We could not get enough of each other. We rolled from one end of the bed to the other, half wrestling, half dominating, and neither caring which role we played.

Our afternoon was spent in my bed as we feasted on each other. Sex with Danielle was amazing, exceeded my expectations and fantasies, and pivoted me into a reality I could easily get used to. Although the sex was hot and we clicked in a way only the two of us could, the intimacy we shared after each climax was even more special. As I blanketed her with my love, she nestled into my arms. Her eyelids were heavy, and she was asleep in minutes. I admired her while she lay in dreamland. Her long eyelashes fluttered, and she stirred for a moment before settling back into a sex-induced nap. How in the world had we not ended up with each other after all this time? No matter what pulled her away from me, she always found her way back, almost steered in my direction from an unseen force. Her allure was bewitching, and like a drug, I had been hooked for years.

I brushed the hair from her angelic face and caressed the satiny skin of her shoulder and arm, which sent her into an even deeper slumber. Her muffled and incoherent sleep talking only made her that much more endearing to me. I was incredibly in love with her.

❧❧❧❧

I peeled myself away from Danielle after my arm fell asleep and Addie needed to go out. Before I left the room, I took one last glimpse at her as she lay there naked and peaceful. Slipping into a pair of shorts and a T-shirt, I closed the door gently and tiptoed away from the bedroom to the back slider.

Addie bolted out the door and ran for her favorite spot to pee. I checked my cellphone for any missed calls or texts because when I was with Danielle, God could call and I wouldn't answer. Not only did I miss a call from Cookie, but I was thrown for a loop when I saw a text from Kylie. I was sure she was finished with me after I basically kicked her out of my tent for Danielle. The text said she wanted to see me and asked if we could get together soon. I felt like I should because of how we left things. I did feel bad about it, but ultimately, Danielle came first in my life. She always had, regardless of whether we were friends or more.

"Where did you go? It was trippy waking up by myself. I was a little discombobulated." Danielle startled the shit out of me.

"I wasn't tired, and you were sleeping so soundly. I didn't want to disturb you."

She saw the phone in my hand. "Crap! I haven't checked my phone for hours." As she dug through her pocketbook in search of her cell, she added, "I need to go home. JoJo is overdue to go outside."

"When is April coming home?"

"Not for a few days. Why?"

"Well, I was thinking. Why go home to be alone? Why don't you go get JoJo and pack a bag? Stay with me for a couple of nights."

"Yeah?"

I grabbed her by the waist, pulled her to me, and planted a kiss on her lips in hopes of coaxing her to stay. "Stay with me," I whispered into her ear. I pinched her ass cheeks; my appetite for her was undying.

So, Danielle and I played house for a couple of days. It wasn't a big deal. Was it? A split reality, a double life, and an affair of grand magnitude took place with my best friend. I would crush *Friendsville* with my own hands. It would die while I tightened the albatross around its pathetic little neck. It was pleasant and comfortable having her here in my home. I lived on my own for a long time, and one might think she would be in my way or be a pain in the ass, but no, I thoroughly enjoyed her. She seemed just as content, and she and JoJo settled in nicely.

For two straight days, when she wasn't at the university, she was busy fucking me. If she wasn't in a suit, she was naked. It was all fun and games as we discovered what made each other tick on a sexual level. Tribbing was at the top of her preference list, and just knowing that April was turned off by it turned me on even more. I let Danielle do it as often and as regularly as she damn well pleased.

The day April was to arrive home, we awoke in the morning and began our routines right away. Danielle went for the shower, and I went for the coffeemaker. Funny how I had been able to sleep at night since she had been here. Growing up the way I did, nighttime wasn't a time to sleep. But with her arms wrapped firmly around me, I even slept with both eyes closed. That had never happened, either. She was my rock. She just didn't know it.

While the coffee brewed, I let the dogs out back, and as I watched them, they sniffed their way behind the shed. They didn't come back right away, and I thought that was odd. I scratched my head and pursed my lips to one side. *What are these dogs up to?* Now they were barking, and curiosity got the best of me. Once I headed in the direction of the shed, barking had been swapped out for growling, and I couldn't get there fast enough. I hightailed it around the shed, and at first, I wasn't sure what was going on.

They were fighting over something, each chomped down, and played tug of war. I was terrified it was a wounded animal they were gnawing at until I realized what it was. A damned dildo! I couldn't believe it took them this long to find it, but those crazy bitches from my insanely wild pool party apparently left behind one of their toys. Each dog had a death grip on either end of this hunk of rubber, lockjawed, and neither about to give up the struggle for possession. I reached and grabbed in an attempt to dislodge the filthy thing from their mouths, but JoJo gave one final tug and took off in the yard with it. I threw my hands in the air, frustrated at my near grab, and took off running after him. However, chasing him was like an asthmatic smoker chasing an ice cream truck. It wasn't gonna happen.

As this spectacle unfolded, I heard my bathroom window raise and Danielle asked, "What exactly am I watching?" There was no time to explain, and later, I realized I must have looked like a comedy show as I ran back and forth after a dog that clearly wasn't going to let me catch him. Like any dog, though, he finally dropped the thing from his jowls and chomped on the treat I offered him instead. I could have saved one of my lungs had I figured it out sooner.

Danielle's first words were, "Eww," when I brought the nasty chewed-up rubber cock inside the house. Then she asked, "Is that Molly?" A knowing grin spread across her face, and her dimples deepened as she did. We both cracked up laughing, and after making several jokes about it, I tossed it into the trash.

Having run around the yard like a lunatic after a dog with a dildo in his mouth, I never noticed what Dani was wearing when she got out of the shower. Once our laughter subsided, I noted that she was dressed in a USF Bulls T-shirt and nothing else. Her backside was to me while she fixed her coffee, and the only thing I seemed to be able to zone in on was that ass. That round, chunky little ass. Before I knew it, I was on my knees with my nose shoved in her crack. I slid my tongue between her slit, seeking out her little jewel and feasted on it.

My face was buried in her ass, and she quietly continued making her coffee. The more she ignored what I was doing, the more aroused I became. My tongue salivated inside of her; it mixed with her own cream and juices and created a lapping sound. It may be crazy, but I'd compared the sound of a woman's wetness to the sound of mixing a can of paint, that sticky sound. It was such a turn-on for me that I let out a moan of hunger. "Mmm," I muttered into her pussy. My tongue was on a mission to bring her to her apex of pleasure and ecstasy. She still was not making a peep, but I knew I had aroused her when she set the creamer down and gripped the counter.

I cupped her meaty cheeks, spread them apart, and sank my face deeper inside of her. Her cum soaked my chin as I licked her clit into a frenzy of sexual heat. I dragged my tongue from her clit and poked her hole as I licked upward and dipped it into her asshole. This finally elicited some heavy breathing. She held in her cries for now, but I would not be denied. She would be screaming my praises when she came all over my face. And that was precisely what happened.

She could no longer tolerate the tongue lashing and whipping her clit received. She let out a cry I had never heard. A high-pitched howl trembled out of her throat as she screamed, "Oh, Parker! Oh, Parker! Yes! Yes!"

Her hand reached behind her and held my head in place. She pushed my face into her pussy as she expelled the last of her sticky wetness into my mouth. "Oh, God!" She slumped over the counter and buried her face in her folded arms. I was still on my knees while my own clit pulsated and throbbed for release. Tender and gentle, I kissed and lightly bit her tight, plump bottom before I rose from the floor. She turned in my arms to face me. I had her pinned to the kitchen counter, and she looked at me in a way I had never seen. Her arms encircled my neck, and she kissed me hard. She thanked me without words. Everything she wanted to say was in that kiss.

Years' worth of affection culminated in that moment, and I fell in love with her all over again. The kissing ended, and we just stood there in each other's arms. She smelled clean of shower gels and shampoo. Her hair was still wet and clung to her face sporadically, curled and matted to her cheek. I peeled the strands away, and her focus was back on my eyes. "I'm sorry I have to go. I can't lie. I've had a really great time," she offered. "I had no idea you were capable of making me feel like this."

"Like what?"

"I can't explain."

"Well, try."

"I have to go." She left me hanging once more.

"I wish I had time to return the favor, but I'm already running late." She smiled and sauntered off to the bedroom to change. I watched her ass jiggle all the way there until she disappeared into my room.

When she returned, she was dressed for work and ready to go. Her hair was dried now and pulled back into a tight, neat ponytail. With her attaché case in one hand and a cup of coffee in the other, she kissed me and walked out the door with JoJo in tow. It was going to be a long day for her. She had to stop at home to drop off the dog, race to class, teach all day, and eventually pick up April from the airport. These last few days had been like living a dream, only to have it turn into a nightmare that ended with April's smug face. We didn't discuss when we would see each other next because we truly didn't know. After fighting the urges we had toward each other, we gave up the fight and instead began an intense affair. I didn't want to be her mistress, her sidekick, but that was what I became.

April didn't go away for two more weeks. It was tough not seeing Danielle, but we made the best of it as we sent text messages when we knew we could and talked on the phone while Danielle was at the school on weekdays. I hated that our routine had been severed by April. She had Danielle under lock and key, and there wasn't a damn thing I could do about it. She was going to have to come to the conclusion that April was rotten all on her own or somehow with a little help from my friends. Friends who still didn't know what happened.

I had two choices: Dorian or Cookie. Cookie couldn't stand Danielle, so there was no use for me to tell her. She would just see it as juicy gossip, instead of the serious threat it was. Cookie's response would be, "Danielle's cheating, too. Minus the inheritance robbing, they're both doing wrong. And April's just making bogus threats on Dani's life. I don't believe she would do something like that. She's trying to scare you." Even if Cookie were willing to help me, Dani would never believe her. Dorian was my only hope, and she was going to be disappointed in both of us for continuing our affair, but I thought she would be so appalled at April that maybe she would be inclined to say something.

⁂

It was time for Dorian to come out of her hideaway with Dahlia. She needed to resurface. So we made plans to have dinner together tonight. Just some pizza, beer, and conversation between two friends who hadn't seen or spoken to each other since the camping trip.

She arrived at my house around seven o'clock in the evening, outfitted in sweatpants, T-shirt, and sneakers. "You look like a slob." I laughed and let her through the front door.

"Stop laughing! I've been in a suit all day, and I haven't done laundry in weeks."

"I can't imagine why. Maybe if you two would leave the bedroom for more than just food, you could get some things done."

I cracked open a beer and handed it to her. I was happy to see my friend. After catching up with her and hearing how well things were going between the lovebirds, there was a small lull in our conversation. I wanted to bring it up. I didn't know how, though. "What is it, Parker? You clearly want to tell me something." She took a big bite of her slice of pizza. "Did you and Danielle end whatever it was you had going on?" We made eye contact, and nothing would come out of my mouth. "Never mind. I see the answer on your face. What are you doing?"

"I don't fucking know anymore, but—"

"No buts. She's supposed to be in a committed relationship with someone else."

"Dorian, I know, but—"

"Listen, no one would have liked for you two to have been together more than me, but it didn't happen."

"Dorian."

"I mean, I thought it was going to happen back when her mom died, but once again, it didn't."

"Can I get a word in?" I proposed.

"Seriously, Parker, you need to end it."

"Seriously, Dorian, will you shut the fuck up and listen for sixty seconds?" I was frustrated with her constant interruption.

"Oh, my! Must be serious."

"It is!"

"Okay, okay. I'll shut up. Shoot!" She chewed on another mouthful of pizza.

"When we were on the camping trip and looking for Danielle the night she got drunk, I ran into April and Cece at the playground. They were making out."

She nearly choked on her pizza. "What? No way!" She was in disbelief and set her plate down to give me her full attention.

"Way! That's not the half of it, though. Before I caught them kissing, I overheard April's plans for after the wedding. After marrying Danielle, she intends to wait for Dani's dad to pass away from the cancer.

Once he does, April is going to divorce her and take half of her inheritance."

Dorian's jaw dropped at hearing that, and her eyes got as big as half dollars. "No fucking way." She found it hard to wrap her head around.

"Way, and when she saw she was caught, she told me if I said anything to Danielle that she wouldn't believe me, anyway. That because I've liked her for so long, she'll just think I'm trying to get with her by making shit up about April." She was about to speak, but I cut her short. "It gets worse. April nearly strangled me to death before she threatened Danielle's life if I tell her."

Dorian let the air out of her lungs in a huff. She seemed to understand that April had me, metaphorically, by the throat. "Wow! That's a lot to take in."

"Oh, and she forbade Danielle from seeing me anymore. She told her she didn't trust me."

"What? Well, how's that supposed to work? You guys are friends, or you were friends, or...or I don't know what the hell you are anymore." She shook her head, confused at Danielle's and my new situation.

I sucked my tongue piercing a few times before I confessed, "Since April forbad her from seeing me, we've been seeing each other when she's away on business. I guess you could say we're having an affair."

"Oh, you're on fire tonight! Anything else you want to tell me? Anything you left out?"

"Well..."

"You're kidding! What else?"

"I want you to tell Danielle."

Her head snapped back a little. "Tell her what, Parker? That her fiancée is cheating on her and has a diabolical plan to steal her impending inheritance?"

"Yes."

"You're crazy!" she asserted loudly and threw her hands in the air.

"Why am I crazy? She'll believe you."

"Maybe she will, maybe she won't, but do you really want to chance April actually going through with her threat to kill Danielle?"

"But..."

"Parker, no. I can't get involved. She's going to have to see it for herself." She took a swig of beer. "I couldn't live with myself if something happened to her because I said something. Either way, you should stop this affair with Dani."

"I'm not giving her up," I said firmly. "There's no going back, Dorian. I'm in love with her more than ever."

"Pssh...I don't know what to tell you, my friend. I don't think any good can come of this affair. I just don't want either of you to get hurt." I knew Dorian was being sincere, and I realized she only wanted what was best for both of us, but the wheels had been set in motion, and there was no stopping it now.

After an hour of discussion, we moved on to a different topic—Dahlia, of course. Dahlia was a good influence on her, and she told me she even slowed down on the drinking. Hard liquor seemed to be the culprit in her odd drunken behavior, so she switched to just beer. "The thing of it is, the more time we spend together, the more I don't even want to drink. It's almost like I don't need it anymore." She only had one beer with her meal and drank water the rest of the evening before she called it a night. That had never happened. I was impressed.

Dorian stood at the front door and held Addie in her arms. "Whatever happens, know that I'm here." She gave Addie a kiss, set her down, and warned, "But whatever you do, Parker, don't tell Danielle. The thought of April's threats is frightening. I don't trust her, and neither should you." She gave me a reassuring hug and turned to walk out the door.

Chapter Sixteen

uring the two weeks Danielle and I didn't see each other, I prepared for Merge's reopening. The renovation was almost finished. We were still waiting on the delivery of my much-anticipated billiards table. A few other touch-ups, and I would be back in business. I couldn't wait. Filling my time had been rough. Sure, I had things to break up the monotony of life like the camping trip and a little thing called an affair, but I was ready to get back to work.

When our hiatus from each other was about to come to an end, April's business trip was postponed two more days. We were devastated. We were so proud of ourselves for the self-restraint we displayed in waiting. However, our patience had worn thin. "I want to see you," Danielle demanded on the phone from her office.

"How? We can wait a couple more days, can't we?"

"But I don't want to wait. I was supposed to see you tomorrow." She lowered her voice as though someone was in the room. "My pussy is aching to feel you."

"Mmm," I responded with an instant image of when I went down her.

"I think you should swap cars with Dorian and come see me tonight."

"What? Come see you where?"

"I don't know. I'll say I'm taking JoJo for a walk, and you can meet me at the end of the block."

"Awfully risky, isn't it?"

"What, not up for a bit of danger and excitement? The thrill of trying to get away with it?" she said.

"Who are you and what did you do with Danielle?"

She laughed that cute laugh of hers. "I can't help it. You bring out the bad in me."

"I don't know if that's the answer I was looking for."

"I don't mean it that way. I mean, I feel uninhibited around you. I don't have to...I don't know. I don't have to change who I am around you, and I like that."

"That's a little better." I snickered.

"Better enough to go get Dorian's Tahoe?"

"Call me when you want me," I replied and hung up. I ended the call absolutely giddy about our secret rendezvous tonight. I was nervous about the prospect of getting caught, but not nervous enough to not go. I wanted to see her that badly.

❧❧❧❧

So after I showered for the second time today, I ventured to Dorian's to exchange vehicles. As usual, she wasn't pleased with our actions, but nevertheless, she caved and coughed up her car keys. Her only request was "Please lay down a blanket." The more I laughed, the more she reiterated her request. "I really don't need either of your bodily juices sticking to the carpeting in my truck. And don't get me started on the leather seats."

"Okay, okay. I promise I'll take your car back all cleaned up. You'll have no idea we fucked all over your entire car, it'll be so clean."

Because the sun set so late, we had to wait. By nine p.m., I got Danielle's call. "Now. Leave now. You'll see me walking JoJo."

"Fifteen minutes. Be ready." I grabbed the keys off the kitchen table and ran out the door.

Fifteen minutes seemed like thirty seconds. I flew down the highway as adrenaline coursed through my veins. Two weeks. Two weeks had gone by since we last gazed into each other's eyes. The yearning was overwhelming, and I couldn't get to Hyde Park fast enough.

It was pitch dark by the time I arrived in Danielle's neighborhood. The light from the crescent moon was dim, and the stars were scattered sporadically throughout the black sky. I drove slowly down the street, looking for Danielle and JoJo to pop up somewhere. Making the first turn around her block, I spotted her as she sneaked from the shadows of the trees that lined the sidewalk. As I pulled over to the curb, I peered in the rearview mirror to see her scoop up the dog while she made a run for the SUV. She whipped the car door open, jumped in, and slammed the door behind her. JoJo hopped out of her arms and into the backseat while he wagged his tail and panted.

"You mean to tell me April didn't find it strange you taking JoJo for a walk after nine at night? You're usually getting ready for bed at this hour."

She didn't answer me because she was too busy climbing over the center console to get to me. She pawed at me like an octopus. "Slow down, babe." I attempted to rope in her hands.

"There's no time for slow. We'll go slow in a couple of days when we can." She lifted my shirt above my head. "Take this off! Come on, Parker! Hurry!"

"Dani, stop!" Having sex at lightning speed was never a turn-on for me. I knew we didn't have much time, but there was no way I would be able to concentrate enough to get off like this. She came to a halt and stared into my eyes.

She wasn't sure how to take my tone. "It's just that I can't be gone long. I'm sorry."

Her sincerity subdued me instantly, and I couldn't be mad at her. "Oh, my God, you are so cute. Let's try this again, shall we?" I lifted myself up out of the driver's seat and crawled all the way to the back, then flipped myself over the backseat and into the rear of the SUV. Once she followed me, we grabbed the dog, pulled him with us, and lowered the backseats to create more space. She was afraid to touch me for fear I would start yelling at her again. Like a runner waiting for the shot from the gun to begin the race, I teased her for a second before I said, "Okay, go!" We smiled and leaned into each other, embracing for the first time in weeks. Her lips were soft against mine as I grazed them over hers. Her tongue danced with mine. "What do you want?" I murmured into her ear.

"I want to rub my pussy on yours." She felt completely comfortable with me in a way she didn't with April. Her insecurities shed when she was with me, and she recognized it, too.

"Do it." I took my shorts and underwear off, spread my legs, and invited her to trib me. It was a good thing the windows were tinted because we were parked on a residential street in an affluent neighborhood. Neither of us bothered to take off our shirts. We didn't have time for that. Once her bottom half was as naked as mine, she straddled my leg and slid up to meet my pussy.

It didn't take long for her to find her groove, and she rode me frantically, pressing her hand into my chest. "Oh, yeah." She moaned as our clits rubbed together, the friction sending waves of pleasure over both of us. Our arousal heightened, and her hips moved faster. Her gaze was zoned in on mine, and she surprised me when she took her hand and traveled the small distance to my throat. She squeezed lightly. This was different and something she hadn't yet done to me. The dominance she exhibited excited her so much that her hips bucked and jerked on me in the heat of sexual fury. The idea of overpowering me released a sex-crazed part of her that I didn't think she even knew existed. It was hot! I took my hand, placed it over hers, held her hand in place, and tightened her grip for her.

She came unexpectedly. "Oh! Oh! Oh, yes! Parker!" She gyrated on me so rapidly, I didn't know if her orgasm would end. Eventually, she slowed and laid her body on me, resting between my open legs. Our skin was sweaty and stuck to each other. I held her close to me as she tried to compose her breathing, and she offered, "I want to go down on you."

"We don't have time," I declined.

"But I haven't gone down on you yet."

I took her face in my hands so I could have her undivided attention. "It's okay. We're going to be together in a couple of days, all right?"

"But I want to."

"You have to wait. Honestly, I don't think I could cum under this kind of pressure."

A chuckle escaped her mouth, and she agreed that tonight wasn't the best night to try. Quite frankly, I didn't think I could have cum while JoJo sat right next to us, staring. We dressed and climbed back to the front of the car. Oddly enough, as Danielle tied the drawstring on her shorts, I noticed someone walking down the opposite side of the street. It was dark, and all I could make out was a silhouette of a person. When the figure appeared from the shadows, I recognized that it was April. My heart raced, and my palms became instantly clammy. Danielle didn't see her right away as she was still straightening out her clothes. I tapped her thigh with one hand and pointed with the other. "April!"

"What? Where?" She was panic-stricken.

"I guess we took too long."

We both looked at the clock. We took way longer than we should have. My first impulse was to drive off in a hurry, but I collected myself and knew we were behind tinted windows. I calmly started the engine and drove in the opposite direction. I didn't know how she didn't catch us because chaos ensued in the Tahoe. Between Danielle freaking out for me to get out of there and JoJo barking his little brains out, it was a miracle I drove as collectedly as I did. I wanted to scream *Shut up!* but knew it was counterproductive to our goal, which was to get the hell out of there.

"What am I going to do? What am I going to do?" Danielle held on to my shoulder and flipped out.

"Dani, you need to calm down! Get it together." I rubbed her leg to bring her pulse down. "You and JoJo are simply going to get out of the car and go inside the house. Period. She's still around the corner. You're going to tell her the time got away from you because you have a lot on your mind."

"What do I have on my mind?"

"Um, your dad."

Time stood still for a moment as she stopped her panic and looked at me. I had struck a chord. Her brain was on overload. She took a deep breath and let it out. "Okay! I got this. I can do this."

"That's right," I encouraged her and pulled over in front of her house. "Now go! Go!" I waved her out of the vehicle.

She jumped out of the truck, picked JoJo up, and before she shut the door, she looked me straight in the eyes, and proclaimed for the first time soberly, "I love you." The door closed, and I was left unable to speak. *Did she just say what I think she said?* I didn't expect it, and I was blown away. I had to go. But damn, I wanted nothing more than to spend the night with her. It was wonderful and shitty all at the same time, and oh, so bittersweet.

I drove off, but April was walking directly toward me. *Fuck!* I tried not to draw attention to myself, so I drove at a normal speed but had to stop at the stop sign. I freaked out in my head. The windshield wasn't tinted, and I felt exposed. She walked right at me, her face looked in my direction, and I was afraid the jig was up. I shielded my eyes with my hand as she came within ten feet of me. *Shit!* Finally, she crossed my path, and I punched the accelerator, a reflex of sheer fear. When I was through the intersection, I peeked in my rearview mirror and saw she turned and looked right at me. I was too far for her to recognize me, but she was suspicious. I knew I was incognito, but I didn't know if it was enough.

Was it possible to make direct eye contact with

someone from a distance? I wouldn't find out until I talked to Danielle, and I could only hope that she was able to pull off this charade. By the time I arrived home, she sent me a text. Obviously, April wanted to know where she disappeared to and what took so long, but she did as I told her as best she could, and April appeared to buy it. I sighed in relief, texted her good night, and told her I'd see her in a couple of days.

I went into my house, probably more confused than when I left. Taking a seat on the dark gray sectional, I stared at the baby grand that stood about twenty feet away from me. That piano held more of Danielle's heart than the entire house. She was everything to me. I began to think, which was no good for me, because I always made things bigger in my head than they really were. I overthought shit, and it never turned out well in my head. No matter what it was. She said she loved me, but I didn't want to read too much into it. She had yet to give me any indication that she would leave April. When we were together, April's name didn't even come up. Our time was our time. Their time was theirs. She made a pretty distinct line between the two. She led a double life, and I let her. The complete opposite of what I said I'd do. But right now, I didn't care.

And what was up with Dani grabbing me by my throat during sex? Even more absurd was that I liked it. I liked being pinned underneath her. I enjoyed her dominance. It excited me. I got off on it, and I didn't know how to feel about that. This dark and mysterious side of her was a turn-on. Who knew?

While I sat there lost in my own thoughts, I received another text. I thought it was Danielle again, but when I glanced down at the screen, I was surprised to see it was from Kylie. Her text simply said *Hi.* So simple and so obvious she was testing the waters. I hadn't texted her back the last time she messaged me. I was too busy playing house with Dani. But I decided there was no harm in saying hello. Once we got through the *hellos* and *how are yous*, she asked me out. I guess she got over what happened on the trip. The part of me that knew Dani was bound to hurt me and leave me in the dust agreed to see her next week. The problem with me was I just never knew how to get out of my own way. Clinging to the possibility of a relationship with Dani yet realizing things weren't changing, I set myself up for a downfall.

❧ ❧ ❧ ❧

Before I knew it, April was Houston-bound and sending her wife-to-be right into my arms. It was Tuesday morning when she left for the airport. Danielle made a beeline for my house. She walked up my pathway with an overnight bag in her hand, and JoJo tagged along behind her. She was my girl for the next three days. Sex and food were the only items of interest on our agenda.

As soon as the door swung open, she dropped her bag and rushed into my arms. "I missed you so much, Parker. This really sucks not being able to see you or talk to you like normal," she said.

"Nothing is normal anymore, Danielle," I said as her hands undressed me. "By the way, what was that chokehold you had on me the other night? That was pretty aggressive, even for you."

She stopped what she was doing and looked at me. She wasn't expecting me to bring it up. "It was, wasn't it?" It didn't warrant an answer, but she continued, "I don't usually have sex like that. You bring something out in me. Something wild that I can't control."

"Whatever it is, you're amazing." I kissed her all over her face and neck.

"If I'm amazing, it's because you make me amazing. I'm so used to vanilla, but you're like rocky road or fudge ripple."

"You're making me hungry."

"Hungry for what?" She got a hold of my arms and moved me backward through the room, her mouth clenched to my neck.

"Um…what are we talking about now? I'm confused. Sex or ice cream?" I breathed into her ear.

She maneuvered me into the wall. "Don't play with me." My neck was sore from the suction of her mouth, and I let out a low, guttural groan. "Uhh… Fuck! It hurts so good!" I had my hand on the back of her head and held her as she feasted on my skin. I felt her teeth as she bit me hard. Then she lifted my hands to press them against the wall. She turned my neck black and blue.

She possessed me in the moment and left my neck raw, claiming my mouth as she bit and sucked on my lips and mouth. No longer nervous or skeptical about my tongue piercing, she tugged and circled around the little ball with her tongue. "My pussy is so wet for you," she confessed in between breaths.

"I'm glad I'm not the only one."

She pulled off her own clothes while she told me what she was going to do to me. "First, I'm going to trib you and cum all over your pussy, and then I'm going to eat you and make you cum all over my face."

"What?"

"Let me show you."

The closest piece of furniture available was the piano. She wasn't concerned with making it sing through its keys today. She wanted to make it sing through me. She hoisted me up, and as she followed, her toes hit a few of the keys. It spit out an awkward sound that was not music but a jumble of abrupt pings and dings. A smile overcame my face, and her pearly whites shone back at me. Her dimples faded, and her smile dissipated as she towered above me and let hair down. Like a golden lioness, her dark blond mane cascaded down and around her face and neck as it fell over her slender shoulders. I swallowed hard as I admired and adored her beauty. She gently straddled my thigh, spread her labia, and rubbed her wetness on me. Her eyes closed. She delighted in the friction on my leg, and I touched her face. I dragged my fingers over her lips before I dipped one into her mouth. Her eyes popped open as she sucked on it, circled her tongue around it, and repeated the action. "I could cum just rubbing my clit on your thigh, you know that?"

"Thought you were going to show me."

"Uh-uh…no. I'm going to cum right on top of your clit." She spread my legs farther apart and slid all the way up to meet me. We were connected at our centers, and she took over. She mounted and rode me into submission. "You feel that? Huh? You feel my clit on yours?"

Her nub was rock hard as it flicked over mine, and our juices blended together. Once again, her hand settled around my gullet and tightened a bit. "You like that, don't you?" she asked rhetorically while her pace quickened. Each thrust created a squeaking sound from the skin of her knees rubbing against the black lacquer of the piano. "Oh, God!" she uttered. As she was about to orgasm, I brought my hand up and wrapped it around her throat, too. It certainly didn't receive a negative response. If anything, she came harder. "Yes!" She gyrated full throttle, and I indulged in the wetness she drained on me.

Without warning, she relocated down my body to give me head for the first time ever. It was a fucking dream come true. Feeling her tongue take that first lick made my nerve endings stand at attention. My skin stuck to the piano, and I shifted back and forth with no give, as if they were sheets on a bed. She cupped my ass cheeks and held me up like a bowl, lapping at me like a kitten laps its milk. Her tongue delved into my opening, and she brought her face up. I saw my stickiness drip from a string of saliva on her tongue to my pussy. "Fuck!" I whooped and watched her hump the piano as she buried her face deeper into my core. She crooned and croaked her hunger for me, her appetite insatiable. She licked me into a tizzy, and I could hold it no longer. "Oh, dear God! Oh, Dani! Oh, Dani! Oh, Dani!" I cried out, my orgasm a powerful explosion, blasting my universe into a million shattered pieces.

I tried to collect myself, but it was almost impossible. Her face lay in my wetness, and each time she kissed my clit, my nerve endings awakened and tingled, which made me jump and push her head away. When she eventually extracted herself from my satisfied pussy, she draped herself over my body. Regardless of how or when this ended, I would always treasure these most intimate moments we shared.

"You tasted so good," she said softly.

"Sweetheart, you are way dirtier than I ever could have imagined or even given you credit for."

"What can I say? I guess you bring out the best of the worst in me." She smiled and crawled off the piano to help me down. "I canceled the two classes I had today."

"What? Why?"

"Well, I know we can't really be seen together around here, but I thought maybe we could spend the day walking around Gulfport. What do you think?"

"Can we go on my bike?"

She rolled her eyes at me. "You know I'm scared of that thing."

"If you can ride with me once, you can ride with me again."

"That was only around the block," she said as if I tried fooling her.

"That was your practice run, and you did great," I asserted. She looked unsure and swayed back and forth in one spot. "You trust me, don't you?"

"You know I do."

Chapter Seventeen

Riding on that motorcycle wouldn't have even been a second thought three months ago, but today, Danielle shocked me by saying, "Okay."

My eyes got big, but I didn't say a word for fear she would change her mind. With her arms securely wrapped around my waist, we took off down the road. I felt her nervousness through her fingertips as they tightly gripped me. She definitely did not like turns because each one came with her hands digging into my side. She finally relaxed after the tenth time of pleading with her. Once we got onto the highway, it was a straight run to St. Pete's and about a half-hour drive. It was a hot, humid day, and the sun was as bright as Danielle's face when she smiled at me. The baby blue of the sky was the perfect backdrop for the calm and gentle waters we passed on our way there.

Gulfport was a small town at the south end of the St. Pete/Clearwater peninsula, bordered by the Boca Ciega Bay. Gulfport's waterfront district attracted all sorts of people, from young and old to gay and straight. Colorful buildings and homes bordered the tree-covered streets, and the town itself was quite eclectic, artsy, and charming. It was a relaxing place to take a peaceful walk or reflect by the water.

I parked the Harley, and we took off our helmets. Danielle pulled her hair back into a ponytail, and we strolled the streets while we dipped in and out of quaint shops. During our window shopping, we came across a darling brasserie, and we went inside to grab a bite. The décor of the place was as artsy as the town itself, and after lunch, we chatted and laughed over a cup of coffee. We talked sports, about Dorian and Dahlia, and reminisced over old times. Anything to avoid talking about the elephant in the room—April. It was nice spending time with Danielle. You didn't realize how much you miss a person until you'd been robbed of them. The time we spent together now was a treasure in ways I couldn't explain. However, it made it that much more difficult when we had to say goodbye, not knowing when we would be able to see each other again.

We both checked our phones, so Danielle could make sure she didn't miss a call from April and that Jeff hadn't called me with any updates about the bar. When I was finished, I set it on the table and went to the restroom. When I came back, she looked at me strange and confused. "What's wrong?" I hoped it had nothing to do with April.

"I didn't know you were still seeing her," she said.

"Seeing who?"

"Kylie."

"Why would you even mention her? Where did that come from?"

"She happened to call you while you were in the bathroom." She pointed at my phone that sat next to my empty coffee mug.

"Oh." I took the phone in my hand, looked at the missed call, and explained, "Honestly, I thought she was done with me the night I chose to take care of your drunken ass instead of spending the night with her. She was pretty pissed off, but she texted me last week to say hello." I studied her face as she contemplated mine. "Why? Are you jealous?" My mouth curved upward into a playful grin as I awaited her answer.

She looked around the room, then our table, and finally at me. She sucked in her bottom lip nervously. "I can't tell you who you can see and who you can't."

"That's not what I asked you."

Again, she scanned the room, fidgeting and clearly uncomfortable with this line of questioning. "It doesn't matter if I'm jealous. I don't have a right to be." Her leg shook so vigorously that it moved the silverware. I casually touched her knee under the table with my hand, indicating for her to stop. Her jitteriness came to a halt, and she gazed into my eyes; everything she felt for me radiated from her beautiful face.

"You're correct. You don't have the right. Yet I know you are, even if you don't admit it, and that's okay."

"If it's happening, I don't want to know about it. All right?" She didn't wait for me to answer. "I don't want to talk about this anymore."

"You brought it up." I realized instantly that I shouldn't have said it that way, and although she struck a chord in me, I didn't want to ruin our day together. We both let it go, paid the bill, and left.

❧❧❧❧

After lunch, we walked out to Williams Pier, a five hundred twenty-one-foot extension into Boca Ciega Bay. It was late afternoon, and we watched the boats sail by as they cut through the smooth surface of the waters with ease. There was a warm breeze coming off the bay, and we strolled the length of the pier. We picked a bench and took a seat. "Oh, you know what I meant to tell you?" she started and crossed one leg over the other in my direction. "I saw my dad this weekend. He was asking for you and Dorian."

"How is he?" I asked, concern sweeping over my face.

"You know it's not easy for me to talk about, but he's hanging in there as best he can. His hair is thinning and falling out from the chemo, and his appetite is lacking. His second treatment starts next week." Her voice cracked a bit with worry, and she repeated, "He was asking for you. Maybe we can see him tomorrow when I wrap up my classes for the day. What do you think?"

"Sure. Yes, I would love to see him. It's been too long, I know."

Her bottom lip quivered, and her eyes welled up with tears. "I'm scared. I don't want to lose both my parents."

I scooped her into my arms and tightened my grip around her shoulder and waist. The tighter I clasped, the more she cried. She needed to let it out, and I knew it. I welcomed being her rock, if only for a short time. She held way too much inside and stuffed down her pain. Running was an outlet. It was bad when her mom died, but she was much closer to her dad. During the rare moments when she broke down, I was there for her with a shoulder on which to cry. Her tears dripped onto my T-shirt. She lifted her head up. "I'm sorry. I'm getting you all wet."

She wiped the wet spot on my shoulder, and I

said, "Well, it certainly wouldn't be the first time, and you're usually able to do that just by looking at me."

Her laughter was a sweet melody in my ear, and as the tension melted away, she gave me a small peck on my lips, got up, and offered me her hand. We walked the distance back up the pier, and as we wandered around, we ended up in the middle of a small carnival, complete with a few rides and games. People crowded the ice cream stand, and children rode the carousel. I was a sucker for cotton candy, and after I bought a swath of it, I tore into it as I watched Danielle shoot hoops. By the time we came across the water gun game, I was so hyped up on sugar that my eyes were popping out of my head.

"You want to play?" she tempted, knowing she plucked a memory from long, long ago.

Around the time we met, she had split with Nicky, and I was dating Allie. Danielle and I had gone to a local carnival. It was almost like a date, or it felt that way. The attraction was still fresh and new at that time, and maybe we were still a little unsure of what the future held for us. We were so competitive, testing each other in game after game, and came away with zero prizes. But when we sat down at the water gun game, we were the only two playing. The guy was nice enough to not make us wait for more competitors since it was the end of his day, and the carnival would be shutting down and moving to a different town the next day. We knew we would walk away with a prize this time. He sounded the bell, and we pulled our triggers. Water burst out of the barrel of the gun that targeted a dot about six feet away. Little stuffed animals raced up the pole, Dani's purple, mine blue. We both white-knuckled the handle of the gun as if somehow that would make our racers move faster. The stream of water spraying the tiny dot was all we needed, and even though she got the jump on me, I quickly caught up. Our racers were tied all the way to the top, and the buzzer rang at the same time.

The guy was only giving out one prize, and we argued over who really won. After several minutes of bickering, I finally gave into her brattiness and let her have it. She picked the same purple stuffed animal that had been her racer. Seeing the smile on her face as she hugged the stuffed bear was enough to soften my heart and let her have her way. To this day, that purple bear sits on her desk at work. Unfortunately, it sits next to a picture of her and that weasel April instead of us.

"I'll play." I sought a bit of revenge. The only difference this time was there were other people playing. We took a seat with three others, picked up our guns, and waited for the sound of the bell. *Ding*! They're off! We both hit our targets right away, rooting our racers on, but as they approached the top, someone else's buzzer sounded. Neither of us won. The teenage boy picked out a pink stuffed unicorn and handed it to his girlfriend. They were young and cute, and I didn't mind losing to him.

"That's not the one that's rightfully mine anyway. That one is sitting on your desk at the college," I teased and set my gun back in its holster.

"Pssh! Yeah, right!"

"Seriously, by all rights, that fucking bear is mine!"

"Seriously, you'll never have that bear, not over my dead body."

The more we went back and forth, the lighter

our tones became, and before we knew it, we were both laughing. We momentarily forgot where we were as we hugged and kissed. When we realized we were in the middle of a crowd of people, we ended our embrace and walked down the street. The last thing we did before leaving the carnival was stop at the photo booth. It was as if we were re-creating that *almost* date from so many years ago. The camera flashed four times, and when it spit out the developed photos, we both looked so happy, smiling from ear to ear. There was no denying our connection.

The sun looked like a fireball against the deep orange backdrop of the sky as we mounted my bike to go home. The ride back was quiet, and the only way I knew she was on the back of the bike was the slight squeeze she gave around my waist. It had been a much-needed great day. The strain April had put on our friendship was draining, and even if nothing was going on between us, our friendship was stronger. Being there for each other wasn't going to change. When we arrived back to Seminole Heights, it was dark.

❧ ❧ ❧ ❧

After a full day of play, Danielle and I spent some time with the dogs before we went to bed. She was surprised that I cleared out a dresser drawer for her. I preferred it that way. Her living out of a bag each time she stayed didn't cut it for me, so it made sense to give her own space. Once she unpacked her duffel bag, we climbed into bed together. The room was dark except for the nightlight that shone from the bathroom. That same light was enough to see more than just the silhouette of her face.

I lay on my back and looked over at her when she turned on her side to face me. She held herself on her elbow and leaned her head on the palm of her hand.

"What?" I asked.

"I had a really nice time with you today. It was nice spending time together."

Now it was my turn to roll onto my side. We mirrored each other, gazed into each other's eyes, and remained silent for a while. Although my mind was still congested with doubts and fears about our situation, I threw caution to the wind. The bottom line was, I would've dived into a roaring fire for her. She was the love of my life, and I wanted nothing more than to be with her, even if it had to be like this.

"Do you remember all of that night?" she asked out of the blue.

"What night?" I giggled.

"The night we went to the carnival, and you lost the bear at the water gun game."

"I did not lose." I was incredulous. "But yes, I do remember."

"We almost kissed that night."

"That's true."

"I was too scared to kiss you."

We never talked about that *almost* kiss and chose to move on and forget about it. Apparently, it was not forgotten. "Why were you scared?" I asked. "It's not like you didn't know I had the hots for you."

"I was afraid I'd fall in love with you, and you would leave me."

"Why in the world would you think that?"

"I don't know. Girls have always been drawn

to you. Maybe I thought you would find someone prettier than me or better than me or..."

I covered her lips with my index finger. "Danielle, I have thought that you are the most beautiful woman on the face of this planet since the day I met you." I brushed my thumb over her bottom lip and stared at her mouth. "And almost twenty years later, you still take my breath away."

Her hands found the back of her head, and she let the ponytail fall loose. She shook it free and raked her fingers through it as she looked at me. I adored her, and as her dimples deepened along with her smile, she said, "Breathe."

Her lids came down swiftly over her eyes, while she batted them and melted my soul. Our faces drew closer with no further notice, and her lips met mine. Her kiss was slow and thoughtful as her tongue traced the fullness of my lips. The pit of my stomach was sent into a wild swirl when our mouths parted, and we connected as one. Time stood still, and all was right in my world in that moment. Every feeling she ever had for me flowed through her lips to mine, and I welcomed it, having died for it for so long.

"I love you," she said softly, letting it roll from the tip of her tongue and maybe not meaning to say it out loud. I didn't badger her about our situation. Instead, I soaked in each of those three words and allowed an intense period of silence to envelop us. She didn't let the silence intimidate her. There was nothing to feel insecure about. She knew I loved her. Every part of me, every fiber of my being loved her.

"I love you, too," I finally said, and our lips drew together again. Only this time, I crawled on top of her. In between each kiss, we disrobed each other until we were flesh on flesh.

I planted a kiss in the hollow of her neck but didn't stop there as I inched my way down to her small boobs and took them each in my hands. I suckled them one at a time. "Mmm" came from both of our throats. Each time I teased one and circled her nipple with my tongue, she pushed it into my mouth. Her long golden hair fanned out over the pillow, and she brought her hands up to her face as she covered her eyes. She peeked down at me, and with one hand, she drew her fingers through my hair and pushed down on my head. "I want you to go down on me," she whispered and forced me down between her legs.

With both hands, I opened her thighs as far as they would go and wedged my face in the core of her. My tongue glossed over her small but erect gem, and I consumed all her wetness while I slid my lips and chin over it. "Oh, God, yes." She groaned as her hand held my head in place. Each lick was met with an upward thrust of her hips. Then I penetrated her hole with the tip of my tongue. "Oh, yeah...eat me and fuck me," she instructed and surprised me with her perversion. "Please," she pleaded, almost begging.

Without further hesitation, I pushed two fingers inside of her and brought forth a cry of sweet pleasure she couldn't contain. My tongue and fingers were in perfect rhythm and cadence as I licked and fucked her until she became unhinged. Her taut body writhed and wriggled under me, and I pinned her to the mattress with my free hand. I pulled her mound upward to get a better angle, but it was impossible to stop her from squirming. Her feet kept pushing at the sheets as if this would prevent it. "Oh, my...Oh, my...Oh, fuck!" She rode my face and fingers uncontrollably, but then,

"What the...Oh, my God!" she shouted to both of our astonishment.

I felt hot liquid burst onto my hand and into my mouth. When I lifted my head up to see what had happened, a huge arc of the same hot liquid streamed into the air a good couple of feet if not more. She had squirted. Female ejaculation. It was incredible, and when I figured out what it was, I threw my face back in front of it and continued to fuck her. The harder I fucked her, the more she ejaculated. After she finished, she was exasperated. "What was that? That's never happened before."

"Seriously?"

"Seriously. What the heck did you just do to me?"

"Uh, you squirted."

"Yeah, I get that. I just didn't know I was capable of it." She stroked my cheek. "That was the most amazing feeling I've ever felt." She kissed my forehead. "You did that to me."

I had only been with one girl who squirted, and I must admit, it was exciting. One might think it was gross, thinking it was urine, but it wasn't. It was just liquid. It had no taste or smell. And if you can make a woman do that, not only was she special, so were you. It was an incredible experience and one I would absolutely welcome again from Danielle. The sounds she made and the way her body reacted were an enormous turn-on for me. I was so hot for her, I never realized my hand had made its way down between my own legs. "What are you doing? Are you masturbating?" she asked.

"You call it masturbating. I call it jerkin' off."

Laughter erupted from her belly at this, and she

took a peek at what I was doing. I was on my side and leaned against her with one arm immobilized under the pillow her head rested on, the other jerked off my clit. "Uh, yeah." I softly moaned and never stopped the rhythm and pace of my finger.

"You can't cum like this. I want to make you cum," she asserted, feeling slighted for not being involved.

But it was too late. My hand slid up and down rapidly, and orgasm was inevitable. "Oh! Oh, Dani! Oh, Dani!" I roared. I was incapable of suspending my own gratification long enough for her to be included.

"That was so not fair!" She crossed her arms over her breasts. "You didn't need me at all."

"Not true, my dear. You were the fucking catalyst. Don't be mad. It was all for you."

The day had been long, all energy had been drained, and neither of us could do anything else but lie there. Conversation turned off for the night, and we eventually curled up in a ball together, not willing to let each other go.

Chapter Eighteen

As planned, when Danielle was finished classes for the day, we went to visit her dad. We pulled into the affluent, gated community in Dani's Roadster, and once cleared by the guard at the security booth, we drove down the street to the Bly estate. The black wrought iron gate to her dad's property slowly opened, and we were buzzed through. We drove up the winding driveway lined with little gem magnolia trees that were in full bloom with beautiful white flowers on them. Rounding the half-moon driveway, we came to a stop at the front doors. As we looked up at the colossal mansion made of terra cotta stucco, the main common area was offset by a wing on either side. The many tall arched casement windows with diagonal muntins gave the mansion a stately appearance.

We climbed the dozen semicircle steps that started out wide and narrowed as we reached the top. Danielle pushed the doorbell, and while it still chimed, the heavy double doors opened. On the other side was their butler, Phineas, who had worked in the house since Danielle was a child. Dressed in a suit like always, he greeted us both and led us through the expanse of the mansion. The foyer was as big as my whole house. We walked the speckled marble floors to a double staircase that led up to the balcony and the nine or so bedrooms. Two oversized urns designed in Japanese art stood on either side of the staircase. An elegant, ornate chandelier hung in the center. We made our way through a set of columns and into the formal living room.

The burgundy drapes were thick and dignified. Phineas led us outside to a view that was even more awe-inspiring than inside. A fifty-foot infinity pool blended in with the ocean and the horizon. The pool was surrounded by lounge chairs, and off to the left, outdoor furniture encircled a fire pit that was outlined with several boulders. Directly next to it was a hot tub made of brown and tan rocks. Under the shade of a suri chair, her dad napped peacefully with his arms crossed and his head tilted to the side.

Her dad was tall. A gene Danielle did not possess. She took after her mom. He was such a good-looking man with his short, neatly combed salt and pepper hair. For his age, he had a full head of hair, though it had started to thin from treatments. Although his eyes were closed, I knew they were the same copper-colored shade as Dani's. Deep, heavy breaths inhaled and exhaled through his straight, Romanesque nose. He had a strong, broad jaw, but his face was haggard and drawn. The illness had started to show on him in more ways than one. His head bobbed as he slept, and his big, powerful hands trembled. He had recently begun to lose weight, a side effect he couldn't afford as he was string-bean thin his whole life.

Danielle touched his hands as gently as she could, so as not to startle him. He slowly came to, and when his eyes opened and adjusted on her, a smile came across his face. "Sweet pea," he groggily greeted her.

"Hi, Dad," she said with an adoring smile. "Look

who I brought to see you."

He looked over and discerned it was me. "Parker!" he exclaimed, straightened himself in the chair, and attempted to get up.

"Don't get up for me, James." I leaned down to give him a hug. Calling him Mr. Bly was short-lived when I first met him. We immediately felt comfortable in each other's presence, and he insisted I call him by his first name. Since I came around all the time when we were in college, it didn't take long for him to see how much I cared for his daughter. He never had a problem with her sexuality, but boy, was he critical of the women she dated. All but me. Granted, we never dated, but he knew early on that I was in love with her. "How are you feeling?" I asked.

"Tired," he replied as he reached for a glass of juice that sat on the table next to him. "If the cancer doesn't kill me, the chemo will." He took a sip and placed the glass back down. "I haven't seen you for quite a while. How are you?"

"Keeping busy. Waiting for the renovation of my bar to be completed."

"That's right! Danielle had told me about that a couple of months ago. I'm glad it's close to being finished and up and running again."

"Is there anything I can get you, Dad?" Danielle interrupted.

"I'll take some more ice for my juice, if you don't mind."

"I never mind." She took her reprieve and disappeared in the house, leaving us alone.

Once she was out of sight, he motioned toward the empty chair next to him and asked me to have a seat. "This wedding is getting closer. Is she happy?"

I squirmed visibly in my seat. "Something seems off when I see her recently, like she's distant. Is she having second thoughts?"

"Not that I know of," I finally replied. I didn't know what to say or how to answer and was unable to admit what was taking place on the side.

"Hmm…Parker, I don't know why, but I have this sinking feeling in the pit of my gut telling me that something's not right."

"As far as I know, everything is all set. She and April are ready to do this thing."

"You know, if I have to be completely honest," he took a slight pause, leaned closer to me, and continued, "I don't trust April."

"Have you discussed this with Dani?" I sat with my fingers crossed under my lap, hoping that he had.

"Sort of, but she blew me off right away, telling me I was just being overprotective. My daughter's pretty hard-headed, as you well know."

"Yes, I do know. Listen, James, about—"

"Is this enough ice?" I heard from behind me, and talk between me and James came to a halt. Danielle had come back before I could get it out. I wanted to tell him he had good reason not to trust April, but Danielle unknowingly cut me short.

We visited for a few hours and spent quality time with him. He listened to her talk of her upcoming nuptials, and he forced a smile through it all. He wasn't alone. It was bad enough he had to fight this battle with a disease that was likely to take his life. He most certainly didn't need to have extra worry, the heaviness of deep concern over his daughter's imminent wedding to a person he didn't deem worthy.

The strain of his illness and the treatments involved wore him out after a while, and he started to nod off. We helped him back into the house and onto a large, cushy recliner in the den. "Take a nap, Dad, okay?" I'll call you tomorrow, and I'll see you this weekend."

He nodded his acknowledgment as Danielle bent down and gave him a hug and a kiss on the cheek. She stepped away, and as she went in the direction of the front door, I gave him a hug, too. When I put my arms around him, he lowered his mouth to my ear. "I always wished she was with you, ya know? You're good for her. It's a shame she doesn't see that." He released his embrace on me. "No matter what, promise me you'll take care of her, Parker."

"You know I love her, right?"

"I've always known."

"Parker! You coming?" Danielle yelled from the door a distance away.

I looked at her dad once more and promised, "She'll always have me." I backed away and turned for the door. I walked away from her dad more determined than ever to expose April for the rotten person she was. It had been a nice visit with him. He was a good man who always took care of his family, and now it was time to take care of him.

When we left, Danielle was bummed out. The thought of her dad's ultimate demise was unbearable, and although she didn't say it, I felt it. I held her hand on the way back to my house, and every now and then, she would tighten her grip.

❧ ❧ ❧ ❧

The next morning, Danielle packed her bag

for home. April would be home this evening from Houston, a city she was in nearly every other week. We said our goodbyes at the door and kissed and hugged longer than usual. Parting had become increasingly heavy-hearted, every departure became more difficult. "Pick me," I blurted out as she was halfway out the door.

"What?" She stopped midstride and whirled back around to face me.

"Pick me, Danielle. We could have a good life. All you have to do is pick me."

I caught her off guard as her mouth dropped, and she was suddenly unable to form sentences. "I-I, uh…You and me, and…I…she…"

"Oh, just shut up and go to work!" I helped push her the rest of the way out the door, completely annoyed by her inability to make a decision and disgusted at her babbling. Through the window, I watched as she wandered back and forth to her car, back up the walk, and to her car again. She seemed to be weighing her options and didn't have an answer for me. Finally, she got in her car and left.

Not long after, I received a text from Kylie. She wanted to see me. It was Friday night and the beginning of a weekend without Danielle. My weekends were fairly boring and lonely without her. I would hang out with Dorian, but she had been preoccupied with getting laid. Cookie was usually around, but she was still trying to fix things with Shady. Hanging out with Kylie seemed a reasonable option. After all, there were no strings with Danielle apparently, and the fact that she wouldn't make up her mind was disappointing and frustrating. I felt rebellious, and I didn't feel like moping around my house all weekend, so I said yes.

Kylie arrived at my house at eight o'clock that night with a bottle of wine in her hand. "Hi," I said as I opened the door. Her entrance into my house was led by a forced kiss. "Whoa, whoa! Easy there, playah," I said and lightly pushed her off me. "What's your rush?"

But an uneasy feeling crept up inside me right off the bat. Something wasn't right. I didn't know exactly what would happen with us tonight, but it wasn't a good start. Deep down, I knew I was just pissed about Danielle's reaction to me earlier. Kylie was only a little payback for Danielle's indecision. The fact was, I wasn't going to sleep with Kylie tonight. All the years I had loved Dani, I never had a problem going out with other women. I always tried to fill the void in my heart for her. Until she said she loved me back. Now it seemed all of a sudden, my lower half belonged to her and her alone.

In that moment, I found my conscience. In all fairness to Kylie, I knew I couldn't let her stay. The idea of betraying Danielle like this made me feel sick to my stomach. She had to go. "Kylie, I think you should leave."

"What? Why the change of heart?" she asked. "I just got here."

I touched and rubbed my temples. "I've got a headache, and it's really starting to pound."

"Nothing a little red wine won't cure." She made no attempt to go and instead went in search of a corkscrew.

"Hey, you need to stop what you're doing and

go," I said more forcefully.

But she had already cracked the bottle open and held it up. "We can't let this go to waste, now can we?"

I shrugged, resigned to the fact that she wasn't going anywhere anytime soon.

"Let's take this to the sofa," she suggested.

While Kylie poured out two glasses of the red, we chatted about nothing in particular. As we were about to have a seat on the sofa, Addie begged me to go out as her tail wagged and her mouth yapped her plea. To the back slider we went. I stepped outside with her and left Kylie in control of the remote. After Addie did her business, we headed back inside. Kylie handed me a glass of wine as I took a seat next to her. We talked for a while and sipped our wine with the TV on for background noise. For the life of me, I couldn't figure out why she was talking about Danielle. She asked when we met and how. Asked if we ever dated. Asked when I saw her last and how often we got together. It was strange to say the least.

During our conversation, I started to feel woozy. Perspiration beaded on my upper lip, and I got light-headed and nauseated. "I don't feel so good." I wiped the sweat from my brow. "I think I'm going to pass out." The room spun, and the voices on the TV sounded distant, almost with an echo.

"It's working," she said.

"What?" I was confused and impaired, and mumbled, "What's working?" That was all I remembered. I passed out and didn't remember anything after that.

When I awoke to Addie licking my face, my head was pounding, and I was groggy and weak, barely able to get it together. *What happened?* I looked around and realized it was morning. Light streamed in through the window and blinded me. I shielded my eyes with my hand as I slowly got to my feet. I scoped the house out and looked for any other signs of life but saw none.

"Kylie!" I shouted. When no one replied, I became aware that I really was alone. "Where did she go?" I asked Addie, who was practically attached to my leg and didn't let me out of her sight. The last thing I remembered was sitting on the couch with Kylie, drinking wine. The glasses were still there. Mine was half full. Hers was empty. I couldn't figure out what happened to me. My phone sat next to my glass, and I grabbed it to text Kylie, but she had beaten me to the punch. *When you wake up, check out Facebook!* Her text was so odd that I immediately logged on to the social media outlet. I had a bad feeling again.

When I saw what she wanted me to see, I nearly lost my mind. There were pictures of us sitting on my sofa, if you want to call what I was doing sitting. She was practically holding me up, with the glasses of wine in each of her hands. One arm was around me, and I leaned into the crook of her arm with a dopey grin on my face. I didn't know what she had said to get me to smile, but my eyes were slits, and the parts you could see of my eyes were glazed over. The next few pictures, my face was in her hands while she kissed me. There were ten photos in all, and in each, I looked completely fucked up! The caption read: *Me and my girlfriend partying hard!* Not only did she post all these fake, crude pictures of us, she tagged me in all of them, so my friends, including Danielle, would see them.

I called her this time, completely belligerent, and screamed into the phone. "What did you give me?"

"Just a little GHB." She giggled. "Relax. You're fine."

"You date-raped me?"

"Well, without the rape, yes."

"Why? Why would you do that?"

"Honestly, it started when you snubbed me for her. And then when I talked to April, things became clearer. When she told me her plans and how she needed you out of the way, I said no at first. Until she offered me a cut of the money. Funny how money changes everything."

"Wait a minute! You're in cahoots with April? To basically rob Danielle?"

"You don't have to make it sound so vile."

"It is fucking vile!" I yelled into the receiver, irate and ready to draw blood.

"Calm down."

"Calm down?" I shouted, my blood pressure rising by the second. "What exactly are the pictures supposed to accomplish? You think Danielle's going to stay away from me because of some bogus pics?"

"She's not going to be too happy with you, thinking you're sleeping with both of us."

"I'm not sleeping with her," I lied as my voice dropped to a more level tone.

"You must think I'm a moron. Well, Parker dear, I have video of little Miss Princess bringing her pathetic overnight bag to your house and only leaving to go to work. Playing house while April is away on business, are we?"

"So April knows?"

"Of course she knows! She will stop at nothing to rid herself of you. One way or another, we will wedge you out of Danielle's life. Mark my words." With that, she hung up. I quickly untagged myself. I would have deleted the post altogether, but Facebook wouldn't let me. I hoped Danielle hadn't seen it. Maybe I would get lucky. With no rights to me, that hadn't stopped her from getting mad in the past. She never liked the idea of Kylie and me hooking up. Her jealousy got the better of her, rights or no rights.

But when my phone rang and Danielle's name and contact pic popped up on the screen, my heart sank to my stomach. "Hello?" I answered.

"She's your girlfriend?"

"Dani, I—"

Click! She hung up. I called back. "You called me, ya know?"

"She's your girlfriend?" Her tone was high-pitched, and her level of annoyance was peaked.

"Danielle, I can ex—"

Click! Oh, for Christ's sake! I called her once again but wasn't able to get the first word out. "Seriously, Parker!"

"Seriously, Danielle!" I hollered. "For starters, you're the one sleeping with someone else, so don't project your shit on to me!"

Click! I'd about had enough of being hung up on, and just as I tossed my phone on the coffee table, it rang. I answered. She said, "How could you? Did you sleep with her?" The upset in her voice was heartbreaking.

"She fucking drugged me! I don't remember taking any of those pictures. I don't remember the entire night.”

“Drugged you? You expect me to believe she drugged you?”

“Yes, I do!”

“You looked pretty cozy with her in the pic of you kissing. That was a great pic! I loved seeing that!”

Her sarcasm stabbed at my heart. Her denial of my truth hurt me more than words could say. “I looked cozy? I looked fucked up! Why can’t you see that?”

“Did you sleep with her?”

“No! But even if I did, it’s none of your Goddamned business!”

Click! “Well, that didn’t go well, did it, Parker?” I said out loud. Even Addie had scampered off as I ranted and raved like a lunatic. I wore out the hardwood around my dining room table. Then I took a seat and shook my head in my hands. She knew me better than this. After all that had arisen between us, the feelings, the heat that erupted each time we were with each other, I would never betray her trust like this. Still, she didn’t believe me, and my hurt feelings made my head pound more.

Once more, my phone rang. I scrambled and fumbled for it around the table, excited it might be Danielle calling me back, but when I finally corralled it into my hand, it was April. *You gotta be kidding me.* “I saw the video of my girl carrying her bag up the walkway to your house and not coming out until the morning. I told you to stay away from her. Didn’t I? I swear I will have her hating your guts in no time, Parker. And don’t forget what I said. Those cards are still on the table if you open your mouth.”

“Don’t you lay one fucking finger on her. And

she could never hate me. She doesn't love you. She loves me!"

Her wicked laugh reverberated and echoed through the phone. "You think she loves you? Sweetheart, she's going to marry me, and there's not a damn thing you're gonna do about it. It's getting closer, you know. Just six weeks out now."

"She's not marrying you!"

Again, an evil chuckle escaped her throat. "You keep tellin' yourself that." *Click! Man, am I tired of getting hung up on!*

Danielle needed to find out about April's affair with Cece and her plan to rob her of her inheritance, and she needed to find out soon. I couldn't accept the dull ache of foreboding in the pit of my stomach. Keeping Danielle in the dark was becoming harder and harder. A whole week passed with me texting and calling her at times I knew I could, but she never answered or replied to any. I didn't think she had ever been so angry with me, and I wasn't sure what to do next. All I could do was wait it out.

❧❧❧❧

The first person I turned to was Dorian. She was stunned and appalled by this new component of April's scheme. "Wow! I thought Kylie liked you."

"Well, I think she did, until she realized she got the boot for Dani."

"Yeah, but to the extent of helping April in fucking over her future wife? That's a pretty terrible person."

"Agreed, but now Danielle isn't talking to me. Her jealousy has gotten the best of her, and she doesn't believe me."

"You're in quite a pickle!"

"That's the best solution you have?"

"Well, Parker, you did start this whole thing."

"Thanks." I seethed with sarcasm. "Because I needed you to remind me."

"It is what it is. Damage control is all you have left."

She was right, whether I liked it or not. Hearing the truth from Dorian was one thing, but Kylie was a friend of Cookie's, no matter how short-lived. That conversation would be tougher. While I wondered if she even saw the post, I powered off my phone. I didn't want to hear anything else from anyone else. A moment's peace could not be had, though. My house phone rang from the living room. I passed by the baby grand and headed for the phone that sat in its cradle on the end table. The base read *Delphina Micheletti...* Cookie.

"Hey, Cook!" I greeted her with a fake, light mood. A fake, light mood she picked up on right away.

"Hey, Cook, my ass! What the fuck is goin' on? Kylie's your new girlfriend? I don't fuckin' understand. I thought you were bangin' Danielle."

"Will ya stop? I'm not bangin' Danielle! Well, I am, but not in the crude way you just described." I sucked my tongue piercing between my two front teeth. "She fucking drugged me!"

"Excuse me? What the fuck did you just say?"

"She put GHB in my wine. She took those pictures of us after I was comatose."

"No way! No. Kylie wouldn't do that."

"Yeah? Well, it gets better," I continued. "She's helping April by trying to get Danielle to hate me. The worst part of it all is that she's in cahoots with April to steal Danielle's inheritance once her father dies from his battle with cancer."

"What's that now?"

"I never told you, but April's having an affair with Cece. She plans on marrying Danielle just to cheat her for money. She threatened to kill Danielle if I tell her. But she included Kylie in her plan to get me out of the picture."

"You don't think she would really hurt her, do you? She told you this?"

"Yes, but I haven't told Danielle because I don't know what April is capable of. I only told her that Kylie drugged me."

"Not that I give a shit or anything, but Miss Priss believed you, right?"

"Sadly, no! Dani saw the post, and she thinks Kylie is my girlfriend now. She hung up on me numerous times before refusing to answer my calls or texts. She knows me better than this!"

"She should! But women are funny when they're jealous."

"She has no right!" I was so concerned with who had what rights and who didn't.

"Doesn't fuckin' matter! You know I'm gonna kill her, right?"

"Who? Danielle?"

"No, ya goofball! Kylie! I knew something wasn't right when I saw that post."

"I thought she was your friend."

"So did I, but friends don't fuck over friends. That bitch is mine!"

"Don't do anything stupid," I warned.

"When have I ever?" She chuckled.

"It's who you are, Cookie. Remember, I grew up with you."

That said, we ended our conversation. The fog that had begun to infiltrate my mind in the beginning of the summer had made a spectacular comeback. I found it incredibly difficult to concentrate, focus, or even get through the rest of my day. I needed Danielle in my life, but things had rapidly changed.

☙☙☙☙

After three agonizing months of construction, Merge was about to have its grand reopening today. Since it was a Saturday, I expected a heavy crowd. I booked one of the most popular and familiar local bands for tonight. New Dawn. Everything in the bar was shiny and new, and the patrons made sure to tell me how impressed they were.

"It's fucking beautiful in here, Parker! The question is, how long will it last before the heathens get to it again?" Buckley jinxed as she took her first beer of the night, fresh from the tap.

"Blasphemy!" I yelled. "Don't say that! Nothing but good energy is allowed in this bar. Now take it back!" While I awaited the reversal of her negative words, I added, "I don't need you putting that shit out there."

"Okay, okay! I take it back!"

The new wood floors glistened under everyone's feet, and the recessed lighting gave off an intimate glow across the room. The two oak bars stood catty-corner to each other. Simone worked one side, and Michelle worked the other. My most prized possession was the billiards table. It was constructed of cherry mahogany wood and detailed with intricately carved side rails and claw legs that made the table classic and timeless. Solid wood beams supported the entire table to make it tournament-ready. I had ended the pool league years ago because the ladies weren't acting very lady-like. They couldn't get along. However, I was willing to give it another whirl to make up for some of the money I lost due to reconstruction. The insurance money didn't cover everything, and I had to tap into my savings.

The swarm of women around the pool table grew within minutes, and even though they were being loud and a little obnoxious, laughter emanated from the pack like hyenas on a moonlit night. The vibe in the room was exciting and positive, and my regular patrons were stoked to have their watering hole back. People were having a great time, and it felt good to be back to doing what I did best—running a bar.

Not only were Trudy and Renee back to bounce for me, but I also recruited another burly dyke to help out with the noncompliant customers. Her name was Katrina, but she went by Kat. There was nothing feminine about her, except her name. Kat stood six feet tall and had hands the size of a catcher's mitt. If her size wasn't enough to intimidate, the look on her face was. She wasn't trying to look mean. It was just her face. The three of them took up posts at essential areas of the room and kept an eye out for troublemakers.

Cookie had been here since the bar opened late this afternoon. She pounded shots with a couple of my drunkard regulars. By the time Shady sashayed though the front door, Cookie was fired up and raring to keep going. That was one of the things I admired about Shady. She could keep pace with Cookie with no problem. That hot-blooded, sexy Latina could go shot for shot with her and looked just as sexy as when she started. My friends tended to fare well with the alcohol. All but Danielle, who looked like a drowned rat the second she crossed from sober to intoxicated.

Dorian and Dahlia came in late. Normally, Dorian would have taken up residence in her corner spot early in the evening. She always wanted the best seat in the house. However, with Dahlia taking up so much of her time lately, those corner seats were no longer available. They found me within seconds of walking in, and as Dorian approached me, she looked around at the brand new Merge. "It looks nice in here, my friend." She gave me a hug. "They did a really nice job. I'm impressed! And I love the two bars, a smart idea." Dahlia ordered a drink for them, and while she did, Dorian realized who the bartenders were. She snickered. "You finally found a way to have them both here, huh? I keep telling you—threesome!"

"Stop!" I smiled and snickered back. "I'm too preoccupied for that."

"Oh, shit! How's that going anyway? I haven't really spoken to either of you."

"We haven't talked in a week, and I'm none too happy about it. She won't answer my calls."

"No chance of her showing up tonight?" she asked and saw the expression on my face. "Yeah, you're right. She ain't coming."

While we talked, I watched as Cookie and Shady danced to a fast song New Dawn were playing. Cookie twirled her around and two-stepped as best she could, always eager to entertain Shady with her silliness. She had that white girl rock, swaying back and forth, and not very well, but she tried. She threw back her head and let out a peal of laughter. Loud enough that I heard her clearly above the music and the crowd. It did my heart good to see them together like this once more.

As the night progressed and New Dawn rocked the house, the crowd tripled in size. Behind the bar, Jules made sure Simone remained fully stocked with plenty of booze, fresh glasses, and garnish. Each time I hopped behind Michelle's bar, Simone shot me a kill look. I ignored it each time because, well, I was the boss. There was nothing to get upset about in the way of Simone. I wasn't in love with Simone. I wasn't in love with Kylie. The woman I was in love with didn't want anything to do with me presently, and I couldn't feel worse about it. Everything was back in full swing. Everything but me. The only hope I had left was that Danielle may show up for our Sunday chess game. I knew April was home. It was the weekend. But I still wondered if she might show. Just holding on to that hope was enough for me to say *no* once again to Simone's usual Saturday night request.

"But why?" she asked at the end of the night. "Don't I eat it good enough anymore?"

"Don't be silly. Of course you do! I just have some things on my mind recently, and honestly, I don't think I'd be able to cum."

"You? Not be able to cum? Parker, even if it's taken you a while, I've always been able to make you cum."

"I can't deny that, but I'm gonna pass this week."

Ultimately, she accepted my refusal for oral sex and took a taxi home for the night. Surprisingly, I received the same invitation from Michelle, who had given up on me a long time ago. I just wanted to be alone. Which wasn't good since I was a true people person. Wanting to be alone was a signal of an impending struggle with depression, and I prayed quietly that the fog would lift.

"It's good to be back, boss!" Jules said as she grabbed her keys, passed by me, and headed for the door. I nodded in her general direction, and she disappeared for the night. She left me alone in a now quiet and eerily silent bar.

Chapter Nineteen

I slid off the barstool and walked to my office. My anxiety level was out of control, and I dug in my pocket. A small dose of Xanax would help take the edge off. I dumped them into the palm of my hand and noticed three pills that were different from the rest. "Oh, yeah!" I forgot that I had put those three Mollys in the bottle to give to Buckley. When she found out I had them but didn't want them, her eyes lit up, and she asked if she could have them. Only I forgot, and so did she. I picked out a Xanie and threw the Molly back in the bottle. *I'll give it to her next time I see her.*

I sat on the love seat with the chessboard in front of me and peered at Danielle's empty spot across from me. The clock in the corner of the room ticked the minutes away. It was six ten a.m., and I was pretty sure she wasn't coming. I hung my head and placed my face in my hands. Tears burned a trail down my cheek and dropped like rain into my palms. Every time I wiped them away, they rebelled against me, insisting they were right to shed and spill down my face. They were right. I missed her so much.

As I grabbed the bottom of my long-sleeve shirt to dry my eyes, Danielle appeared in front of me. "Oh, my God!" I exclaimed, so happy to see her. I got up from the couch, wrapped my arms around her, and squeezed hard. She hesitated at first, but then gave in, and hugged me back. "You came," I muffled into her shoulder.

She had yet to say a word, and with my eyes still wet, I searched her eyes, wanting to see forgiveness in them, even if I hadn't done anything wrong. "I came because we need to talk."

"Does April know you're here?"

"She does."

"She's okay with that?"

"Only because of why I'm here."

"Okay, you're freakin' me out here, Danielle. What is it?"

"Maybe you should sit down." She pointed to the sofa with an open hand.

"What the fuck, Dani? What is it?"

I took a seat, and she sat beside me. We faced each other, and without blinking, she said, "I can't see you anymore."

"What?" I spouted with a misery so acute that it was a physical pain. I bit my lip until it throbbed my pulse and gave a choked, desperate laugh. "You're kidding, right? You must be kidding because you would never say that seriously."

"I'm serious."

"No. No, don't say that."

"Parker, there are a bunch of reasons I can't see you anymore."

"But we're friends. We've been friends for so many years."

"I know. And maybe we can be friends again down the line, but right now..."

"Is this because April doesn't want you to see me? Or because you don't want to see me?"

"A little bit of both, I suppose, because..."

She pulled her cellphone from her messenger bag. "Receiving these photos last night really pissed me off. They made me jealous, and they made me insecure, but most of all, they made me think that girl is nuts! Why is she sending photos to my phone? And photos like this?"

I took the phone from her hand, and I couldn't believe my eyes. There were about five pictures of Kylie basically molesting me. I was so out of it I didn't remember a thing. I surely didn't remember her hand down my pants. In the photos, she was making out with me, feeling my breasts under my shirt. My face was emotionless in them, my eyes barely open. "Danielle, I told you, she slipped me a mickey. Look at me," I showed her the phone and pointed. "Look at me! I'm wasted."

She looked at the phone again. "So you got drunk. It's not like you've never been drunk."

"I was unconscious. Why won't you believe me?"

"Why would she drug you? It doesn't make sense. And is she trying to make me jealous by sending these to me? Does she know something about us?" She asked a series of questions I couldn't answer, but she continued, "It doesn't matter, and I can't take the stress of this anymore. She's the one that's free. You should be with her."

"I don't want her. I want you. I've always wanted you."

"You can't have me. I belong with April."

All at once, a fury built up in me, and April's conniving plan had to be revealed. And I was going to be the one to reveal it—now. But before I could get it out, she hit me with another sharp blow. "Her company offered her a promotion and a transfer to

Houston," Danielle said, her voice emotionless. "She's taking it."

"What? You're moving?" A wave of panic swept through me. "No!" I placed my hands on her shoulders. "No! Danielle, no! Please!"

She finally looked into my eyes, and that familiar zing of passion passed between us as it always did when we looked at each other. However, when I leaned in to kiss her, she leaned away from me. "No. This ends here and now."

"What about your dad? Holy shit, Dani, what about your dad?"

"He'll come with us."

"Oh, I'm sure that'll go over well. He doesn't want to move from his home and everyone he knows, especially at the end of his life. Why would you uproot him like that?"

"Don't tell me how to care for my father! I'm sorry you're mad, but I am marrying her."

"Dani, you can't!"

"What are you talking about? Of course I can." She turned to go, and as she reached for the doorknob, I uncorked the dam and let it flow, "She's cheating on you!"

Her hand stayed frozen to the doorknob, and she slowly turned back around to face me. "Excuse me?"

"April is cheating on you with Cece. They're involved in a full-blown affair." Instead of speaking, she allowed me to go on. "I walked in on them making out on the camping trip. She told her to be patient. That she was going to marry you, wait for your father to pass away, and take half of your inheritance. And on top of that, she said she would kill you if I told you."

There. It was out. She stared at me in silence, doubt visibly taking over her face. "I cannot believe that you would make up such a story just to keep me from leaving." She gazed into my eyes as though I had let her down. "Not only do you expect me to believe that a woman you've been attracted to, kissing, and hugging all over drugged you, but now you expect me to believe April is going to rob me and threatened to kill me?" She shook her head. "Just seems too farfetched. This isn't the way to get me to be with you."

"I'm not making it up. I heard her! She's gonna marry you and fuck you over!"

"No, she's not. I am so disappointed in you, Parker."

"You're not going to do this! You need to believe me before it's too late!" I reached for her arm, but she shrugged me off.

"I have to go!" She turned for the door once more, and my panic was replaced with anger. I was losing her, and I had no control over it. I knew she was serious when she opened the door and began walking through it. I spewed my rage and grabbed for a tumbler glass, chucking it at the door as she closed it behind her. I was so enraged that I took every one of the glasses sitting there and winged them at the door one after the other, glass shattering all over the floor with each strike. "Yeah! That's right! Run! Run away! It's what you do best, anyway!"

My body was shaking uncontrollably from the inside out. I collapsed to my knees as my rage turned to sadness. I wept into my hands. Tears dripped to the floor. My cheeks were flushed and warm, and I became light-headed. I almost hyperventilated from the hysteria I felt. Danielle left me. An acute sense of loss overcame me, and I felt a nauseating despair. It was a raw and primitive grief. I balled up on the floor in a cocoon of anguish. I was unable to get it together. All that April had predicted had come to fruition. I was trying to save her, but she was like a skydiver jumping with a knapsack on her back, insisting it was a parachute. All these years of loving her, of being her friend and confidante were over in a few seconds.

I eventually calmed down enough to stand. I dusted myself off and straightened myself out. A switch flipped, and the part of me that cared was flushed into the wind. I didn't want to feel. I wanted only to be numb to the hurt I was feeling. It was hard to accept defeat, and the lack of control over the situation drove me crazy. No further thought was involved when I pulled my cellphone from my pocket and scanned my contact list.

"Hey! I changed my mind. Can you come back?" That conversation over, I went back in my contact list. "Hey! Are you awake? Why don't you come back to the bar? I want to talk to you about something." Phone calls made, I tidied up, both myself and my office, as I swept up the broken glass and discarded it. I kept glancing at the chessboard on the coffee table, a constant reminder of Danielle. One fluid motion of my hand, and I sent it flying through the air, the pieces scattered in every direction. So much for tidying up.

One-third of my mind-numbing plan showed up a half hour later. "I'm glad you changed your mind. I haven't tasted you since your pool party," Simone said as she walked through my office door.

"You haven't tasted me, and I've missed being tasted."

"Well, let's get down to business then, shall we? Pants off!" she commanded as she pushed me onto the love seat where Danielle usually sat. However, just as she was about to drop to her knees, the door to my office swung open. "So what did you wanna talk to me about?" Michelle asked as she walked in.

"Wait! What the fuck is she doing here?" Simone asked indignantly.

"Relax!" I exclaimed and stood back up. "You're both here for the same reason."

"Oh, really?" Michelle's voice was sharp. "And exactly what reason would that be?"

A shit-eating grin spread across my face as I explained, "You're both here to pleasure me."

They looked at each other and back toward me. "Um…no, I'm not sharing you," Simone refused.

"Yeah, Parker! I don't even like serving drinks with her. I'm not about to have sex with you with her. So, no!" Michelle barked.

"Are you sure? It could be a delightful time." I opened the palm of my hand and showed them the three little pills I had hidden there.

"What are those?" They simultaneously chimed in together, intrigue getting the best of them.

"Molly."

"What?" Michelle drew out. Her eyes nearly popped out of her head with pure excitement as she practically drooled.

"I take it you like them?" I offered my hand to her. She picked one up, and I grabbed a few bottles of water and gave one to Michelle. "What about you,

Simone? You don't want to be left out, do you?" I placed my open hand in front of her and tempted her with my sweet, sinful proposal.

"Could be fun," Michelle said and popped the pill into her mouth.

I tossed mine down my throat, too. I had never taken it before, but I wanted to find out what it was like because I didn't want to feel this way anymore. I just wanted to let go and float. Facing Simone, I said, "Come on. Take it. Let's have some fun! This is a great way to bury the hatchet between you two." I paused for effect. "And a great team-building exercise."

That caused genuine laughter among the three of us, and the ice finally broke. Simone swallowed the Molly, and I cracked open a bottle of wine. "Something to take the edge off while we wait for it to kick in," I said and distributed the wine among us. They were still a bit cautious in each other's presence, so used to hating each other. We all had a seat on the sofa, sipped from our glasses, and attempted to have an adult conversation. It was somewhat forced at first, but as the time passed, conversation became easier. When we started laughing and talking more fluidly, I realized that the drug was working.

Everything felt so good suddenly. Every fuck I gave about my situation with Dani dissipated. Even the cushions on the couch had a new feel, plush and soft against my skin. There was no time for feeling the couch up. Michelle welcomed the effects and was the first to start touching. "It's been so long." She rubbed my arm and moved closer to me.

Simone, though high, shot Michelle a dirty look. She was jealous since she never had to share me, especially with someone she despised. But I squashed that immediately and pulled her softly toward me. I was in the middle of two hot women, both wanted me equally, and while my head floated with giddiness, they started kissing my cheek, one on either side. Tiny kisses led to my lips, until the three of us were making out. Tongues swirled and circled as we explored the recesses of one another's mouths.

Simone's desire grew rapidly, and she climbed on top of me while still making out with Michelle. *Whoa!* All my senses were heightened. Every nibble, every kiss, every touch sent a tingling rush over my entire body. My nerve endings were alive, and I shed all the negativity the past week had thrown at me. "Oh, my God, you feel so fucking good," I announced as I trailed my fingers up and down Simone's thighs and backside.

Michelle was not to be denied. She pushed Simone over to my right leg while she straddled my left. "Nice." I indulged in two women grinding their pussies on my thighs. Our clothes were still on, but that didn't stop any of us. Simone was the first to grab for my pussy and cupped my khakis. The slightest graze of that area sent my clit screaming for touch. The grinding, the riding, all of it slung us into a mind-blowing euphoria.

Sapphic moans bellowed from us. Our hands were like an octopus as we rubbed one another into a frenzy. "Take off your clothes," I directed since I was the ringleader of this sexual circus. They undressed while I scrambled to rid myself of my own clothing. The only thought in my mind was feeling their silky, soft skin sliding all over me.

Our clothes were thrown and scattered across my office, and with magnetic force, we fell directly to the floor in a heap of bodies aching to be felt, rubbed, and tickled. My main objective was to have them go down on me together, but now that I was in an altered state, I decided I wanted more than that. I wanted to get them off, too, and I wouldn't be satisfied until I did. We formed a circle, knelt on the carpet, and the fondling got underway. We groped one another in ways none of us thought possible. The beef between these two dissolved right before my eyes as they made out again.

They were so attractive while they sucked on each other's tongues that I couldn't resist placing my hand behind their heads and forcing them closer. When I pushed my fingers between Simone's legs, slipping them between her moist folds, she jutted forward and slid back and forth over them. Her clit was hard as I rubbed over it, and she cried out, "Uh, yeah! Uh-huh...yeah!"

Her pussy was so wet and her urge so great that she grabbed my hand and forced those same fingers inside of her. "Oh, fuck yes!" I indulged and fingered her hole.

"What about me?" Michelle asked while her tongue licked at my ear. I turned my face to her and allowed her to shove her tongue in my mouth.

I pulled my sticky fingers out of Simone and immersed them into Michelle's awaiting wetness, which gobbled up my fingers whole. "Fuck!" I wailed again as I delighted in the sensation of her drenched pussy.

"Uhh...Uhh...Fuck me!" Michelle yelled and wrapped her arms around my neck. She opened her legs wider to give me better leverage.

I didn't think I had ever been so horny in my

life. The pleasure induced by the Molly shattered any previous joy from any other drugs that I had ever done. But even high as hell, Simone's jealousy compelled her to wedge between us. She wanted the attention back. And I gave it to her as I retrieved my fingers from between Michelle's thighs and plunged them deep back into her.

She tried to ride them again, but I took hold of the reins this time. I fucked her hard, and her wetness slapped against my hand. "Oh, fuck me, Parker!" She circled her arms around my neck and commanded my attention as she orgasmed for the first time this morning.

My appetite for sex had sprung to a fiendish level, and I pushed Michelle to the floor, parted her legs, and dived in face first. "Oh, fuck yeah, Parker! Eat me!" she barked out and pushed my face farther into her core. "Goddamn, that feels good! Lick it! Yeah, lick it!"

While I ate away at her erect gem and lapped up the puddle of sticky nectar she produced, Simone set my bottom half on its side, opened my legs, and devoured my pussy the way she knew how. That slurping sound she made while sucking on my clit created a reverberating vibration between her lips and my nubbin. "Oh, God, yes!" I moaned as my face was still buried in Michelle's crotch. Michelle's thirst was only quenched when Simone lay on her side, opened her legs, and invited Michelle's mouth to entertain her tortured pussy that begged for release once more. I was amazed at how willing Simone was to be felt, let alone licked by another woman. I knew she had it in her. All inhibitions shed away because of the Molly.

Michelle got off first, my mouth firmly in place

as I licked her fervently. "Don't stop! Don't stop!" she screamed out as her orgasm transported her to heightened levels of pleasure. The Molly-induced climax did nothing in the way of satisfaction, though, and she went right back to eating Simone out.

Seconds later, it was Simone's turn to feel the nirvana of having her eyes roll back in her head at the pleasure she succumbed to. "But you're a woman," she cried out. "Oh. My God! I'm cumming!" They both indulged in an orgasm, but I hadn't got mine yet, and they knew it. I got up from the floor, fell backward onto the couch, and opened my legs wide. They stared each other down before they raced to their knees and dug in immediately. They found my clit with their tongues and lapped up my juices.

"Oh, fuck yeah!" I shouted out at the feel of two wet tongues on my drenched pussy. They licked in unison, then off canter, and it all felt…so…good. From the cushions on the couch rubbing my backside to the two women giving me head, it all felt like paradise. As they went at it, I noticed they pushed each other out of the way, each of them wanting my pussy all to herself. "Ladies, please! No fighting! There's plenty for both of you." I grabbed their heads and brought them together between my legs once more.

Their tongues slid up and down the shaft of my clit and made my nerve endings stand up. I moved my hips to meet their every stroke, but once again, they nudged each other out of the way. Michelle took a turn at me and flattened her tongue, as it slid over my clit with one big swoop. She did this several times before she took it into her mouth and sucked lightly on it. I hadn't felt her mouth on me for a couple of years and had forgotten how good she made me feel.

But the hunger of Simone's addiction to eating pussy possessed her in a way she couldn't control. She gave Michelle one good shove and sent her tumbling to the floor. She was so crazed that she clamped her whole mouth around my pussy and started licking me like a madwoman, unwilling to stop until I came for her. My orgasm came in waves of heightened pleasure. "Oh, my God! Yes!" I screamed and fucked her face savagely while I held her head in place.

Michelle refused to be frozen out. She quickly got up and fought for position. She tried to lick up the last drops of cum I had to offer. My howl blended in with the sound of the door opening again. The voice shuddered with surprise and dismay. "What the..." I heard. The three of us turned to see the woman standing in the entryway. Danielle. "Is this what the fuck you do?" she yelled incredulously. She was visibly shaken. Her eyes were wide, but her expression was one of pure repugnance. "Just how many women are you sleeping with?"

I immediately pushed Michelle and Simone out of the way and rushed to get up. Danielle wasn't waiting. She stormed out of my office and slammed the door behind her. I was hot on her tail and attempted to pull my pants up. Doing two things at once was almost an impossible feat as fucked up as I was. After tripping over my pants and my own feet, I stumbled up behind her. She reached for her car door. I grabbed her hand and spun her around to face me. "Dani, wait!" I clamored.

"No!" She jerked away from me. "I had come to try and talk this out with you, but I can see there's no talking to you. I made the right decision."

"No, you didn't! You belong with me! This was

just me being pissed at you."

"So every time you're pissed at me, I can expect you to fuck other women?"

"Why are you using that word? It doesn't even sound right coming out of your mouth."

"Isn't that what you were doing? Fucking? It's dirty and gross! Threesomes with your bartenders?" Her face became a marble effigy of contempt, sickened by the thought of her words.

"Danielle, please let me explain."

"I thought you just did."

As I stood there with my pants still unbuttoned, babbling like an idiot, the Molly surged through me again, made me tingle all over, and tightened my jaw. The colors in the morning sky were so lovely behind her as she yelled and shouted out her displeasure with me. Even the warm breeze that coursed through the morning air brushed over my skin and teased my clit. My body was confused, feeling every nerve ending seethe for touch. Yet my brain needed to be sharp right now. I needed to get it together before it was too late. But I choked on the very words that would save me, that could save me. Truth be told, there were none. My only defense was that I loved her and couldn't have her.

"I don't ever want to see you again," she said, her eyes beholden to mine, pain and hurt still flickering there.

Suddenly, all life drained from my face. All pleasure left my body. I felt like I had been struck by a freight train. How could she? I dropped my lashes quickly to hide my own hurt. The animation left her face. She gathered herself and spoke calmly with no lightning in her eyes, no smile of tenderness. "This is really over."

She slid into her convertible, drove off, and left me standing there like a washed-up hooker. I finally took the time to button and zip my pants and headed back into the bar. I was sullen and still high and didn't want to be. Feelings of joy depleted in me, and the touch of anything that made me feel good only annoyed me.

I walked back into my office to find Michelle and Simone twisted into a sixty-nine position. Whatever feelings of hatred they had for each other changed to desire as they ate each other out like their lives depended on it. I gathered up my shit, picked up my Jeep keys, and headed back to the door. Before I left, I turned to look at them once more. They were so involved in what they were doing, they never even heard me leave. I shut the door behind me and left the bar, upset and on a mission of self-destruction. Fate was about to show its ugly face, and I welcomed it.

Chapter Twenty

I didn't remember what happened after I got in my Jeep and started driving. Going home wasn't an option. A sad song was playing on the stereo, and a single tear turned into sobbing as they clung to my eyelashes before they splashed down my face. I rocked back and forth to the gloomy, melancholy melody, hanging on tightly to the steering wheel.

However, sadness yielded quickly to anger and resentment once more. My iPod was an arm's length away, and I snatched it from the passenger seat. I sifted through my playlists and settled on a list titled *Rage.* Hard guitar riffs and thundering drumbeats pounded out of my sound system, and before I knew it, I was headbanging. I was feeling nefarious, wicked even, and when I was in a self-destructive mood, there was only one person I sought out. Cookie.

I leaned to the side, wiggled my cellphone out from my pocket, and dialed my corruptive friend. "Hey!" she greeted me abruptly, and I could already tell something was wrong with her.

"Hey! What's goin' on with you?" I asked as I got off the exit to her place.

"I'll tell you if you tell me first," she said while we assessed each other's anger.

"Outside of Kylie fucking me over and then me fucking myself over, Danielle doesn't want to see me anymore. She ended it," I bristled with indignation.

"Now you!"

"Shit! Okay, me. So I just got a voicemail from Shady. Wherever she was, there was a bad signal, so her message was broken up, but I distinctly heard her say she decided to go back to that fuckin' whore. Twice… Twice, Parker, she's fucked me over for that girl! So I called her back and left a voicemail for her, telling her to stay where the fuck she is. She's been calling me ever since, and I won't answer her calls or check her voicemails. Fuck her!" She continued, "I'm about to go out and do some fucked-up things. You wanna come with me?" I was already pulling in her driveway. She peeked out the window, and I waved. "Well, speak of the motherfucking devil!" she exclaimed agreeably.

"It's on, bitch!" I shouted as I busted through the front door of her tiny ranch-style home.

She greeted me with a fist bump. "Lickety split, we're about to get into some shit…bitch!"

After a succession of *bitch this* and *bitch that,* we settled at the breakfast nook in her kitchen. She had a rather humble home as it was. It wasn't that she wasn't clean, but my friend had a bit of a clutter issue. Shady had been good for her in this way. She needed someone to take care of her, and Shady did a great job of it. But when she left, Cookie went right back to her cluttering ways. She moved a pile of mail and papers from the table onto the kitchen counter and began rolling a joint. I started to come down off the Molly and fixed myself a cup of coffee from the pot she had brewed that morning.

She lit the joint and handed it to me. "Don't say *no,* either! You look like hell, by the way," she said, and I took the joint with no more fight left in me. I put it to my lips and pulled hard from it as I pursued numbness and wanted to release my pain.

"Tell ya what, Kylie better fuckin' stay away from me at work. If I didn't need my job, I'd jack her the fuck up," she confided.

"Ya know, Cook? I'm not even mad at her at this point. I'm mad at Danielle for not believing me. After twenty years of friendship, she didn't believe me."

"Wow! You'd think she would fuckin' know you better than that. You'd never lie to her. Even I know that!"

While telling me her story, Cookie pulled a bong out of a hiding space behind her couch and came back into the kitchen. She filled the bong with water, packed the bowl with quality weed, and handed it to me. I took it like a pro as I lit the bowl, watched the base fill with smoke, and pulled the stem up to suck it all in like a vacuum.

"I thought we were falling in love all over again, like we might have a second chance. I don't know what this girl has on her, but she can't seem to let her go. She fuckin' cheated on Shady's ass! Why does she want her back?" Cookie asked.

I answered immediately. "She cheated on you, and you want her back," I pointed out.

"That's different."

"How?"

"I've never stopped loving her." She looked away, then moved restlessly while she squirmed in her chair. She seemed uncomfortable exposing her vulnerability. However, her guard went right back up as she repacked the bowl with more weed.

"More? Really?"

"Always more, and we're gonna take a ride, too."

"Cookie, I haven't even been to bed yet. I've

been up all night."

"I have a cure for that. Besides, I thought you wanted to be bad."

"Well, I do."

"Then let's go!"

"Go where?"

"I've got just the place."

She got up and expected me to follow as she went into the garage, which was bigger than her entire house. Her passion was motorcycles, not just riding them, but fixing and refurbishing them, too. Unlike her house, the garage was immaculate. Each tool had its own place in a huge rolling toolbox that sat next to a bike she was working on recently. Her Harley was tucked away with a cover draped over it—overkill since it was already in a dry and well-kept place. Her fire engine-red Honda VFR1200F stood uncovered and raring to go. The thing was loud and fast with its megaphone exhaust, and her eyes lit up whenever she saw it. It was her favorite bike to ride when she wanted to stir up some trouble.

"Come on." She pulled the cover off her Harley for me.

"What do you mean come on? My bike's at my house."

"So? What, my Harley's not good enough for you?"

"Well, she's not exactly my Fat Boy, but she'll do."

"Snob! No wonder you and Miss Goody Two-Shoes get along so well."

"Not anymore." My anger swelled once more. "Fuck it! Let's go!" I chose one of her many helmets, put it on my head, and fastened the chin strap. However, before I climbed onto her hog, I looked down at what I was wearing. I was still in my khaki pants and long-sleeve shirt. My sleeves were rolled up, but I was hot, and I wanted shorts and a T-shirt. "You got a pair of shorts for me at least? I'm roasting."

"Nah, I'm down to the pair I got on. I need to do some fuckin' laundry."

Accepting the fact that I was going to remain at a boiling temperature, I threw my right leg over the engine of the cycle and took a seat. She opened the garage door, and we idled out. "Where are we going?" I asked.

"Don't worry about it. Just keep up with me." Cookie full-throttled it out of the driveway, raced to the stop sign, peered back at me. "What did I just tell you? Keep up!" She looked forward and squealed wheels through the stop sign. I chased, hot on her tail, and was about to pass her. The power of her Harley was immense, but I was used to my Fat Boy, and I missed it right now. She wasn't used to me riding as carelessly as she did, but my destructive mood had just begun, and she hadn't seen the last of it. I would shock her several times that day.

❧ ❧ ❧ ❧

It was about three p.m., and not much was going on in Tampa on this warm, sunny Sunday. I let Cookie take the lead and was surprised when she rode toward East Central Tampa, not far from the city's center. I was even more concerned when she turned onto Nebraska Avenue, a street known for its nightlife and prostitution. The nightclubs were closed, and it was too early to see hookers out doing their thing.

Strip clubs and dilapidated properties lined the street, and I couldn't imagine where she was taking me. We stopped briefly to be entertained by a woman, clad in a bikini, doing a little dance. It was her best attempt at a street performance, and she was terrible at it. More than likely, she was a drug user trying to collect some change for her daily fix.

I followed Cookie down a side street, then a back alley loaded with bags of trash and congregating homeless people. We came to a stop in front of an old, decrepit building. Several windows were boarded up or busted out, and graffiti was splattered randomly across the walls. Nicknames were spray painted in big bubble letters along with various gang symbols. The building was evidently abandoned, and I watched as Cookie started to get off her bike. "What are you doing?" I asked, bewildered at why we were here.

"I'm going in." She walked toward the door. She hesitated and looked back over her shoulder at me. "Come on."

I scanned my surroundings. I was uneasy about the kind of people milling around. Not making eye contact with anyone, I followed Cookie closely. Before we went in, she pulled cash out of her pocket and handed it to a toothless crack whore. "Watch over those bikes." The junkie stared at her before she added, "I'll take care of you again when I come out." The woman, filthy from head to toe, glanced at the twenty in Cookie's hand and took it.

"How do you know she'll actually watch the bikes?" I asked.

"Because she watches my bike for me every time I come."

"Wait! You frequent the place?"

"I don't know about frequent, but yes, every now and then, when I'm in a foul mood, I stop by and take some aggression out." She climbed the steps to the front door. "Now come on already!"

I followed her through the rickety, broken-down door and was immediately hit with the stench of urine. "What the fuck is this place?" I asked as my nose scrunched up from the odor.

"You'll see."

We walked down the piss-soaked hallway. When we got to the end of the hallway, we entered the last room. The first thing I noticed were different groups of people huddled together in separate areas. I followed Cookie through them to a small crowd crouched on the floor in a circle. They were a rambunctious group, some cheering, some squawking their disapproval. Then I noticed what was taking place—a dice game. I looked at Cookie, almost panicked, because I knew I shouldn't be here. "Don't worry. It's not a card game," she said while she pulled more cash from her pocket. "Poker's your downfall, not dice." As if one was any better or worse than the other. Both were gambling, and the effects of it were never positive for me.

Sadly, the mood I was in was unruly, and my temperament was anything but subdued. "Just for a little while, to get your mind off of her," she said as she was greeted by a couple of people she knew. "You said you were in the mood to be bad. Well, be bad!" She tossed her money into a pile in the center and rolled the dice. I didn't get in the game right away and chose instead to watch for a while.

Not everyone in the room was gambling. Some were chatting and doing drugs as if this was all so normal. I wasn't talking about smoking pot, either.

I watched one guy tie a shoestring around his arm as he tightened it with his teeth before injecting heroin into his veins. I stared as he nodded in and out of consciousness. Then there was the group in the corner of the room. Men and women alike snorted, smoked, and banged meth, or what I'd always called crank. I hadn't done that since I was just out of high school. I also hadn't been to sleep in over twenty-four hours by this time, and quite frankly, I was jealous. "Seven come eleven!" Cookie shook the dice and rolled them on the floor against the wall. "You getting' in?" she pushed.

"In a minute." I walked over to a guy who was a part of the speed party. "Dude, you got any of that for sale?" I knew I shouldn't, but I didn't care at the moment.

His eyes bugged out of his head. "How much you want?"

"Just a twenty."

He pulled a big baggie out, filled with a bunch of little baggies loaded with the off-white, chunky substance, and handed me one. I took it, gave him the twenty, and started to open it.

"What the fuck?" Cookie said in a huff. "I hope you're fuckin' sharin'!"

An empty cardboard box was in front of us, and we used it as a makeshift table. I wiped it off with my hand and dumped the contents of the bag out onto it. It was so thick, chunky, and sticky that it was hard to form a line as it stuck to the credit card I was using to cut it. Lines made up as best as I could, we took turns snorting it through a rolled-up dollar bill. It was harsh and burned the inside of my nostril. The taste dripped down the back of my throat. It was disgusting. I had forgotten how horrible it tasted, and I practically gagged. However, as disgusting as the taste was, I welcomed it, fully aware of the effects it would bring in seconds. "Ow! Ow!" I snapped my head back and rubbed my nose, as if this would somehow help the burning. "Fuck!"

"Gimme that bill!" Cookie insisted. She reached for the made-up tube and quickly inhaled her portion.

"I have a question." I looked around the room at the junkies doing their drugs of choice. "Aren't you afraid these people will rob you?"

I thought I had spoken low enough, but the gambling section of this area of the room all turned to me, and without saying a word, they raised their shirts to show me the pistols buried in the waistband of their pants. "How about you?" I asked Cookie directly and never expected her to do the same, but she did. "What the fuck are you doing with that?" I asked, almost panic-stricken.

"You asked." She squatted back down to get back in the game.

The men and women she was associating with were rough. There were about eight of us, half were men. The other two women appeared to be gay. The men, not so much, but they didn't discriminate. Our money was green, too, after all. Tattoos, guns, cigarettes, drugs, and dice were the menu of the day. When I asked Cookie why she didn't just go to the Seminole Hard Rock Casino, her answer was, "I don't need to wait ten minutes between rolls for people to place bets all over the table. That's craps. This is dice! Straight up street dice! Basic craps and no minimum or maximum bets. Besides, look at all the added treats I get here."

"Seriously?" I asked.

This wasn't who I was anymore. I said I'd never gamble again, but the temptation was too great. Even though this was way grimier than the back rooms I used to frequent, the drugs and the draw of gambling compelled me to join in all the same. "Slide over." I nudged her over and squeezed between her and the guy with huge ear gauges. His stretched-out earlobes were adorned with huge spikes sticking through them, and although he freaked me out some by his appearance and a small, but constant facial tic, he ended up being a nice guy. Just goes to show that looks could be deceiving.

The crank renewed my energy, and for someone who hadn't slept in over twenty-four hours, I was feeling fresh and awake. I was racy and jittery, and even though I hadn't smoked a cigarette in years, I found myself asking the guy with spikes though his ears for a smoke. He lit it and handed it to me, and I dragged off it fiercely and blew the smoke into a cloud that already hovered over the clique of gamblers. We shot dice, smoked, and shared in a flask of whiskey. Hours passed without our knowledge, consumed in addiction. After all was said and done, I lost a total of five hundred dollars, Cookie just a little less. I was winning for the better part of the game but gave it back in the last hour we were there.

❧❧❧❧

After yet another line of meth, Cookie and I decided to pack it up. It was time to go. We headed back down the hallway, outside to our bikes, where the homeless crack whore was keeping watch over them.

Just as Cookie said she would, she handed her another twenty-dollar bill. It was dark, almost eleven already. I had been up for thirty-six hours now, without an end in sight. The speed would have me up for hours longer, but when I'd finally come down from this hyped-up high, I'd probably sleep for days.

We were both high and drunk with nowhere to go but still looking to make some trouble. Neither of us paid any mind to our number one rule of *no imbibe and ride* as we started the engines. Self-destruction was right around the corner waiting for us. Cookie was drunk enough that her sensitive side was coming out, alternating between sadness and anger. "I wanna go past her fuckin' house!"

"Who?" I asked.

"Shady."

"Why? What good would that do?"

"I just wanna see her."

"It's a bad idea! Just as bad an idea as me wanting to ride by Danielle's."

"But maybe I could change her mind," she said, desperately clinging to the idea of *them* once more. "She played me all over again. I don't understand."

"I'm sorry she hurt you again," I said sincerely. "I know how much it hurt the first time she left."

"Well, I don't fuckin' care! I wanna fuckin' see her! Follow me!" she yelled, revved her engine, and took off. She hightailed it down the street with me in chase mode, trying to keep up with her. The night air was exhilarating, and my heart raced as I trailed her down a pitch-dark, deserted back road.

The road wasn't exactly smooth. It was an old, narrow road that weaved through marshes and reeds. The grass was tall as the headlight from my cycle shone on it while I rounded a bend. The warm air was humid, and I was sweating under the helmet. I regretted wearing long pants and the long-sleeve shirt that clung to my body. The stars were covered with clouds, and fog had settled over the narrow road. It was pitch dark with no streetlights.

Cookie whizzed back and forth, crossing over the double yellow line, slowing just enough to allow me to pass, then accelerating past me again. Then she shot off like a rocket, traveling at speeds so fast that her taillight appeared as a small dot, then disappeared in the mist and fog in the distance. I wished she would slow down, all the while I increased my own speed to try to catch up. We were pumped, and I could hear her screaming at the top of her lungs while she rode twenty-five yards in front of me. I chimed in, screaming my own insanity. Each time I heard Danielle's voice in my head, uttering the words *I don't ever want to see you again,* I charged forward, breezing by Cookie like a ghost rider burning a trail behind me. This went on all the way down the long stretch of winding road.

When we came across a piece of road that was a straightaway, she shot past me again, giving me the finger as she did. I laughed under my face mask, which steamed up the shield and blurred my vision for a split second. Just then, the road curved. I didn't notice how close I had come to her bike, and a fairly large pothole suddenly appeared and was unavoidable. The front tire of her bike hit that hole with such force that it stopped dead, tossing her forward and into the air. It was like flying down a snow-covered mountain on a pair of skis and running into mud. The skis stopped, but the skier kept going. Everything happened so fast, and my reaction time was slowed. My bike slammed into hers, metal grinding against metal and making a hideous, loud sound. Just like her, my body was propelled through the air, spinning like the propellers of a helicopter. And then a large tree stopped my momentum, breaking my helmet in half, and nearly my body, as well. I didn't remember anything after that.

❧❧❧❧

When I awoke, I looked around, confused and scared, not knowing where I was. There were machines and tubes, and a loud beeping sound surrounding me. I finally realized I was in the hospital, and slowly, the events that preceded this knowledge came back to me. *The crash!* I turned my head to the side and immediately recognized Cookie lying in the bed next to me. She had all sorts of tubes connected to her, and a thick tube connected to a machine was sticking out of her mouth. It had been taped there to keep it immobile. The machine was breathing for her. She had bruises and lacerations all over her face, hands, and arms, and was basically held together by stitches and bandages. Her whole head was bandaged, too, from an apparent head injury. The machine made a loud breathing noise each time the air was forced into her lungs.

I was so disturbed by the image of my friend barely clinging to life that I jumped up from my own bed and hurried to her side. I touched her arm and wiggled it some to rouse her, but she didn't move. She lay there motionless, and I shouted out, "Cookie!" She needed to wake up. I needed to know she would be okay. Again, I squeezed and wiggled her arm.

"Cookie!" I yelled once more, filled with trepidation and fear.

"Why the fuck are you yelling?" I heard from behind me as I gasped and grabbed my chest out of sheer surprise.

"Holy shit! You scared me!" I exclaimed at Cookie popping up out of nowhere. "How are you standing here if you're there?" I pointed to the Cookie lying in the bed.

"Same way you are." She pointed to the bed I just got out of, but when I glanced at that bed, much to my horror, I was still lying there, or at least my body was. A breathing machine was attached to me, as well, and I damn near lost my mind. "What the fuck!" I shouted, terrified.

"Calm down!"

"Calm down? We're both out of our bodies, and you're telling me to calm down?"

"That's what the fuck I'm telling you, yes!"

"But...but I...but you..."

She took hold of my shoulders and shook me. "Get a hold of your fuckin' self, Parker!"

"This can't be real! This is a dream, right? It's gotta be a dream!"

Just then, a nurse entered the room. She checked the machines we were hooked up to and took our vital signs. I tapped her on the shoulder, but she ignored me. I tapped her again. "Hey, lady!" No response. "Hey, lady!"

"Parker, she can't hear you," Cookie explained.

"But I don't understand what's happening," I said, baffled by the concept of another realm. "Why aren't you more freaked out? Aren't you scared?"

"Nah! Not really. I feel eerily peaceful actually."

"You do?"

"Yeah. I don't feel any pain, and by all rights, I should," she admitted and looked over at her broken body.

"Well, I don't feel any pain, either, but peaceful is something that's lost on me."

"I left my body before you did and saw my Aunt Judy," she told me.

"Aunt Judy?"

"Yeah. She's dead."

"What?"

"She told me we're in some kind of staging area."

"Staging area for what?" I asked.

"For heaven, of course!"

"Excuse me? Did I just hear you right? We're in a staging area for heaven?"

She chuckled. "Yes, you idiot!"

"Well, what do we do now?"

"You're asking me? How the hell should I know?"

While we waited, for what I didn't know, I observed my body more thoroughly. Although my eyes were closed, they were black and blue and swollen. My head was immobilized by a halo neck brace, and the tube coming out of my mouth looked so uncomfortable. I was fortunate enough that my arms had mostly been saved by the long-sleeve shirt I was wearing. The fact that I went flying through the air helped in the way of minimum road rash. I didn't really know the full extent of my injuries, only what I could see from where I stood.

Cookie was in way worse shape than I was. Her arms and legs were covered with bandages. She had flown, as well, but she landed and skidded on the road for a good twenty feet. Most of her teeth were missing, and there wasn't a part of her body that wasn't in a cast or wrapped in bandages. "I'm a fuckin' mess, ain't I?" She laughed as we examined our bodies.

"How can you laugh?"

"Because I don't feel any pain, and quite honestly, I don't know what else to do."

"Aren't you concerned to know if we're going back?"

"Sure, but there's nothing we can do except wait it out." And that was what we did—waited. Whatever realm we were in, there was no time. All stood still, and although we both shared in a peaceful awareness, it was unnerving not knowing what was going to happen. It was like we were half in heaven, half on Earth.

While we waited, the first of our visitors finally arrived. The news was slow moving as I had no next of kin to notify, and Cookie's wallet had been thrown from her person, landing in the thick reeds by the marsh. But eventually, the news did get out. The first to arrive was Danielle. Cookie and I watched as she crept through the door, almost as if she was trying not to wake us. Her face was somber, mournful even, while she glanced from Cookie to me. She covered her mouth with her hand at the horror of seeing the seriousness of our injuries. She was timid, walking over to the side of my bed, scared to see me so vulnerable and motionless. Her hands trembled as she reached down to touch my arm. I couldn't feel her hand, but I could feel her heart while she caressed my bruised skin.

Tears formed and dropped from her eyes on to me, and I found myself stepping closer to her. "Dani,

I'm right here," I said, trying to gather her attention, but she couldn't hear me.

Her tears muffled her words as she spoke, but she didn't let that stop her. "Parker, I'm so sorry." Her tears fell in torrents. "You were right. You were right about everything!" I stood attentive by her side while she spoke to my smashed body. "After you told me April was cheating on me, I decided to investigate a little further. I went into our iCloud." Her voice shook as she choked back tears. "Every text to Cece she had deleted was there. I read them all. She had no idea that we shared a cloud. I even found naked pics of Cece that she had sent to her. I guess she thought they disappeared into nonexistence when she deleted them." She took a moment to wipe her eyes and look at me, taking in the reality of it all. "Oh, Parker! Why didn't I believe you? I'm so, so sorry," she said, her emotions welling up inside of her. "I left her."

"What?" I asked, stunned by this turn of events.

"I left her because of what she did and because of my father. But mostly, I left because of you," she said. "I left her because I love you. I think I've always loved you."

I couldn't believe what I was hearing. She was speaking the words I longed to hear for so long, and all I wanted to do was jump back in my body, hug her, and tell her I loved her, too. But there was no jumping back into my body. I didn't know how. She pulled up a chair and sat next to me, silently for a while and incapable of not crying. Every time she looked at me, she shook her head in disbelief. "This is because of me. It's all my fault." Her chin quivered, and snot bubbled at her nostrils. "The last thing I said to you was I never wanted to see you aga...I never wanted to…" She couldn't finish the words as she choked on her tears once more. "I didn't mean it. Please come back." She gently placed her hand on mine and gave it the lightest squeeze. "Parker, please come back."

Silence enveloped the room. So silent, her tears could be heard splashing to the floor as her shoulders drooped forward and her head bent downward. She caressed my hand and fingers for hours. The clock on the wall said so. Time was speeding by, but where we stood, it didn't feel that way.

Danielle didn't leave my side that night. Instead, she lay uncomfortably in a pleather recliner with a thin blanket on top of her. She started out where the recliner had been when she first arrived, but once the nurse gave her permission to stay, she moved the chair as close to my bed as possible. Her face was tight, and her mouth was set in a permanent frown. Her concern for me was genuine, but the regret of her final words to me weighed on her in a visible way. The lines on her forehead deepened as she attempted to close her eyes, and all I wanted her to do was sleep restfully, untroubled.

I got as close as I could to her, and just as she was in that in-between state of sleep and consciousness, I leaned in close to her ear and whispered, "I love you so much, Danielle." And as I swept my hand over her forehead and down her cheek, she stirred and snapped back to consciousness.

"Parker?" she called out. She scanned the room, pausing on Cookie, then me. She wiggled and squirmed in the chair some, repositioned herself, and shrugged off the feeling of my presence. She closed her eyes once more. Her exhaustion and the heaviness of the situation as it stood finally drove her to sleep.

"Well, that's just great! Nobody came to see me!" Cookie announced, a little perturbed.

"That's what you're worried about? Not how we're supposed to get back into our bodies?" I asked, resentful of her lack of concern of the relevance and seriousness of our circumstances.

But then, I noticed something flickering in the upper corner of the ceiling. I pushed Cookie out of the way to examine it further. It wasn't much, just a miniscule dot of light that flickered for no apparent reason. Maybe Cookie was okay with being in this new and strange dominion of awareness, but I wasn't as trusting. Looking into that dot of light made me feel better, calmer as it entranced me.

"What the fuck is that?" Cookie's eyes finally connected on the focus of mine.

"I don't know," I admitted. "But if this is a staging area for heaven, I sure don't see any of the perks." There were no white, puffy clouds or angels flying by. There wasn't even fairy dust or unicorns to speak of. No, it was just Cookie and me trapped in some parallel universe and clueless as to how to get out.

Chapter Twenty-one

In a flash, night turned to day, and Danielle was awoken by the sound of praying coming from the bed next to mine. It was Cookie's parents, her brother, and Shady. They were holding hands, forming a circle around Cookie's body. But Cookie's attention wasn't on her family, who were clearly devastated by witnessing her barely clinging to life. No, it was on Shady, who was praying over her in Spanish, eyes closed.

"I don't even know why the fuck she's here," Cookie said, dismayed at the woman who left her for a second time. However, when Cookie's family took a small reprieve from the room, Cookie's dismay was about to make a U-turn.

Shady knelt by her bed and stroked her cheek, looking at her but not saying anything. Her eyes brimmed with tears, and they spilled over when she finally said, "I only went back to her house to collect my things. You misunderstood." Her cheeks glistened with wetness. "I just went back to pack. I was coming right back to you." She could hardly catch her breath. "I was stupid to leave you the first time. I wasn't going to let that happen again. Cookie, I was meant to be with you." She leaned her head against Cookie's body and softly said, "I love you."

Like a shot through the heart, Cookie looked at me wide-eyed. "Parker, we gotta go back!" she said frantically, touching her own body, attempting to find an entryway. "Parker! Help me get back! You gotta help me get back!"

"Enough!" I grabbed her by the shoulders and shook her until she stopped. "I don't know how to get back, but poking at your body isn't it!"

"She wasn't leaving me! I had it wrong!" She wiped her face with her hands in pure frustration.

When Shady left, leaving Danielle alone in the room once again, the doctor came through the door, clipboard in hand. "I'm Dr. Kreilan, the head neurologist here at Tampa General. Since you're the only emergency contact listed in Morgan's wallet along with her ID, I'm here to give you an update on her status."

"Morgan?" Danielle seemed confused and maybe a bit groggy from the unrest she had all night in that chair.

"Yes. Ms. Parker."

Her face flashed acknowledgment, and she corrected him. "I'm sorry. We just call her Parker. As you were saying?"

"Yes, well, Ms. Parker," he said, then realized he misspoke. "Parker's spinal cord injuries are pretty serious."

Danielle glazed over and didn't seem to return until he summed up. "If she somehow comes out of this coma, she'll have a tough row to hoe."

"Is she going to come out of it?" she asked with desperation in her eyes. "Please don't lie to me. Don't give me hope if there is none. I would rather be given the truth than false hope."

He took a deep breath, looked at me, and back over at Danielle. "Anything could happen. Stranger things have occurred, but the odds of her survival are slim."

She thanked him for his honesty, and he left the room to talk to Cookie's family. Alone again, Danielle came near the bed and observed me, examining the machines that were breathing for me, and with a heavy heart looked back at me. "You need to wake up. We can deal with everything if you would just wake up. Parker! Can you hear me?"

"I can!" I yelled. "I can hear you!" But she couldn't hear me, and at that moment, my eyelids fluttered for a second, and she saw it.

"Parker?" She looked around the room. Again, they fluttered. "Parker?" she went running out the door. "Doctor! Doctor!" she screamed.

He came rushing back into the room with two nurses in tow. "Her eyes! Her eyes were moving! She's going to wake up!" Danielle said. But the doctor insisted these were involuntary reflexes of the body. He explained it wouldn't be completely abnormal to even see my hands or fingers twitch.

When he left the room, Danielle came closer to me. "I know you're in there. I know you are." She leaned over the rails of my bed and gently kissed my bruised hand. "I have to pick up Addie, bring her back to my house, let JoJo out, feed them, shower, change, and I'll be back. Okay?" she asked as if somehow I would answer. I watched her while she wearily walked to the door and left.

"You're still looking at her ass, aren't you?" Cookie grinned.

I looked at her with disdain and wonder at how she could say such a thing. "Yeah, totally! I'm sorry, but she has the cutest ass."

After attempting various ways and methods to reenter our bodies, I noticed the glowing dot in the corner of the ceiling stopped blinking and became much bigger. It was about the size of a softball, and the light swirled within. I was fascinated by it and stepped up on the end table to get a better peek. The aura of the sphere radiated different shades of blue and purple with a touch of yellow. Like a whirlpool, the colors swooshed around in waves, and I was enthralled. I put my hand out to touch it, but it went into it and through it. My hand disappeared inside the light. There was nothing on the other side. I didn't feel anything. "Take your hand out of there! You're fucking making me nervous!"

"Maybe it has something to do with us getting back!" I argued. But the hole was still too small to truly find out.

While Danielle was away, Dorian came by. She was with Dahlia, but after moments in the room, she asked Dahlia to step outside. As soon as she was out of sight, Dorian lost herself in a sea of emotions. Her tears were mixed with sadness and anger. Every time she tried to speak, she was suffocated by her heart. It took several minutes for her to finally calm down enough to say, "You look like shit." She was trying her best to keep it together, speaking to me as if I were awake, but the tears kept coming, anyway. "I don't know what happened exactly, but you need to come back. Can you hear me? Things would never be the same again if you left me. You said you would never leave me as long as I needed you." She spoke of something I had said a long time ago during one of her drunken rants about me being such a good friend. "I still need you. You have to come back." She touched my arm. "Besides, who's going to tell me to stop talking to trees?" She slumped forward and muttered, "What would I do without you?"

I placed my hand on her shoulder, and the charge that passed through me to her was electric. I was positive she felt me when she put her hand on top of mine. She looked from me to Cookie and back to me, her face glistening from the abundance of tears accumulated there.

When Dahlia returned, Dorian lost it completely and buried her face in Dahlia's shoulder. It was all Dahlia could do to calm Dorian down as she rubbed her back. It wasn't long before Dahlia took her home. Things were a mess, and it was looking less likely that we would be returning to the dimension in which we lived. I didn't know how to grasp that, and I didn't want to stress Cookie out even more by giving up.

So quickly the clock chimed to the next morning. I waited as patiently as I could, under the circumstance I was in, for Danielle's return. No sooner did I envision her face than she showed up. The color had drained from her face, and all energy was depleted with the acknowledgment and acceptance of the crash. She took on full responsibility for what had happened, and she shouldn't have. No one forced me to get on that bike high and drunk. No one made me ride at speeds that well exceeded the speed limit. I did all of it of my own free will. There was no one to blame but me.

She couldn't stay in the room with me without crying. Worry and sadness consumed her as she strode to my bedside. She studied me for a while in silence, a mix of hope and despair spread across her face. She set her messenger bag down and sat in the chair next to me. She took my hand in hers and just sat there caressing each of my fingers and tracing over the veins protruding from the top of my hand. I could tell she was trying so hard to keep it together, to not cry, but not breaking down seemed almost impossible every time she looked at me. "Parker, please come back to me. If you just come back, I'm sure everything would be okay. You just have to come back," she said softly, trying to convince herself as the tears flowed from her beautiful brown eyes. The gold flecks in her iris created a copper luster that had been dimmed and faded now. But even with the whites of her eyes bloodshot from weeping so heavily, she was still the most beautiful woman I had ever seen. She was my queen.

Her voice shook and cracked as she reached down to her bag and pulled the little purple teddy bear from it. I was confused about why she had it with her. The stuffed animal was worn, his stitching frayed, and the color faded from sitting in the sun for so many years. A flood of emotions drowned my heart as she placed the bear in the crook of my arm. "It's yours," she sobbed. "All you have to do is come back, and it's yours. I know I said I would never give it to you, that you could have it over my dead body." She sniffled and gasped on the words. "I'd gladly give my life right now for you. It was always yours, ya know? The bear. It was just my way of keeping you without actually having you." She yielded to the low, tortured sobs that shook her entire being. "How am I supposed to go on without you? Parker, please wake up."

But pleading soon turned into praying. She wasn't a religious person, to say the least, but whether she believed in God or not, praying seemed the only thing left to do. She raised her face and petitioned for

God's mercy. "I know we're not on the best of terms, and I know I haven't always done the right thing in my life, but…" She tried to smother her sobs to no avail. The floodgates were open, and negotiations weren't off the table. "But if you let her live, I'll do anything you want me to do. I'll be a better person. I'll volunteer my time to good causes. I'll…I'll…" Her head dropped to her hands, defeat near, but one last plea. "She's the love of my life, and if you just give me one chance to make it right, I'll never let her go. We were meant to be together, and I hate to think I ruined my one chance."

I knelt between her legs and wrapped my arms around her waist, laying my head in her lap. "Parker, is that you? I swear I can feel you." I could see the hairs on her arms stand straight up as my energy embraced her.

"Yes," I whispered. Her eyes closed, and her eyelashes feathered out upon her cheek. She could feel me, and I knew it from the goose bumps that popped up all over her skin. We stayed that way for some time.

In real time, though, the clock moved fast. Each time Danielle came and went from the hospital, the sphere of light in the corner of the ceiling would grow. By the time Dani started staying every night in the recliner, the ball of light had grown to the size of a window. As it grew, Cookie and I were too nervous to examine it further.

However, once it reached the size it did, Cookie became brazen. "What are you doing?" I asked as she stuck her head into the light. "You didn't even want me sticking my hand in there."

"Curiosity has the best of me."

"Do you see anything? I don't like that I can't

see your head when you peek in there," I said, getting more anxious with each passing minute. "You're making me nervous, Cookie! Get out of there!"

"I don't see anything but mist. Whoa!"

"What?"

"Holy shit!" she exclaimed and climbed into the glowing hole.

"Cookie!" I freaked out as she disappeared. "Cookie!" She was gone. Just like that, she was gone, and I didn't know if she would return. I was scared, but I, too, poked my face into the light. It was true. There was only a mist. I couldn't see a thing, but climbing in wasn't an option. I wasn't leaving Danielle for anything. All I could do was wait, the same way I had since I got myself into this mess.

❧ ❧ ❧ ❧

By the look of the clock, days passed with no sign of Cookie. I was alone and afraid I would never see my crazy friend again. Loved ones came and went, visiting both of us as often as they could. Two months had gone by, and Danielle only left to shower and take care of our dogs. She took off the rest of the semester, dividing her course load among a few kind colleagues.

Most days, she played one-sided chess with me, moving the pieces for both of us. When she wasn't playing chess, she read to me one of her favorite classics, *The Catcher in the Rye*. Other times, she just talked to me, telling me how difficult the split with April had been and how hard it was getting her out of their house. Apparently, April begged for her forgiveness, but after all the disgusting things she had found out about her, there was no room for reconciliation. She admitted to my comatose body that she didn't love April. She loved me. Every day began with an apology and a prayer for me to wake up, explaining how beautiful our new life together would be.

The biggest news she revealed to me was that Dorian had resigned from her job. Sometime after finding Dahlia, she decided life was too short to work herself to death at a job she couldn't stand anymore. When my crash occurred, Dorian took over my responsibilities at the bar. She decided that running the bar made her happier than accounting ever did, and if I ever came out of this, she intended to ask me to be a business partner. I never thought in a million years she would give up her gig at the accounting firm. It was a blessing I could never repay.

One day, as I watched Danielle read to me, Cookie reappeared through the circle of light, which had grown to the size of a door. She walked through it, and I immediately hugged her. "Oh, my God! Cookie, where did you go? I was worried sick."

She looked different than when she left. Something in her spirit had changed. Everything about her appeared and felt peaceful. There was a calm about her I had never witnessed before. "I'm not going back," she announced. "But you are."

"Excuse me? What's that now?"

"Parker, it's time for me to go home. It's my time."

"Right! Your home in Tampa."

She shook her head and pointed to her broken body lying in the bed. Only when I looked this time, she was surrounded by her family, Shady, and a priest. The priest was giving her last rites before the doctor, assisted by two nurses, pulled the plug from her life support. The machine flatlined, and Cookie took her final breath. She would never be in her physical body again and only returned to say goodbye. She watched as the people who loved her wept and mourned for the loss of a wonderful soul.

"No! No!" I refused to accept the death of one of my dearest friends.

"It's okay, Parker."

"No, it's not!" I said, devastated by this news.

"It is."

"How can I go on without you? You've always been there for me."

"You will go on, and I will always be there for you, just in a different way."

Tears welled in my eyes. "What happened in that light?" I needed to know.

"I saw my grandmother." She smiled. "She came to take me home."

"But what's to become of me?" I asked with genuine concern.

"Parker, you're going to go back, and you're going to live out the rest of your life. You have a long, happy life ahead of you," she foretold, glancing over at Danielle. "You're going to spend the rest of your days with that lady right there."

"Wait. She's a lady? Not Miss Priss? Or Miss Goody Two-Shoes? You usually have a negative name for her for every day of the week." I laughed.

"There's no negativity over here. It's amazing," she explained. "Danielle is a good person, and if I've learned nothing else from being on this side, it's that that woman loves you."

I peered at Danielle, who empathized with

Cookie's loved ones. "I love her, too. But how do I get back?" I asked, genuinely worried for the outcome of my own situation.

"I don't know. I'm sure you'll figure it out. I have to go." She started for the light, and I stopped her.

"I don't want you to go," I confessed.

"I know, but you're going to be okay without me. We'll see each other again when it's your time."

My life was a series of moments that always depended on time. Not the right time. When it's your time. I was sick of time. I'd like to smash the clock hanging on the wall, laughing at me as if it was a joke, but what would it matter? Time marched on whether I liked it or not, whether I was here or not.

"I love you, Cookie. You've been my savior and my death," I said and embraced her once more.

"Don't go gettin' all sappy on me," she began but changed tunes immediately. "I love you, too, Parker. Live your life." She turned and disappeared into the misty orb of light that was quite large now.

Again, I looked at Danielle. Everyone else was gone from the room now. Time marched forward. They took Cookie's body, and it was just me left in the room with Danielle. She stopped reading and softly kissed my hand. In silence, she stared at me, her thoughts so focused on me. Once more, she placed her lips on my hand and kissed it repeatedly, as if her kisses would somehow rouse me to wake.

"Morgan Lynn," I heard from behind me, not used to anyone using my first name, let alone my middle name. When I whirled around, I was astonished and flabbergasted at who I saw. My mother.

My eyes widened into half dollars, and my heart leaped to my throat. "Mom?" I asked, awestruck by her angelic presence. Like a child missing her mother, I practically jumped on her and hugged her as tightly as I could. "What are you doing here?"

"I wanted to talk to you before the light fades away and I miss the opportunity." I had never seen her look so healthy, happy, and at peace. Her smile radiated joy as she surveyed her middle child. I smiled back, but my smile quickly faded; my face was long, and my frown deepened. "What is it, Morgan?" she asked.

"It's just…It's just that I couldn't save you. I wanted to, but I didn't know how." I sobbed as tears streamed down my face at the guilt I felt over my mother's abused life and tragic demise.

"You weren't meant to save me. You were just a child. I should have saved you, but I was imprisoned in my own mind, like someone jailed with the cell door wide open. I couldn't see it," she spoke honestly and sincerely. "You couldn't save me, dear."

"But I wanted to."

She wiped the tears from my cheek. "If you want to honor my memory, stop doing the things you do when you get mad or upset. Stop with the gambling, especially. It's not who you are, and you need to find another outlet to cope with your depression." She looked at Danielle, who was resting her cheek on my hand. "She's your saving grace, you know? She may not have realized it before, but she loves you with all her heart. Let her be your gambling. Let her be your drug. Let her carry you when you need carrying. Most of all, let her love you."

"But I don't know if I'm going back."

"You're going back because it's not your time."

"Still, I don't know how to get back," I admitted,

having tried several times.

"When the time is right, you won't have to try. It'll just happen."

My eyes filled with adoration for her. "I miss you so much, Mom. I damn near destroyed myself when you died."

"I know. But you see, I didn't die. I merely left my physical vessel. Our energy never dies. Our soul lives on for eternity. I miss you, too, but I've never left you. I love you, Morgan Lynn."

"I love you, too, Mommy," I spouted, crying as if I was still ten, needing my mother so desperately in my life.

She embraced me once more, and I felt all her love surround and hold me. And then, she was gone, disappeared from my arms and faded back into the light. I was stunned to have just conversed with my deceased mother but even more so when the light closed like a sphincter and faded into nothing. Just like that, I was left alone. No more Cookie, no more Mom, no more light. Only me, alone in this strange and unusual realm with no clue as to how to get out.

❧❧❧❧

More time passed. Each day, the nurse would change the date on the board that indicated what nurse was on duty. One night, a storm rolled through town, rain came down like a monsoon and pelted the windowpane. The thunder was loud, and Danielle jumped each time it clapped like an explosion. The moon was full, and the mood in the room became intense. When the lightning lit up the room, I noticed her eyes moisten. She hadn't cried for a while, almost accepting what had happened to me. But tonight, she was feeling my absence in such a way that she broke down in tears. "Why won't you come back to me?" She squeezed my hand in hers.

"I want to come back. I just don't know how," I answered, even if she couldn't hear me.

I tried everything to reenter my body, looking for any hole through which to enter. Forcing myself into my ear canal didn't work, just as trying to squeeze through my nostril didn't work. I even attempted bouncing up and down on my body, as though I were jumping up and down on a bed. Nothing worked, so I sat by Danielle and did the only thing I knew how to do—love her. I wrapped my celestial arms around her and clutched her. "I miss you so much. I can't imagine life without you," she whispered through her tears. I wiped them away, each one that fell, and caressed her cheek as I did. "I need you!" she wailed now. "Parker, I need you in my life!"

Like magic words, I felt a warm tingling sensation, then a buzzing noise. With a loud *boom*, I felt my soul being sucked like a vacuum back into my body. Violently, I was forced back into my human vessel. There was no smooth transition. I was zapped back into being, pulled through a vortex. My eyes sprung open, and I was instantly confused. Confused by the pain I had avoided since I got here. Confused by the sensation of the plastic tube inserted into my throat. I thrashed around as much as I could, having been restrained by the machines I was attached to and the halo that was supposed to keep my head immobile. Attempting to speak was impossible, but it didn't stop me from trying. "Oh, my God! Someone, come quick!" Danielle screamed as loud as her lungs would allow. "She's awake! Someone, please help!"

A series of *Oh, my Gods* came from Dani's mouth before doctors and nurses alike came running from every direction. She was pushed aside, and they began working on me right away. The feel of the tube sliding out of my throat was harsh and uncomfortable. Each time I tried to get out of bed, I was reminded of the paralysis from my knees down. Through the throng of medical staff, I saw Danielle, speechless and aghast, scared to death and crying. Her hand covered her mouth, horrified at seeing me struggle so hard. Although I was in pain like I'd never felt before, I was here, and I knew I was here. I was alive. Granted, I was in pretty bad shape, but I was alive with a chance to get better and live.

❦ ❦ ❦ ❦

Rehabilitation was slow. They told me I had a good chance of walking again if I put in the work. Every day was grueling. Learning to walk again hurt. There were times when giving up seemed to be the only option, but Danielle wouldn't let me. Bones and bruises healed slowly, but they healed. Friends visited me every day. I had the full support of not only Danielle, but of everyone who ever cared about me. Dorian and Dahlia came most mornings. Even some of my bar regulars like Buckley and Sherri came by to see me. None of it seemed to matter. Every day was a new realization that Cookie would never be one of my visitors. Survivor's guilt was real, and it was immense. Depression was inevitable.

You would have thought I would have been thrilled by the news that April had hanged herself through the same device that had allowed for her affair. She learned more about iClouds than she probably cared to know. I was as thrilled as I could be in the awful state I was in. Danielle was free, free to be with me now, but I couldn't get past the remorse of surviving the crash. Danielle was so patient with me. It was like she knew what was at the end of all this, so it didn't matter how fast or how slow we went. We both knew that when I was fully capable, physically and mentally, we would be together. I was hers, and she was mine. Nothing more needed to be said. There was nothing left standing in our way.

Don't get me wrong, I was grateful to be alive, but I sank to the depths of darkness still. I couldn't bring myself to smile, feeling as though I had no right; guilt blanketed me like a black cloud. Memories of our friendship ruled my mind. Seemed Cookie was always saving me from something. Whether it had been making her family take me in when I was a teenager getting my ass kicked by my father or driving an hour to pick me up on the side of the road when my car broke down or just being there for me with a shoulder to cry on whenever I needed it and willing to kick someone's ass. She was always saving me. But I couldn't save her, and just like it killed me not to be able to save my mom, it was the same with Cookie. She was my best bud.

After a month of wearing that stupid halo brace, it finally came off. Danielle was there when they released me from the uncomfortable restraints. Ever since I opened my eyes, she had done nothing but smile, so happy I had returned. Unfortunately, she hadn't been able to get very close to me—literally. The contraption I wore was a huge obstacle and not very friendly to hugs, but today…today was different. When the doctor took it off me, Danielle looked to him for confirmation that it was okay. A smile and a nod later, and she practically did a cartwheel into my arms. Her embrace was firm as she securely held me, unwilling to let go. "Don't ever leave me again," she said softly in my ear. Dating while rehabilitating wasn't easy, but there was no choice but to take things slow, so our first hug was our first touch. When she held me, my body became alive again. My desire for her was undying, and though I still couldn't feel my legs completely, I could certainly feel the heat permeating through my shorts. The feeling was seemingly mutual as she slowly released me from her grip, her gaze glued to mine. Yes, the attraction was still there and still as strong as ever.

Wanting to feel her naked body on mine was reason enough to suffer through the grueling physical therapy I endured on a daily basis, but the depression veiled and masked that determination. Any feelings of happiness were quickly squashed by guilt and regret over Cookie's death. I hadn't even been physically well enough to get out of the rehab center, let alone attend her funeral. I never got the closure I needed to end a chapter of my life I didn't want to end. Every time I closed my eyes, I saw her lifeless body, beaten up and broken from the crash. I couldn't stop seeing her lying in that bed. The quiet despair and desperation I felt left an empty space in my heart. Everyone did their best to lift my spirits. They tried to get me to recognize that I had no control over the outcome of the tragic events that took place. Sadly, nothing they said got through to me. I wasn't ready to accept things the way they were. Until one night while I cried myself to sleep, stricken with internal sadness, Cookie appeared in my dream.

"What are you doin', ya dumb fuck?" She chuckled to herself.

"What do you mean what am I doing?" I was confused by her question.

"You've been given a second chance at life, and you're blowing it."

"Second chance? What about your second chance? How am I supposed to be happy when all I can picture is you lying there dead?"

"Then don't picture that! Jeez!" she exclaimed, almost comically. "Parker, listen to me." She took hold of my shoulders and demanded my full attention. "When you think of me, I want you to think of all the happy memories we shared. Life is made up of moments, some small, some big, but it's those moments that make life worth living. It's those moments that you'll hang on to, that you'll turn to when life isn't going your way. Don't remember me dead. Remember me alive. I'm always going to be with you. You may not see me, but you'll feel me." She pointed to my heart. "You'll feel me here."

"But going on without you just seems wrong," I said as tears fell from my eyes.

"But it's not wrong. It's just as it's supposed to be. Everything happens in perfect time."

"Time? Time hasn't been so good to me."

"Give life another try. I think you'll see that's about to change."

Just like that, she faded away, and I awoke in a pool of sweat. I wasn't sure if she had been there. It was a dream, right? Except that when I awoke so suddenly, the pungent smell of pot hung in the air.

I smiled through my tears, knowing full well that Cookie's spirit had just visited me. For the first time since coming out of my coma, I slept soundly the rest of the night.

Morning came and, with it, a new attitude and a renewed love of life. Gratitude was the new word of the day. I was grateful to open my eyes to see the sun streaming in through the window blinds. Cookie's blessing to go on without her was a life-altering experience, giving me a reawakened passion for living. It was a slow start, my progress, but with a swift, hard kick to my ass from Cookie, I was open to things getting better. Granted, it wasn't exactly like a light switch. The depression stayed with me on and off for the next few months, until it eventually switched off for good.

The feelings in my legs started out as tingling but soon turned to pins and needles, and finally, I took my first steps without the aid of balance bars. Sure, those first steps were with the support of a walker, but it wasn't long after that I was able to walk with just a cane. The doctors said that eventually I wouldn't need the cane, but I would walk with a slight limp the rest of my life. It was a small price to pay for my life.

Spending almost a full year at the rehab wasn't a cinch, but it did come to an end. When Danielle took me home, Addie and JoJo nearly knocked me over, unable to contain their excitement. Addie almost lost her mind, panting, barking, wagging her tail, and genuinely ecstatic to see her mama. I missed my dog. I missed my house, too. It felt great to be home. I was eager to start my new life. Looking around, things seemed different, but in a good way. Walking past the baby grand, I couldn't help but notice a picture, framed, and sitting solitaire on it. As I looked closer, I recognized one of the pictures from the carnival photo booth. Danielle had it enlarged and framed and placed it in the center of the piano.

"Is it okay that I made the piano its new home?" She pointed to the photo and awaited my approval.

"Of course," I said naturally.

She stepped in front of me and with the tips of her fingers guided my chin and face around to her, taking my attention away from the picture and setting it on her. "Is it okay that this is my new home, too?"

"What?" I grinned, unsure of what she was saying. "Wait…did you move in?"

"I did, and I hope you're okay with it. I just assumed, but if you're not—"

I stopped her mid-sentence and covered her mouth with my fingers. "You assumed right." I moved closer to her.

"Are you sure?" She moved closer still.

"Are you kidding me?" I adoringly scanned over her pretty face. "So what does this mean exactly?" I pulled her all the way to me, our mouths just inches from each other.

"It means it's finally our time," she breathed and pressed her lips to mine. Our first real kiss in a year was about to turn into a lifetime of them.

About the Author

TL Dickerson resides in southern New Jersey with her beautiful wife, Gail, and their lazy housecat, Sweetie. When she's not writing, she enjoys spending time on the beach where she finds a peace one can only find at the ocean. One of her favorite pastimes is studying the American Civil War and visiting as many Civil War battlefield sites as possible. Her most prized possessions are artifacts she's collected from the era. She loves horror and comedy flicks, and her all-time favorite sitcom is Friends. She enjoys a wide variety of music, but her favored preference is old-school rap and hip-hop. There are a lot of female rappers she likes, but her favorite is Missy Elliott. Above all else, TL makes a mean pot of gravy. Not sauce, gravy.

TL has written two previous books to Hearts Under Siege. Writing in the Lesbian Fiction, Romance/Erotica genre, she has two self-published novels, the debut Servicing the Rich, and sophomore effort A Breath in Time. Both are available at Amazon and on Kindle.

IF YOU LIKED THIS BOOK...

Share a review with your friends or post a review on your favorite site like Amazon, Goodreads, Barnes and Noble, or anywhere you purchased the book. Or perhaps share a posting on your social media sites and help spread the word.

Join the Sapphire Newsletter and keep up with all your favorite authors.

Did we mention you get a free book for joining our team?

sign-up at - www.sapphirebooks.com

Check out TL's other book

The Coffield Chronicles – Hearts Under Siege: Book One – ISBN – 978-1-952270-12-3

The year is 1862. The war between the states has been raging intensely for a year now. The country is in complete and utter turmoil, and brother is fighting brother to the death, dying for what each believed. It seems it's all the townsfolk of New Albany, Indiana can speak of, and Melody Coffield is paying attention. Through a series of heartbreaks and sorrow, she settles on the decision to cut her hair and don men's attire.

Going under the alias of Melvin A. Coffield, she leaves her childhood home, the only home she had ever known, and enlists in the United States Army. Chewing tobacco and drinking liquor were ways of men, and she learns quickly how to behave like one. She would soon know the horrors of battle, and what was called the glory of war, through roads that led straight to Vicksburg, Mississippi. However, her biggest concern was making sure she was not detected by the others. Keeping her secret would not only be challenging, but trying as well.

Will she remain in this solitude the rest of her life, never allowing anyone into her heart again? Or will she find love, once more, in a world that was intolerant and unaccepting of who she truly was?

The Coffield Chronicles – Hearts Under Fire: Book Two – ISBN – 978-1-952270-30-7

1863 opens with a bang! President Abraham Lincoln issues his Emancipation Proclamation, freeing all slaves in the rebellious states. Independence Day is won twofold, when the Yanks win battles in Gettysburg, Pennsylvania, and Vicksburg, Mississippi. The Union Army is thoroughly exhausted by the time the siege at Vicksburg is won and the Stars and Stripes proudly wave atop the trenches they now possessed.

Melody Coffield, a.k.a. Lieutenant Melvin A. Coffield, survives battle, fighting even when the fear had threatened to overwhelm her. The Livingston Plantation in Vicksburg is now a Union headquarters, where Melvin is an aide-de-camp to General John Robert Frommer. Still holding the secret of her sex, she meets the beautiful and intriguing Becca Chamberlain. The Southern belle possesses an air of mystery and a bit of arrogance that Melvin finds charming, even bewitching. Honoring her role as a soldier is becoming increasingly difficult. Hiding her true identity is detrimental, but with her feelings for Becca come carelessness and a need for love that was all but forgotten.

Other books by Sapphire Authors

My Home is on the Mountain by Caro Clarke- ISBN - 978-1-952270-40-6

You can make your life extraordinary, if you have the courage.

Cecilia Howison, the rich and well-known daughter of a prominent East Tennessee family, appears to be the perfect Southern girl, cultured, gracious, virginal. The actual lesbian she is feels restless and ready for something new. She finds it in a high mountain meadow: a girl, wearing nothing but overalls, asleep beside a violin. Cecilia accepts the challenge.
Airey Fitch is the mainstay of her family's hard-scrabble hill farm. She has no love for the Howisons or any their kind, who now, in 1931, are evicting the mountain folk to create a new national park. Despite them, she will hang on, despite them, she will seek a life in music. When Cecilia offers to make that happen, Airey dares to trust her. And wonders at Cecilia's hold on her thoughts.

Cecilia understands all too clearly the risks she runs by wooing Airey Fitch but cannot stop, lured like a moth to Airey's flame. Airey wants more than the passion Cecilia gives her—wants her heart. But the world they live in forbids it, and Cecilia is faced with a choice that only love can make.

Curtain Call by Kim Pritekel - ISBN - 978-952270-42-0

What do you do when you come from a long line of

dancers that spans the globe and generations, yet you can't tell your right foot from your left? You fall in love with a dancer, of course!

Gray Rickman is an awkward seventeen-year-old when she first sets eyes on Christian Scott at the dance studio/theater Gray's parents own and run in Denver, Colorado.

Though only a handful of years older than Gray, Christian carries herself with poise and wisdom far beyond her years. A woman of few words, she speaks volumes with her body.

Before Gray even really knows what her type is, Christian stars in endless daydreams and even fulfills a couple of her fantasies before vanishing out of thin air, leaving Gray in an empty bed with nothing but bittersweet memories and broken dreams.

With no choice but to move on, Gray attempts love, even moving with her college girlfriend to New York City to pursue a career in journalism. But her standard has been set, the bar way too high for any other woman to reach or clear. It's an unexpected encounter in an obvious place when Gray sets eyes on her dancer again. Will the bright lights of Broadway illuminate the way back to the woman of her dreams? Or will they blind her to any other possibility of happiness?

Break a leg, Gray. The Great White Way calls.

Laying of Hands by Patricia Evans - ISBN - 978-1-952270-49-9

Nestled in the Adirondack Mountains of upstate New York lies a picturesque retreat for the conservative young women of the Sanctity Covenant religion, surrounded by crisp, pine-scented breezes and the endless blue shimmer of Coyote Lake. But dark secrets lurk behind closed doors at Valley of Rubies, and what emerges from the summer shadows is nothing less than terrifying.

Adel Rosse, an investigative journalist for Vanity Fair looking for a way to stand out in the cutthroat world of Manhattan journalism, has just been handed an assignment that will catapult her career—if she can survive as an undercover Creative Writing tutor at Valley of Rubies and get the scoop on what really happens there. Just as she starts to uncover the gritty truth behind the shadowy cult running the organization, she falls in love with the one woman who holds the key to the story.

Grace Waters is an old maid at twenty-six, at least by Covenant standards, and her annual idyllic summers spent teaching at Valley of Rubies are suddenly imperiled by the news that she must marry the man chosen for her at the end of the session. If she refuses, she risks being excommunicated—or worse—but a mysterious new writing instructor at camp makes her wonder what would happen if she dared to write her own story.

Pushing their boundaries in search of answers, Grace and Adel seek to redefine themselves to save their futures—and maybe each other.

www.ingramcontent.com/pod-product-compliance
Lightning Source LLC
Chambersburg PA
CBHW061042190726
48286CB00006B/1576